Copyright © 2025 A S

All rights reserved

The characters and events portrayed in this book are fictitious. Any similarity to real persons, living or dead, is coincidental and not intended by the author.

No part of this book may be reproduced, or stored in a retrieval system, or transmitted in any form or by any means, electronic, mechanical, photocopying, recording, or otherwise, without express written permission of the publisher.

ISBN-13: 9781969239038
ISBN-10: 1969239034

Cover image by: A L Watson
with additional design by: A S H
Printed in the United States of America

OTHER BOOK BY
THE AUTHOR

A White Rabbit in Summer

Lovelife of a Deathdealer

Twisting the Turall

Ether

Voyage

Gold

Empathy

CONTENTS

Copyright

OTHER BOOK BY THE AUTHOR

Title Page

Book 1

An Introduction 1

The First Chapter 4

The Second Chapter 14

The Third Chapter 30

The Fourth Chapter 43

The Fifth Chapter 53

The Sixth Chapter 64

The Seventh Chapter 78

The Eighth Chapter 94

The Ninth Chapter 101

The Tenth Chapter 111

The Eleventh Chapter 119

The Twelfth Chapter 125

The Thirteenth Chapter 134

The Fourteenth Chapter 145

Book 2 157

The Fifteenth Chapter 158

The Sixteenth Chapter 170

The Seventeenth Chapter 184

The Eighteenth Chapter 197

The Nineteenth Chapter 205

The Twentieth Chapter 220

The Twenty-First Chapter 229

The Twenty-Second Chapter 241

The Twenty-Third Chapter 252

The Twenty-Fourth Chapter 266

The Twenty-Fifth Chapter 280

The Twenty-Sixth Chapter 291

The Twenty-Seventh Chapter 301

Book 3 311

The Twenty-Eighth Chapter 312

The Twenty-Ninth Chapter 328

The Thirtieth Chapter 343

The Thirty-First Chapter 357

The Thirty-Second Chapter 373

The Thirty-Third Chapter 383

The Thirty-Fourth Chapter 397

The Thirty-Fifth Chapter 404

The Thirty-Sixth Chapter 412

The Thirty-Seventh Chapter 424

The Thirty-Eighth Chapter 429

The Thirty-Ninth Chapter 444

The Fortieth Chapter 456

The Forty-First Chapter 472

The Forty-Second Chapter 486

The Forty-Third Chapter 495

The Forty-Fourth Chapter 503

TWISTING THE TURALL

Collection 1

ASH

BOOK 1

Ether

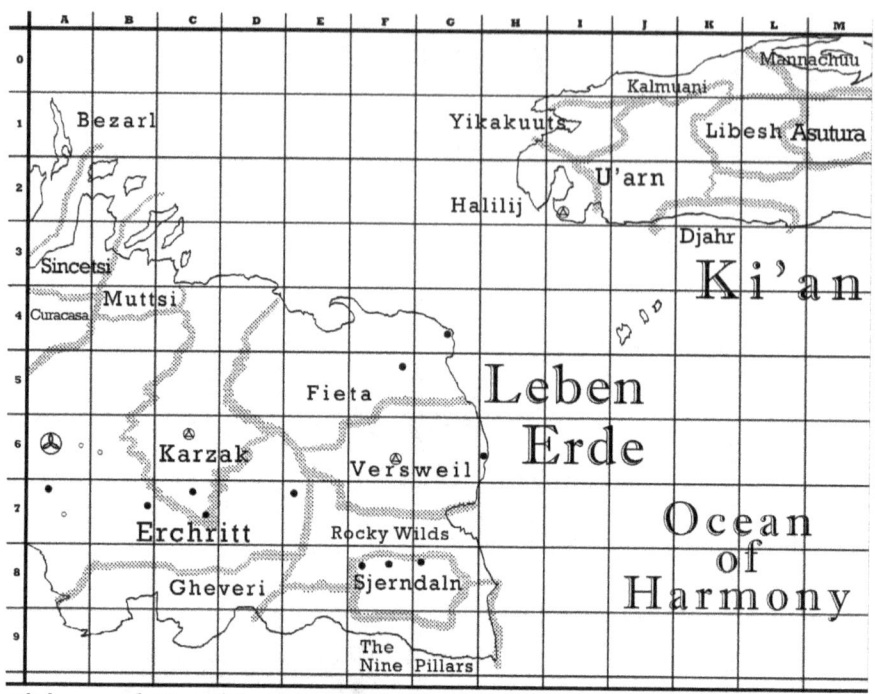

Cities and Notable Locations

`================================================`

Schlabaum	--	Ozalto	C6	Situ	I2
	(left) A6	Voro Serek	--	Vergebaum Heff	G4
Vomdaus	--	(top) C7	Taulge	F5
	(right) A6	Befenji Vrost	--	Rokenrook	F6
Oras Groon	B6	(bottom) C7	Raakt Wolkust	G6
Hochel	(top) A7	Wicklarb	E7	Sjernport	G8
Monfel	(bottom) A7	Skeevaukt	--	Mublom (right)	F8
Schlanicht Weis	F8	(left) F8		

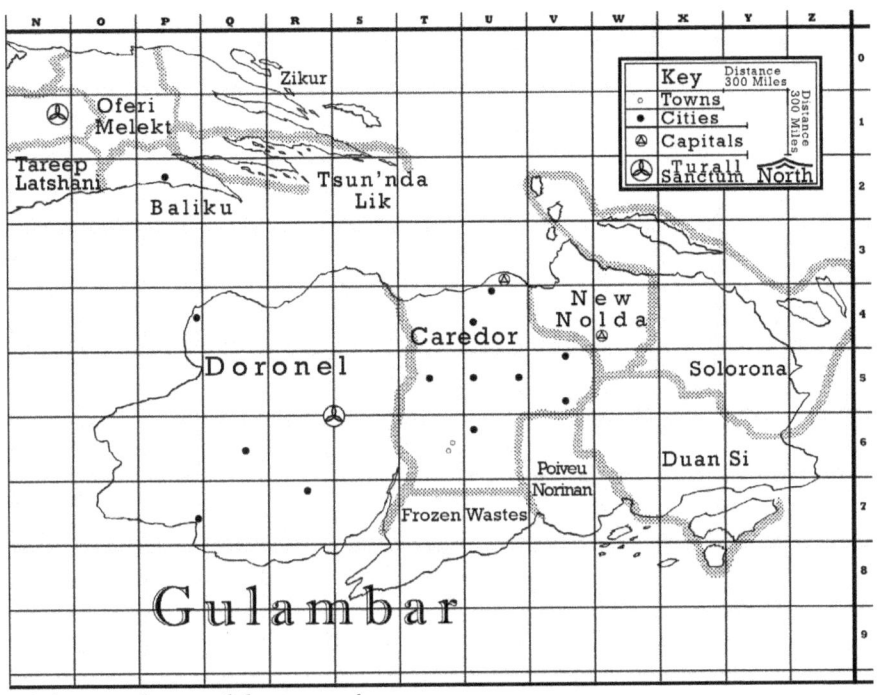

Cities and Notable Locations

==

Mu	N1	Norsant (bottom) U4	Caredor City	U3
Qirshod	P2	Lirond T5	Belegoth (top)	U4
Faigovaidon	P4	Centrosto (left) U5	Dothyiairiaid	W4
Vytur Castle	--	Sothlen U6	Yuron (right)	U5
	R5-S6	Risgwa (top) T6	Lake Itacaima	--
Farnimb	Q6	Yestepor (left) T6	(top)	V5
Azgrova	R7		Araswoods	--
Olphram	P7		(bottom)	V5

AN INTRODUCTION

Long before the time of words, when historians recorded stories, the sages preserved dreams. The sages of old were the first to see the Grand Dream and they knew not what it meant. By the time they recognized it for prophecy, evil had already descended upon the world. Off to the north, where the air was more fire than water, evil had taken over the continent of Ki'an.

Ruled by the "little evil," Hultur, the people set their sights on the land of gemstones and magic, Gulambar. The people of the Eastern continent, Gulambar, were ruled by the "wise ruler," Ngoltur. She saw a river of blood and abdicated to Hultur to preserve the life of all people. Hultur sought to marry Ngoltur and combine their powers, and when she refused him, Hultur turned his violence onto the people of Gulambar.

Not satisfied with Ki'an and Gulambar, Hultur set his sights on the Western continent, Leben Erde. It was a land of plenty and prosperity, where neighbors hugged children, and strangers tended fields. They knew nothing of war and learned slavery quickly. But one boy had dreamt of war. He'd lived war a thousand times and knew that this evil wouldn't survive without Hultur. This boy was the "courage door," Muttur. He faced evil where he found it and traced the wickedness back to Gulambar.

With the knowledge of the Grand Dream complete in Muttur's mind, the Sages were given the design of a great sword, Magoloiherdir. Muttur united the people against Hultur and freed Ngoltur. With Hultur deep in enemy lands, the people of Gulambar were able to kill him with minimal casualties to all. The invaders from Ki'an retreated to their lands. In the eyes of the people of Gulambar, Ngoltur should marry her savior Muttur, but this was not to be. Muttur gave Ngoltur the great sword, Magoloiherdir, and returned to Leben Erde.

This story was repeated many times throughout the history of the world, though with each occurrence there were slight variations. The three chosen came to be known as the Turall. Sages were born on each of the three continents and watched for the coming of the Grand Dream.

Always born first was Hultur. He was recognized by the drive to conquer when the strong woman of Ki'an denounced her fertility and became male. In that rejection of birth, she became Hultur, and all knew that the Time of Conquest was upon them. The people of Ki'an always followed, because the war of the Grand Dream never ravaged their lands.

For many, the coming of the Grand Dream was foreseen by the coming of Ngoltur, who was born to the royal line with skin white as the clouds, hair radiant and white as the sun, and eyes blue as the sky. Her birth came like a beacon, letting all know that the Grand Dream was upon them. For none in Gulambar are born with skin so fair, nor hair so bright.

Yet the birth of Muttur was always a mystery. He was in a town so remote that any could be the one who slays evil. He was born with a name like any other and only announced his birthright when Hultur laid siege to Leben Erde. For the boy didn't know he was Muttur until evil brought about the nightmares of the Grand Dream. From the moment nightmares broke his sleep, he knew the skills of those that have come before him. In his mind shone the design of magnificent weapons and tools that only the people of Gulambar could create. Muttur was always the last to reveal himself, for his appearance meant the cycle was, at last, nearing its end.

Many scholars have sought to make sense of the magic that brings the Grand Dream back to the world, but none can feel its flow. The Time of Conquest is known by a woman rejecting her womb. The Time of Loss is foreseen by the birth of an albino princess. The Time of Liberation begins when a deaf boy wakes with the skills of a thousand heroes. Only the Sages know these times are coming and they work in small ways to guide the hands of fate.

But what happens when the Sages misread their signals? What happens when the conqueror wants a future without war? What happens when the pale princess lives her life in exile?

This is the story of that unforeseen outcome.

THE FIRST CHAPTER

In Which Ngoltur is Named and Meets the Bringer of War

Ena Syndril Theolass Vamqinsys knew nothing of her destiny nor of her place in the royal family line. Ena had only known that her parents once lived in the royal palace and that they left to start a life anew in the central nation of Caredor. Once a duchy to the Pearlescent Line, the rise of democracy had transformed the land into a modernized thaumocracy. During Ena's life, she saw villages transformed into ethereal repositories, shamans and healers taken to the cities for "a brighter tomorrow," and golden coins replaced with ether-infused crystals called gulda. She only knew that her parents were born with great power, the rest of her birthright was taken from her.

In Caredor, all who could touch magic were put to work. Some worked the ether-chains to focus their will along the transit lines. Some meditated in the spires, transforming raw ether into cricketbread and chewsticks. Most gave their time to the repositories, focusing their energy into gemstones that made up the land's currency. Ena worked the fields on the edge of progress. Her natural talent as a Caster gave her the power to preserve huge stores of grain and meat or to imbue batteries with living lightning. To the villages she attended, she was a fixer of problems and an ender of famine.

Ena traveled a circuit of forty villages. If troubles were

light, she'd visit each three times a year. When problems multiplied and spread with the wind, Ena might only attend each village once that year. The year of her twentieth birthday had begun slowly, with each village needing nothing more than recharges and fixed wainwrights, but the coming of summer brought a plague of pustules, swarms of sealouse, and fieldhands met more than their fair share of monsters.

Leaving the small village of Risgwa, Ena found it hard to say goodbye. Infected children were bound to bedposts and trees to keep from opening their sores, elders tilled farmlands while the healthy hunted with shield and wand, and a handsome man of twenty asked for her hand in marriage.

Ena didn't deny Haenir's request because he was cruel or ugly. The man had a good head on his shoulders, and was still alone because he'd given up on love long ago to care for his aging father and lame mother. Most painful of all, Ena found him easy to talk to. Jokes came easy when he was around and every morning she awoke remembering the feel of his hand from the night before. They laid on a hill watching the stars dance across the sky. Loving Haenir came easy, but Ena knew they wouldn't have an easy life. As a Caster in a Band of Brokers, she did good for the nation, but as the wife of a farmer, the Supreme Magus might send for her before the year's end. So it was with a heavy heart that Ena rejected Haenir's proposal.

Their hug goodbye lasted a year in the moment and a heartbeat when his skin left hers. The smell of his sweat and sun-baked wheat in his hair stayed in her nose, beckoning her to return to his arms. The way their embrace left a lock of errant curls over his eye pulled at her hand to fix it. The bittersweet smile on his heartbroken face parted her lips in anticipation of a kiss she dared not seek.

"Why are you smiling?" she asked with half a chuckle and half a sob.

"Because I know you'll be back." His smile widened twice as much, making his handsome face boyish. "I know this isn't our last goodbye."

She gave a coy smirk. "Maybe it should be. People usually say everything when the end is near."

Dark as he was, blush barely kissed his skin, but she knew it was there for the parting of his lips and his audible pant.

They bit their lips in tandem.

Ena looked back to the wagon. The Band of Brokers, her coworkers, were all packed up. More villages needed their aid. She'd run out of excuses to say the words.

"Goodbye, Haenir."

"I love you."

Ena bit her lip and lowered her head. She couldn't echo the words.

He leaned against her and kissed her cheek soft as the first snowflake of autumn.

Her brain ceased all function. Words failed to form in her throat. She watched him turn around and go. A whip cracked. The Band of Brokers left without her, giving her the chance to change her mind. She could run to him, throw her arms around him, kiss him, and love him for the rest of her days. But she couldn't. She kept remembering the sight of her parents boarding the black wagon to the capital. Maybe they could live in obscurity for a time, but their peace wouldn't last. Sooner or later the Mages of Caredor would find Ena and bring her to the capital. On that day, Haenir and their children would be all alone. Loving him would be cruel.

Ena ran up to the departing wagon. Sal held out a massive dry hand. She pulled herself onto his leg-sized fingers, and the rocky man effortlessly brought her into the wagon. The big Boulba was the closest thing she had to an older brother. All the Band of Brokers were like that to her, a family. Huddled in the wagon, they all looked at her with sympathy and curiosity.

"So what happened?" asked Visk. She was a red-skinned warrior from the northern continent of Ki'an. As a guard, she was an important part of any Band of Brokers, but Visk didn't always pick up on the subtleties of Gulambar society. The band groaned at her. "It is a question we all mean to ask!"

Narla patted Ena on the back. She was an older woman, but young for a tinker, being only in her mid-forties. She was a greasy friend drunk and a sleeping friend when sober. "Tough break, kid. You made the right decision. It's better to have sex and leave. The first time you fall in love you think it's everything, but love is the greatest teacher of heartbreak."

Pale Ena couldn't hide the blush on her skin.

"Oh, you didn't..." Narla reached for her flask and offered it to Ena. "Maybe you need this more than I do."

She waved the drink away. "Thank you, Narla. Thank you all. I just want to get some sleep. They'll probably have half a year's worth of stuff for us to do at the next place we hit."

There was no talk after that. They all knew where they were going and had a long ride ahead of them. Ena leaned back against Sal and closed her eyes, though sleep was far from her mind. Boulbas weren't hot unless their bellies were full of rocks. His rocky skin was warm like stones at the end of a long day in the sun. He cooled with her sweat and the gentle breeze about them.

~ ~ ~

It was dark when Ena awoke. She hadn't remembered drifting off, or what she dreamed about, but her shoulders were tense and her tunic was soaked with sweat. Torno was standing over her, illuminated only by the light of the moon reflecting off the lake. Torno was three years older than her, a point that neither of them could forget. He was handsome in a rugged bastard kind of way, and every year he seemed to push the boundaries of what was or wasn't a beard. The gray hairs on his face stood out in the dim light like stars in the night sky.

"Bad dreams?" he asked.

Ena shook her head. "Was I sleep talking? Ow!" She stood up and saw stars, one side of her was all pins and needles.

Torno helped Ena back down and sat beside her. "A little. Visk says you were fighting something. She thought we should pull over to keep you from evoking us into an early grave."

She wiped at the drool on her cheek and took a whiff of her rank pits. "Where is everyone?"

"Inside. Me and Narla burned some ether to get us here early."

"I wish you wouldn't do that," Ena grumbled.

"I know," he acquiesced.

Ena leaned out to cool her damp hair in the wind. Crickets and night fowl serenaded her. The silence outside the wagon was altogether more pleasant than the tense unspoken words inside. Her history with the man made things complicated in their little family.

Torno broke the silence by snapping a flame onto his thumb. He lit a cigarette and let it sputter out. "So why didn't you stay with him?"

"Because I'm in love with you, Torno, is that what you're fishing for?"

He sighed smoke out his nostrils and looked away. "You really have no problem playing with a man's heart, do you?"

"My apologies, sir. I had no idea you were so fragile. Next time I shall handle your tender heart with gloves of velvet."

"And here comes the sarcasm." She could feel the roll of his eyes even in the dark. "Is it so hard to believe that I'm here to check on you because I genuinely care about you?"

"That all depends. How far away are you from your fifth confession of love, or will this be your sixth? I'm beginning to have trouble keeping track."

Torno sighed again. "Fourth if you don't count the last one--which I don't."

"I believe your exact words were, 'Beautiful women have beautiful destinies, and I don't want to leave yours.' You're right, that was hardly a confession at all, it was closer to a marriage proposal." She was grumbling. Her arm was finally starting to regain feeling. Ena could leave him alone in the wagon, but his concern sounded genuine for once. He didn't sound like he was trying to use her pain as a pretense to get closer.

Ena dropped her arms onto her knees and her head followed. "I almost stayed behind."

"Why didn't you? Really."

"Fear."

"What? You being too scared to take a chance on love? Say it ain't so."

"I know, it's shocking." She chuckled. "It's not like I don't have feelings for him, I do. I could've spent the rest of my life with him. I just kept thinking about how bad it would be for us. If I abandoned the Brokers to marry him we'd be happy for a time. I'd help his village, maybe even find a way to help his mother recover, but it wouldn't last. Sooner or later the Supreme Magus would come for me and take me away to work in the capital."

Torno put his hand on her back.

"Don't touch me, seriously."

He raised both of them. "I was just trying-"

"I know what you were trying and regardless of the intentions, I don't want you to touch me. As much as you think I don't care about your feelings, I do, Torno. I don't want to hurt you any more than I already have. Especially now."

The concern was evident on his face just from the glow of his cigarette.

"I might even know how you feel now," she sniffed

back the threat of tears.

"Did you sleep with this guy?"

Ena sighed and pulled herself out the back of the wagon.

"Seriously! It matters."

"Why does it matter, Torno? So that you can know if I'm still perfect wife material?"

"It matters because when you love someone sex matters, and when you don't, it doesn't." His reply came out sheepish, he couldn't even look at her while he talked about something everyone does.

"And this is something you would know?" Ena asked, skeptically.

"Of course." He snickered. "I grew up in the capital, remember?"

It was time for Ena to walk off and leave that smoke stack to his growing pile of ash.

"Ena, nothing would make you less perfect," he called out more as a jab than a compliment.

She flashed him a rude gesture.

Torno's words kept repeating in her mind while she bathed in the lake; not his words about her being perfect, but his comment about sex. Twenty wasn't too old to be a virgin, no matter what Torno said. Growing up, she'd thought no one would love an albino like her, but that all changed when she left the chantry. Away from the gossip and scheming Ena met real people, people who didn't care who her parents were. They liked her for who she was and it wasn't long before boys were asking to kiss her. Torno had been the first one that she liked back, but he was too old, too gross, and too Torno. She'd never kissed anyone and before this last trip to Risgwa, she hadn't cared.

Visk waited for her with a fresh pair of clothes, a lamp, and a spear. The Ki'an woman kept her eyes on the lake while Ena changed.

"You keeping an eye on me, Visk?" Ena asked.

"Only to see what men crave in these lands. Your flesh is too thin for me."

Ena couldn't help but laugh. "I'll try not to be disappointed. I meant to ask if you were guarding me."

"I was. The sealouse could be this far south as well as any other slimes or slizzers. You should think more before you talk, it would make it easier to understand you."

"That it would," Ena tried to agree without mirth. "I guess we both have a long night ahead of us. How bad are things inside the Sorcerer's Hall?"

"It is like a drawn bow inside. Now that you are dressed, we should arrive to release that tension."

"You're not going to keep watch for Torno?"

"If he is killed, I will fetch a dish to hold the single tear I will shed." She said it just as serious as everything else that came out of her lips.

Ena giggled. "Yours might be the only one."

There was indeed tension inside the Sorcerer's Hall and it released with an exuberant, "surprise!" Villagers from all over the region had come to meet Ena in celebration of her twentieth birthday. The celebration might've been a day early, but that was nothing a few hours wouldn't fix. So many familiar faces and reasons to celebrate, but Haenir wasn't one of them. It made sense. If Haenir knew about the party, he wouldn't have been able to leave anyway, not when his parents needed so much of his support.

"Friend Ena," Sal came up to place a hand over her entire back. The wide-mouthed Boulba had a voice like an avalanche. "These are times of celebration! Come, open up a present or three. Narla says she brought hers in from Doronel!"

"Narla probably purchased an overpriced spirit! After I refuse to drink it, she'll spend the next week emptying the bottle!"

"Yes, but think of how much joy that will bring her." Sal laughed and Ena joined in. "And who knows, maybe this will be the year that you taste a spirit and enjoy it!"

"Maybe," she chuckled. "I guess it wouldn't hurt to-"

Ena bumped into someone. She turned to apologize to their face and found an elbow. Up and up her eyes went until at last she saw the red-skinned face of a Ki'an man. According to Visk, the men of their people were more peaceful and gentle, favoring jobs like carpentry and smithing instead of combat. By the inquisitive eyes and tiny round spectacles on the fellow, Ena could believe the rumors, but not by the bulk of him. He was built wide, wider than any Ki'an she'd ever heard about. If he was of a size with Torno, he'd be a stronger man twice over.

Silence had appeared just as suddenly as the stranger and all eyes were upon him. The man slowly removed his hat and placed it over his heart. "Evening and apologies, Lady Vamqinsys."

Ena hadn't meant to tense up. She hadn't meant to walk back into Sal's chest either. The Boulba took her response as a call for help and clenched his rocky fists. "It's alright, Sal," she muttered, and thankfully he let his sluggers fall. It was the name that had shaken her. Only at the capital had anyone referred to her by her family name. It was the name of an exile.

"I had no intention of robbing you of your celebration, but I don't have the luxury of time. Is there somewhere private we can talk?" The Ki'an man spoke calmly, without the bite of Visk's matter-of-fact tone.

After a few reassurances to her friends that she wasn't in danger, she went outside for the two of them to talk in "private," while a hundred eyes watched from every window. The man was smiling apologetically with too many teeth showing, the white in the dim night was unsettling. "Again, I apologize for the interruption."

"Well, what is this about?"

He put his wide-brimmed hat back on his head. "It is a delicate matter, and I'd find it easier to relax if your friend wasn't aiming a deathstaff at me."

Ena arched a brow and the Ki'an pointed to the wagons. There was Torno just as he said, laying inside the wagon with his long ranged deathstaff in hand. She gestured, "No," and waved for him to put it away. He took his time doing it.

"Sorry about that. Maybe it would help if you told me your name."

"That's just it, Lady Vamqinsys, it's my name that is somewhat of an issue, just as yours is. I was born Eres, first blood of the Volain clan, but I took another name when I cut out my womb."

"What?" Ena whispered in horror. She stepped back, not believing what she was hearing.

"I am Hultur reborn, just as you are Ngoltur come again."

"What?!" she shouted.

Visk jumped off a balcony and landed with her spear at the ready, Narla appeared out from behind the bushes with a sparker in one hand and a banger in the other, and somewhere in the darkness Torno was taking aim with his deathstaff. The three of them were ready to kill Hultur, Bringer of War, Commander of Conquest, and Master of Evil. If Ena was as wise as the legends said, she'd be gathering enough ether to turn him into a memory, so why was she hesitating?

THE SECOND CHAPTER

Where Ngoltur is Told an Obvious Truth and Commits to a Shorter Life

Hultur showed no signs of fear behind those tiny spectacles. If Torno's deathstaff made him feel threatened, surely Narla's bomber and Visk's spear made things worse, but the Ki'an giant didn't even take a battle stance. Visk imbued her spear with red lightning and illuminated the face of a man who regarded this danger with disappointment. His feelings weren't directed at his would-be attackers or even the situation. No, it was Ena who disappointed him. If she truly was Ngoltur reborn as he said, then it was her destiny to view the devastation of two armies clashing and surrender.

Fuck that!

Surrendering sounded like madness. Ngoltur's surrender was the stupidest part of the Grand Dream. It was why Ena always hated Ngoltur. Here she was, a woman with power at least equal to Muttur and Hultur, and she didn't even try to fight. But wasn't that what Ena was doing right now? No, her hesitation was far worse, it was a hesitation born of fear. She could feel her knees shaking!

"Ena!" Visk snapped. "You must focus! He will unite my

people by bringing out their greatest evil. He turns hunters into assassins, protectors into executioners, and smiths into warmongers! In his presence evil blooms like saplings after the flames. He must be killed!"

Ena didn't see any of that in his eyes. This wasn't a man looking to corrupt the world, this was a man trying to have a conversation who got interrupted.

"Fuck!" Visk swore and launched the attack unaided by Ena.

The red lightning around Visk's spear grew to the width of an arm span. While amplifying the power of her enhancement to maximum, she hopped forward to clear the last of the distance between her and Hultur. Coming in low, she stabbed at his gut. It was a practiced strike, backed with a power that pierced house-sized monsters.

Hultur knocked the stab away with a backhand.

Red lightning shot out, striking the fields and the side of the ranch house, leaving flames in its wake. But around Hultur the concentrated bolts of ether merely crawled over his spherical shield. He ducked and a concentrated spiraling ray of green light struck the base of the Sorcerer's Hall. The force of Torno's ranged blast took out a chuck of the wall and put out the fire where the winds burst outward.

Visk shifted, bringing the tip of her spear close and above her shoulders. Hultur chased her. When she tried to strike his heart again, this time he sidestepped and grabbed the shaft of the spear.

"Ena, move!" Narla yelled.

Ena unfroze enough to take one step back. Swearing, Narla tossed the bomber at Hultur. With his free hand, he gripped the black orb. Though Ena knew it was exploding in his palm, it looked like he was creating the most concentrated burst of fire she'd ever seen. It glowed like a ball of pure light. Narla didn't give Hultur a chance to do anything with it and clapped to let out a spray of flames.

Ena was in the way of the raw burst of fire, at last

forcing her to evoke. Her cold shield was shaped like the edge of a glacier. Flames rebounded off the unseen wall, focusing the blast toward Hultur. Though it turned the grass to ash, the devastation stopped there, doing no more damage to his spherical shield than a punch did to a mountain.

But the attack at least had split Hultur's attention. He held Visk's spear, blocked the red lightning, contained the explosion of a bomb, and blocked a gout of flame. Even if it hadn't taxed him magically, and Ena didn't think it had, it split his body enough for Visk to bring her arm under his chin. She pulled back on the taller man, twisting as she tried to choke the life out of him.

Still, Hultur didn't strike back but instead pointed his hand upward to give the explosion a harmless direction to release. He was glancing back at the Sorcerer's Hall, worried about the spreading flames of Visk's first attack, and the people inside.

Though Visk was putting all her effort into choking the taller man, she was twisting him with purpose. She exposed his front to Torno. At a glance back, Ena saw an orb of light building where Torno lay on the grass. She placed herself between them to ruin his shot. Ena pulled at the wind around them, binding it to her vocal cords.

She shouted, "Stop!"

The sound of it drowned out the struggles of the fight, the crackling of lightning, and the sputter of flames.

Visk was still putting everything into keeping the shot lined up and a desperate attempt to choke Hultur. "What are you doing?! He needs to die!"

"Visk, he hasn't made a single attack."

She loosened her grip slightly.

Narla spoke up. "Ena, we might never get another chance at this. Hultur-"

"Hasn't done anything to us. If a Band of Brokers were able to kill him, do you really think the world would've needed Muttur? Stand down. All of you."

Visk got off him and recovered her spear like a child on time out. Grumbling, Narla repeatedly squeezed her sparker. Off in the distance, Ena could swear she heard Torno scream, "Fucking Ena!" His large orb of power unraveled into ribbons of light. Sal guarded the double doors into the Sorcerer's Hall, his massive hands extended to keep everyone inside.

"Sal, is anyone hurt? Where's Myrrel?"

"She went out to treat the sick, they're some time away. We're okay in here. Everyone got away from the windows when the fighting broke out." Sal was going to say more, but Ena turned her attention to the Ki'an man.

The man who called himself Hultur was still undaunted. Ena found his glasses on the floor within the circle of unburnt grass. She picked it up along with his hat, only to find that most of his fedora had been outside the circle. She held out the glasses and the still-smoking remains of his hat.

Hultur took his glasses. "I liked that hat."

"Sorry." She glanced around at the devastation. "Maybe it would've been better if we talked somewhere private."

He eyed her and Ena chuckled sheepishly.

They all went to work undoing the damage they'd wrought. Hultur helped to clean away the debris with his hands but refused to use any magic in the effort. Torno was acting like a pouting child the entire time, but he magicked some water where the walls had been while Ena froze it into place. The wall could be fixed with ease, but it would take time and manual labor without a spire. Once everything was settled everyone went inside. All in attendance were gathered around the giant man. People were sitting on the floors so that everyone could be in the same room.

"This is a mistake, Ena," muttered Torno while the gathering was still settling.

"You're just disappointed that you didn't get to fire that shot."

"I had a lot of ether behind it. Master of Evil or not, that was going to hurt him."

She rolled her eyes.

Hultur clapped his hands once and all silenced.

"Thank you all for giving me a chance to speak. As I'm sure you all know by now, I am Hultur. The revelation came with a great deal of disappointment to me. As a child, I'd been grateful that the world had gone a hundred and fifty years without the coming of the Turall. Ki'an, Gulambar, and Leben Erde had all made great strides toward creating a better world just within my parent's lifetime. To think that all of that would be destroyed in a handful of years..."

He shook his head ruefully and then got a sense of the atmosphere in the room.

"Though I've accepted my destiny as Hultur, I deny the call to conquer. I came here because I met with Theo Qinsys, the last King of Doronel. He lives in Caredor City as an exile." Hultur pointed at Ena. "That is his daughter. Born with white skin and hair, her eyes are blue, her blood is royal, and it is her destiny to play out the Grand Dream just as it happened before."

"Ena is Ngoltur?" asked the voice of an excited child.

Some laughed at the child's tactlessness, but all eyes went to the daughter of the exile. It was a question they'd half considered in the past, but now that their suspicions were confirmed, they were ready to bow to her and follow her to the capital.

"I am no Princess and I am no hero. I'm a broker and a caster, and that's all I've ever been. My father isn't Theo Qinsys, it's Althene Vamqinsys. While he is an exile from Doronel, he worked at the royal castle as an illusionist and nothing more. The King died in the March of the People, this is a history that everyone knows."

Hultur and others were smirking at her.

"What?"

"Baby Face, Vamqinsys means not Qinsys," said Narla. "It's the name given to an exiled family when they renounce their claim to hereditary lines. Your father might not be the King now, but he was born a Prince, just as you were born a Princess."

"How can you say that with such certainty?!"

"Because Liberation Day in Doronel comes in two days," came the voice of Yestepor's Sorcerer. "Doronel officially became a democracy twenty years ago, one day after you were born."

Behind her, Torno let out a single chortle. "You really didn't know."

"Of course, I didn't know!" She looked back at Torno, and then back to the villagers of Yestepor. An hour ago they'd all been friends and acquaintances. They were people she helped and never the other way around. Now they were all looking at her like they were her subjects.

"So what if I was born a princess and born albino! I'm not Ngoltur and I never will be. Ngoltur is always given that name at birth." When several hands raised to object to the truth of her claim, she cut them off with a fluttering of fingers. "Regardless! Even if it's my destiny to lay caged in a tower while I wait for my hero, I won't have any part of it! I refuse to take up my birthright and play out this story that has done no good in the history of the world!"

"Then we are of one mind," Hultur said it like he was celebrating. His wide smile didn't appear any less unsettling in the light. If anything, it looked even more unnatural poking out of his ebony beard. "We can only be agents of destiny if we follow its guiding hand. If only I desired to change the Grand Dream, then my efforts would be for naught. United, we can keep these entropic winds from deteriorating the work of generations. Are you committed to our preceding course of action?"

Visk leaned over to Narla. "What is he saying?"

"I don't know. Some people just like to hear themselves talk," she muttered.

Ena bowed her head to hide her chuckles. "If you truly

are against our destiny, then why have you come here?"

Hultur blinked. "I thought it was obvious."

Ena showed her empty hands.

"He wants to take you to Leben Erde, Princess, and it's not going to happen." Torno stepped up, his hand on the pommel of his sword.

Ena smacked his hand off the weapon. "The only thing that's not going to happen is you going around calling me Princess. My parent's exile means an end to my claim to the throne, and I don't want it anyway. Stop acting like a bandit, you're embarrassing yourself."

"I'm afraid I must share Torno's attitude," said Visk, stepping forward. "You can't risk a trip with this man, regardless of what he says."

Ena pulled Visk back by the forearm. "Were both of you not paying attention to that fight outside? No one got hurt because he didn't attack us a single time. If he wanted to kill me, he could do it now. Hultur showed up to talk and we tried to kill him. I'm supposed to be this Maiden of Peace. Think about what would happen if he went to talk to Muttur by himself. The kid would kill him outright."

"Okay. Yeah, that's cute and all, but what if he changes his mind and wants to kill you along the way?" Narla took a nervous sip from her wine. "What better way to change destiny, than to give up on marriage? For all you know, this long-stemmed pepper is doing all this to try and get the two of you to fall in love. If he starts his quest for evil after your marriage, then I don't know if even Muttur could stop the two of you."

"That settles it," Torno decided. "She's not going with you and you'll have to try your luck with Muttur by yourself."

"Excuse me!" Ena snapped at Torno. "What gives you the right to decide what I'm doing with my life?"

He pulled open his jacket and showed off his Broker's Captain's patch. "In case you've forgotten, I'm in charge. I decide where we're going and when, and a detour to Leben

Erde isn't on the itinerary."

"Well, last time I checked, Fallen Princesses outrank upjumped brown nosers," she snarled at him.

"So you're a Princess after all. That didn't take very long, did it?"

Ena was seething.

If it wasn't for Visk putting an arm between them, she might actually smack him. "I think we can all agree that all of this goes well beyond our contract to work as brokers."

"Friends," Sal said in his kind way that was somehow never condescending. "I don't know if we should be discussing this in front of everyone else."

They looked at the villagers in various states of awe, panic, and sleepiness.

"Whatever decision you make will affect these people," Hultur said. "You were bound to help them. If you leave, you're leaving them behind to survive a year of turmoil on their own. I think it only fair that they have a say in their future."

"Very well." Yestepor's Sorcerer rose. "I think she should go with them."

"What?" Torno growled.

"But your village..." Sal pouted.

Ena put a hand on the Boulba's head-shoulder.

The sorcerer continued. "Times are tough right now, there's no denying it. We've never seen sores like these pustules before, and there's enough evil in the air to breed a horde of monsters, but these tragedies are nothing new to us. We lived before without the brokers, and we'll find a way to live without them again."

He raised his hands to quiet the protests of Ena's friends. They did eventually quiet down. "It won't be forever, and many of us were going to have to go the year without your help anyway. Now if I had my say, we'd be gathering our wands and gulda and storming the capital to demand our people back. That self-made Supreme Magus has taken our sons and mothers and they had no right to it, none at all."

Murmurs of agreement went up throughout the Sorcerer's Hall.

"But it's not my place to tell women what to do, Princess or not. If you don't want to be a force for revolution, I won't push you into it. The way I see it, you've helped us all more than you needed to, and you don't owe us anything. So whatever you're going to do, just do it." The Sorcerer sat down and then immediately stood back up. "And a Captain has no right to order Ngoltur around, Torno, you know better than that."

The grumpy ruffian rolled his eyes but didn't voice whatever snide comeback was scraping at the back of his mind.

With that, the Sorcerer sat down, and all eyes were on Ena once again.

"I don't want to be a revolutionary, even if it is justified. I may have been born a princess, but I'm not a leader. If you all want your family back, then unite and storm the capital together. You don't need me to do that and you never did. You all might think that you're the only ones who feel this way because you live in the outskirts of Caredor, but you're not alone. Your complaints are echoed in every bar, in every town hall, and in every bedroom in every city. If you want to start a revolution, then do it, but that isn't my calling."

She looked to Hultur. "I don't know if I am Ngoltur reborn, but I know one thing, this man is Hultur. There's no denying that. I've never seen anyone wield such power with so little effort. If he thinks that we can keep the world at peace, then I'm going with him. I have to try."

Ena looked to her fellow Brokers. "By doing this, I'm making myself a traitor. That's a decision that I'm making and I don't think you should come with us. I don't have the right to put any of you at risk."

Narla leaned against the head-body of Sal. "Isn't that cute, she still thinks we're not going to support her?"

"It must be the folly of youth I've heard so much about," Sal agreed with a chuckle.

"Please be serious about this," Ena pleaded.

"They are being serious, Pr-"

Ena glowered at Torno.

"-ecious." He paused to grin. "We've been together every day for three years. Any one of us could've requested a transfer to another post or to service an area with more prestige. Wherever you're going, we're going with."

"Besides, you'll need someone to watch your back," Visk said, never taking her eyes off Hultur.

"Okay. Thank you all." Ena bit back tears and leaned in to give them all a hug, even Torno.

The double doors to the ranch house flew open. Myrrel stood on the threshold. She was, in every way imaginable, the mother of the group. Her hair was a wavy rat's nest because she was too focused on helping everyone else to look in a mirror. She had a perpetual look of worry that only disappeared to give way to an ever-approaching wave of sleepiness. The woman had thick shoulders, a tough jaw, and an attire that was all utility and no flash. The healer had a battle wand in one hand and an axe in the other. She lowered both and blinked at the passive assembly.

"What's going on?"

Narla answered fast. "Ena finally figured out that she's Ngoltur reborn. We're breaking our contract to the Supreme Magus by following Hultur to Leben Erde. Oh, and we were in the middle of a group hug."

"Oh. Well, count me in." The people laughed but Myrrel walked up and threw her body over Ena's back.

"Um, Myrrel, we were kind of done with the hugging," Ena mumbled with her face smushed into Sal's arm.

"Ssh. The group hugs don't end until I say so. You know that, Camellia."

Ena laughed at Myrrel's enthusiasm and her nickname as the white flower. There was nothing to do but lean into the hug until she pulled away. Even if she was next to Torno it didn't have to be horrible. He was risking his life for her, that had to count for something.

Myrrel leaned back and glanced at Hultur. "So, you're the big evil, huh?"

"It would appear so."

"Funny, I thought you would look more menacing."

"I used to have a hat," Hultur offered with a shrug.

People laughed. Sighs of relief went about the room.

"I'm drained from healing eight people back from the brink of death and I see bottles of wine. Is this a birthday party or isn't it?" Myrrel asked.

Nods and jovial shouts went about the room and the crowd either jumped back into festivities or fetched their horses to go to bed. It was incredible how quickly Myrrel changed the flow of the room. If anyone should be a lost Princess, it should be her.

Visk put her arm around Ena's shoulders. "You know we cannot trust him."

"I know, Visk, but this isn't about him. This is about the fate of the world and maybe even breaking a cycle thousands of years old. I have to try to do this, and it'll be a lot easier to sleep knowing that you'll be watching my back."

She nodded and raised her head with pride. Her glower was trained on the only fellow Ki'an in the room.

Torno was also lurking about, his dark eyes waiting for an opportunity to swoop in and voice his opinion.

Ena confronted him. "Can you spare me the 'you're making a terrible mistake' speech? I'd like to enjoy what's left of my party."

"Actually, I was going to praise you."

Ena leered at him.

"I'm serious. That was a good speech. I know you don't think of yourself as a leader, but that was a pretty impressive start to an epic quest."

"Well, with any luck this won't be a story that needs to

be told. There's no reason Hultur and I won't find Muttur and keep a massive war from erupting on the three continents."

Torno had one of those annoying looks on his face.

"What?!"

He almost patted her on the head, but thankfully stopped himself. "It's good to know you still haven't lost your idealism."

He walked off to grab a drink and Ena couldn't care less. She was done worrying about him, done thinking about her destiny, and done mulling over the fact that her parents had lied to her. She was going to follow Myrrel like a shadow and have the best birthday of her life if it killed her.

Around the time that Ena and Myrrel were getting hungry, everyone else was falling asleep on the floor. Hultur hadn't been the partying type, choosing to retreat into a bedroom the moment drinks started pouring. Everyone was nervous about waking him up, and they knew they'd have to get him into the wagon before Visk because she would definitely want to kill him in his sleep. All things considered, it wasn't the worst idea, but Ena had given her word that she would work with Hultur to keep this era of fraught peace going. Myrrel volunteered to wake him and the giant came out a moment later, ready to ride.

Ena had a brief conversation with the village sorcerer and her friends in Yestepor that were still awake. They meant what they said and urged her to not look back and think about the duties she was leaving behind. It bit at her stomach worse than Narla's birthday present. People were going to die because she was leaving on this fool's quest, but then people were going to die no matter what she did.

Torno was half-drunk and half-asleep and kissed Myrrel three times on the cheek while she led him back to the wagon. She teased him flirtatiously and the drunk gnave showered her with compliments. The lighter patches of Myrrel's skin lit up from blush. When Ena caught her staring, the woman looked away in shame.

Hultur had brought two "gerhat" horses, which were some kind of enlarged breed native to Ki'an, known for their speed. He had brought the second one for Ena, but Visk took it so she could watch the rear. Having the two of them off the wagon made it easier for Ena and Myrrel to relax in the jockey box.

After a glance back at the sleeping Brokers, Ena smiled wide at Myrrel. "So what was that about?!"

She sighed. "I knew you weren't going to let that go." She sat up and closed the tarps to the wagon's innards, making sure everything was tight as a tourniquet.

"How could I? Have you and Torno..."

"No. Love spells be real, I'd have cast one on him," she giggled.

"How long have you had feelings for him?"

"That depends on if you believe in love at first sight," Myrrel mumbled.

"Myrrel!"

"What, he's an attractive man! I know you don't like him and think he's this greasy rogue, but I like that about him. If it wasn't for you, something probably would've happened by now."

"You mean because he's hung up on me?" she asked.

"No, because he's obsessed with you. He only ever flirts with me if he's drunk. If it wasn't for the fact that so many of the men I treat are so..." she cleared her throat, "grateful about my healing, I might've got him drunk and had my way with him."

"You're not worried about the two of you changing the group dynamic?"

Myrrel scoffed so loudly it almost turned into a snort. "Why because he's the captain? Ena, the man has never once questioned my judgment calls. I'm a healer, I know what's best for the people we're helping. Torno is a Lord's bastard. He knows what he has is a good thing and he isn't going to ruin that by making unnecessary drama."

Ena was staring at her.

"What?"

"I didn't know he was a bastard," Ena grumbled.

"But you call him that all the time. The first time I heard it I thought you were being a little cruel, but let's be honest, you've called him worse."

"Well, I didn't know he was a bastard." She sighed. "I thought he grew up in the lap of luxury with servants fanning his back and feeding him grapes."

"Those things might've happened, but there's a lot more to high-class living than being waited on hand and foot. You're probably a sweeter person because you didn't grow up in that life."

Ena was smiling at wagon mamma.

"What?"

"You really think I'm sweet?"

She kissed her on the forehead. "Of course I do, my sweet little camellia."

Ena pulled herself away from the awe Myrrel projected. "So what are you going to do about Torno?"

"There's nothing to do. He likes you, you hate him, and I'm not so old that I can't still make men melt over me like butter on bread."

Ena thought about that. She'd suspected that she had been hooking up with injured men here and there, but she didn't think it happened so often. "Myrrel, has anyone ever proposed to you?"

"Oh, all the time. There's nothing like healing and sex to make a man think you were crafted by the Gods to please him. When I really want something to happen, I sweeten the deal with a meal and mead."

Ena laughed. "That works?"

"Like a love spell. Listen, we all want to be magical beings full of higher thoughts, but most of us is animal. This flesh hungers, it hurts, and it gets horny. When you can tap into the first two, the third is rarely far behind."

Ena only contained her guffaws because she had no intention of waking the others. "You sound like a hunter!"

Myrrel rolled her eyes. "Camellia, these men know what I'm doing. If a man's married he'll talk about his wife or look away when I'm treating him and I know to leave well enough alone. But sometimes a man smiles at me the same way that I'm smiling at him and everything feels right. The simple truth is that some men are a little shy and they need you to make it easier to make the first move."

Ena bit her lip and changed course.

"Planning a little detour, are we?" Myrrel shot her a knowing glance.

"Just a little."

The women giggled.

Hultur rode to their side. "Is something the matter?"

"We're gonna need supplies," Myrrel said like that explained everything.

"I don't like all these delays," he grumbled.

"The woman's given up her entire life to join you on this quest and so have all of us. Give us a little bit of slack."

He considered it, nodded, and rode off.

"That man's a virgin," Myrrel said with certainty.

"Good! Can you imagine what it would be like sleeping with the Master of Evil?"

"No, but I'm sure I'll be dreaming about it soon enough," she said, fanning her neck and chest.

They laughed again.

~ ~ ~

Myrrel shook Ena awake. It was close to sunset outside. Narla was the only other person in the wagon's interior, and she was dead asleep. "We're coming up on Risgwa now. What's the plan, lover girl?"

Ena rubbed the sleep out of her eyes. "I'm gonna grab one of those fancy horses and I'm gonna say goodbye real proper this time."

Myrrel smiled. "I'll stall the others as much as I can."

Ena grabbed her arm. "I don't think you understand. You're gonna convince them all to get rooms for the night."

Myrrel chuckled. "Oh, Ena. I'm liking you at twenty."

Ena couldn't believe how naughty all of this felt. Her heart was pounding in her chest, but so little of it was from shame, and the blood was straying far from her cheeks. If she was going to die far away on some foreign continent, she wasn't going to do it without finding love. It was still her birthday, and she was going to make it one that she never forgot.

THE THIRD CHAPTER

In Which Ngoltur Loses Her Virginity

Ena felt like a child riding a horse so large. It was rigid in gallop, the flesh only moving and shaking as hooves met ground. Leaning forward and pressing her body along the mane of his neck, she could feel the motion of his body in perfect harmony. She was the horse, galloping to outrun the sun. When he breathed in, Ena felt her legs lift. Her chest and head moved with every little change in direction. And when it came time to slow, they lifted their bodies in tandem.

Haenir's farm was a simple place. The silo, kikaa coop, and goat pen were all the same building; attached to an empty two-horse stable. The stable was crafted years ago by Narla the first time the Band of Brokers arrived to help the family of three. It was made to welcome Ena's return.

Ena cast an aero spell, tossing a ball of wind into the middle of the stable. She popped it early and cleaned the place of cobwebs and dust. Some remained and she cleaned the last of it with a smaller aero resting over the tip of her finger. Her new friend wasn't happy about his accommodations, but they were all they had. She latched him into his cell and he motioned for the road, eager to gallop again. She put her hand against his neck. He ceased stirring, but the pounding of his heart remained.

Feel.

She focused her will on the word. Ether tingled up and down her spine like the moon shimmering on the lake. Touching her heart, she pulled out a single strand and twirled it into the horse's mane. Excitement. Gallop. A love of the wind. Cramped space. This was all that passed through the boundary of species. Ena could understand how he felt, but it was time to rest. She told him with her eyes and by brushing his cheek and neck. Gale was a good name for him. She could feel it in his heart and naming him aloud settled the beast.

Trouble? Stranger.

Haenir stood by the entrance, a bucket of feed in one hand, a basket of grooming tools in the other. Shadows made the man into a stranger. Gone were the dimples in his cheeks at the end of his smile and the excited lift of his ever-somber eyebrows. She'd never been alone when she met him. There was always more to a person than what they showed the world. Somewhere inside Haenir was rage, covetousness, jealousy, and other dark feelings he kept hidden even from himself.

Fear pulled at Ena's heart. Once she went to him there was no going back. No light would reveal the face she'd known. Kindness was something she'd learned to appreciate and if she walked forward she'd never again see his smile and know that kindness lived in people. This friend would never again be able to greet her, there would be someone else there in his stead. Death wasn't guaranteed. She could still come back to the Haenir that always thought to bring her water or a handful of gulda imbued with the slivers of ether he could focus. Nothing had to change.

She took a step forward.

Gone were her memories of his smile and the smell of their past. They were replaced by a stomach that quirked and churned. Blood rushed through her. Every blade of grass came into focus. That shadow wasn't a mask, it was a barrier keeping him from her. She was still afraid. She could feel the fear cutting through the kiln of her heart, letting the heat out as everything precious cracked under the sudden gust of raw air.

He put the supplies down.

Cracking. That's what was happening to her. She was cracking from the inside. Something around her protected her from the harsh elements and memories of isolation. That unknown shell over her heart was cracking and the fear inside was pushed out. It gave her commands, but she could only hear the undercurrent of its voice, like a conversation heard from the other side of a wall.

She touched his face.

He was hot to the touch, warm with life. Slowly, she ran her fingers to the back of his chin and felt the harsh stab of stubble against skin soft as water. Ambient light broke through the darkness, the sheen coming off her bright complexion. This wasn't a boy unsure of his place in the world, overwhelmed with gratitude and awe for her. Haenir looked every bit as guilty as he looked hungry. The soft chestnut of his eyes was dark and sweet as burnt sugar.

His hands touched her hips, moved not an inch inward, and stopped.

He knew fear too. Doubt crawled over his face. Seeing his trepidations brought out all of her uncertainty. She wasn't holding his cheek in her hand, but his heart. She knew what it felt like to watch as a loved one left and never returned. How could she put him through that?

"I haven't stopped thinking about you," he admitted. His voice came in deep and husky, he sounded like a man on his deathbed. Where were the assuring flits in his voice when he spoke?

"I'm not here to marry you."

Stabbing him would've been kinder. His hands fell to his sides. Pain replaced fear on his brow, and it brought out that anger that Ena had always known was there. He looked away. Ena tried to touch his face, to bring his eyes back to her, but he stepped out of her grasp. He picked up the supplies and went to care for Gale.

"Haenir..."

"I...I love you, Ena. You know I do, but you can't say it back, so why are you here?" Cruelty wavered his voice. He was readying an attack, trying to find a way to hurt her the way she'd hurt him. Before he'd only ever sounded like he was searching for the best way to make her smile.

"Because I can't stop thinking about you either. Months ago when I was coming back to Risgwa, you were all I could think about. I couldn't sleep on the way here, and I couldn't sleep that first night back when you asked me to dance and we only stopped with the music. If things were different, I would've married you, Haenir. But we never would've had a life together. The second I became a farmer's wife, they would've sent someone in from the capital to bring me back." She was shaking. She cast back the cold with a spell, but no warmth came to her.

He worked the brush over Gale's ashen coat.

"I do love you, Haenir. I didn't want to say it because it would make everything real. Because then every time we'd see each other we'd have to know that we could be together. It would've been too painful to live a life where I could never be with the man who holds my heart."

He'd stopped caring for the horse. Confusion, pain, and hope all fought to dominate his expression. Pain was winning. "What changed?"

"I don't have a future to worry about anymore."

Worry pulled him closer. He closed the gate and moved to comfort her.

She held up a hand to stop him. "I have to leave. I'm breaking my contract and becoming a fugitive."

"What-"

"I'm going to Leben Erde, Haenir. I don't know if I'll ever be back. There's a good chance that I'll be killed. Even if I survive, I don't know how I can ever return to Caredor."

Her eyes had dropped to the floor and her head followed, bringing her chin to rest on her sternum. He touched her cheek now. Eyes met again. There was an amber light in his eyes, it was such a beautiful hue, but altogether too fragile. With the slightest tilt of his chin or a minute shift in his focus that stellar color disappeared. But his eyes stayed on hers. His hand was warm, warmer than Gale's coat, warmer than the sun's rays on her back, but oh so much colder than the pounding in her chest.

"I came to say goodbye."

He shook his head. "Whatever's going on, you don't have to do this alone. I can go with you."

"And leave your parents behind to die alone in that sad hut?" She shook her head ever so slightly, his gentle hand on her cheek moved along without hindering. "Besides, I'm not alone. The others are coming with. I just..." She swallowed hard. "I told them to wait back at the inn."

He swallowed and kept his lips parted.

"I want to spend the night with you." She ran her hand over his arm, feeling the strength in his muscles that he only used for work and never to grab her. His fingers found hers and they interlocked intuitively. "If I can't spend my life with you, let me have one night. I know it's selfish, but-"

His lips came before hers. Ena didn't remember tilting her head or bringing her hand around to the small of his back. She'd never seen that look in his eyes, nor any man in her life, but she knew it. The heat in those glowing amber eyes matched the flames inside her. With that kiln cracked, the blaze caught and spread down. Her head was fuzzy with smoke. There were no more thoughts of words.

Lips came together gently and parted quickly. The feel of him peeled back like a wound and she stung where he left her. They kissed again, just as tentative, but a force came between them. It lasted a single moment and lingered in her mind even as their lips came apart. She kissed him repeatedly, searching for that force, feeling the shape of him against her. He chased a kiss and held her head still in his firm grip. Their tongues embraced and she found that yearning; it pressed down into her mouth and poured through her like a river breaking a damn.

Pangs of guilt pulled her hand back but he stayed firm, his fingers never once unwrapping. She pushed back and he met her, keeping his resolve steady. He meant to love her. He had a lifetime of love ready to give her, and with the smallest encouragement, his passion pushed into her. There was assurance in that strength, there was safety in his arms. She forgot about tomorrow, or the feel of the stable threshold pressing against her back, or the tickle of sweat rolling down her neck. She wanted to feel the flesh of this man, and his lips and arms were so much less than everything he had to give.

Panting, they stared into each other's eyes. He searched for confirmation. She brought up their hands, still interlocked, over her heart. He swallowed. Doubt gave rise to nervous shimmers in those chestnut eyes. She pressed the back of his hand against her heart. She inclined her head and he brought his forehead to rest against hers. Their sweat intermingled. Their breaths came out in tandem. She pressed against his hand to move it down, but he resisted. She kissed the side of his lips.

He let out a wince of protest.

She kissed along his cheek, slowly working her mouth over to his ear. His panting came out labored. Not kissing him completely, she pressed her lips to his ear and slowly parted them. Gentler than a dandelion seed on the wind she whispered, "Touch me."

He ran his hand over the curve of her breast so gently, she thought he would pull it away to wave out a burn, but it remained on her tunic. She leaned into his hand and he followed the motion of her down to her belly. He ran his hands over her ribs and came to touch her neck. She met his lips before he'd even finish tilting his head. His opposite hand found her breast and his fingers sunk into her naturally as any glove.

She pulled at his shirt and worked her hands under the fabric. She squeezed at his pecs, rolled over his sweaty skin, and grabbed his flesh wherever she could get her fingers in. His hips were so close, but something deep inside told her no. That way led to danger, the death of safety, and the end of good feelings. But everytime she broke these laws he grunted deep in her throat. Every little trespass of her fingers brought this man closer.

Fear stilled her lips. The shaking returned in her knees and wrists. She grabbed the sides of him. He looked at her with concern but in a heartbeat the worry and doubt disappeared like they'd never been there at all. Anticipation stilled him.

Fingers slipped under the hem of his trousers and ran the length of his hips. She pushed into him, giving her the leverage to work her fingers over the curve of his hips. She touched the damp curls of his hairs. He kissed the side of her face and pressed into her hand. Then she felt him, not against her fingers, but along her arm.

There was a wetness that found her, and it stayed. Twisting, the skin of her forearm came to rest against the length of him. She touched taught testicles and felt them pulse in her fingers. He kissed her slowly and pulled back to leave his lips there. He was there for the taking, all of him. His heart ached with love and passion and she could feel its beat in his erection.

Tentatively, inquisitively, she pulled up. He grunted deep and it took his breath. He shook and gasped against her cheek. She chuckled and they laughed together. Before he stopped laughing, she tried her hand again, moving it up and down in small motions, seeing how it awoke that yearning he never showed with words. Without warning she stopped. He gasped and let out a simpering protest.

They laughed again and she ran her hand over the depth of his abs.

"Can we go to the silo?" she asked him innocently.

"There's a fresh pile of hay," he said between gasps.

She took his hands and giggled. "Well, what are we waiting for?"

They broke off into a run, laughing all the while. He closed the barn doors to the silo. She willed the light crystals on and found a river of ether surging through her.

His skin had never been so flush with life, his eyes never so attentive. He was staring at her with love, frozen by the familiar awe of his captivated gaze.

"I want to see you naked," she told him honestly.

"Should I go slow?"

She giggled and worked off her top. His hands were frozen on the hem of his breeches. With a smirk and a tilt of her brow, he got back to it. Breeches and underthings came off in a single motion. Seeing him only in a top, he looked embarrassed to show off his thick erection. Ena wiggled out of her brassiere and pants, and laid them on the hay. Biting his lip, he let go of embarrassment and took off his shirt.

He was gorgeous. Each bead of sweat caught the light like stars. Somehow this handsome man was staring at her with wonder. It made her smile to see him so enamored. She walked up without a care for her stride. He took her head in his hands and she found the base of his penis again.

In a way, they went back to how they'd been before, with her stroking and him kissing and panting, and yet it was nothing like before. That playful streak that had taken hold of her was gone. Now she pulled at his erection to encourage him. If his kisses slowed, if his hands lingered on any part of her naked flesh, she gripped him tight at the base and pushed down. It worked too well for Ena to let go. There'd be no more thoughts of tomorrow or fearful confessions. She wanted his body. She wanted his passion directed only at her, and the more he gave, the more she stroked.

He gripped her arm at the elbow and finally gave up on

being weak. He pulled her hand off him and pressed forward. Her heels hit hay and he lowered her down with one hand along her back. He was so strong. He touched her to knead her flesh and adjust her body, and the way he moved her took the breath out of her lungs. She was laid down and parted. He pulled at her hips to ready her. This wasn't the man she'd known, and she couldn't wait for him to enter her.

With a single hand, she steadied his hips. "Let me," she whispered.

Panting, he nodded. Sweat dripped off his dark brow. Meeting his gaze, she ran her tongue over her hand. With one hand she gripped the base of him while the other rubbed saliva and precum over that swollen head. She parted her wet lips and spread her legs apart as far as she could. She throbbed to meet him but knew this pleasure would come with the pain of losing her virginity.

She moved her hand to the back of his hips and kissed him.

The feel of his lips and tongue let her focus on him, and she wanted that. She wanted to pay attention to his excitement, to feel the strength in his arms, the yearning in his hips, and the quiver of his heart. He kept grunting and gasping and it made it easier for her to wince. The first came out as a shriek. Gripping him tight, she grit her teeth and let the sounds escape her lips. He was deep inside her, so much deeper than her finger had ever gone. She caught her breath and everything shifted around her. Her entire body unclenched. She held onto him, the only thing that was real. Every breath flowed through her like she could feel every individual vein. At the peak of her breathing, before the next gasp, she felt her passions returning.

The beat of her heart took hold of her, moving her hips ever so slightly. He pressed against her this way and that, holding steady as she worked herself against him. She grunted a pleading, desperate sound and he moved those glorious hips. He worked into her, pressing hip to hip before pulling back.

Kissing became impossible. There was room for grunting, moans, and hissing, but no words. Entwined in each other's arms, driven by the hunger of their flesh, they'd finally found the rhythm that they craved. She fought to find her breath, to take hold of him and gaze into his eyes. Gasping, she kissed the side of his face and found him. There was so much pleasure and disbelief there. This was real. Everything she felt for him was real, and those feelings wouldn't let go. They gripped her heart. She squeezed his back. She embraced every part of him from his back to his rigid excitement deep inside her. She held him with everything that she was and screamed a breathless scream that pulsed through her.

Orgasm wracked her body. Each breath she found only through a gasp and had to wince and struggle to get another. He was holding her back, keeping her as close as possible. He never wanted to let her go, and she wanted the same. She wanted to stay in his arms forever and feel this pleasure every day of their simple life together. She didn't want to go. She didn't want to die. She held him long after they'd come. Every kiss he laid on her head and neck was something she wanted to keep forever.

One night wasn't enough for the love he held for her.

Haenir pulled back and gathered his clothes. It couldn't be over yet, the sun hadn't even set. He must've seen the fear on her brows, because he returned to kiss her forehead. "I just need to tell my parents that I'll be sleeping out here. I'll get some blankets and something to eat, too."

Ena was digging her nails into his arm.

He caressed the back of her hand. "I'll be back."

She let go and watched the natural light drown out the crystals of the silo. Ena sat up and took a meditative position. She placed her hands on her belly and brought them low, feeling the sperm and eggs fighting to find life. It was easy to still them. They were such fragile things, barely able to exist, their only purpose was to create something that they would never be. But she couldn't afford to be a mother now, just as she couldn't stay behind and love this man with everything that she was.

Haenir returned with blankets, pillows, and a basket of goods. He had a bottle of wine their parents had been saving for their wedding. Ena knew he was giving up on their future, but she was going through that same pain. They talked about every moment they wanted to kiss each other. They confessed how they'd dreamt about having children and growing old together. They drank the wine, kissed, and confessed their love through the dance of sex. None of it was ever enough to ease Ena's guilt, nor her sorrow, nor her fear of the journey ahead.

She lay on his chest, absently running her fingers over bare skin and short hairs. "I don't want you to wait for me."

"I'm going with you, Ena."

"You're really going to leave your parents behind?"

"They'll find someone to take care of them. They could even live with the sorcerer if it came to that. My parents, they don't want-"

"I don't want you to go," Ena confessed. She tried to keep him from sitting up, but he kept pushing until she relented.

"Why? You love me, you told me you did," Haenir said.

"But we're not going on a honeymoon. I'm traveling to a foreign country to try and talk sense to a person who was born to fight for me. I'm fighting against a destiny that's been going on for thousands of years. I'm probably going to die, Haenir, don't you get that?"

"So don't go."

Ena looked away and he took her hands.

"Please, Ena. Just don't go." He kissed her cheek.

Ena kissed him back. She took his head in her hands so he wouldn't look away. "I have to do this."

He let out a long, slow sigh. "I know."

"I can't have you coming with me. If you're there I'm going to spend the entire time worrying about us and all of us will have to invest too much ether protecting you."

He leaned back and scowled. "So I'd be a burden."

"Yes."

He got up.

"Haenir."

"I need to relieve myself." He left the silo.

Ena sighed. This was always going to hurt him. She knew it, but she still came back here to say goodbye in the way that she wanted. If they were quiet and kissed then they could be happy, but if they stopped and thought about the future for even a moment everything fell out of focus, like the amber in Haenir's eyes.

He came back after too long. He joined her under the blankets and rubbed her back. His cool hands were shocking, but brought comfort as they warmed. "I don't regret tonight. This was so much more than what I thought it would be like. I just don't want you to leave, Ena."

"I don't want to leave either."

Haenir wrapped his arms around her and she settled into his embrace. "You're right about my parents. They'd be miserable having to leave the farm and live with someone else. Mom's snoring would make her enemies wherever she went. But I'd give all of that up if you ask me to. I'd leave behind my parents, I'd leave my home and spend the rest of my days with you if you only asked. I don't care how dangerous it is. I'd rather die by your side than live without you."

"But I don't want that," she confessed. "I don't want to watch you die at the spear of some murderous Ki'an, or chewed to bits by a monster, or watch you killed to fulfill some twisted prophecy. You can have a great life here, Haenir, I know you can. If you let me go, you'll find someone who will love you just as much as I do. This is your home, please don't leave it behind to be with me. Promise me that you'll fight to be happy here. Promise me."

After a long time, he sighed, kissed the back of her head, and promised.

~ ~ ~

Deep asleep, Ena didn't hear the horses ride up. She didn't hear the goats screaming at the people surrounding the building. She didn't smell the torches lit. She didn't know anything was wrong until the doors of the silo were cut open. Two Ki'an women kicked the splintered wood off the hinges. They ducked under the entrance and entered with swords drawn. Ena tried to scream, but the words didn't escape. She was moving slowly, hindered by a chrono-bubble. Haenir leapt at them, not a piece of cloth on him.

One woman lifted him by the neck while the other slit open his belly. Guts poured onto the ground and they tossed his corpse aside. The pair knelt before the viscera on the ground. They ran their hands through the guts, holding up bits of his intestine and discussing the contents. Haenir's body was still. There was no color in his eyes, only white pools where life had once been. Ena tried to cast, she tried to scream and run up and attack them, but her body only thrashed uselessly against the sheets and straw.

A lone figure walked through the hole in the silo where the doors had been. He held a flaming sword in one hand and a shield in the other. His skin was the faintest blue. His ears were long and pointed. The Ki'an held up Haenir's guts in celebration. The short man of Leben Erde laughed.

THE FOURTH CHAPTER

In Which Ngoltur Says Goodbye

E na pulled out of the sheets. Hands quirked and strained through the gestures of temporal magic. The slow spell was broken, because it had never been. The silo door still stood on its hinges. The dirty floor was only covered in straw, bedding, and clothes. There were no signs of any blood.

Haenir wrapped the sheet around her shoulders and held her from behind. "You were yelling in your sleep. Are you alright?"

Normally, when someone expelled that much ether they were drained from the effort. Ena took on the look of fatigue by staring at a distant point on the horizon. It was a simple deception, but one she needed to perform. Or at least she had.

Ena snuggled into Haenir's. Cool skin took from the comfort he offered, draining her of anything like serenity. She got her arms around his flesh and squeezed. "I dreamt you were killed."

"I'm here."

Ena squeezed as tight as she could and the man didn't even wince. He just held her back, gently kissing her cheek and neck.

"Please don't come with, and don't try to follow us,"

she whispered. "If anything happened to you...Promise me you'll stay here."

Haenir let out a slow sigh. "I can't do that."

She pulled back to argue her point, to plead and beg if she needed to.

"But, I promise that I won't follow you on your quest. Wherever I'm going, whatever I do, I'll do it for me. I promise you."

That stilled her heart. She closed her eyes to push out the vivid nightmare, but it remained. Her lips found his chest. She kissed her way up to his waiting lips. They embraced. Past the point of panic, his flesh became inviting. That one kiss only stopped for their passions to take over. Glances and grunts passed between them, but no words were said. This was about love and they wouldn't ruin that by starting their goodbye.

Panting above him, her breath came back slowly. It wasn't out of elation or exhaustion that she came to rest on his chest, but a kind of defeatism. Poofs of her unstyled hair came to rest on his body. Those mangled curls were a mark of her destiny, curly locks that supposedly looked like pearl and gold. Their color was closer to that of wheat and salt or maybe common dandelions. He was the one who looked beautiful. Every pinch of his flesh mesmerized her.

Ena's breath brought a companion back to her chest, panic. The time for sweat and passion had ended. Sweat trailed down her brow and rolled over trembling lips. Again and again, she reached for the words, but she would've found it easier to grab the sun and shove it back under the horizon. Haenir took her hand, their fingers interlocked.

The ecstasy had left his face, but so had the fear. It was okay. He wasn't upset at her. He wasn't broken. He would find a way to live without her and she didn't need to say goodbye. He kissed her fingers. She kissed his. Ena climbed up his chest and joined their lips. This was a kiss without lust or need. It was a kiss of apologies and gratitude. It was a kiss of their love that could never be fulfilled.

Ena thought they'd have time for breakfast, so they went out to the bath. Haenir took his time scrubbing her back. With every touch, he admired a new feature of hers. He was enamored by the pink flush that broke through her impossibly white skin. He adored the ridge of her elbow, which seemed particularly pointy. He giggled at the way her stomach lurched back when he surprised her with a kiss. He didn't voice all his thoughts. That was the feeling that gripped Ena when it was time for her to wash him.

She was silent. She might never feel the touch of a man like this again. Even if she did, would she ever love one the way she loved him? He was so much more to her than she'd ever known. Fear had kept her away and Ena still understood that fear. They weren't alone in this world. So many troubles could've come for them, but they all seemed small compared to the Grand Dream that called to her.

They dressed each other in slow reverence. He held out her pants and she stepped into them as his hands slid over her skin. She put on his shirt as he ducked down. She swept back his wet hair and raised his chin to bring him into a kiss. Haenir presented her a single flower growing by the edge of the water spout, a duskshade.

The flower was a small, selfish thing that sucked the nutrients right out of the soil. Its petals ran a gradient from day yellow to sunset red before ending in a black stripe. Bothersome things weren't supposed to be beautiful. He moved to place the flower in her damp hair. She started to shake her head but tilted it away from him instead. The thick stem fit right into the strands of her hair. His hand slid over her cheek. Approaching horses stilled them. They didn't hide from the coming wagon, but neither could they look at each other.

The Band of Brokers had returned. This time there would be no return trip.

"I want-"

Haenir took her hand and squeezed. She risked a look and found his gaze steady. "It's okay, Ena. I'm going to be okay. I'm not going to live like how I was. I'll make something great of my life, I promise you. And if love finds a way to me, I won't close my heart to it."

His conviction was reassuring. She could imagine this handsome man in a suit of armor or a lord's clothes. He would find a life without her. She could let him go. Knowing that suddenly made it all the more painful to leave his side. "I'm sorry I didn't kiss you sooner."

"I'm not." He ran his hand over her cheek. "I don't regret a single moment with you."

She kissed him. She didn't care if Torno was watching or if Narla was going to start hooting and hollering. She loved him and wanted to say goodbye with a kiss. But it struck her that she wasn't saying goodbye to the Haenir she knew. No, that man had left her sometime yesterday. He was different. There was so much more to him than he'd ever shown her; than she'd ever known to seek. Ena had come to say goodbye, but instead their night together only felt like saying hello.

"I'm sorry, Camellia. It's time."

Ena looked back to Myrrel. The wagon was upon them. Visk had saddled and mounted Gale. They were all there waiting for her. She must've been kissing him for close to ten minutes. Everything was happening so fast.

"I'll always love you, Haenir."

He smiled to hear that. "Love your life, Ena. Whatever time you have left, no matter what impossible things you have to do, love your life."

She nodded. "I'll try. Good luck on your adventure, wherever it takes you."

They waved at each other. She climbed into the wagon and turned around to look at him. What a handsome man he was! Had he always stood so tall or looked so brave? She wanted to run back and kiss him. She wanted to spend just one more night with him. She wanted to spend the rest of her life with him, but she couldn't. If he came with them, if she stayed behind, something would tear them apart. She had no doubt about which of them would be made to suffer.

"Save the world, Ena. Save us all from this cycle of violence. You can do it, I know you can. I believe in you," he called out to her.

Ena laughed back at him. "Stop it, you're making me nervous."

Torno cracked the reins from the jockey box.

Haenir was falling out of view quickly now. "Don't be nervous. You're Ngoltur reborn. It's your destiny to do good. Believe in yourself, Ena. I love you."

"I love you," she called back. He said something else, but she didn't hear it. It couldn't have been what she thought. This couldn't be the last time they saw each other. She leaned back in the wagon and whispered, "Goodbye."

~ ~ ~

Ena sat before the campfire late that night. No one had inquired for details or offered their sympathies. Instead, the wagon had been alive with talk of Leben Erde, each of them trying to remember a different fact about the continent far to the west. She hadn't been able to contribute to the conversations. It wasn't just that Ena missed Haenir, or that she was remembering their night together. It was that they'd loved each other so much in a single night, and she hadn't kissed him sooner. Ena didn't share Haenir's view. She regretted the last year of her life now, maybe even the last two. She'd known he was interested in her since at least then, but she'd always had another reason to look away or busy herself elsewhere. At the time, Ena always told herself that she was being sensible but she couldn't escape the thought that she'd been afraid.

"Mind if I join you?" the towering Hultur asked.

"Huh?" Recognizing the question, she shook her head.

The red-skinned man was longer than her by strides. Sitting seemed an unnatural thing for one so tall. He looked up hopefully, staring at the crimson splash of the jargon nebula. "Do you have a wand?"

For a second, Ena's mind was back in training, reaching around for a wand that should always be at her side. She closed her eyes and recalled. "It's, uh, in my bag. Back in the wagon."

He nodded. "You don't need it, do you?"

"Not normally, no. Most threats I can handle without it. Wands just reduce the strain of holding onto that power, after all."

Hultur grunted. "Yes, but you're the only Broker that doesn't use one."

Ena shrugged. "I guess. Narla uses wristbands and Myrrel casts with an amulet. It's not that big of a deal."

That smile again. "Yes, but you don't use anything to focus your power."

Ena felt that familiar cut of being laid out for dissection. "What does it matter? Why do you care?"

"Because if anything goes even slightly wrong, we will have a great many threats before us."

"Then I'll just bring out my wand."

He raised his hands in surrender. "I apologize for bringing this up. I hadn't realized it would be a point of such pride and identity."

"Pride and identity..." Ena shook her head. "What are you talking about?!"

"As I said, I apologize." The giant rolled onto his feet and rose to his full height. "Enjoy the night, Ngoltur."

"Don't call me that," she grumbled.

Hultur took his leave and passed the other Ki'an in the group. Visk sized him up as he passed her, her spear at the ready. She walked to Ena's side and crouched down to talk. "What happened?"

Ena shook her head. "He was just asking me about my magic. It was weird."

"Weird how? Was he sizing you up for weaknesses?"

Her tone was intense even for Visk.

"He could've been. I don't know him yet."

Visk brought her eyes to Hultur, a deep scowl on her brow.

"Visk." She didn't look away from him. "Hey. Have a seat. Relax with me."

With theatrical resignation, she took a seat.

"What's going on with you and the big guy?"

"He is Hultur, the-"

"Yeah, I know, he's the Master of Evil and a dozen other monikers, but why do you hate him so much? I thought the Ki'an loved Hultur; that they celebrated his return."

"Ah." Visk stared into the flames. "You wish to know about my past."

"Yeah. I guess I do." She thought back on what she knew of the guarded woman. "I mean, I know you left your home to get away from your church, but I don't understand what that has to do with Hultur."

"Geshuri are Hultur's servants. They worship his deeds and sacrifice the elderly to bring about his return. Not all in Ki'an are controlled by Geshuri, but in the old city of Mu their word is law. They killed my grandparents and forced my lover to marry a man. I left because of the church, but Geshuri are what they are because of Hultur. Hultur's blood may be spilled on Gulambar soil, but it stains the heart of every Ki'an."

That gave Ena a better sense of what Visk escaped. She barely ever spoke of her homeland, and every time she did, the tragedies of her life were explained with similes and a complete lack of emotion. The proud woman had a bitter scowl on her face, but her eyes were pink and shimmering with tears. Ena offered her hand and Visk gripped it like a spear.

Tears flowed from her hard eyes. "Forgive me, I've stared too long at the flames."

"You can look a little longer."

And she did.

~ ~ ~

Endless fields lay between the Band of Brokers and the nearest city, Sothlen. Much of the land had been unsettled before Doronel splintered into Caredor, and much of it was unsettled still. Far to the west, the barest hint of the Faingarre Mountains showed the edge of their nations. These untilled lands had little value to Doronel and it meant less under the Supreme Magus's rule. Torno had taken to riding Hultur's big Gerhat, Li'at. He rode far ahead looking for monsters stalking the fields. Once the man-child found them, he stood in the stirrups and took long shots with his deathstaff. The wagon passed by and he ignored all offers to help. All his focus was on sniping the monsters while he rode, though his mind was surely on other things.

Monsters were an endless problem, and no one knew where they came from. Some said they were born from the nightmares of children. Others believed that they crawled out of the ground when the night was darkest. On the southeast side of Gulambar, in the frigid country of Daun Si, Clerics claimed monsters were born from wickedness and excess. But no amount of devotion, lighting up the lands, or swaddling children ceased the creation of monsters. They were a cruel part of life, and none had ever seen them breed, nor witnessed their young at play.

Torno was coming into view again, and the Band picked up their heads. Ena rounded the back and hung off the ropes to watch Torno's display with interest. It wasn't that she was interested in his shooting, just that pull of boredom. The deathstaff was tall as Torno, save his head. At the tip of it, the battle staff was no thicker than a pinky. On the opposite side, the padded stock was thick as a man's arm. Torno kept the stock stiff against his chest and aimed up a shot with one eye. Deathstaffs worked more like wands than actual staffs, the thin length of the core designed to harness incoming ether into the tip of it. The deathstaff could hold tremendous amounts of power before releasing it into a single, focused beam of energy. Each shot from the deathstaff filled the air with a satisfying sizzle. Monsters fell to the ground dead and broke apart into a swarm of the strange clouds of dissolving black they called mottle.

"Eyes forward," called out Narla from the jockey box.

A rider was approaching with haste.

Hultur put a hand up and magnified the rider's image before them in a circle. Again, his power left Ena awestruck. It wasn't that she'd never seen a magnification so large before, it was that he'd done it without any magical gestures, words of incantation, or objects of magical focus. Most Ki'an could barely cast utility spells.

Visk was returning at a gallop.

Torno shot down the last of the humanoid Ramaliers just as Visk was returning.

"Has he been doing that the entire time?!" Visk asked.

"It's Torno," Ena said, to explain his stupidity.

"Foolish fuck."

"What's the malfunction?" Narla asked.

"There's a mega coming for Sothlen!"

Sighs and groans went up throughout the wagon.

"What's a mega?" Hultur asked.

Visk gave him the word in Kest.

Mega monsters were about as bad as things could get. The smallest of them were forty feet high. They came in all shapes and sizes, with many of them reaching hundreds of feet in length. Megas ate everything they came across, including other monsters. The longer they rampaged, the bigger they became. The only sign that they had any intelligence at all was that they seemed to have an internal compass that pointed them toward cities.

"You all missed my last shot," Torno said like he was ready to brag. The fool got a sense of the mood and asked, "What's wrong?"

"We're coming up on a mega," said Narla, throwing up

her hands. "We can either ride around or wait for it to destroy half of Sothlen. The timing of this couldn't be any worse. I'm all out of booze!"

"What happened to my birthday present?" Ena asked with a pout.

"We kinda drank it," Narla reminded her.

"The mega is in our path," Visk explained. "Any attempt to get by will make it follow us."

"Hey, wait just one minute," grumbled Sal. "We're not a normal Band of Brokers anymore. We are an entourage of righteousness! We got Hultur on our side, don't we? I say we ride to Sothlen with haste and save the city."

"Sal's kind of got a point," Narla agreed.

Torno mulled it over.

"There's one problem with your assessment," Hultur told him. "I'm not going to fight."

THE FIFTH CHAPTER

In Which Ngoltur Fights a Mega Monster

Problems came like rainstorms in the best of times, and the Band of Brokers did not have the time to deal with all of them. Priority had to go to the mega between them and Sothlen. Narla was the Band's resident monster expert and went forward to scout Gale. In the meantime, the Band needed to prepare. Though Hultur wasn't going to fight--and they would talk about that--he was willing to invest ether into the fighting. Which was good, because Captain Likes-to-Show-Off was nearly depleted. The Band had little more than 500 gulda, and in a pinch they could draw from it, but the gemstones would be valueless until they were reimbued. Recharging individual gemstones was a pain, but Myrrel had an idea to get around that.

"Get me all the water we've got," she told them. It was a little more than three pitchers' worth. "Okay, that'll have to do. Torno, I need your help. I need you to gather all the water into an orb and try to keep it steady."

Torno grumbled. "I told you I don't have that much juice."

"We don't have time to discuss this," Myrrel hissed. "Just keep it going as long as you can. My aeromancy isn't as good as yours, so I need your help. Please."

He nodded and might've mumbled an apology. Using

half a dozen rings, Torno collected the poured water into a sphere.

"Okay, Ena, I'm gonna need you to freeze the inside of the sphere, but keep the power low. Most of the water should be close to freezing."

Ena did as directed, manifesting the cold directly in the center. Branches of ice spread out from the center in gorgeous spikes. When they connected with the edge of the sphere, they spread out fast, freezing the edge.

"That's too much. Try to keep the edge from freezing until I've reshaped it."

Ena nodded. The ether required to keep the chill in the center was so small and delicate, like holding a piece of paper vertical against a breeze. It took almost no power whatsoever, but so much concentration.

"Visk, melt the edges," Myrrel commanded.

Visk held her hands up like knives, red lightning ran over her knuckles and arms. She struck close to the sphere of water to melt it, but with every stab the wind wobbled and the shape of the sphere slumped.

"Please hurry," Torno said through his teeth. He swiped at stray wisps of air until he was able to return to a calm circular rhythm.

"Okay, I'll need quiet," Myrrel whispered.

Smoothing her amulet along an invisible plane, she pulled at Torno's shaping. The wind pushed against the sphere to create a solid surface. Water reshaped into a semisphere. Myrrel worked another plane against the surface, then another. She was shaping it into an ethereal chamber, one surface at a time. The more planes she added, the harder Torno gasped to keep his will alive.

"Can't..." he spat out right before his arms dropped. Though not unconscious, he had to lean against the wagon wall to catch his breath.

Myrrel was in the zone. She hadn't broken her stride and kept adding smaller planes to add detail to the shape of the surface. "Little more cold."

Ena pressed a second finger into her thumb and pinched the threads of ether inward to direct the cold. The tendrils of ice spread out slowly, adding just enough to gently freeze the crystal's outer edge. But the ice was brittle, soft enough to be cracked and pushed by Myrrel's shaping. At long last, Myrrel gave a quick nod and Ena froze it solid with a casual divining wave. The pair let out a sigh of relief.

Hultur took it into his hands. "Impressive. This should hold a decent supply of ether."

"It better, for all the trouble it took us." Myrrel wiped her brow.

With very little coaching, Hultur was able to grasp the simple principle of tying ethereal threads together inside the ice crystal. Myrrel talked him through the process. Her background as ether-store lead gave Myrrel the confidence to answer questions and corrected his forms.

Narla was back. "Which do you want first, the good or the bad news?"

"Bad first; always," grumbled the exhausted Torno. He was sweating and pale.

"Look out the front, we can see the mega from here. Whatever you're doing, you better hurry."

Most everyone poked their heads out to take a gander. The monster cast a mantis-like silhouette against the rising cloud of dark smoke. Its back end was large and seemed to trail behind its body. The mega glowed with ether, winter colors illuminating the smoke and village homes.

"What could possibly be the good news?" Sal asked from the jockey box.

"See those buildings over there at the edge of the outskirts? The distillery's in there. So assuming we pull this off and make ourselves heroes, we're gonna be celebrating with a fresh batch of gin," Narla explained with a mad chuckle.

Visk and Ena shared an annoyed look.

"How's Torno?" Narla asked, poking her head in.

"Don't worry about me." Torno placed a gloved hand on the ice crystal to start drawing on the ether. "Finish the report."

"Okay, well, remember how I said we should just wait for the mega to hit Sothlen and see if the city's defenses can handle it? I'm renewing that suggestion. It's chewing through the city's outskirts like they're an appetizer.

"Working name: Wand-Breaker, Classification Vurn-Slizz. Most of the body is vurnglek, and its ether-sucking ability is on full display. The large plates over its body are magically charged. It keeps flashing through the elements, but it seems to favor cold magic. I didn't get close enough to see the underscales, but I'd say they were prism-sealed, more of a focus on magic defense.

"The slizzer part of it likes to break things apart, but I think it's too slow to attack a moving target. It offsets its top-heaviness with these spider legs on its top. Lots of spider features at the front of it, too. Wand-Breaker's mouth is like a nasty mashing hole of pedipalps. When it starts taking significant damage it has this twisted little recharge move."

"Why does she sound excited about this?" Hultur asked.

"This was why she took this job," Sal explained. "She wanted to learn more about monsters."

"Yeah, and this monster nerd is telling you stuff about how to kill it, so maybe let me finish." She tried to take a drink from her empty flask and glared at its treachery. "As I said before, the ether plates over its body glow with different elements. I don't know why it changes elements or how, but it's pretty easy to tell what spells are going to be spitting out of the edges of the oversized scales.

"When it's taking a lot of damage, that's what we need to watch out for. It backs up and acts like it might be running away, but I think it only does that to lure out strong attacks. The glow of the scales dims down and then it opens up its mouth and most of the slizzer body's chest. It becomes this big open ether sink. This is one horrifying mega. I know they're all dangerous, but I don't know how we're going to beat this thing."

"I have an idea," Torno said.

The crew looked incredulously at their Captain.

"Myrrel, are you going to be ready to fight?"

"Absolutely not! I'm staying with the wagon to heal everyone when we're running for our lives," she grumbled.

"Not necessary." Torno stood up. "This crystal might not be a one-to-one copy of a gemstone ether store, but it's good enough to store a thousand gulda worth, maybe more. Hultur might not be fighting, but I'm already full of ether again. We need him back at the wagon recharging that ice block. Ena, slap a heat wall on it."

She obeyed, keeping her terse comments to herself. Whenever things got tense, the knave lost all courtesies. With the hard edges, it was an easy matter to shape ethereal strands into a barrier.

Torno was in full "I'm in command" mode now. He barked out a series of orders. Then he looked to Ena and snapped, "With me."

She crossed her arms and leered.

Torno rolled his eyes. "Please."

She stopped at the back of the wagon. "Hey, you know how you do that thing where you tell us a bunch of things to do, but you don't actually tell us the plan? Can you tell us what the plan is?"

Torno shook his head. "I don't know if it's going to work. If I tell you the plan and have to try a new one it might lower morale, and nothing dilutes magical attacks like doubt."

Ena grit her teeth. The only thing more annoying than bossy Torno, was bossy Torno with a decent point.

"Now hop on the horse. We don't have time to waste arguing."

Ena grabbed his arm. "Wait."

He damn near swooned at her.

Yikes. Ena pointed at Gale. "I want that horse, we've kind of been bonding."

They switched horses. Torno lead Ena into the devastated outskirts. People were fleeing on foot or crawling among the blood and rubble. Everywhere they looked wands, staffs, shields, spears, and bows lay unattended. This wasn't an undefended village. Wand-Breaker was clashing against the Sothlen's casters and turning them into corpses.

Torno was leading them away from the carnage, riding into roads full of abandoned carts and wagons. "I'm glad we're being so open with each other today, Ena, because I'm gonna make an observation about you."

"This should be good," she grumbled.

"You know how you always hold back your power and then act like you're about to pass out even though you're fine?"

Ena looked away from that fucking prick!

"I need you to not do that, Ena. I need you to put everything you can into this fight. If things go bad we can escape just like Narla said, but I'm going to let you in on a little secret; two in fact."

"Torno, I already know you're impotent and brain-dead."

He ignored her jab and continued. "I actually care about people. This has my blood boiling. No matter what happens, I'm not running away. I'm gonna do everything I can to stop Wand-Breaker, even if it kills me."

That caught her off guard. She'd never seen Torno so worked up. He wasn't even smiling. The fucker always smiled. "Please don't tell me that the second thing is that you love me, because I don't think I can deal with a fourth love confession right now."

"I'm scared, Ena." He rounded a turn and shot her a terrified glance. "I don't want to die."

Oh, fuck. Ena was feeling sympathy for this blowhard.

Torno slowed the horse to a stop. He took his deathstaff off his shoulder and held it out to her. "When that thing opens its mouth to absorb power, I need you to put everything you have into shooting it."

"What?! That's madness, Torno, even for you. You heard what Narla said, it can create an ether sink. All that will do is power Wand-Breaker up!"

"You wanted to know why I don't tell people my plans, well now you know." He chuckled. "No ether-sink is complete. If you fire a bolt of concentrated ether strong enough, it'll be too much energy for it to absorb all at once. Ice magic has always been your strength, Ena. Pour all the cold you can into that shot. You need a boost getting to the roof?"

Ena dismounted. "Yeah."

"On three."

"Three."

Ena called on the wind, pushing her up by the legs and hips. She got a little off the ground, but Torno took over, taking her almost a full story over the top of the building. She waved a hand to form a pillow of air and landed softly. Torno gathered Gale's reins and looked up at her. She'd seen that forlorn look in his eyes before. She hated him for looking at her like that. It was never her fault that he loved her.

This all sounded like madness to Ena. Bolts of energy were shooting at Wand-Breaker from every angle. There were plenty of mages firing at it with deathstaffs of their own, and theirs were probably of a higher quality. Every flare spell and dark shot smacked into thick glowing plates. Hails of arrows rained down along with levitated boulders, doing nothing but directing the mega's attention away from the core of the city.

There wasn't any time to take in the chaos of the battle. She needed to climb the highest perch.

The mage towers had been the first to fall. Away from

town square, most buildings were about three stories tall, with one obvious exception: the Spires. Great pointed towers surrounded by depots and silos, the Spires were a central part of Caredor's infrastructure. There, ether was transformed into food, planks, and blocks, though none were of the substance they were made to emulate.

The ground shook but settled. Ena took in the carnage. A huge plume of smoke rose where businesses and row houses once stood. Wand-Breaker lowered its slizzer chest and raised its back. The multicolored scales glowed and cast a myriad of spells at the fighters. Her friends might already be in that chaos.

Ena sprinted towards Wand-Breaker. There was a spire between them and the last thing she needed was for her attack to miss. Doubling up on gestures, Ena wrapped herself in a bubble of fast time. She cleared a full road in a single leap and then another. Ena tweaked up the haste and was clearing rooftops in two steps, one to land and one to kick off. The spire up ahead was at least three roads away from the closest roof.

Wind rushed against her speeding form and she gathered it behind her. Preparing for the final leap, she cleared the last road, landed with both feet, and cast the wind behind her. She thrust her hands forward and shouted, "Aero!"

In the time it took her to jump and somersault, she flew over the gap. The spire came at her like a stone thrown. Crossing arms and legs, she gathered wind to stop her approach. Her face hit the conical tower with a smack. Though dazed, Ena kept her gripe on the spire. Explosions and screams grounded her in the world of the living. Wincing through the pain, Ena climbed.

The mythril-lined focusing stripes gave Ena handholds on her ascent. Reaching the top, Wand-Breaker looked close enough to slap. It was several roads away, but large as it was, the mega could reach her in a few steps.

Ena didn't have any trouble getting her legs around the tip of the spire. The focusing stripes kept her secure at the top. All of her wobbling ended the second she brought the deathstaff into her hands. She'd never used one, but they were designed to be intuitive. The padded stock of the deathstaff slid off the ball of her shoulder and stayed rigid against her chest. Even though the weapon was comically long, she found it easy to aim when held properly.

Letting out a long sigh, she started pouring her ether into the long core of the deathstaff. The tip of the weapon glowed a faint blue, but a small ball of pure ether glowed at its center. Ena let the deathstaff dip and focused on her breathing. Down below, her friends were fighting for their lives.

Visk and Narla were mounted, riding between alleyways and buildings torn asunder. Staying far from Wand-Breaker's scythe-like arms, they harried the mega with spells directed at armored magic plates. Wand-Breaker's plates shot out spells with chromatic ether trails that exploded into bursts of frigid cold and searing light. Their red lighting and bursts of fire weren't doing any damage to the creature, or even getting its attention, but they changed the color of its scales and the magic of its attacks.

Sal rolled around Wand-Breaker's side. The headless boulba rolled fast as horses in their boulder form. An innate use of geomancy not only generated the force they needed to move around, but a tactile feel for their surroundings. Sal hopped a good ten feet in the air to avoid any obstacles and Myrrel used her wind magic to fling him at the joints of the Wand-Breaker's spider-like legs. Yet the attacks weren't constant, they were keeping Wand-Breaker's attention and nothing more.

Ena couldn't spot Torno, but the feel of the fighting had changed. Battle magic all around the outskirts shifted fire magic. Red casting streams flew out in volleys, bursting into flames as they struck the creature's face. It was working, the mega was starting its retreat.

The time had come to pour everything into the deathstaff. Torno had been right about Ena holding back. She had to. If the wizards of government knew Ena had a strong source of ether inside, they would've hauled her off to the capital and turned her into a living ether charge just like her parents. Just like how they were using Hultur now. Anger, disgust, loneliness, and fear all focused her will on the long core of the deathstaff. But these emotions were nothing compared to the limitless pain of her parents abandoning her.

She knew they never had a choice, that they were carried off by the Supreme Magus's requests, but that didn't explain why they never wrote her. That didn't explain why they could just forget about their daughter and start a new life in Caredor City. She honed in on the chill of her Arcanum Instructor sharing the good news that she had a brother. They had moved on. They didn't care. It was why Ena was so attuned to the power of ice magic, she was intimately familiar with the cold. The chill of her skin and the locking of her joints were nothing compared to the ice inside.

Wand-Breaker backed onto a marketplace and shuffled. Plates along its back went from autumn hues to solid red. Its mantis arms parted, its dozen pedipalp fangs moved aside, and the mega monster's front split open. The ether sink glowed a destructive red inside.

Ena had amassed not a ball of power, but a crystalline snowflake of blue ether. She took aim at the red inner core of Wand-Breaker, directed a tiny sliver of power outward, and the energy snapped. The spell erupted out of the deathstaff's core with such force that it shattered the weapon from the inside out. Ether shot forward not in a directed ray, but like a tendril of ice following the coldest path. The white-blue light pierced Wand-Breaker and came out the other side. An explosion of snow shot up and clouds of ash halted and fell like snowflakes.

The force of the deathstaff shattering knocked Ena backwards. Her legs slipped and she slid down the length of the spire. One of the twisting focusing stripes hit her hip. She rebounded off the spire and went end over end. Splintered bits of deathstaff gave her more than cutting pain, they broke up the curl of her fingers and the flicks of her wrist. Her efforts to cast continued to fail. Her shoulder hit the spire with a crack. She rolled down, hit a focus stripe again, and flew off the lip. Ena's last thought before she hit the ground was, "I'm falling."

THE SIXTH CHAPTER

Where Ngoltur Receives No
Credit Despite Risking Her Life

As a child, Ena spent a lot of time moving around. Her earliest memory was playing with a whirl-bob in the shape of a fairy. An older child, a cousin of some kind, used wind spells to keep it aloft, but young Ena could only use her hands to play with the doll. She ran her fingers over the air-catches, spinning them along the body as she imagined it hovering in the air. She spun the whirl-bob and tossed it into the air, not understanding that she needed to cast magic to keep the toy aloft. When the toy was separated from her, an older woman grabbed her. Though a relative of some kind, Ena didn't know who she was. Trying to escape did nothing, so she screamed and bit at the woman's clothed arm. The toy was left behind on the floor and the woman refused to listen to her.

Mom took hold of Ena. So distraught from the abduction, young Ena was sobbing too much to explain what this awful woman did, let alone the particulars of the toy. She could only hold onto her mother and cry. Ena knew that babies cried. She didn't want to be a baby, but she couldn't get the tears to stop. Mother was in a hurry, carrying her out to the front of the house where a carriage waited.

Placed on her feet, Ena grabbed at her mother's skirts. When that didn't work she pulled at her hand to get her to notice. But she only looked at her daughter to tell her to quiet. Father came out of the house lifting eight bags with gravitic magic. He was talking to people too, one writing on a ledger, the other in fancy servant's clothes. Father only looked at Ena because Mom asked him to silence his daughter.

He stomped over to her, picked her up, and placed her in the carriage.

"If you do not behave yourself, I will take away your voice. Do you understand?"

Ena looked at her dust-covered skirt. The triangle pattern was starting to fray.

Father closed the door and chided his wife for her impotence. The doll had been a gift, she knew it had. Her cousin had said so when he handed it over. It was the best thing to happen on that entire trip. Ena finally had something of her own, something she could play with when she was on the road.

Mother and Father joined her in the carriage shortly.

"Momma," Ena started, but she met her father's glower. She looked back to her skirt. The doll was back there on the floor. No one would care for it after she left, they didn't have little girls at that house. Someone would probably just throw it into the fire.

After the fall off the spire, Ena awoke thinking about the whirl-bob designed to be like a fairy. She'd given the toy a name, Princess Skyler. It was a silly name, she knew. But toys were allowed to have silly names, especially when those names were secret.

Thoughts of the mega monster came back slowly. Panic was the only thing keeping her up, but Ena felt far too close to sleep to move. There wasn't any pain in her body, but neither was there a sensation of any kind. Something pulled at her skin. Maybe they were ripping her riding clothes. Ena didn't want them to take her clothes off, but someone placed their hand on her head and calmed her. They were using magic on her.

~ ~ ~

Myrrel's face came into view first. She was bathed in a deep blue light closer to the navy of heraldic azure than the light of the sky. Close as she was, Ena could make out every freckle on her face. Weak and dazed, her eyes lingered on the lighter patches of her skin. It was rude to stare, some part of Ena knew that. She'd seen so many children stare at her growing up. Children asked why she was different even before saying "Hi," or asking her name. But Ena couldn't help but stare. The white pattern over her right eye and mouth almost looked theatrical, as if she was done up in makeup to perform a play. This must've been the play, "Let's Heal Ena." It was a production Ena was familiar with and she never liked the beginning.

Ethereal light faded, replaced by the yellow glow of a tableside lamp. Myrrel pet Ena's head and smiled at her. "You're gonna be okay, just try to get some rest."

"I can see why so many men kiss you after this," Ena grumbled.

Myrrel chuckled. "You just think about the men you're going to kiss. Matter of fact, dream about them."

Ena tried to grab her hand, but only her fingers twitched. Myrrel took her hand in both of hers and gave it a firm squeeze. "You're beautiful, Myrrel."

She gave a hearty laugh. "Oh, I know. Just get some rest and we can talk about how beautiful I am in the morning."

Ena closed her eyes. She sank into the warm blanket and felt a gentle kiss on her forehead. Myrrel wasn't like her mother. She was there for her when Ena needed her.

~ ~ ~

Sal rolled out of his ball shape and flicked on the lantern. Ena couldn't see him, but she heard him fine. Solid rock touched the other side of her. She leaned into it and turned to see Sal cast in a long shadow, his massive hand blocking the lantern's light over his face-chest.

"How you doing, Slayer?" Sal asked with a chuckle.

"Thirsty." Ena wanted to say more, but the boulba stomped off to pour her a glass.

"You need help sitting up?"

Ena tried and found pain. It jumped out of her shoulder and radiated down her back. She winced through the effort. A drink of water helped her throat and gave her a chance to orient herself to the small medical room. It was a private box with a wash basin and privy inside a smaller room. The walls were decorated with old Doronel script for healing magics. Though Ena could barely heal the scrape from a hang nail, she knew enough to recognize it.

"Hungry?" Sal asked.

"Probably. I can't feel it if I am. I'm in pain though, so that's good."

Sal smiled. "It's good to know you still have your optimism."

"Where is everyone?"

"Most everyone is off celebrating; except Myrrel. She's been working herself like a golem." Sal gave a little frown. "I'm worried about her, but she won't hear it. She always said that her body could heal people for days if only she had the ether. Now that Hultur's helping her, she seems determined to prove it. I'm tempted to break that ice crystal you made."

"Can you get Torno? I want to give him an earful for lending me a faulty deathstaff."

Sal looked away.

"What?"

"It's...gonna take some time for him to visit. I'll let him know you want to talk to him though."

Ena placed a hand on his brow-shoulder. "What is it, Sal?"

Sal gave a long sigh. "Don't do this to me, Ena. Myrrel told me not to get you worked up about anything. You're not one hundred percent, you know."

Ena nodded. She could feel how far she was from fine under the bandages around her shoulder.

"I'm gonna grab you something to eat." Sal forced a smile.

"Please don't. I wanna talk to someone."

"Good Ole Sal. Worth as much as a wall of rock."

She would've punched him if it wouldn't have broken her fist. "Stop that! You know I hate it when you say things like that. I wanna talk to you, you know that."

He nodded but also looked away.

There was no point in trying to talk him out of his pity parties. The more someone pushed him, the more he retreated into his feelings of inadequacy. Ena forced herself to smile so her tone would come out chipper. "Did I ever tell you about my childhood?"

"I think so. Did you leave out all the parts where you were a princess covered in diamonds?" he joked.

Ena pursed her lips in disgust.

His laugh rumbled the bed. "I believe you moved around a lot, going from house to house. I don't remember why."

"I never knew why. I always thought it was because my dad couldn't find work. My parents were always worried about money back then and my dad was always on edge. Now that I think about it, they might've been upset because gold was being replaced with gulda." She shook her head. "I don't know. Ever since we met Hultur I've been rethinking my past, trying to look for some sign that I was a princess on the run."

"Did your parents talk to anyone important?"

Ena nodded. "I think they did. Maybe we kept moving to these different houses because those people were monarchists. We always went to big houses with lots of rooms in them. I hated them. The second we arrived, Mom would push me into the arms of some maid. They would smile and try to be nice, but I knew I was just a burden to them."

"Did you have any good memories?" Good Ole Sal, keeping Ena from getting too worked up.

She gave him a knowing smile and chuckled. "I had a couple, yeah. It might sound a little strange, but I was a maid."

"The exiled Princess was a maid?"

"Yeah," she said, wistfully. "We all were. Dad worked in the big house doing something with the books and Mom stayed behind with me to work refrigeration and the furnace. She only ever liked working the fires. She'd turn it into this game. We'd say something we were mad about and chuck it into the flames. During the day I always had something to do. It was hard work, but I got to do it with friends.

"They were all my secret friends. We couldn't talk when anyone was looking at us. If the head maids saw us playing we'd get a switch and scullery work. If my mom saw me, she'd make me work alone. We found time to play, though. There were always days when there wasn't that much to do, so we could go out and play."

Ena's smile soured to grief.

"What happened?"

"We were playing this epic game of tag where each of us had a stone tapped with ether. Because each of us had imbued a stone into everyone's pocket, we could track them into the woods, or into the house. Jolly was always terrible at those games. He was younger than us. He couldn't outrun us and he wasn't that good at hiding. Jolly had the bright idea to hide in the big house. The other kids knew better than to go after him, but I didn't. I wanted to get him, not just because I was mad at Jolly for cheating, but because I wanted to win. If I came back with my stone from him, it'd be an easy way to win.

"The thing was, work was slow that day because the Lord and Lady of the manor were entertaining this big shot. When I saw Jolly, he ran off to where there weren't any servants, and I was fool enough to follow. He ran into a big room and I chased him down and grabbed him. He didn't want to give up any stones, so we got into a scuffle. The commotion brought out the big important guest and she was just standing there staring at us. Oh!"

Sal waved his hand in front of the suddenly silent Ena.

"I think she figured out who I was," said Ena, putting pieces together with enthusiasm. "There weren't many albino children in the land, and my age couldn't have helped. Dad came to get me and the butler gave him a thrashing. I was screaming bloody murder for them to stop hurting my dad, but it didn't help. They led that big shot out of the room and Dad walked me back to the beds. We packed all our stuff, and once that important woman left we had to move again.

"I think that was when we fled to Caredor, because that was the last time we were at a big fancy house. Dad told me it was my fault that we had to move again, but I didn't know how right he was. It wasn't just that I was playing where I shouldn't have been. My skin gave us away."

Ena picked her head up. A burst of ether was let out. It must've been over a thousand gulda's worth of ether released.

"Did you feel that?" she asked the unmagical Sal.

He just kept staring forward.

Of course, he hadn't felt that. "Oh, umm, somebody let out some ether. Maybe a crystal in a spire broke." Ena cleared her throat. "Can I get some more water?"

"No problem."

Sal came back with water and a neutral expression.

"Thank you." She drank half a glass.

"I want to ask you something, Ena?"

"Sure."

"Does it feel better knowing that your parents were running from people to protect you?" The rockman placed his hands on the floor to stand inert.

Ena chewed on the thought. "I don't know. I mean, they were still mean to me so I don't think it excuses how they treated me. Things did get better once we moved to Caredor. Dad was always working at the house and Mom worked out in town. I never knew what she did, but she had to wear these really drab straight clothes, the kind that went from her collar to her ankles."

"Enchanter's garb?"

"I guess so." She shook the thought away. "We must've lived at the farm for four years, but I hated it there. I had no one to play with and I wasn't allowed to go into town. The only time I saw other kids was when I snuck outside."

"Did the people of Caredor find out about you?" Sal asked.

She shook her head. "I don't think so. Dad said he made a mistake because they were struggling to pay for the farmhouse. He went on this trip in the winter, right after that really bad blizzard." She shook her head again. "I don't know. I could probably think back on every single moment in my life and think about how it changed why my parents did what they did, but they were never nice to me. My dad hugged me when he had to say goodbye. That could've been the only time he hugged me. I can't think of another."

Sal looked to her with pity.

She hated that look. "Anyway, what about you? What was your childhood like?"

"Well, you know–"

Myrrel stormed into the room. Her brow was covered in sweat, her hair was more disheveled than normal, and her healer's apron was covered in blood from her hip down. "That arrogant blowhard! I'm going to kill him!"

"Who?"

Sal moved to calm Myrrel and she sidestepped him to pace about the room.

"Hultur! Do you know another arrogant blowhard?"

Sal and Ena shared a look and told her in tandem, "Torno."

"Oh, he is so much worse than Torno! Torno can at least be reasoned with! That man thinks that every idea he has is sent from the Gods! Did you tell her about why he wouldn't fight?!"

"You told me to keep her calm," Sal reminded her.

"Myrrel, why don't you take off your healer's clothes, take a seat, and tell us what happened?" Ena suggested.

She ran her hands through her matted hair, sighed, and took off the apron, folding it to keep the gore off the floor. "I might as well! I'm not gonna be doing any more work today!"

Sal poured Myrrel a glass of water. She glowered at the thing, but took it and drank.

"How late is it?" Ena asked. "It's so dark out."

"It's about three in the morning," Sal informed Myrrel more than Ena.

"This hospital is full. You get that. You understand what that means. There are rows and rows of people out there in need of healing. A thousand people or more are crying out for help. Some of them are children, and that fucker tells me to take a break! They can't take a break. They can't choose to stop being hurt!" Myrrel was pacing again.

"Myrrel, you've been working for almost two days," Sal said as calmly as he possibly could.

"So what? That gives him the right to break my crystal of ice?!"

"What?!"

"Oh, that's right! He didn't just lay hands on me to keep me from going inside the wagon to get more ether, that fucker shattered it! He shattered it like an empty bottle of wine!" Myrrel grabbed her hair, gripped it, and groaned in frustration. "He says that I'm unhinged, that I'm too tired to keep going! Do I look tired? Do I look unhinged?!"

Sal and Ena stared long at the deep bags under her eyes, the swell of the vein on her forehead, and the flush in her skin almost matching the pink of her eyes.

"Nope," Ena said.

"Not at all," Sal agreed.

Myrrel groaned and sat down. "Fuck you both for

taking his side." She sighed and looked around. "Where's Narla when I need a drink?"

"Out drinking, I assume," Sal provided.

"So what happened with Hultur?" Ena tried to sit up but the pain kept her down.

They glanced at each other with one part annoyance and one part worry.

"Just tell me," Ena insisted. "I'm already up and Myrrel's screaming certainly isn't keeping me calm. What's going on out there? What have I missed?"

"You killed the mega, for starters," said Myrrel. "That shot of yours went right through it. Narla was practically wet talking about how much power you threw out. But we've been keeping that knowledge to ourselves. If anyone asks, you were nowhere near that spire."

Ena nodded.

"That's Hultur's idea, not mine. He thinks it's a really bad idea for people to know that you're Ngoltur reborn. That's actually why the maniac doesn't want to fight. He says that if people see him flinging spells and killing megas, they're going to know that he's Hultur and we'll never get to Leben Erde."

Sal interjected, "At this rate, we may not get there anyway."

"Not this year," Myrrel said deadpan.

"What about Torno?" Wincing, Ena sat up. "Why isn't he here?"

"You tell her." Myrrel went off to the restroom.

"He's taken credit for the destruction of Wand-Breaker," said Sal.

"What? How in his mind is anything that happened because of him?"

"It was his plan," Sal reminded her. "Legally he's got more of a claim for glory than anyone else. Everyone saw him rallying the city's defenders."

"So I almost get killed using his defective deathstaff

and he gets the credit for destroying a mega because he was running around telling people what to do?"

"That's the short of it, yes."

Ena groaned and tried to put her head in her hands. But the act of moving forward filled her body with pain. Whatever happened to her shoulder, it wasn't even close to healed. "Ow. I really shouldn't have done that."

Sal walked over to the washroom and knocked on the door. "Myrrel, I think Ena needs a spell to numb the pain and fall asleep. Myrrel?" He placed his hand on the door to listen. He glanced back at Ena and chuckled. "I think she fell asleep."

They shared a laugh. Sal went off to grab her a meal. Ena was halfway through the stew and bread when Myrrel stumbled out of the washroom. She mumbled something about "told-you-so," climbed into bed with Ena, and fell asleep. It wasn't long before Ena joined her.

~ ~ ~

It was a jarring and altogether unpleasant experience falling asleep staring at Myrrel and waking up to see the smug asshole mug of Torno. Disgusting as the man was grungy and disheveled, he looked positively repulsive clean shaven. Ena pulled back so fast that she put pressure on her shoulder to get away. The pain was more like touching a bruise than sticking her finger into an open wound, so someone must've healed her, but it still hurt. Torno put on affectations of concern and Ena couldn't peel her eyes off him. It wasn't just that he'd shaved. Instead of his usual brown leather jacket, he was wearing an officer's suit jacket. His hair wasn't just trimmed, it was styled.

"What the fuck happened to you?" Ena asked.

He chuckled. "Promotion."

"Seriously?!"

Torno nodded. "The ceremony is today, so I'm looking the part of an obedient cog in the Supreme Magus's machine."

"You have a funny way of turning traitor, you know that?"

A sigh of acquiescence rumbled his lips. "Tell me about it. This'll probably help us in the short term. As a Wizard, I shouldn't have any trouble getting us to the capital."

"Wizard? They're going to make you a Wizard!" Ena started choking, testing the limits of the healing on her shoulder and ribs.

He reached out to rub her back.

Ena caught her breath, leaned back, and glowered at the man, bulging her eyes as she did.

Torno held up both hands and let her cough and choke in peace. When she was done, he gave her a glass of water. "We don't have time to chat. The Mages are sending a couple of Acolytes over to investigate us. They're Gulambar, so I doubt they'll be using any strong empathy magicks. Are you gonna have any trouble hiding your emotions?"

"I can share a room with you without puking, what do you think?"

Torno smiled. It was one of those warm smiles that could be called affectionate. This man really couldn't take a hint.

"Wait, what were you going to do if I said I couldn't suppress?" she asked seriously.

Torno held up a vial about as big as his thumb. "Iltwyr. I already asked Myrrel about it, she said it shouldn't mess with your recovery. It'll calm your emotions without raising anyone's hackles."

"Are you on it?"

He shook his head. "Growing up in the capital is all the emotional suppression I need. Do you want it?"

She really didn't but held out her hand. It tasted like sage and licorice, with an aftertaste of burning butt. It made her stomach churn, but there was nothing there to empty. She went to the washroom to use the facilities, casting mute to keep her sounds from squeezing through the cracks in the door. It was difficult to keep the spell going when she was filled with so much disgust and paranoia. Wind magic responded to a carefree attitude, others called it joy or whimsy, but it was the feeling one got as a child when the autumn breeze blew pleasantly through their hair. Ena had so few memories of times like that in her life. Even her time with Haenir hadn't been that kind of happy. She tried to focus on her birthday, trying the expensive brandy Narla got her. Times were casual enough then.

Suddenly, it got a lot easier for her to keep the spell going. She didn't even have to focus on the memory of leaning against Myrrel and laughing at Narla's stories. She could just look at her hands and admire the smoothness of her nails and the way she could see her veins. Washing her hands was like an art project, and she had to keep telling herself to turn the water off and dry her hands.

Outside, Torno was waiting on the chair by her sick bed. In a suit with his hair clean, it was easy to forget that he was Torno. As much as he tried to cultivate an air of being some ruggedly handsome scoundrel, there was a boyish charm in the way his emotions played off his face. One of the reasons she'd been so quick to distrust him was because he was skilled in light magic. Light magic was the magic of lovers. It had always come difficult for her, and those who excelled at it were always the most sheltered and pampered children in the world. Still, there was a sorrow that hung around Torno. She hated him for finding love in a place so sterile and unforgiving.

"You're feeling it, aren't you?" Torno asked with one of his annoying smiles.

"Yes," she pouted. "Don't you come near me, or I'll flick your nose."

He laughed.

"And don't laugh either. Let me be serious."

He raised his hands in defeat.

For some reason, Ena didn't really care that she was in a patient's garb. It didn't exactly hug her form, but it showed too much. Yet, Torno hadn't been staring at her body. His eyes were always on hers, watching to see what she was feeling. She swallowed. "Can you-"

There came a knock on the door. The Acolytes were here.

THE SEVENTH CHAPTER

Where Ngoltur Meets the Biting Shadows

Torno waited for Ena's okay to open the door. Her lips curved in odd directions, confirming nothing. Baffled, the well-dressed Broker Captain hesitated, and that was all the approaching Acolytes needed to act. The door flew open, and a man of average height jumped into the room. Though he was supposed to be an Acolyte, he wore the chest plate and shoulder guard of a Mage. Yet, the armor was an odd shade of amber and bone instead of the Mage's ebony and crimson. The man's gambeson was a dark black, decorated with personal effects of red added on in a flattering fashion that was anything but formal. Done up like a dandy, his ebony curly hair was short on the sides and back but else wise long enough to give his appearance a kind of gravity. Most noticeably, a patch of carmine-dyed strands trailed down to his chin.

This oddly dressed man jumped into the room and shouted, "Got you!" When he found Torno and Ena standing in the room doing nothing, he squinted at them with exaggerated suspicion and held the door open with a foot.

His companion was a woman just as strange as himself. The sides of her head were shaved down to the scalp, but a thick single braid ran from the front of her brow down to the small of her back. The elaborate braid not only broke the regulations of an Acolyte's attire in its length but by the cyan and lavender strands intertwined around the natural black. She, too, wore the same strange amber and bone cuirass and pauldron as her compatriot in arms on top of a regulation black gambeson.

The woman marched into the room not as a Mage or Acolyte, but as a baton-twirler marched in a parade. She ignored Torno and Ena and examined the room itself. She went straight to the closest corner and held a sensing crystal over the wall's trimming.

Torno tried to cut through the tension. "Morning, Aco-"

"Silence!" the man yelled.

Torno and Ena throw their heads back in surprise.

The woman finished sweeping one corner for hexes and listening spells and proceeded to scan under the bed, sticking up her posterior as she did. When Torno glanced at her odd posture, the man yelled again.

"Eyes forward! Hands on your legs!"

Torno and Ena did as they were told and risked a look to check if each was as befuddled as the other.

After crawling halfway under the bed, the woman Acolyte proceeded to climb over the back of the bed rather than walk around it. She made her way to the next corner and then followed the seam of the ceiling into the washroom. Making quite the racket, the woman apparently saw fit to empty the washroom cabinet. She returned to the threshold of the washroom and shouted, "Magical sweep complete!"

"Stand up!" the man shouted at them. "Arms out!"

The confused pair of brokers stood and assumed a t-position, glancing at each other while the woman patted them down and ran her sensing crystal over their persons. The woman finished and shot to attention. "Interrogation of their persons complete!"

"Sit down!" yelled the man.

Torno again tried to diffuse their hostile nature with a casual tone. "Listen, we–"

"I said, sit!"

Torno found his chair and Ena had to awkwardly walk around the woman standing in violent attention to sit beside the window.

"Secure the room," the woman snapped.

With a salute, the man kicked the door closed. He then went through the motion of a full body aeromancy cast to seal the door, before returning to an Acolyte's salute. "Room secured!"

The woman pranced over the bed again and came to stand at the empty corner before making a military about-face to glare at the wall. This time she spoke like she was talking to someone in another room on the other side of a very large house. "You stand before your country accused of dereliction of duty, breaking position, assuming command above your station, and illegal obfuscation. How do you plead?"

Ena, unsure of who the woman was addressing, looked to Torno.

"We were told this was an inquiry and not a military tribunal," said Torno.

"Answer the question!" the man shouted.

"Innocent, we plead innocent."

"The defendants have entered a plea of innocent!"

The woman's entire face scrunched up as she stared at her compatriot with a punitive scowl.

"Innocence! The defendants have entered a plea of innocence!"

"Listen, we don't have to conduct things so formally, Acolytes. We–"

"We are Junior Mages," the woman said with a head held high. "I am Cerrano and this is my compatriot, Iodize!"

"You will answer the questions we ask, and only when we ask you to respond. Any attempt to answer before we are finished will go on your mark as an act of willful obstruction of the judicial process. Do you understand?" Iodize barked out.

"Yes," said Ena.

"Yeah. Would it kill you to lower your voice? I'm right next to you."

"One mark of willful obstruction," Cerrano remarked with a sadistic smile. "Note it, Iodize."

"So noted!"

"Now, let us begin with the interrogation of the so-called innocent."

What followed was the most bizarre series of questions that may have ever occurred. Cerrano ran through an exhaustive questionnaire regarding the placement of people at times far too specific for anyone to answer with any degree of accuracy. She drilled them about physical details like articles of clothing, the placement of personal possessions, and their position relative to the sun and true north. Iodize would randomly interject with direct accusations of treason, intent to murder the Supreme Magus, and inciting rebellion. These accusations always came in the form of a question, and many of these interjections were shouted in their ears.

When they were finished, Iodize ceased his pacing and stood by the door.

"It is the opinion of this official inquiry that the accused are guilty on all accounts," said Cerrano with sadistic glee. "This matter will be reported to a senior mage shortly. Any attempt to leave the city will be added to your growing list of crimes. Though we are leaving you, you are not safe, nor are you absolved of any guilt. We will follow you like shadows until justice is finally served by carrying out your sentence."

Iodize dismissed the spell of silence, opened the door, held it open with one foot, and saluted. Cerrano proceeded to walk out of the room backwards to keep her eyes on

Ena and Torno. When she inevitably backed into the wall, Torno's suppressed laugh escaped his nose in a snort. The pair of Junior Mages glowered at him. Iodize tried to help lead Cerrano out of the room and she slapped his hand away.

Iodize walked out, stomped to attention before the threshold, and shouted, "We'll be watching you!" He slammed the door.

Torno laughed into his hand.

"I can't believe you're laughing!" Ena huffed. "They said that we were found guilty! Didn't they say we were accused of being traitors?"

"Relax," Torno composed himself. "Acolytes don't have the authority to pass judgment and I've never heard of any...Junior Mages."

"So we're gonna be okay?"

Torno shrugged. "I mean, we are traitors. We're about to leave the country without orders and some of the things they accused us of we did actually do. But those two jokers won't have the authority to do anything."

Ena let out a long sigh.

He put a hand on her arm. "We'll get out of the country, Ena, don't you worry."

"Okay, thanks."

"As for me, I'm probably late for whatever pomp proceeds this promotion ceremony. Listen, whatever happens, we're leaving the city as soon as we can leave the building. Make sure the others know that," Torno said moving to--and lingering by--the washroom.

"Can do." She was forced to wait for him to use the facilities. The interrogation had gone on for so long that Ena needed to go herself. When she thought about it, the Junior Mages hadn't asked them any questions that might've been relevant. They never told the pair why they were in Sothlen or even who Hultur was. Which, all things considered, was a good thing. If Hultur had a fake name, Ena didn't know it. She felt like they'd left the gallows with nothing but a sore neck.

Torno came out with haste, making his way to leave.

"Hey, wait."

"I gotta go, Precious."

"Yeah, so do I." She pointed to the facility. "But you owe me an explanation for your deathstaff breaking."

"You're Ngoltur reborn." He left her.

Ena was too desperate to pee to hunt him down and beat the answer out of him.

~ ~ ~

After the needless pomp and procedure from the Junior Mages, Ena was happy to be out of the hospital in record time. Too many wounded were forced to sleep outside on cots and rugs for them to scrutinize her departure. On Myrrel's word alone, she was released.

Outside, the devastation had left a hole in the city's outskirts. Scavengers and survivors picked through the remains of homes and businesses alike. Close by the hospital, makeshift tents and rowhouses were set up to care for the wounded and displaced. Acolytes assisted wherever and however they could, but many simply stood around preventing petty squabbles.

Visk was first to run up and hug Ena.

"I'm okay, Visk, but I might not be if you keep hugging me this tight."

"Apologies." She stepped back and bowed. "I'd never seen you so thoroughly battered. I thought we'd lost you."

"Nah, it'll take more than that to kill..." Narla looked about the crowd. "Her."

Ena looked around for Sal and Hultur. "Where are the others?"

"They're in the hotel 'getting ready,' whatever that means for men." Narla rolled her eyes. "We'll meet our glorious Captian at City Hall."

Ena took stock of the four of them. "Huh? I can't remember the last time it was just us girls."

"That's because we're going into the city to look our best," Myrrel said with unbridled excitement. She threw her arms around Ena and Narla's shoulders. "We're buying dresses and getting our makeup done!"

"Fuck. I could even get my hair done." Narla touched the short strands poking out from behind her goggles.

Ena's eyes lit up. "Wait, are we gonna see Visk outside of her armor?"

Visk made her face hard. "It is an unavoidable outcome."

"We only got three hours to spend five hundred gulda, girls, so let's get this wagon in motion!" Myrrel giggled.

"Isn't that our entire treasury?" Ena asked, jumping into the back.

"Oh, that's right, you weren't there for all the celebrations," Narla smacked her head. "They were practically showering Torno with gifts after the mega went down. I'd never seen him so happy."

"I have. It's like this." Ena exposed her lower teeth in a grimace.

"He was beaming, Ena. You wouldn't have recognized him."

"Hey!" Myrrel shouted from the jockey box. "This is the first time in years I get to feel like a woman outside of the bedroom. Let's not ruin this by talking about men."

"Fine with me," Narla said.

Ena noticed the scowl deepening on Visk's brow. "Hey, I'm okay. Really."

"I know." She nodded.

Ena grabbed her hand. When Visk kept staring forward she looked at Narla. "How bad was I?"

"You were limp when Visk found you. There was a lot of blood on the ground from where you..." Narla touched the back of her head.

"I made sure none moved you," Visk told the wall of the wagon.

"You did good, Visk," Myrrel praised. "Everyone did. Even Hultur."

"Oh, have you finally come around to forgiving him for making you sleep?" Narla asked.

She stayed suspiciously silent when faced with shame.

"Hey, about Hultur," Ena spoke up. "What are we supposed to call him anyway? We can't just go around calling him Hultur."

"Vamere," Visk told Ena. "He picked the name himself."

Something about Visk's harsh tone silenced the wagon. It was clear she hadn't warmed up on her feelings about Hultur. Ena supposed that she should start thinking of the man as Vamere. He never really lined up with the vision of the legend in her mind. Hultur was large and powerful, but he was also a ruthless destroyer. Vamere didn't have that look of malice she'd always imagined Hultur having. He looked far too calm to be the Master of Evil.

The Band of Brokers visited Sothlen once a year to drop off their status report and pick up new orders. Year after year they received the same instructions and never spent any real time in the inner city's marketplace. There were baths, beauticians, boutiques, and bazaars that took Ena's breath away. Everywhere she looked merchants were selling styles and fashions from all over the three continents, and some beyond. The simple thing would be to adorn herself in the style of Doronel or Caredor City, but the gowns looked too austere or old-fashioned. Ena might never again have the chance to wear a dress.

Her wandering eyes caught the attention of an Encomium, little girls who patrolled the fashion districts in search of patrons with money to spend. They were named such because of their tendency to speak at great lengths of the beauty of not only their clients but the stores that paid their commission. Many considered Encomium a nuisance, but they helped well-to-do travelers manage the stress of finding their way through crowded marketplaces. Besides which, the children had a reputation for earning gulda with gifts rather than beguiling it with a grift.

"Gorgeous and eloquent madam, your very countenance contributes to a world of grandeur and majesty. Never before have I seen a woman born with so many splendors that can't be purchased, who was wrangled by such an economic exigency to acquire attire." The girl's flamboyant vocabulary was delivered not only with great enthusiasm, but she was also evoking over the sounds of the market to make sure she was heard.

Ena couldn't help but giggle. "I don't know if I'd call my exigency economic, but I'm definitely in a hurry. What kind of stores have their hands in your purse?"

"Only the best kinds, madam, I assure you! I'm known in this fabulous circle as having an eye discerning as an eagle and am not shy about voicing my revulsion for vendibles very much below the beauties our great city gathers. Mallino Peet was a seamstress and tailor of great renown before she came to start up her own business in this very quarter. Every single one of her garments was crafted by her design down to a thread. Their patterns and fabrics compose attire far too elaborate to be called dresses."

That sounded like the kind of store Ena couldn't pass up, and she found the girl's enthusiasm infectious. If this was going to be her last shopping trip, it might be worth it to put her beauty in the hands of this little lass. "And are you known by a name?"

"Lu Maudmerry as it pleases you, and surely you must be Ngoltur reborn!"

"I suppose I must," Ena said with a coy smile.

Once Lu understood how little time they had, she rushed her to a bath and barber. As her hair was cared for, the energetic Lu came back with armfuls of gowns and accessories. She'd go through each one describing its history with a story and a smile, and she transitioned to the next like the previous item never touched her hands. The barber hadn't the time to tame Ena's hair, so she agreed to cut it down from a storm extending past her shoulder blades to a manageable length under her chin. The stylist healed her scalp as she damaged it, pulling at the thick hair to work her fringes back into an elaborate braid.

Lu dragged her to a boutique covered in a smock and a slip and no one gave either of them a second glance. Mallino Peet was every bit as creative and inventive as the girl had boasted, and she outfitted Ena in an elegant navy gown accented with a flowing half cape to hide her bandaged wounds. The makeup artist gave Ena thin reeds to bite and went right to work drawing gold branches over her face. The angular bits brought out cheeks Ena didn't know she had, and the curves did a surprising job of flushing out the roundness of her eyes. With the detail work finished, the master went to work on another client and two understudies finished her lips, eyes, and nails. Once she stood, Lu affixed bits of jewelry in quick succession until she looked every bit like Ngoltur from a stage production.

All in all, the 150 gulda Ena spent felt like quite the deal. Little Lu celebrated her final showing and pushed the crowd aside with evoked flashes and bangs as she announced that Ngoltur reborn was leaving the bazaar. Meeting up with the wagon and the women, Ena turned about to thank her Encomium.

"Thank you, Lu. You truly made me feel special today."

"But you are special, Ngoltur! None could look at a woman such as you and feel anything but wonder! I do hope that everything goes well at your party tonight."

Ena inclined her head in appreciation. She went back to the wagon and reached for some more gulda to give the Encomium, but when she turned back Lu was gone. A passing gentleman offered to help Ena rise to her wagon and she accepted. So many eyes were on her and none gazed at her white skin with revulsion. She sat in the jockey box and looked at the admiring gentleman. He placed his hat over his heart and watched her go with stars in his eyes.

The Brokers were exquisitely dressed and each had nothing but praise for their friends.

Myrrel had opted for a traditional look in a Doronel ball gown that hugged her ribs and chest close as any corset. The reds and golds of the ruffled skirt continued up along patterns on her sides that matched the gold script on her arms and the blush of her cheeks. Strong magicks had been employed to ease her hair into natural curls that bounced in the wind and framed her face.

Narla found a burgundy suit with a delightful pink undershirt that popped out of the lapels and cuffs to show off its frills. Her makeup was done in a Leben fashion, lacking any script, glyphs, or true linework. The woman's chaotic curls were sheered down to a clean frohawk tinted the subtlest of oranges.

Visk surprised them all by dressing in a traditional Ki'an style. The green gown had a thrice-cut ankle skirt and a cross-back top that only came around the front to conceal her breasts. Woven into the fabric of the emerald number was a lace of geometric patterns that covered her chest and back. From ankle to neck, the cherry-skinned woman was oiled to show the definition of her athletic body. Braces around her calves and arms were tight to accentuate their thickness. Her long braided hair was wrapped into a topknot held together with a mesh matching the lace of her gown. It wasn't all traditional. Visk's attire lacked the veil of an unmarried woman and the markings of one spoken for.

The men were alright.

Sal wore a formal vest and pants, and even though he insisted he'd had his face stones sanded down, none saw the difference. Hultur was wearing the same expensive travel suit he always wore, but he had no plans of attending the party. He would be riding the wagon around in a circle, stopping by only to pick them up after Torno received his accolades. He didn't say anything about the attire of the women, nor did he give any of them a second glance. Sal tried his best to give compliments but claimed he lacked the vocabulary to properly express his awe.

Once they arrived at the steps of city hall, all their swagger and raised chins were put in check. Every guest arriving was dressed just as formally, and many of them more so. These were people used to affluence, and their attire spoke not only of their wealth but their station. Ena tried to hold onto Lu's praise. She told herself that she deserved to be there, but every sideways glance brought back memories of classmates calling her "bone bitch," and "spit bastard."

Visk did her rounds to find every exit. Narla glanced at the pillars and the painted ceiling on her way to the bar. Sal wobbled over to the other boulbas. And Myrrel grabbed Ena's arm tight enough to pinch her skin.

"Can you believe these men?" Myrrel whispered into her ear. "If I start to salivate, don't hesitate to give me a good flick in the ear."

"I don't know if I can do this?" Ena whispered back. She was backpedaling, retreating back to the entrance. "I think I should stay in the welcome room until the speeches start."

"Are you mad?! You can't leave my side now!" she seethed more than whispered.

"I can't be out here wearing this, Myrrel. Everyone can see me." Ena turned around, probably drawing in more gazes than she was avoiding.

"I know, that's why you can't leave my side! These men can't take their eyes off you! If I'm standing in your aura, they might just take a second look at me," she snickered. Their eyes met and Myrrel felt the severity of her panic. "What's wrong, Camellia?"

"I'm a freak, Myrrel. Everyone in here can see that I'm an albino."

"And I have vitiligo. Why does it suddenly matter that you're a freak?"

"Because these are city people, the magic elite. They're

the reason I've been working out in villages that no one important will ever go to!"

"Ena, I want you to take deep breaths and listen to me. Okay?"

She nodded.

"We were sent away because a bunch of snobby bitches didn't like our faces. We've known that for a while. That's why we're in a band with a boulba, a Ki'an, an alcoholic, and Torno. But you're wrong about something. Someone important did go to those villages, you did. We're here because you killed a mega monster. You did that, Ena. No matter what happens, no one can take that away from you. You know what else?"

Ena shook her head but kept it low, almost to her chest.

Myrrel took her chin and raised it. "You're gorgeous and everyone here knows it."

Ena tried to look out at the faces, but only made it to their shoulders. Someone was approaching, a man who knew how to wear a beard and earrings. He looked like a true gentleman, cultured, handsome, and kind.

"Evening, ladies. Can I get the two of you some water?"

Myrrel sounded weak, her voice lacking any power. "Oh, that would be so sweet. Thank you so much."

The man bowed with one hand on his back and left.

"That sexy man came over here because he's interested in you, they all are. When he comes back we're going to tell him that you're upset because your mother forced you to go to parties. She died when the mega attacked and you haven't had time to mourn."

"Why would we tell him that?" Ena chuckled.

"Because we can tell him anything. You don't have to be Ena today. You can be anyone from anywhere because you'll never have to see these people again."

"I'll go along with you, but I don't want to lie about who I am." Ena let out a long sigh. She tried to look out at the partygoers again. Some of the women were pointing at her, but they were also pointing at each other. There wasn't any malice in their eyes. No one was looking at her with jealousy or spite, only curiosity. When she looked at the men, they turned away from their friends and tried to catch her attention with a smile.

"Here you are." The handsome gentleman came back with two glasses of water. "Is there anything else I can assist with?"

Ena took the glass and drank slowly.

"I hope you can," Myrrel said. "We don't know anyone here. Maybe you can introduce us to some people."

"It would be my honor."

The man's name was Rien and Ena made it a point to remember it. All the other names that flew at her that night, she struggled to process. He wasn't there alone, and Ena appreciated being shown to a table full of friendly faces. They were all a little bored and curious about Torno, so they lit up when Ena explained that he was their Band Captain. It was strange hearing them talk about Torno like he was this grand hero but thinking about him helped her forget about her time at the academy. She could focus on their questions about her dress and their gossip about the politics of the Great Generation.

Ena did eventually leave Rien's table, but only because she had to relieve her bladder. She rounded the hallway corner to return to the ballroom, but the sound of ceramic clattering on wood stopped her. Torno was standing there in his pompous officer's uniform, a scroll unraveled at his feet. His boyish shaved face hung open. She snickered at him and he blinked a hundred thousand times as he tried repeatedly to compose himself. There was a strong temptation to simply walk back to the ballroom, but Ena couldn't pass up this opportunity to tease Torno.

Focusing on the heel-to-toe motion of walking in heels, Ena reveled in his stupified expression. She steadied herself against a wall and leaned over to pick the scroll off the ground. She glanced up at his staring eyes and Torno shot them skyward like a Cleric in devotions. He kept opening his mouth to say something but only succeeded at making himself look like a basking fish.

"I believed you dropped this," she told him casually.

He might've nodded, but it was a little hard to tell with all the involuntary motions shaking his body. Torno shook his head firmly and took the scroll. "Thank you. I was just...trying to prepare for my speech."

"Do you feel ready?"

Silence from the awestruck man.

"You better get everything together, Torno. If they see you acting like this, they'll think twice about giving you a promotion for courage and leadership. Has all of that Capital training to suppress your emotions failed so easily?" She smirked.

"Completely. Ena, you look...I can't even find the words."

"Careful, Torno, if you keep looking at me like that, you might just give me your fourth confession of love."

"I'll give my fifth, sixth, and hundredth if it means I can share one dance with you." His voice came out strained and his excessive swallowing did nothing to settle him. The poor thing.

"A dance might be sweet," Ena said with a smile. "But I think it might kill you. Look at you now, you're shivering."

The Captain nodded. "A happy death is one worth fighting for."

A side door opened. "They're ready to go." It closed without another word.

Torno looked to the door and then back to Ena. His hand fell off the doorknob. With a sudden twist, he directed his full attention to her. Long strides closed the distance between them. She backed up until she was up against the wall and still he came. Ena placed a hand on his chest, but only to stop him. His lips were obnoxiously close.

"You better back up, Torno. I can smell your aftershave."

"Is that what you're worried about, my aftershave?"

"At the moment, yes. Though if you stay this close, I might be able to guess what you've had for dinner." But she couldn't smell anything on his breath. She could indeed feel his breath on her face, but nothing about his gasps unsettled her.

His heart was pounding against her palm. Surely, all of this excitement couldn't just be because she was beautiful. They'd known each other for so long, seen each other in so many different situations, but she'd never seen him like this. Strange how the feel of him against her skin wasn't unsettling. He was warm in a way that Ena hadn't known before her birthday. Somehow that heat had worked its way into her cheeks. There was a tilt in her chin that she hadn't planned. Air struggled in her lungs and it only escaped when her lips parted.

THE EIGHTH CHAPTER

In Which Torno Ruins Everything

Strength drained out of Ena's arm. She'd always meant to stop him. Her arms were primed to push him back. At least she thought she was. There wasn't anything holding him back. Those hands of hers were resting against his chest when they should've been applying resistance. Torno moved forward ever so slightly and her hand slid down to his ribs. No boyish enthusiasm colored his face now, nor could she see any of that cocky, self-assured exuberance. His eyes never strayed from hers and they were so close to closed but so full of light. Lifting her chin, Ena prepared to receive his lips.

"Marry me." Those words came out with such certainty.

Ena pulled her head back. "What?"

Torno caressed her cheek. "I don't care if this gives me another confession or ten. I love you, Ena. I don't want to spend my life with anyone else. I want to love you forever."

If Ena hadn't been leaning against a wall she would've fallen on her ass.

The stage door opened again. "Torno, they're waiting for you."

He didn't acknowledge the intruder. He was so sure of himself, so sure of them working as a couple even though they'd never even kissed.

"They're calling you," Ena said with a point.

"I don't care. The whole world could catch fire and I wouldn't notice right now. Say the words and kiss me." He sounded weak with lust and raw with emotion.

"No," she said. She took his hand and brought it off her face. "I'm not going to marry you, Torno. I don't love you back."

He leaned back ever so slightly.

"Torno!" The interloper snapped.

"In a minute," he called back.

Ena used that glance to slip away. She could already see the pain in his eyes, feel the familiar anger radiating off him. "I'm sorry. I didn't want to hurt you."

"Hurt me a thousand times, but don't lie to me." His pained expression wasn't softening.

"I'm not, Torno. I don't want to marry you." Whatever impulse had grabbed her, had left her. She walked away.

Ena had no idea how that happened. All she wanted to do was mess with him, not touch his chest and let him kiss her! He always thought he was so cool and strong, but he was a coward. Torno was a knave to the bottom of his disloyal heart. But how virtuous could she be if she was going to let him kiss her? Something had changed between them. No, that couldn't be right. Torno was always staring at her, always confessing his love to her. It didn't matter that he proposed. When a man confessed his love, it was the same thing as asking a woman to marry him. Ena had been the one to change. Maybe having sex with Haenir awakened something inside. Maybe all of this was happening because she was going on this journey to meet Muttur. Maybe none of this would matter in a year.

Everyone was having a good time in the ballroom. Myrrel was dancing with the handsome Rien. Narla was drinking with a striking woman about her age, the Mage's long hair was coated gray, but still black enough to look like a raincloud. Sal was laughing and chatting with the only boulbas in attendance. Even Visk was talking to two women. They were standing on either side of her, taking turns running their hands over the lumps of her abs.

Ena quick-stepped over to a table at the back of the room. Lights dimmed as she found a seat. Curtains pulled back and an older woman stepped up to the podium. She was a Magus, the ultimate magical authority in the city. For years now, Magus Yersen had kept Captain Torno and all the Brokers out of the public eye. Every time Ena met her their interactions were brief. She was practiced at faking a smile and she could even conjure up a convincing laugh. This speech was no exception to the woman's endless charms. When the room was full of polite chuckles, she welcomed Torno to the stage.

Hanging crystals shone light onto him, but Ena couldn't look at the man. She couldn't risk him seeing her in the corner. It was better to look around the room and glance at the people standing up to applaud his arrival. They wanted to believe that heroes were men like Torno, men with visions of tomorrow that lacked the courage to live today. Ena spotted Myrrel walking out of the ballroom, the handsome Rien leading the way.

"Wow, thank you all for your support. Thank you." Torno cleared his throat but they kept clapping.

With so many people standing and him basking in the stage lights, Ena could risk a look. She could see him happy to be surrounded by sycophants. But when the people in the way sat down she didn't see the man smiling. He looked severe and close to tears. He glanced at his scroll on the podium and then he looked up to scan the room.

Ena dropped to the floor. She didn't care how silly she looked or if people were looking her way, she couldn't have him know where she was sitting.

"I've made a lot of mistakes in my life, but this one might go down in history as my best." He paused and they laughed. "I wasn't supposed to be in Sothlen when the mega attacked. My band and I were stationed in the villages south of here treating pustules and fighting a very real outbreak of monsters there, but we'll get back to that before my speech is done. It was fate that brought me here. A friend of mine had an unexpected visitor and we were escorting him back to the city because the roads this far from civilization have become treacherous. Perhaps we should all pause to applaud fate."

Even though Torno paused to give people a chance to clap, no one did.

"Because the simple truth is that I didn't kill the mega named Wand-Breaker, and I never could've. I didn't study monsters enough to identify their hybrid properties. That was the work of my mechanic, the talented Narla. She's probably somewhere by the bar."

They didn't sweep house lights over the floor, but Torno looked and she raised her glass to a spattering of claps.

"I may have identified that the mega retreated before activating an ether sink because it was synching its scales to absorb incoming attacks, but it was the work of Visk, Narla, and so many other casters here today that created an opportunity. Many of them are absent because they died following my orders. And so many others died before I even arrived. They didn't die because they were working towards my great plan, but to save a son, or a friend, or to give their infirmed mother the smallest chance of survival as she ran for city hall."

He pointed to the heraldic sigil of Sothlen. His wrath for the city and the system were uncaged.

"Those people died heroes, but there will be no monuments or awards for them. It does no good to celebrate the accomplishments of the dead. Hold up a hero and make him a Wizard, and the people will believe that our thaumacracy is worth fighting for. That's why I'm here, to be a symbol.

"They want to make me a symbol so that everyone

can look to our spires and ether-chains and write poetry about how glorious the achievements of the modern age are. They don't want you to look outside the city limits. They don't want to talk about how downtown was full of capable spellcasters who hid in their homes and businesses, because they knew they were safe. If that mega came closer, an ethereal barrier was already charged. It was ready to withstand the attacks of the mega for days if that's what it came to.

"What do they call them, siege weeks?"

He shook his head with disgust.

People were shouting at Torno now, most of it incomprehensible.

"I hear you. I hear you. I said I fucking hear you!" Torno shouted, amping up wind magic to spread his voice. "None of you were at fault. You weren't trained to fight. Many of you were trained to feel whatever emotions come naturally while living a life of monotony and pour those thoughts into generic, formless ether. And you should all be celebrated because without you this system of magical dependency breaks down. So here's to you."

He clapped. He was the only one.

"Go on. Join in. Give yourselves all a big round of applause."

Narla, Visk, and Sal had all made their way back to the door.

Sal spotted Ena hiding under a table and came over to ask, "Where's Myrrel?"

"She might need another minute," Ena said, looking towards the door.

"I don't know if we have that!"

Torno's speech continued over them. "Because that's what all of this control is about, symbols. I've been a symbol for a nation that does nothing but take, but we aren't so cruel as to leave their villages defenseless. I'm a Broker Captain, a great hero that solves the problems of villages. Problems that little villages of a hundred have been capable of handling themselves for generations!"

"Is he drunk? What the fuck got into him?" Narla asked Ena.

"I turned him down again." She grimaced.

"Oh fuck! We're actually going to die."

"But it's okay," Torno assured the grumbling masses. "Because we have symbols of the thaumacracy's power and the Supreme Magus's right to rule. As long as people like me are here, we don't have to think about the fact that our infrastructure is incapable of helping villages against hordes of monsters, let alone a rampaging mega. Little villages like that are what we in leadership call acceptable losses. Three days ago, we learned that anything outside the city's main production of power counts as an acceptable loss. And so I accept your applause as a loyal patriot who was here to minimize an acceptable loss."

He stepped back from the amplifying net and raised a hand.

"Yeah!" Narla cheered to silence. "Go Caredor!" She grabbed Ena's arm and pulled her out of the double doors. "Couldn't you have just said, 'we'll talk about it later?!'"

Ena winced. "I didn't think that he was going to incite rebellion!"

Visk clicked her tongue with disapproval. "This is going to be a very unpleasant trip."

Sal walked over to the washrooms and saw Myrrel and Rien. She was daintily wiping her mouth with a handkerchief. Sal asked her, "Where were you?"

"I got busy." Myrrel glanced at Rien and a smirk broke through his calm composure.

"No time for chiding, we need to find Torno and get the fuck out of here. Which way to the backstage?" Narla asked.

The hallway opposite the washroom exploded in flames and Torno ran out with a bloody sword in one hand.

"I think it's that way," Visk said, pointing.

"It could be the other way, I think I did see a door by the washroom," Myrrel added with a straight face.

"Oh, you guys are funny. You're a fucking laugh riot!" Narla screamed.

Ena leveled her hand with the floor and wall and felt for the flow of water. Pipes moved water below. She waited for Torno to break into a run. Tapping into the earth remotely, she pushed the pipes up through the ground. Water sprayed into the hallway and she froze it into a wall with a snap.

"If Narla is panicking things are bad," Sal said.

"Of course things are bad! Torno just disrespected Magus Yersen!" She pulled at the frills of her chest just so she would have something to break that wasn't Torno.

"Hey," Torno said, meeting up with the group.

They followed him outside at a sprint.

"Torno, that was by far the stupidest thing you've ever done!" Narla snapped at him.

"Then you're going to hate what's waiting for us outside."

They came out to a city in chaos. Everywhere they looked spells were flying in high arcs or exploding against buildings. People with pikes were clashing into rows of Acolytes and the city guard. Flung spells were deflected, countered, and landed to launch people into the air.

"Did you start a fucking rebellion?!" Narla screamed.

They all turned to look at their fearless Captain.

A smug smirk twisted his face. "Why do you think I've been in such a good mood?"

THE NINTH CHAPTER

In Which Ngoltur is Forced to Accept Her Destiny

There was no time for the Brokers to give an appropriate response to Torno's act of insurrection. Revolutionaries weren't just out in force, they were attacking City Hall. Guards formed a perimeter past to defend the Magus with their life, and the Band of Brokers found themselves defended by the people Torno betrayed. Sal layed hands on the ground and signaled where Hultur was lost in the crowd. Avoiding the chaos as best they could, they rounded a corner only to find a barricade locked in mortal combat. Torno tossed his blood-covered sword onto the ground and moved through the gestures of a pyromantic attack. Holding his hands over his head, a ball of flames emerged. Anger flashed over Torno's eyes and a look of zealotry took him as he poured ether into the inferno.

"Isn't the first rule of warfare, don't fight in a gown?" Myrrel asked the group sardonically.

"Funny, I thought it was don't kill your allies!" Narla snapped back.

Torno brought the fireball down on the backs of the city's defenders. Flames erupted catching wands and staffs along with their clothes. Their now traitorous Captain directed the explosion into a wall of fire that made its way through the makeshift barricade. Screams of elation added to those of death.

"Behind me!" Sal yelled.

They did as Sal asked, with Visk making sure that she was taking up the rear. She had to pick up Torno by the collar of his shirt. He'd reached his limit with that attack and his eyes were glazed. Revolutionaries ran past, patting and shoulders on their way in to continue the killing. Sal held tight, moving against the crowd.

Up ahead, rays of ether exploded against the side of a spherical shield of magic. Inside that impenetrable defense was their simple Broker's wagon. For the most part, revolutionaries were avoiding the wagon, focusing their efforts on tearing apart ether stores, wand shops, and other places of arcane power. Those that tried to push in on the wagon were tossed back by a wall of wind that cycled around the wagon's base.

Hultur was sitting on the jockey box, controlling the impenetrable wall of wind and protective sphere with a single raised finger spinning. The Ki'an giant caught sight of the Band and beckoned them forward. He seemed to care more about his new black fedora than the fighting.

Rising a bit of the wind cyclone four feet off the ground, Hultur let them inside. When others saw Sal push through the wall, they tried to follow them in. Visk grabbed a big man by the arm and pushed him back into the masses. "Go break things."

Torno struggled to climb up to the jockey box, so Hultur lifted him like a child. "Go right. Do what you can to avoid hurting people."

"I've been doing that for some time," Hultur grumbled.

Rather than whip at the four horses tied to the front of the wagon, Hultur let out four threads of ether to explain what needed to be done. Gale and Li'at were standing in front of Missie and Chen. The aging draft horses hated to have anyone ride ahead of them, so Hultur must've done some convincing to get them to obey.

Ena joined Hulter in the jockey box. By accident, her bare foot found Torno in the back of the ribs and she didn't mutter any apologies. He glanced back at her and neither said a word. People were running in all directions, trying to escape the chaos or participate in a way that was impossible for the eye to follow. They learned to avoid the wagon fast though. No matter what anyone threw at the wagon, Hultur kept up the barrier with the casual twirl of his index finger.

"Okay, so something I don't get," said Narla, poking her head out from the back. "Why did the Magus let you make your little speech? How were you even able to escape her wrath? You're resourceful, Torno, but you're nowhere near strong enough to compete with a Magus."

"Remember when I shook her hand?" he asked.

"Yeah?!"

"I injected her with a semi-paralytic." Torno sounded calm as he described his act of insurrection. "It took effect a little after she sat down."

"What the fuck, Torno?!" Narla spat.

"Wait, that's why you had that calming elixir because you'd been to see an expert in toxins?!" Ena shouted at him. "That's also why you were there at my interrogation. You needed to know the Acolytes didn't have any suspicions about what you were planning."

"More or less," Torno confirmed with a weak nod.

Myrrel reached over to hand Torno a purple gem of twenty gulda to restore his ether.

Narla grabbed her arm. "Oh, no you don't! Don't give this madman any more ether. He's already got us into enough trouble as it is!"

"I have to say, I share Narla's outrage," Sal piped in. "We weren't prepared for any of that. Your stunt, your secrets, put all of us in danger!"

"Ena was with you. As long as you're with her, you're not in any real danger." He put a hand on his head. Even leaning against Ena's leg, she could feel him swaying back and forth.

"Why, because I'm Ngoltur reborn?" Ena asked incredulously.

"Tell her, Narla," said Torno.

Ena looked at the irate woman for an explanation. She glanced at Ena and then lowered her eyes apologetically.

"When you killed the mega, I calculated that you put out over seven-thousand gulda of ether. That's not counting whatever you spent to get onto the spire." She let out a sigh. "There's no denying it anymore, Gorgeous. You're Ngoltur reborn."

"Narla, if Torno doesn't get some ether, he's going to pass out," Myrrel said seriously. "Bad as things are now, how much shit are we going to be in if he's not conscious and powered up when we get to the monorail?"

Narla let go of Myrrel and she gave the revolutionary his magic juice.

"Thank you," Torno mumbled. He grabbed the purple gemstone with the arm covered in blood to the elbow. Gulda over his mouth, he sucked in the ether with slow breaths.

"Why was your sword bloody, Torno?" Ena asked.

"Because I killed Magus Yersen."

The wagon got quiet. Everyone had been leaning forward to hear the nonsense coming out of Torno's mouth and the news kept them that way.

"Which way?" Hultur asked.

Bodies were marching in to depose the Magus in smaller numbers here. Looters were just as common a sight as citizens fleeing for their lives. The Band reached a slight fork and neither path was going perfectly straight.

"The right one," said Myrrel. She rubbed Torno's back. "You going to be okay?"

He nodded. "It's only exhaustion. I'm not used to these. They yanked the ether right out of me." He pulled back the cuffs of his suit to show off military-grade casting bracelets.

"I can't believe you planned a revolution to start

with your speech. How fucking arrogant can you be?" Ena snapped. "You probably have that entire speech written down on that scroll you were carrying."

"Yep. I figured if I died it might give people the tiniest bit of hope to rise against this twisted system. You know, I thought you saw my speech earlier," Torno chuckled. "Did you think I was giving a speech like that because you rejected me?"

"No," Ena pouted. "Narla did."

"Speaking of which..." Torno dabbed his brow and glanced back at the fuming mechanic. "Why are you so upset about this revolution anyway? Since I first met you, you've had nothing but bad things to say about the Supreme Magus and his plans for the Great Generation."

"That didn't mean that I wanted to be a revolutionary, Torno! That didn't mean that I was going to be okay with burning Acolytes from behind! Those men were just doing their job, Torno! Are you really telling me that you don't feel an ounce of guilt over what you did to them?!"

He shook his head. "It'll keep me up at night. Probably for the rest of my life...however short that is."

"What's this Great Generation?" Hultur asked from the front.

All the Caredor natives let out an exasperated sigh.

"Just keep driving," said Ena.

"Torno, none of us have any love for the Supreme Magus," Sal agreed. "We all drank to his failing health more than once. I think most of us are surprised. We would've preferred to know this was coming."

"At the very least, I would've worn better shoes," Myrrel said with a chuckle.

"I couldn't risk anything happening to Ena and Hultur," Torno said. "I had to put my faith in strangers. If one of them decided to sell us out, I needed all of you to be able to slip out this unharmed and get Ena and Hultur to find Muttur."

Myrrel slapped Torno on the back of the head.

"Ow."

"So you were just going to sacrifice yourself?! After everything we've been through, you thought that we'd just watch you executed for treason and continue without you!"

Torno gave a slow grim nod. "It's hardly the most selfish thing I've ever done."

Myrrel closed her eyes. She swallowed back a long rant and just turned her head away in disgust. Myrrel busied herself by finding a comfortable pair of shoes.

"What about you, Visk?" Torno asked. "You haven't said anything."

She watched the back. Without the flames illuminating clouds of smoke, the gray would be lost in the night sky. "No, I haven't."

Torno brought his eyes to his lap and sighed.

Ena found it hard to conjure up any pity for him. He did so many bad things today. He'd hurt each of them in one way or another and the worst part about all of it was that he knew it. He knew what he had done was wrong and he hurt all of his friends because they fit some twisted metrics of morality in his warped mind.

The Band came up to the monorail station; a congregation of people were waiting at the top of the steps. They held up flags of black with a red bull, the flag of the democratic revolutionaries used to overthrow Ena's parents. All eyes went on the wagon and Torno. Their great Captain jumped off the jockey box and revolutionaries gathered like flies to Torno.

He told them the news with a smile. "Magus Yersen is dead!"

They cheered. "Death to the magus! Death to the magi!"

People Ena had never seen before helped her down. They stared too long at her white skin. When they finally met her eyes, they busied themselves emptying the wagon. These revolutions were far too organized to be gathered by Torno, and he lacked the charisma to bring them together besides. This revolution was coming one way or another. Torno had been a catalyst for the action and maybe it wasn't even him. Maybe the true catalyst had been the mega monster, Wand-Breaker.

"I want those horses!" shouted Hultur.

The revolutionaries parted in fear as the seven-and-a-half-foot-tall giant rushed forward to take Li'at's reins.

Torno put his hand on his arm. "Relax, big guy. They're just bringing them to the monorail's cargo. The other horses are going, but we're keeping yours."

Hultur stared Torno down for a long time before releasing the reins and nodding.

"Wait, what do you mean we're getting rid of Missie and Chen?!" Ena asked. She walked right up to Torno and pushed him. "Those horses have been like family to us, Torno! You can't just give them to these...you can't just sell them!"

The other Brokers had rallied behind Ena to share their outrage. Missie and Chen had been with them since they were first assigned as Brokers. They'd been to the edge of death and ran at monsters to protect their humans. No one could ask for better horses.

Torno silenced them with a raise of hands. "I know how you all feel, believe me, but we're not going on a gentle tour through the fields of Leben Erde. They served us well and they've been nothing but loyal to us. Do you really want to see Missie die from an arrow through her throat or watch as some monster devours Chen? Bad as things might be here, taking them with us would be a death sentence."

Myrrel walked up to a man in conductor's garb. "Do we have time to say goodbye?"

"The monorail's already behind schedule." The man nodded despite his words.

They all gathered around the horses and hugged their

chests and necks. Visk reached over heads and pet Missie's snout.

Ena pressed her face against Missie's mane. "You were a good horse. I'm sorry you never got to raise a fowl."

She went to Chen and rubbed his cheek. The mare had never expressed any fondness for Ena, but Chen still respected her as part of her herd. Visk had always been her favorite and she pushed hard into her nearly bare body. Visk held her tight and cried into her mane. They stepped back but Visk held on. Myrrel was the one to move her along, and she did so with a gentle touch. Visk parted with a solemn expression and cheeks glistening.

The conductor led them up the steps, while a team of monorail operators ran ahead with their cargo. Heads poked out of the twenty-cabin machine aimed northward. Judging by the confused and irritated looks on their faces, they'd been waiting there for some time.

Narla turned around and blocked Torno.

"Narla?" Myrrel asked.

"He can't come with us. Not after this," she growled.

"He's our Captain, Narla," Myrrel said out of habit.

"No, he isn't! He's not our Captain and we're not Brokers, not anymore! We're not anything!" She was losing it. Her voice was ragged. Tears of rage rolled down her cheeks.

"But it was already like that," Ena reminded her.

Narla glanced back to sneer, but then recognition dawned on her.

"You decided to give up on being a Broker when you sided with me. We all did. Torno might not have done right by us, but he didn't make us traitors. We turned our backs on Magus Yersen without any word from Torno," Ena said gently. "As much as we might not like how Torno lied to us, he was right about one thing: Magus Yersen deserved to die."

Ena paused to see if any would argue with her, but none did. They'd spent the last three years of their life seeing what Magus Yersen's selfish decisions had done to the villages they served. They knew what the Supreme Magus's plan did to the people of Caredor.

"Besides which," Hultur spoke up. "No matter what's happening here, it is nothing compared to our mission. Ena and I don't have a choice but each of you do. There's no guarantee that any of us will survive what is to come. Your Captain accepted that. We must all share his conviction if we're going to succeed in changing the world."

Narla looked from Hultur to Ena and back again. "Fuck." Fuming, she entered the monorail.

The others followed slowly, bowing their heads at the grim realization that this wasn't a simple tour of duty, but an act of treason. They all stepped into the monorail without even glancing at Torno. Ena followed Hultur in, but stopped at the door. Visk was standing on the platform. Her hands were balled into fists.

"Visk, you said that you wanted to come and protect me. If you don't want to die to do that, I respect that. I won't hold it against you. After everything we've been through, you're still my friend no matter what. I promise."

Visk shook her head. "You're right."

She was the last inside. The doors shut behind her and the ether-chain below hummed into life. The monorail left the station slow at first, giving everyone time to find their cabins and seats. Torno and his revolutionaries had secured a private cabin for each of them. Ena's stuff was inside her room along with three presents sitting on a desk.

At the bottom of the stack was a letter bearing the wax seal of the Magus' Office. The middle was a black box with a red ribbon. When she slipped off the ribbon she found the red bull of the democratic revolution. Inside was a case of cigars and a small card that read, For the Slayer of Wand-Breaker. The Liberators Will Never Forget Your Heroism. On the back of the card was the same red bull surrounded by the six quills of democratic voice.

The top box was from Torno. She didn't know how she

knew, it just had his stink. The box was white and tied up with a ribbon of blue and gold. Judging by the weight, it was a magic weapon or jewelry. It was too small and too light to be anything else.

Red light crystals blinked to life inside her private cabin. Besides the light was a warning for guests to find a seat quickly when the light went on. She sat on her bed and looked over the desk. There was a small chair attached to the base, able to slide in and out. The wood of the desk was nice and the personal lights were better than any she had at the chantry where she learned her magic. The monorail sped to max, pushing her back into the wall.

Soon, the acceleration stopped and the red lights were off. She was free to read the formal letter from the dead magus, or what was probably another confession of love from a man who had far less sense than she thought he did. Ena hadn't the strength for any of it. The day had been too long and she was tired of thinking. She made sure the door to her cabin was locked, laid down in her fancy gown, and let sleep find her.

THE TENTH CHAPTER

In Which Ngoltor Swallows a Bitter Lullaby

Nightmares didn't haunt her, but neither did dreams visit her to make the trip pleasant. A man's words resonated through the too-thin walls. His voice was deep and unfamiliar. Though she couldn't make out his words, he sounded apologetic. Narla talked back to him. She couldn't be sure of what she was saying, but Ena recognized her voice through the wall. They talked for a bit before the sounds of smacking lips and grunts of passion took over.

Ena decided it would be best to check out the rest of the train.

Silent communities hid in the dark. Ena knew they existed if not their people and their struggles. She'd seen them over three years before when she came down the rail to first meet Magus Yersen and Torno. She knew what he was and why he was banished to an obscure job serving the needy. Back then, she was convinced that the man would be just as sadistic as the people of her chantry.

Visk was in the dining car, a single cup of tea resting in her hands. She was back in her light leather armor. Visk met Ena's eyes but lowered them back to her tea. Ena decided it best to let the woman have her privacy. A bartender welcomed Ena with a demure smile and got straight to work.

"What'll you have?"

"I don't know. I'm not a drinker," Ena admitted.

"We have night tea. It's supposed to help you sleep, but no one who ever drinks it ever does," the woman admitted in a conversational tone. She was comfortable with this time of night when big thoughts were put to rest and privacy was a matter of course rather than something one had to fight for.

Ena took a seat. "Why do you sell it if no one buys it?"

She smiled. "Oh, they buy it, the problem is the brew doesn't help. A sleeping tea gives people the illusion of control or maybe it just gives them something to complain about. Outside the monorail, people say the tea works like a charm. One hot cup and they're out in ten minutes. When people come back from a trip they can gripe to their family, 'I had three cups of night tea and I couldn't sleep at all!' Maybe we sell it just to add to the myth of the rail.

"Thing is, travelers never sleep well. Nothing easy making people get up and change their life. Plenty of awkward conversations come with a trip across the country. 'I met a man.' 'I'm pregnant.' 'I lost my job.' Some say they can't sleep because the monorail is too quiet, but they can always open the window."

Ena was staring at the bottles of spirits.

"You don't talk to your parents much, do you?" the woman asked.

"Am I that easy to read?" Ena asked with a chuckle.

"It's just my job. I can try my best to get a read on people but sometimes I make a mistake and say something I shouldn't, so I've gotten better at reading my mistakes. My mother says that our family has some Leben blood in us, but I just think we have naturally pointed ears." She tried to start a chuckle but gave up on it. She reached for a bottle with nothing but text on the label. "You want to try something different?"

"What is it?"

"It's a gin, but it doesn't taste like a gin. Gin drinkers

love it, but casual drinkers hate it. Maybe since you don't like to drink, it'll give you something to think about." She took out a shot glass. When Ena didn't answer one way or the other she smiled. "Of course, there's always the night tea."

Ena pointed at the gin that didn't taste like gin.

The bartender poured a shot and gave her a glass of water as well. "Take a small sip of the gin and don't take another lick until you can't taste it anymore. It's kind of like reading a book for your tongue, you gotta take your time with it to appreciate everything that's going on."

Ena reached for her gulda.

"No charge," she said with a smile.

Of all the smiles Ena had seen from her, she liked that one the least. She paid something anyway and found a seat.

Ena wasn't sure if she liked the woman or hated her. Maybe she was just one of those people who didn't have any friends, so she didn't care if she made any enemies. Ena took a sniff. It smelled like someone had spilled a bottle of liquor in the woods. At least she had some water to drink.

Narla entered the dining cabin. She was wearing the dress shirt from before, but the frills of the collar were torn clean off. She stopped to chat with Visk, but didn't join her. It didn't take Narla long to find the bar. A quick order, a fast pass of a red gulda, and she walked over to Ena with a glass of whiskey.

"How's it going?"

Ena tilted her head in a noncommittal way.

"Oh ho! What do you have here?" Narla said of her glass. "You mind if I?"

Ena shook her head.

Narla's face soured and she stuck her tongue out. "I keep forgetting how much I hate gin. What made you get it?"

Ena did her best to explain her encounter with the bartender without being loud enough for her to hear.

"A book for your tongue. That's rich. I guess you gotta do what you can to move product." Narla sipped from her own glass. "That's better. You can never go wrong with a good whiskey."

Ena tried to be casual when she asked, "How's the guy you found?"

"Oh, fuck! I didn't wake you up did I? I'm sorry." She sighed and then smiled. "He's fun. I think he's widowed or something. It's been awhile for him, you know? But...he's sweet."

"I don't know if I've ever seen you hook up with a guy before."

Narla nodded. "Yeah. I, uh...haven't wanted to. I'm sure you know about the miscarriage from someone."

Ena said, "Just that. Myrrel didn't want to tell me any details."

"Myrrel. Heh. That woman sure does love her goss. It's fine. I get it. I only talk about it when I'm five shits to the wind. I haven't gotten that drunk since Rachak broke things off with me. How old were you when that happened, eighteen?"

Ena nodded. "Do you still think about her?"

"All the time, but I'm not like Visk. When your heart's good and broken, sex helps." She let out a long sigh and drank. "What about you and Haenir?"

"I don't know. I haven't had any time to think about him." Ena scanned the dining cart; Visk had taken off. It was odd that Ena hadn't noticed her departure. "I still love him. Like, when I think about him it hurts to think that I'm never going to see him again, but it's not at all how I thought it would be."

"You mean because you're not bawling your eyes out over him?"

"Yeah."

"Grief has a way of sneaking up on you."

Ena put her hands under the table to hide how much they were shaking. She really didn't want to talk to Narla about this, but maybe she needed to. "Back in Sothlen before…"

"Before everything went to shit?"

Ena nodded. "Torno didn't just confess his love to me, he proposed to me."

"For all the fucking good it did him," she was happy thinking about Torno with some egg on his face.

"I almost kissed him."

Narla glanced back at the mostly empty cart. "Were you drunk?"

"No, but I did have some Iltwyr earlier in the day. That doesn't last a day, does it?"

Narla shook her head. "It's not good for more than nerfing your spells and it won't last more than an hour. I can't imagine popping that to get in the mood."

"I don't know what happened, Narla. He waltzed into my personal space like he always does, and I stood there and let him. I could've pushed him back or slapped him or froze him into a million tiny pieces, but I let him get close. The more I kept looking at him, the more I wanted him to kiss me. If he hadn't proposed to me, I would've kissed him." Ena whispered all of this, scanning the room between every few words as she told Narla about her secret shame.

"Tell it to me straight, Ena. Did you back him today because you like him?"

"I don't think so."

Narla arched a brow.

"I don't. I don't even know how I feel about him after that mess he made at City Hall. I'd always known he was trouble, so why was I gonna kiss him? I feel like something's wrong with me, Narla."

Narla reached for Ena's gin, but then thought better of it. "Did you and Haenir…?"

"We had sex."

"And it was good?"

Ena bit her lip and looked away. Damn her transparent skin for showing every little blush.

"Well, that's probably it. You're horny, girl."

"Wait, so you're saying that now I've had sex I'm just gonna start throwing myself at every hottie?" Ena was choking on the words. The thought sickened her.

Narla snickered. "Look, like it or not, Torno's a handsome man. Worst than that, he knows it. In all the time we've been working together, I've seen women undress before him and he turn them down like it was nothing."

"Because of me?"

A laugh burst out of her.

It renewed the blush in Ena's cheeks and made her shift in her seat.

"Ena, he's obsessed with you. You've never gotten drunk with him, so you don't know, but it's no secret. The man isn't playing a game when he says that he loves you. If you want something to happen with him, it will." She snapped. "Just as fast as that. He probably killed Magus Yersen in some sad attempt to impress you."

"What? What does that have to do with me?!"

"Because of that speech you gave on your birthday. Fuck, girl. Do you think he doesn't listen to every little thing you say? We had to restrain Torno when you went off to fuck Haenir. Between you and me, I don't think you should mess with Torno. If you kiss him, he's going to name every one of your children in his head. As bad as he is after you've rebuked his advances now, he will be a thousand times worse if you fuck him and leave him."

"Are you still mad at Torno?" Ena asked.

She looked back at the bar.

"I need to know, Narla."

"We all are. You are too. He can't just pull something like that and not tell us." Narla reached for the gin and drank, disgust rolled over her face. "As my friend, sure. I'll put it past us. I'll drink him under the table and he'll apologize with tears rolling down his face and I'll forgive him someday. But as a leader? No. He's done. Someone else has to start calling the shots."

"Why not you?"

Narla had the gin up to her lips. She held up a finger and put down the glass. "I know you're young and cute and all, but you can't just say absurd things like that when a woman is trying to choke down gin. One second later and I might've died."

"But why not, Narla? You're the oldest and you have experience on the battlefield."

"Yeah, on the side of the liberators. I wasn't smart enough to figure Duke Urson was the type to betray everyone and look where it got me! You want me to lead? I couldn't even lead my family out of Caredor." Her eyes were frantic, spinning fast enough to jump out and run on their own. She got up and walked back to the bar.

"Narla, I'm so-"

"It's fine."

Ena sighed. She could only sit there and feel the weight of her mistake. One of the first things Ena learned about Narla was to never bring up the liberators or the rise of the Supreme Magus. She knew that about Narla, so why had she made such a basic mistake? Nothing made sense anymore.

Narla came back with a tall glass of whiskey. She stared at it with a wide grin. "Ah! Now there's a drink." She sipped. "You wanna talk about the revolution, and how I killed people as a grenadier, I'm ready for that now. But if we keep following Torno he's gonna try to get us to kill Urson, I guarantee it. Listen, there's only one person to lead us now, and we all know who it is."

"Who?" Ena chuckled at her tone. She made it sound so obvious.

Narla kept staring at her.

"Be serious. I'm the kid of the group. I don't even like the taste of liquor." She laughed.

"You're Ngoltur reborn, Ena. Hultur doesn't want to do shit, fine. We can't make him. Fuck him anyway. But it's your destiny to rule, not just a little Band of Brokers, but the entire continent."

"I'm not Ngoltur reborn," Ena groaned.

"Do you think deathstaffs break all the time? They're not wands of bone! Seven thousand gulda of ether, Ena. Seven thousand! If I poured every ounce of ether out of me, it would take me half a year to output that much power. You expelled that in one day, and it came out of you in maybe five minutes. No one in the world has that much power, Ena. You're chosen by the Gods. We don't have time for you to deny your destiny. We need you to lead us because following Torno will get us killed."

Ena's stomach churned. Her skin felt clammy.

A large fat man in a robe and slippers entered the dining cart.

Narla looked back and waved at the man. She picked up her glass and stood. "Listen, I know everything is changing too fast, but we need you. I love you, Ena, but you gotta take charge. You're not a little girl anymore, no matter how much you still look like one." She left the table.

The man awkwardly turned sideways to let her through or lead her back by the hand. Narla hooked her arm under his and brought him in for a peck on the cheek and then a deep kiss. It lit him up. He was full of happiness and appreciation. He looked proud as he turned around to rest his arm on her shoulders.

Ena finally tasted the gin. It was sour and burned her tongue. What kind of a story was that?

THE ELEVENTH CHAPTER

When Ngoltur Sees Her Parents

The former Band of Brokers left their cabins with luggage in hand. Torno hadn't shaved and he seemed to have deliberately messed up his hair. The brown jacket was back so he was basically Torno classic, except without the power of being a Captain. Matter of fact, everyone was back in casual wear except for Narla. She'd opted to wear a long fog jacket with a shoulder cape. When she spotted the group gathering by the end cars, she kissed her night's paramour and hustled over.

Torno clapped his hands to grab everyone's attention. "Alright, I'm sure we all have tons to do in the Capital. Our friends in Sothlen should've done everything they could to stop communications, We should still have access to our funds. Anyone want to volunteer to their time to a bank run?"

Narla raised her hand.

"All of you know the drill. Hand Narla your signet rings and bank statements. Did everyone receive their letter from the glorious Magus Yersen?" It was chilling to hear Torno joke about someone he'd murdered. He paused to make sure the letters from Magus Yersen were icnluded.

"Don't the people of Leben Erde still use gold?" Myrrel asked. "How useful are the gulda going to be?"

"You won't find a sailor alive or a port town in the three continents that won't exchange it," Sal said with confidence. "Just don't expect to get a fair deal out of the trade."

"A few hundred gold will be better than nothing, I think we can all agree to that," Torno nodded. "I don't know how many of my contacts in the city will be happy to see my face, but I should be able to get us a discrete ship sailing out of Sapphire Cove."

The comment was directed at Visk more than anyone else and she bowed her head appreciatively.

"Hultur, are you going to have any trouble getting around the city?" Myrrel asked.

"I doubt it, but I wouldn't mind the company."

"We can take the horses along with everyone's bags," Myrrel volunteered. "I'll just need ten or twenty gulda to rent a wagon."

"Money won't be an issue," the massive Hultur assured her. Each of them looked at the two double-sized suitcases in the man's arms, wondering which held his riches.

"Sal or Ena, do either of you need anything?" Torno asked.

They looked at each other and shook their heads.

"In that case, I'll meet you all at Sapphire Cove in three hours. There's a shipyard by the name of Raised Sails. It's made out of a capsized ship, you can't miss it. Dismissed."

Everyone split up. Ena overheard Hultur asking Myrrel about getting some Dreamcasts about the Great Generation, and she took far too much amusement at the idea of him breathing in the memories of people having sex.

"Ena," said Torno. He'd fallen into step beside her. "Can we, uh, have a word?"

"I didn't read your note, Torno, so we can keep your love confession count at way too many." She tried to up her pace to lose him, but the taller man had no trouble keeping step with her.

"Oh, that. Yeah, it might be better if you just got rid

of that," he chuckled. "I kind of thought I was going to die and that maybe all of you were going to end up detained by the Mages, and...Forget it. Not what I wanted to talk to you about."

"I have a lot to do. I'm sure you do too, Torno, so how about we sideline this conversation for another time?"

"Ena, please." He sounded small and sad.

She got outside, held the door open for him, and stepped out of the flow of traffic.

He lit a cigarette.

She gave him an impatient, expecting look.

"Look, I...I meant what I said about wanting to marry you. That wasn't just something that I felt in the moment," he muttered.

"Yeah, no shit! You're in love with me, I get that. I meant what I said too. Besides, there's a good chance that all of us are going to die, so what does it matter if we get married anyway?" She was finding it hard to keep up her normal levels of outrage. Surrounded by the glitz and lights of the Capital, he was something normal and comforting by comparison.

"I'd get to die happy." He put his hand on her arm. "And maybe you would too."

"Torno, I..." Her exasperated voice caught in her throat.

He stepped closer.

She had a wall behind her again, but this time she wasn't backing up. She grabbed his wrist and took it off her arm.

"You were going to kiss me."

Ena rolled her eyes. "You seriously wanted to talk to me about that?"

"Of course I do."

Ena moved out of the range of his hand and out from the corner as well. "You know, Narla had this silly idea that you started that revolution because of me. That you killed Magus Yersen as part of some immature plot to get my attention. That wouldn't have any truth to it, would it?"

Torno glanced around to make sure no one was listening, and shrugged. "You inspired me."

She groaned and walked away.

"But I didn't do it to impress you. I did it because you were right. The people have always had the power to rise against the Magi, we just needed a push. I needed a push. I'm done running from my emotions and hiding who I am." He made that sound like a good thing.

Ena turned around to look at him but kept walking away. "When have you ever hid who you are? You've always told me that you loved me and you've always tried to control people with your little plans. I don't have the mental energy to keep rejecting you and to keep having to explain a hug that went on too long or a sleepy look that didn't mean anything. I need to focus on our mission, Torno. I need you to make that mission as easy as you can by giving up on me."

"You want me to give up on you? Really?" The fucker sounded incredulous.

"Yes, Torno! A million times yes. Give up on me. There are so many women out there who like you. All of those things you want to do to me, they want to do that to you. You're in the Capital! It shouldn't be that hard to find a woman who has seen your Dreamcasts and wants to turn her fantasies into a reality. Go make one of those women happy, but leave me alone. I..." She was going to say something more, but she couldn't; not anymore. She walked away, and this time he didn't follow.

She was lying about having a lot to do. She might've been lying about a few things, but it would be easier if Torno finally stopped hounding her. So what if she wanted to kiss him? That was just that one time. That didn't mean that she had feelings for him. She didn't need him and he certainly didn't need her. It wasn't her fault that he'd spent the last three years turning women down.

Ugh! Why had Narla told her any of that? She was

supposed to talk her out of liking Torno. But in a way she had. Torno couldn't just kiss her and walk away. He'd never be able to let go of her if Ena let something happen. Even if he was handsome and passionate, kissing him would only hurt him.

Ena had walked into the city's lower estates. Though still owned by the powerful Magical Elite, these were where the lesser lords had been when Duke Urson declared his duchy a sovereign nation. They traveled from their homes to attend parties rather than host them and people only knew their faces if they watched the dances of the Great Generation. It was how Ena had first learned her parents were still alive because she'd seen them in the Dreamcasts.

She hadn't meant to walk to their house, not consciously, but now that she could see the spired roofs, she couldn't turn around. Her parents were in there. They were planning what to wear at their next grand dance or discussing the best snide comment to make when their rival approached.

Ena's time at the chantry had been nothing but suffering. Boys shoved her into a privy fresh with urine. Girls pretended to be her friends only to pinch her skin and laugh at how red the marks were. Instructors lashed her for every small offense and made her balance a pitcher of water on her head while she magicked a rat to hover in the sky, all because she'd bled on her skirts in the middle of class. Every day they invented new cruelties for her to endure, and her only solace was watching the Great Generation dance, laugh, and live this great wonderful life that she might one day join.

But those dreams of a better future died the second she saw her parents and knew that they were not only alive but happy. She was made to suffer for being a freak while they drank away their nights at parties.

Laughter broke Ena from her ruminations. People were walking down the street. It was a family of three, her family of three. Father was there, his goatee trimmed and styled to accentuate a protruding mustache. He was fit and well dressed, and if he had a single care it did not show. Mother was thin and gorgeous as she'd ever been, only now she knew how to smile. She was happier than when she was a maid, and her face looked tired from all the smiling.

He was between them. A perfect boy in perfect clothes with perfect posture. His skin was sepia and hazel and perfectly smooth. There wasn't a scratch on him. This was a boy who woke up every morning with a smile and went to bed every night with a full belly. If he knew what suffering was it was only because he'd read about it or seen it through a Dreamcast.

Ena's parents didn't see her standing down the street, because they never once looked away from their son. They were smiling to see him and laughing at every small change in his inflection.

And Ena's anger was gone. The fight in her had vanished. She was hollow inside, shaken by the knowledge that she would never be loved in the way that they loved him. She didn't have the pain to cry, she didn't have the passion to yell at them. She just stood and listened as their voices carry on about all of the small pleasures that she had never known.

THE TWELFTH CHAPTER

In Which Ngoltur Faces Her Guilt With Sweat and a Bit Lip

When Visk had her first period, she was given her first dagger. Though she'd trained with spears, swords, axes, and knives, none had ever been hers. With her first dagger in hand, she was sent to fetch her greatest friend in the world. Duli was Visk's chosen, a girl of a similar age, only one month older. She bared her arm before Visk, Visk's parents, and their head matriarch. When Visk drew the blade across Duli's skin, she didn't cry or wince. Several months later, when Duli's time had come, Visk received her cut with pride. In returning the gesture of protection, they became Urahatu.

In many ways, the bond between Urahatu was deeper than sisterhood. They rode together, trained together, and fought together. When one was sick, they cared for each other. They were always welcome at their family's table and inside the other's bed. Many Urahatu shared their first kiss, and many still shared their first orgasm. So it was for Visk and Duli. Though other women would come to fight for the favor of Visk or Duli, neither ever gave the challengers the right to test their bond. Such Urahatu were rare in Ki'an. Women looked to their love with envy, and parents pointed to them as a model to follow.

Duli and Visk stayed together into their twenties and won many battles for Geshuri, priests following the old religion born from the teachings of Hultur himself. After their greatest battle, Visk and Duli had each killed forty women. They were honored with a great feast in the largest church of Mu. But in the celebrations, a Geshuri man looked to Duli with lust. He declared his intention to marry her and demanded that Duli lay down her spear of steel and take into her the spear of flesh. She refused, and so they took away her choice. Women Visk and Duli had fought alongside their entire lives turned the tips of their spears onto their friends and forced Duli to give up her life as a warrior. They were wed in a glorious celebration. On that night, while Visk lay in prison, Geshuri weighed bride-gifts to buy Visk's hand in marriage.

But all was not lost.

Visk's compatriots in arms, the same that turned their spears against her, sought redemption. They freed Visk and begged for her forgiveness. She would forgive them for their cowardice, but only if they freed Duli from her bonds of matrimony.

And so, the great old city of Mu was turned to chaos. Sister fought sister and warriors turned against the Church, but it was the families that ultimately sided with Visk. Old women who'd given up the spear long ago took up arms and fought the men of the church. Duli was rescued, and her husband was castrated and hung by broken hands.

The unbroken Urahatu were united once again, but the women's victory would not last. The great leader of Asutura, Zular Sanin, Zular of the Diamond Sands, brought her armies to retake the ancient city of Mu. Strong as Visk and Duli were, they knew they could not stand against the might of the Zular. So they took Visk's bride-gifts and traveled south to leave Asutura. Mu surrendered, but Zular Sanin rallied the survivors under her banner. Her wrath wouldn't be satiated until she had Visk and Duli flayed and quartered. Visk and

Duli knew they would never be safe in Ki'an. Sooner or later, the politics of nations would demand that they be sent to Zular Sanin, and so they purchased a boat to Gulambar.

The boat ride was long, and the women struggled to keep down their food. As days turned into weeks, their bodies withered. But Duli was worse by far. What they thought was a simple sea sickness was in fact a great illness. She could no longer hold a dagger, she could no longer stand, and her eyes became cloudy as her vision failed her. Visk could only watch as the love of her life withered.

When the boat finally came to land on the docks of Sapphire Cove, Visk was filled with hope. They'd come to the great city of Caredor, heart of the new nation filled with the greatest healers in the world. She took Duli into her arms and carried her off the docks. But even before Visk had stepped foot on Gulambar soil, a great tremor had taken Duli. She was cold and weak and wanted to be put onto the ground to rest. So Visk laid her down and stroked her face. Duli asked her to get closer, close enough for the blind woman to see her face. But she could see only white and died looking for her love.

Nearly seven years later, Visk knelt before the same spot on the pier.

Ena had intruded on her mourning, but only at a distance. The woman didn't move. She laid her hand on the old wooden planks and gave an unspoken prayer to the love of her life. There was no way of knowing if she was speaking to Duli directly or if she was asking the Gods to watch over Duli. Visk never spoke of her views of the afterlife, and the stoic pain on her face made it clear that she didn't want to.

Shame pushed Ena away from the pier. She had no right to look upon the woman's grieving, but she came anyway. She wanted to see her friend consumed by sorrow because Ena couldn't find her own. Inside was emptiness and a numb, scraping feeling against the walls of her heart. The sensation could've been sorrow for the life she never had or anger for the way she was cast aside. The pangs of her heart were too diluted for her to identify, and no thought nor force of will would bring them to the surface.

Ena ended up in Raised Sails. As it turned out, the place was more of a marketplace than a shipyard. Buildings thrust out of the capsized ship like errant growths and vendor stalls divided the floor into lanes where tables were absent. Sailors between voyages bartered on the floor and it was a common sight to see displaced merchants hawking their wares from an absconded table. Any signs of excitement or haggling repulsed Ena and she wound up in a dim bar.

Whiskey or wine made no difference to Ena, but she tried sipping fancy grape juice nonetheless. From listening to Myrrel, Narla, Torno, and Visk, she was led to believe that drinking would somehow make her feel better. It didn't. Neither the act of sitting alone with the juice or the singe of alcohol on her tongue brought any comfort.

"Brooding alone?" asked a stranger.

Right, she was alone at a bar. This kind of thing happened. Her instinct was to tell the guy off, but there was a playful self-awareness in his voice that made her look at the man. He wasn't tall, but not as short as Ena. His eyes were concerned and lacked the glossy stare of a drunk man. There was a proper beard on his face and his attire was semi-formal but not as luxurious or austere as the magical elite of the Great Generation. All in all, he was handsome, kind, and probably older than her by ten years.

"I was." She leaned back to offer the seat next to her.

He was nursing a mug of suds and refused another when the bartender shot him a look. "Name's Ve'an."

"Ena." She offered a hand and he gave her a proper shake.

"You bothered by anything you want to talk about?" he asked kindly.

"Just trying not to think about it. I've got too much time to kill, really."

Ve'an took that in and proceeded to prattle on about

common things. News of the pustules had reached the Capital. The act of insurrection in Sothlen was only known as a disruption of the ether-chain. The eastern Kingdom of Solorona was in another feud of succession that they hoped to resolve by wedding sister to brother. A new Marineld Warlord was attacking trade routes to the Far Lands. Clerics in Daun Si were being granted the right to wed prisoners. Some Cleric was on a pilgrimage to Vyltur Castle to pull Magoloiherdir.

Ena placed a hand on his and the man silenced. "Will you help me?"

He swallowed and grew serious. "However I can."

"I want to feel alive."

~ ~ ~

By chance or fate, the man lived close by. Ve'an's occupation, Ena didn't care to ask. At a look, she knew he lived alone. The bed was large and soft, and that was what mattered. He closed the door and ran a hand over the back of his neck. He muttered something about a drink, and she took him by the arm. All his hesitation melted when she put her lips on his. He brought her close, embracing her with one arm. She slid his hand under her shirt.

He moaned with pleasure, his breath warm on her face. Their lips parted and he kissed at her cheek and neck. She found the flesh of his belly and rubbed him through the fabric. She pulled his shirt up just enough for the skin to touch. Warmth took her. Glorious warmth spread from his lips to his hand to her groin. But she was still so cold. She needed more of him and brought his other hand onto her front.

As he embraced her from behind and felt up her front, Ena leaned her head back into him. She smelled his sweat mixing with tobacco and the salty ocean spray. She breathed in short and only let her exhales come out as gasps and whimpers. She wanted her heart to work to get those breaths; she made it fight to grasp a handful of air, and only relented when something warm touched that frigid core inside. He was eager, consumed by the scent of her and the feel of her body, and she could feel the warmth of his erection pressing against the small of her back.

Her hands only touched the hairs of his arm or the flesh between his thumb and index, but he touched so much more of her. Every time his caressing hands rubbed a bit of life out of her ribs or along that flesh clinging to her frigid heart, she pressed in so he'd not only touch her, but grab her. She wanted him to melt her body with friction, but he moved slow and strong, and wasn't shy in reaching down to her loins.

Something like a scream escaped her lips. There was still life inside, there was a heart that strove to pump blood down into her clit. She knew she was melting there because a wetness was soaking her. Cracks must've formed in that solid piece of ice that lay under her breast, because her chest was at long last moving. It heaved with every pant, and she no longer had the power to keep back its cycle of life.

Life had found her. It pulled at her hips and drove her, grinding, against his teasing fingers. Oh, but they promised to do so much more than tease and she was impatient to feel his skin against her lips. She pulled off her breeches and climbed onto his bed. He took her by the hips quickly and pulled her back to the edge. His strong hands ran over her belly, brushed against her legs, and spread apart her ass. Without a shirt she could feel the full length of his arms, and the strength of his muscles as they leveraged her.

Biting her lip, she awaited that painful press of penetration, but felt the tickle of his tongue instead. She yelped and rolled onto her side. Fear. It had been there all along, a timid fear of the unknown. This man was kissing at her legs, rubbing at her inner thighs to ask for permission. There was hunger there now, not to force himself into her, but to pleasure her. He was being dutiful, and she didn't want to deny him.

No, she wanted very much to know what his mouth would do to her.

She closed her eyes and felt his lips kiss their way to her vagina. She grabbed a hand and forced her fingers between his. It gave her no comfort and spread no love into her heart. She felt exposed atop a spire. She was surrounded by ice, a moment away from falling. There was nothing for her to grab onto, so Ena spread her legs and fell.

He had her by the legs. His lips went right to the swollen arousal of her clit and kissed her. Her hips arched up in shock and he held firm. She squirmed and thrashed, but those scratching sensations of shock gave way to electricity. Her legs came together around his head and squeezed to find some security, but there was only this surge in her body. It built and built until it felt like her entire body was going to spasm.

Fingers penetrated, and the electricity ignited. The flames were burning, hurting tender flesh that was too used to the feel of cold. Heat took her, making her pant to find water or a fist full of dirt to quench it. There was nothing to relieve the burning of her body except that glorious button that this man licked with rapid flicks. All she could do to fight through the blaze was to scream, and she screamed and let her sweat turn to steam and her body turn to ash.

Feeling the tension in her hips and legs at last die down, his relentless tongue, at last, licked her with kindness. Tender hands spread her sweat across her skin. He kissed his way up to her stomach and came to rest his head atop her ribs. She gasped for life and he panted from exertion.

She'd gotten what she came for but had done nothing for him. She was too relieved to feel shame. Every drop of sweat kept her body tingling and every gasp for air let her feel the pain in her heart. He shifted and crawled up the bed. Ena ran her hands over his belly but knew not what she was going to do when her hands reached his swollen erection.

He brought a hand to rest on her wrist. "You don't have

to."

"But..." She tried to kiss at his sweaty flesh and felt nothing for him. She rolled back and looked at the ceiling. It took her a long time to let out a sigh. "You really don't mind?"

"No." He leaned down to kiss her head but stopped himself. "That was great, really. I haven't felt this satisfied in a long time."

She took him in, looking for some sign of a lie or resentment, but there was a serenity in his eyes. She nodded and got up to dress.

~ ~ ~

Visk was waiting at the tables of the Raised Sails when they returned. The woman saw her, recognized the closeness between her and this man, and looked away. Ena turned to look at him and bit her lip. She struggled to think of something to say that would remove the burn of embarrassment or the guilt for doing something so completely selfish.

Ve'an just smiled. "Thanks for a wonderful lunch break."

"No problem." Her eyes fell, and when they rose again he was halfway to the bar where she'd found him.

Ena walked to Visk and sat beside her. The Ki'an woman was drinking a fruit from its hollowed center. She slid it over to her friend and Ena drank deep. The juice was tangy and refreshing.

"Are you going to tell anyone?" Ena chirped.

"It's not my place to say anything about what you do with your time," she said.

The silence was painful. Ena looked around for the vendor that sold those fruit drinks.

"Not that long ago, I might've looked upon you and that man and thought less of you," Visk admitted.

"Because of me and Haenir." It wasn't a question, Ena knew that was why Visk felt the way she did.

"But maybe I am wrong to think that a person should

only love one person in their life." She sounded heartbroken.

"I don't think so. I mean, what I...that wasn't love, you know?" The only good thing about the sweltering heat of the capital was that she couldn't blush.

Visk snickered. "Yes, I have heard. But I was raised to believe that love and sex are like the spear and the shaft. One is useless without the other." She sighed. "But I have killed with a spearhead and evoked with a length of wood. And..."

Visk looked like she could puke or cut off her own hand.

"And?"

Shame lowered her head to her chest. "I have looked to other women with lust in my heart."

"Oh!"

"This is also something that shouldn't be shared," she snapped.

Ena raised her hands in surrender. "Yeah, no problem. Your business is your business." She swallowed, and Visk said no more. "Does it hurt to admit that?"

Visk shook her head. "It hurt more to feel it. It hurt to ask Duli for forgiveness, but talking to a friend is always good."

"I feel the same way." Ena offered her hand and Visk took it.

"Sometimes I feel Duli. I feel her looking at me or holding my hand when I am with my tears," Visk whimpered. "She is sad for me."

Ena rubbed her back and Visk hugged her tight. Visk cried into her shoulder and onto the side of her head. Visk was a very tall woman and Ena was not. Hugging her made the pain of loss come alive. She could see Haenir's smile again, she could hear the sound of his love, and feel his hand in hers.

Ena hoped he'd moved on because she felt like shit for doing it so fucking fast.

THE THIRTEENTH CHAPTER

In Which Ngoltur and a Lion Have a Chat

Torno was the last to arrive, to the surprise of no one. He was moving in a fast walking panic, as usual. Nothing was ever simple when it involved Torno's plans. Groaning, everyone got off the table and prepped their legs to run and their hands to fight.

"I don't understand the look of agitation on all of your faces," said Hultur.

"That's because you haven't known Torno long enough," Narla snapped. She shot Ena a glance that Ena pretended not to see.

"Fuck, what is it now?" Myrrel sighed.

"Perhaps Torno simply impregnated a woman, and now she has demanded that he take on his role as a father," Visk suggested. They all looked at her. "It is a possibility with him."

"What?!" Sal yelled at Torno, raising his arms.

"Trouble," Torno mumbled. He walked around the horses and checked to make sure all the cargo was secure in the cart.

"We need details, Torno!" Narla chuckled. "We can't just improvise every time your plans land us in a slime!"

"It's what I have to do," he mumbled again. He grabbed

Li'at's reins and led horse and crew down the dock. Ena grabbed Gale's reins to assert her ownership over him. Not that anyone tried to fight her for the beautiful gerhat, but this was supposed to be a long trip. When they'd gotten clear of the Raised Sails, their glorious former Captain finally opted to fill them in.

"Ena, remember those two weirdos from Sothlen; the Junior Mages?"

"Yeah..."

"I spotted them in Caredor and I'm pretty sure they were following me."

Narla got as much in his face as the shorter woman could. "Fucking shit, Torno! You're telling me someone followed us from Sothlen?"

"Yes."

"And they know we started a rev-"

"Yes, Narla! Be sure to say it nice and loud so that everyone in the cove knows," he hissed.

"Maybe things aren't that bad." Ena didn't know why she was trying to defuse the situation. Torno was the one who lit it. Every bad thing to come was entirely his fault. She shook her head and did her best to catch the others up to speed. "We met these two Acolytes who called themselves Junior Mages. They weren't that perceptive. It took them close to two hours to interrogate us and they didn't ask anything important. I don't think they pose any threat."

"Right, because suddenly my luck has just turned around," Torno grumbled.

The pier was clear, which either meant commerce avoided this part of the city or they were walking right into a trap. Turning into the main dock area, the sight and smell of commerce eased Ena's nerves. Hawkers insulted each other's goods with mirth-filled jabs. Gold-accented alchemists handed over powders to cure invented problems. Prostitutes in powdered faces danced between bites of street food to lure the midday crowd into the brothels. It wasn't exactly classy, but none of it looked like a trap.

At the base of a gangplank, a Marineld waved both arms in the air. He had a bombastic red shirt, a tricorner hat, and three head tails coming down the back of his fishy head. Marineld were fish people from head to toe, but the most distinctive thing about them was their eel-like skin and fish-like faces. It was fairly common to find them at docks, and even more common to find one captaining a vessel. This man had firmer skin than most, and his green flesh was marked with black tiger stripes. Even among the Marineld, he stood out.

"Ah, Torno, tell me this is your lovely crew."

"Yeah. Sorry, we don't have any time for proper introductions. How fast can we be anchors up?"

The Captain pursed his lips and shrugged. "As soon as you're aboard."

"Great. Everyone get up there," Torno shouted. He took out a very cheap wand.

"Please ignore our friend," Myrrel said cordially. "I'm Myrrel, a healer renowned for her beauty and grace."

"Truly you are a delight for the senses and my sea-shaken sensibilities, m'lady." He bowed and spun his hat in a flourish. "I am the great Captain Fascinosa, but you may know me better as the Rogue Prince Fascinosa Beribet."

Everyone crowded around the Marineld.

Sal's eyes widened. "You're Fascinosa Beribet?! The prince who forsook his birthright to stand up to his father's tyrannical regime?"

"One and the same."

"Hey! We're in a hurry, remember? Get on the ship," Torno snapped.

"Oh, calm down," said Myrrel with a wave of her hands. "Everything's fine. Look, Hultur is already on the ship with the horses."

Hultur waved his hat to show that he had already made it aboard. Actually, he was trying to get their attention.

An outstretched hand pointed past rows of waiting vessels to an accord of Acolytes and no less than six Mages. Each of the black-clad officers was selected for their superior ether reserves and fanatical devotion to the Supreme Magus. At the front, a figure in red accents drew the eye. This wasn't some arbitrary group of peacekeepers out on patrol. They were following the lead of an Archmage.

"Ah, I'm afraid we must save our introductions for later, my boulba friend. Worry not, this will not be the first time that I fled a port with spells flying," Captain Fascinosa said with a chuckle.

"It could be your last!" Torno shouted.

"Men, we leave with the wind," Captain Fascinosa called out to his Marineld sailors.

"But boss, Teetee's still looking for her cat," a tough woman with an eyepatch called out.

"What? Teetee was supposed to be on the ship!"

"She snuck off!"

"Oh, this isn't good." Captain Fascinosa slapped his cheeks. "Well, uh, do what you can to ready the ship without me, then. Worst case, I will jump onto the ship at the last possible moment." And then Captain Fascinosa ran off into the shops surrounding the docks.

"Congratulations, Torno, I think you finally found a Captain less competent than you," Ena teased.

But Torno didn't have any witty retorts. The Archmage and her squadron were clearing the path by the sheer force of their presence and with good reason. Ena recognized the Archmage. She'd seen that silhouette a hundred times in borrowed memories sucked in from dreamcasts. It was Archmage Kalta Minquet, Torno's ex-girlfriend.

Among enthusiasts of the Great Generation, Kalta and Torno were the premier young couples. They would pose for paintings staring into each other's eyes with fiery passion. Kalta composed dozens of variations of the most popular songs that doubled and tripled the length of pieces so that she could dance with her beloved for as long as she wished. Torno recited custom love poems in the middle of ballroom dances to win her back after fights that none could remember. Their famed disappearances during dances were the object of constant speculation, and every act of indecency titillated the imagination. Kaltor, as their couple name was known, was a topic of constant conversation, and their image became synonymous with the Great Generation itself.

When Torno cheated on her, the scandal was all anyone talked about for weeks. Kalta became a symbol of the betrayal so many in the nation felt and Torno was so thoroughly scorned that the great goss stopped talking about him almost overnight. While Torno ended up the Captain of a Band of Brokers in a remote part of the nation, Kalta stayed in the spotlight and rose through the ranks to become the youngest Archmage in Caredor.

She was gorgeous even in the crystal-lined uniform of her office. Her face was sharp and expressive, her body full-figured and fit, her hair brought up into a front-facing top knot held down with the red hairpin of the Archmage. It was impossible to not look at her, and harder still to not stare at the sheer presence she exuded. This was a woman who set the standard of excellence for the Great Generation and the expression on her face was far from loving or nostalgic.

"Ena." Torno grabbed her arm. "Ena! What are you doing? Blast her!"

Ena yanked her arm away. "I'm not going to blast her. We're on a mission of peace. Did you forget that?"

"Yeah, so are they," Narla chuckled. "Peacekeepers don't get their name and titles by having a winning personality."

Kalta caught Ena's eye and regarded her not as a serpent looking at a meal, but a lioness meeting a rival across the watering hole. Beside her, one of the Mages brought a deathstaff's butt to his shoulder. With a raise of her hand, he lowered it.

"It looks like she's willing to talk," said Sal.

"Of course, she is," said Torno. "She's an Archmage, a member of the Great Generation. Everything she says is a lie and a ploy to win you over to their side."

"A lie and a ploy all at once," Myrrel snorted. "How does she manage it?"

"This isn't a joke!"

"We getting on the ship or what?" Narla asked from the gang plank.

Most of Captain Fascinosa's crew were on the boat. Somewhere out in the maze of the docks was a Marineld looking for a girl who was looking for a cat. They needed time. Besides, Torno was being far from forthright.

Kalta wasn't just "an Archmage." He was keeping his past with this woman a secret from the Band. This time Ena knew why. This time Ena had all the information. Ena might not be ready for leadership, but she wasn't about to br dragged into another one of Torno's mistakes.

"I'm gonna parlay," said Ena.

Again, Torno grabbed her arm. With a look, he let her go. Palms out, he breathed through his teeth like a child given his first douse of discipline. "I think that this is a really bad idea."

"Then get ready to run for your life. That was your plan anyway, right?" She scoffed. Ena went forward to talk to Kalta Minquet.

A few steps out, Ena could hear the creak of planks underfoot. That was the fear the Acolytes and Mages commanded over Caredor. With a single word Kalta could lawfully destroy any business. With a single evocation, she could end the lives of any in her path. This woman was a magical monster and a political powerhouse, but Ena knew she was so much more than that.

She had spent time with Kalta. She had been inside her head. Through the magic of dreamcasts, Ena had worn her skin and felt her desires. The only reason Ena knew what praise and admiration felt like, was because she'd felt it from inside her mind. Inside Kalta's body, she'd learned about the Great Generation, the politics of the needy, and about the pleasures of sex. This woman was so much more than a role model to Ena. When she dared to dream that she had rich dark skin and a tall athletic physique, it was Kalta's body that she saw.

Stopping halfway between their groups, Ena waited for Kalta to close the distance. The first step made Ena's heart leap into her throat. Shaking knees melted away to jittery hands. It was happening. Ena was actually going to meet and talk to Kalta. She was five strides away. Three! Somewhere in Ena's mind, she was already imagining the two of them sharing a glass of wine and talking shit about the bonfire of feces that was Torno Beren.

Kalta didn't adjust the red bejeweled headress that marked her station. Nor did she smooth any fabrics, finger her wand, or adjust her gloves. She was perfect and she expected the world to live up to her standards. A serene roll of her arm summoned the air about them into a controlled tempest. She'd cast a silence spell and in a way that looked effortless.

Standing tall, she brought hands together and regarded Ena with a polite smile. "I have heard an unsettling rumor about your Captain, Broker Ena. Given what I've heard, I'm relieved to be talking to you instead. I don't know what he's telling you, but he hasn't been permitted to end his tour of duty nor leave the country. You and your Band will be given safe quarters while we make sense of the confusion. I will handle this matter personally. Our office will pay for the seafarer's wages in the interim. The Mages have an office close to Foundation Station, we can discuss things in private there. Come, let us gather your Band."

Given a command, it was Ena's impulse to fall beside Kalta and let herself be ushered forward away from the stress of this conversation and the curious eyes of cowering locals.

She turned about to fall into step but then quickly stopped herself. Kalta regarded Ena with a raised brow.

"I know who you are," Ena said. She'd meant it casually, but the words came out like an accusation.

Maybe it was a response to Ena's tone, but there was a moment, an instance shorter than a breath when Kalta's eyes seemed to narrow and ignite. It was gone just as fast, replaced with a playful mein.

Kalta squared her shoulders and smiled. "In what context do you know me?"

Faced with her wrath, Ena stammered. "I..."

Kalta's smile turned brilliant and personable. "You've seen my dreamcasts. I'm flattered and humbled, believe me, but this isn't the time. When we get to the Mage's Office, we'll have plenty of time to talk and get to know each other."

"I'm sorry that he hurt you." It was a strange thing to say and hardly the most pressing, but those were the words that came out of Ena's mouth. Confusion played on Kalta's brow and Ena felt that warm betrayal of blood marching into position on her cheeks. "I've had to deal with Torno for the past three years. He doesn't make anything easy."

"No," she said formally. After a smile, her voice lulled into something more conversational. "No, he doesn't."

"I know that..." Ena tried to pick the right words and her past at the Chantry reminded her that she was the wrong person to convince anyone so gorgeous, brilliant, and mystical of anything. Still, she had to try. Ena's mission wasn't one of survival but for the peace and prosperity of the entire world. She had to risk embarrassing herself.

"As I said, Broker Ena, we can discuss things in a more relaxed manner back at the Mage's Office. We're not interested in punishing you or your Band. We know that you were simply following the chain of command."

Ena continued forward with her speech. "I know that the Supreme Magus has been good to you. I know that life must seem grand from inside the Great Generation, but

Caredor is suffering."

At the first mention of politics, Kalta's demeanor grew stiff. "There is no country without suffering."

"He has broken up families. He leaves people unprotected and-" Her voice was silenced by her own uncertainty.

Kalta took Ena's trepidations as an invitation to interrupt her. "Are you planning to overthrow the government?"

"What?"

"I received a rather sparse account of what took place in Sothlen, but Torno's actions don't surprise me. He's always been a man of broad ambitions tempered by the most selfish aims. Our past makes this difficult, but I will do what I can to make sure that he is given the full extent of Urson's mercy."

Something about hearing the Supreme Magus's name from Kalta's mouth put Ena at ease. She believed that Kalta could get a request to his ears.

Kalta continued, "As I said before, I have no interest in seeing you punished.

"We are allies, you and I. We serve the same people and work towards the same cause. What you know from me, you probably have seen from a dreamcast I made when I was barely an adult. I am not that person any more. I have gone through a great deal of maturing. I've learned a lot about responsibility and leadership. I can see those talents in you.

"You told me that you know me, but I know you, Ena." Her voice came out familiar and comforting.

"You do?" Ena couldn't help the childish quality that rose in her throat. At Kalta's words, she imagined her parents talking to the Archmage with warmth or scorn.

"A little," Kalta said with an almost apologetic tone. "Life was hard for you growing up and harder still at the Chantry. I do not share the small jealousies and resentments of your classmates and instructors. I can understand why you would conceal your power."

"How did you..."

Kalta stepped forward and offered a hand with a smile. "Let me help you find your place in this world."

Her fingers reached out. Looking past Kalta, she saw Hultur standing on the ship. Supplies were loaded. Everyone was waiting at the dock to see what Ena would do. Kalta had blocked Torno from her line of sight, using her tall statuesque physique to sever that link. Ena stepped back, closer to Kalta's Mages.

"This isn't about my problems," Ena muttered more to herself.

"Then what is it about?" she asked like a friend.

"The Grand Dream has begun."

Kalta's sisterly charm slipped with every annoyed twitch of her brow.

Ena went on, "That man out there, the Ki'an on the ship. That's Hultur. He has come to me with a mission of peace. We're going to Leben Erde. We're going to find Muttur and bring about a new age of prosperity. I can't help him bring about an era of peace if I'm stuck in a room waiting for bureaucracy to decide the best path forward."

"I will oversee this matter personally. Your Captain-"

"Torno had reasons to do what he did. The people of Caredor have every right to rise up in rebellion. The Supreme Magus is not a judicious benefactor. He is a tyrant who positions bodies like bricks in his castle. You can help me by getting every able body you can rally to join our cause."

Frustration pulled Kalta's brows to center. Then, like coiled lion giving up her pounce, genteel grace washed away the expression. Smirking like an old friend, she said, "How do you know this 'Hultur' isn't-"

Nothing happened. Ena didn't move or breathe wrong or alter her expression in any way. Kalta simply gave up on whatever idea had struck her. Throwing her arms back, the air shimmered from a sudden rise in heat as flames came to life. Air shifted breaking not only the silence spell, but working around Kalta to suck the oxygen straight out of the flames.

Torno was straining to pull at Kalta's spell, cancelling the evocation by literally casting against her. Beside him, Visk jabbed out her spear sending a blast of red lightning. Narla pushed out with both hands, adding gesture and weight to a gout of flames that joined Visk's attack. Kalta turned about and hopped. She used Torno's spell as fuel, converting it into a barrier right before Ena's eyes. She protected those eyes a moment before Visk and Narla's combined attack exploded, tearing apart half the dock and most of a nearby ship.

A vortex of wind brought Ena across the space, pulling her close to Torno. She rolled over the planks, the parts of exposed skin scraped from every abrasive bump on the wooden floorboards. Kalta landed beside her Mages like a dancer moving into the next number.

Ena couldn't take her eyes off her even as Narla helped her to her feet. Every flick of her finger and twist of her wrist looked better than the form chart taught at the chantries. Her gorgeous golden bracelets and rings glowed with activated ether.

"Ena, do something!" Torno shouted.

She'd already lost a battle of words. Somehow Ena wasn't convinced this conflict was going to go any better.

THE FOURTEENTH CHAPTER

In Which Torno's Past Blocks Their Future

Ships and piers broke up the curls of the ocean. Around the docks waves were small and choppy. One swell worked against the backlash of another. For all the chaos on the surface, the bay was close to stagnant underneath. Water was a terrible impetus for motion. So it was up to Ena to evoke the ocean to life.

Hydromancy was high magic and took a steep ethereal cost from the caster. So Ena reached down to the bottom of the bay and geomanced a tremor. Switching to kinetic force, she pulled up hard at the water. The splash came out larger than a house. Clawing at the sky, Ena's nails dug into the image of the spray and froze it against the deck.

With three spells and a little bit of physical thinking, she'd managed to create more than a wall, but a solid fortress of ice. It covered the hole in the dock and connected the smoking debris of a ship to the shopfront. Ena allowed herself a sigh of relief; even if it was pre-emptive.

Kalta fired right through the fortress.

A spiral of flame drilled through the spires, cracking what wasn't melted down to steam. The flame only increased in size as it spiraled through the sky. The front of the blaze coalesced and reformed into the mouth of a lion, the lower part of its jaw scorching planks.

Panicked, Ena shouted, "Cryo!" and crossed her arms. Ether cut across the sky in streaks and spread out to form a glacial wall of translucent blue. The top of the lion's jaw snapped down over the barrier and barreled down on Ena, still frozen in her hasty defensive stance.

Torno yanked her back with one hand and aeromanced the flames away with a twirling motion of his bracelet.

Kalta's Mages and Acolytes ignored Ena's ice blockade and attacked the ship directly. Dozens of ethereal strands shot out of wands and death staffs. Ena clawed at the air, forming an icy blue web of ethereal energy. Strands connected and manifested into bursts of flame and bolts of lightning. Both tested the burning point of the ship's hull and left it smoking.

"Put the ship in a haste bubble!" Torno shouted.

"I can't," Ena growled back.

"Yes, you can, you-"

"Shut up!"

Her friends were still hurrying up the gangplank. Their escape made her panic. They're abandoning me! But it was a strategic retreat. They needed to get on that ship and fuck off. Even with Torno and Visk giving it their all, they weren't going to be able to stop three Mages, to say nothing of Kalta the Archmage.

Another volley of wand shots streaked out toward the ship, too fast for Ena to react. The ship was going to be torn apart. They were fucked!

But the strands of ether hit a spherical shield and popped harmlessly into elemental bursts. Right, Hultur was there, he just wasn't going to fight. She needed to focus everything she had on blocking Kalta's attacks.

Lightning arced up and around the spires of ice. With a snap of thunder, the bolt split and forked again, filling the sky with jagged tendrils of electric death. Torno met the attack with a flick of his wand. Light burst out and seemed to rip the energy right out of his ex-girlfriend's attack.

With one hand to her mouth, Kalta sucked in a gulda. The other raised a staff.

Myrrel aeromancied one of Narla's grenades skyward. A volley of wand shots burst the explosion in the air, but their magic didn't stop on the defensive. Rings of ether pulled on the flames, twisting the explosion into a spiral of fire for them to use as fuel. Ena clawed it away, freezing the burst into nothing more than a puff of smoke.

Torno shouted at her. "What the fuck are you doing, Ena?! You-"

"I said, shut up!"

Wand shots flew out again but from the sides. Ena shrieked and brought up another wall of ethereal energy, but they sailed by to hit the sphere at the back of the ship. Those spells weren't anywhere near her. Ena fought to regain her composure, flustered and burning with shame.

"Get on the ship!" Torno shouted.

"But..."

Grabbing her by the arm and shoulder, he shoved her towards the gangplank. She was halfway up before she realized that Torno was getting flanked. Two figures posed on the roof of the nearby stores. One wore a distinct long braid with green and blue running down the length, the other a wild-haired dandy with a distinguishing forelock of red. It was the two Junior Mages from Sothlen.

Iodize struck a pose with his hands on his hips. "Cretin! Your villainy comes to an end on this day!"

Cerrano let out a burst of light with a pop of sound. "Let all know that you've been stopped by Iodize and Cerrano, the heroes of the people!"

Torno blinked at them. "Okay."

With his bracelet hand, he gathered up a ball of wind and flung it at their feet. It exploded and sent them flying end over end and out of sight.

His attention was so fixated on the screaming couple that he didn't see the Mage peeking out from the hole in Ena's ice wall. With a flick of his wand, five strands of ether spiraled out. Ena frantically batted the ethereal strands with claws of cold. Exploding with a pop, the spell coalesced out of the wand shot into a concentrated vortex of cold. Matched element for element, Ena's attack did nothing to stop the Mage's spell. Torno's training was top-notch, at the level of Katla's and he was able to bring up a shield. The cold pushed through, slamming into Torno's side. He hit the dock on the shoulder and rolled far from the gangplank.

That's when things got really bad.

Kalta lifted her staff over her head with both hands. Staves were longer, thicker, and designed to work differently from wands. Instead of drawing only from the caster, staves used the power of the caster to synchronize with the nearby area and pull in ether from the very air itself. Ether poured into the length of the glyph-covered stick, forming a small thin disk over her head. Twirling the staff, she danced, pivoted, and cut Ena's barrier with arcing blades of fire. The sound of ice splashing back into the bay was Ena's only warning. Tendrils of flame bore down on her faster and too split for her eyes to follow.

She screamed and brought up a glacial wall to block the human-sized burst of flames. Light flashed in her peripheral vision. She turned to claw at the oncoming burst of flame. Close as she was to the source of it, her spell split the burst like claws attacking a branch, except the leaves that broke through were flames. They spread over her, burning her skin and catching her hair. The attacks kept coming, merciless. She spun and clawed away spell after spell, and more flicks of fire struck at her clothes. She was losing her balance on the gangplank, and the lure of the cold waters below called to her. Maybe if she jumped in, the others could get away without her.

Wind overtook her. It sucked the breath right out of

her lungs. Before Ena could even grab her throat, a gust of wind pushed her up and onto the ship. She rolled over the planks and her side smacked against a mast. Coughs overtook her body. The burns seared, but she couldn't even scream out in pain. Myrrel was on her, pouring healing into her flesh. There was a soothing quality to the cone of restoration that mended her flesh but it felt like licking sweat to fight dehydration.

"I gotta help, Torno," Ena coughed.

"You-"

Ena shoved Myrrel back and got to her feet. She stumbled and almost plummeted face-first onto the dock. Sal yanked her back to the edge of the ship. What sailors had finished with their tasks were leaning over the side, firing wand shots at the Mages and Acolytes on the dock. And there was the Marineld Captain, holding up a spiraling disk of water to protect Torno, and a little Marineld girl with a kitty in her arms.

Pain was something Ena could deal with; she just had to scream and pretend that she wasn't about to pass out. Time magic was the only thing that was going to save Torno. The problem with time magic was that it wasn't an innate magic. Chrono effects demanded extensive knowledge of temporal scripts, glyphs, and geometric structures. Like all high magicks, chronomancy was cerebral and demanded an incredible amount of concentration to effectively pull off. It was like reciting a poem in your head as fast as you possibly could, and Ena had to do it while her entire body burned and stung.

The mnemonic device for the chants and figures poured out as a scream. Her hands flicked from one form to the next, concentrating on the basics of the spell's foundation. It coalesced into the river of time like a boulder flung into the stream. Ena held it there, and the flow came about the blockage like an eddy. Haste took the three of them, four if one counted the cat, and sped them up.

They made their way up the gangplank like they were sprinting, but Torno was holding his side, probably nursing several broken ribs. Even still, magical effects flew at the four of them, slamming against Captain Fascinosa's wall of water. But his defensive spell held. They were going to make it.

That was until Kalta and her staff had something to say about it.

Fire came in from the opposite side of Captain Fascinosa's defenses, flinging him up into the air. He was steaming when he fell into the water.

"No!" Ena screamed. Concentration slipped and her haste spell vibrated out as a ripples on the river of time.

Sal was there, putting his spherical form between Torno and the marineld girl. Bursts of magic slammed into him, but the ice and electric spells were equally useless against his rocky body. Water splashed up, froze, and a slicing disk of ice spun through the air. It cut the plank close to the dock. Sal jumped forward. He grabbed the edge of the ship with one massive hand and held onto Torno, Teetee, and the cat with the other.

Flames manifested off the sides of the deck and threatened to overtake the ship, the sails, and everyone on board. Fear was easy for Ena to find just then. manifest that terror into ethereal fuel, she grabbed at ether strands like they were piles of blood-soaked hay. The flames of Kalta's attack hit a glacier-shaped wall of ether that went from the water to three hundred feet above the top of the ship. The attacks rebounded, finding no place of entry. Ena brought up another barrier on the opposite side of the ship but found no attacks coming.

Ena ran to the back of the ship and took in Kalta's mages. Their attacks had ceased. Archmage Kalta was staring right at her, sucking gulda into her mouth as casually as any socialite drinking the night's refreshments. With a single command, the Acolytes focused their attacks on a single volley of orange ether. They curved down, striking not the ship or Ena's barrier, but the water.

Electricity spread out over the bay in all directions. It hit the hull of the ship harmlessly, but anything submerged was bound to be fried.

"No!" shouted Teetee. The wide-shouldered woman with one eye held her back. She cried out and struck at those constricting arms. "We have to go in there! We have to save him!"

"Stop it!" the woman shouted. "Either it's too late or he's already gotten away. Your tears aren't helping!"

She ran downstairs, the black and gray tabby following behind.

Myrrel was focusing her healing on Torno, and Ena was glad she was. Torno looked bad, and Ena needed that sting of pain. She'd fucked up. She had panicked and cast defensively. She'd acted like a child thrown into their first fray. There was no excuse for her failure.

Hultur caught her eye. She grit her fists tight enough to crack the burned skin. Despite searing pain, an adult of weight between them, and common sense, Ena walked up and slammed a fist on his flat, muscular chest. It would've been a lot more satisfying to slap him, but she'd have to jump up to get there.

"What the fuck was that?!" she shouted. "We were fighting for our lives and you just stood there and watched?! What does it matter if people know who you are now?!"

Hultur glanced over at the ship full of strangers. They were going to be on a very long voyage with them. Ena didn't know how far away Leben Erde was exactly, but the trip was bound to take at least a week.

One of the deckhands pulled Ena off of him. "Ma'am! I don't know what your relation is to this man and I don't rightly give a fuck! His defensive sphere was the only thing keeping us alive back there. You owe him our thanks. Whatever his past, I don't care." The portly man looked to Hultur. "You're welcome on our ship any time."

Hultur doffed his fancy black hat.

"We got trouble!"

Eyes flashed up to the lookout and followed her pointing finger. Caredor's naval ships were changing course, and they looked to be moving to intercept. The crew of the ship jumped to life. The one-eyed Marineld barked commands as she ran below deck. She had to be the first mate of the ship, which made her the Captain now. Fascinosa had defended Torno. He'd given his life to save him. Ena couldn't imagine why he would do that for a stranger.

Myrrel came to Ena's side and healed the burns on her skin. The stinging cooled fast. She placed an empty gulda mark in Ena's hands and whispered, "Pretend to suck this."

Right. Ena had thrown out hundreds of gulda worth of magic and she was still standing. If the crew didn't know she was Ngoltur reborn before, they certainly suspected now. "How's Torno?"

"Bad." Myrrel only said that when there was a chance someone could die.

Nearby, Torno lay on his side. Wet coughs wracked his body while Visk looked over him.

"Why aren't you healing him?" Ena whispered.

She shook her head. "He won't let me. He insisted that you were treated first."

"Why?"

"Because you're the only one that can get us out of this, Ena! You saw what..." She glanced around at the crew of the ship and thought better of risking his name. "You saw how useless the big guy was in that fight."

There was something unsaid in Myrrel's words. Ena was useless, too. She knew that.

"Captain coming up aftside!" shouted the lookout.

People ran to the back of the ship to watch. Water split as Captain Fascinosa approached, leaving a wake big as a galleon's. The crew cheered. "Wasn't even worried," the portly man mumbled. Laughter rang up and there was talk of opening a barrel of rum.

Captain Fascinosa dove under and the crew backed up. He jumped out of the water with a spin and a somersault, a spray of ocean water following the trail of his body. He flew above heads and came to land beside Ena. His red uniform looked pristine and his smile was charming. The only concern on his gallant face was for the tricorner hat hanging around his neck. Removing the hat, he returned it to his head with a flourish. For some reason, he watched Ena during all of his showboating. She was glad he'd survived, but all that splashing didn't do anything to impress her.

His crew crowded around to pat his back and welcome him. A cheer rose as the First Mate returned with reinforcements.

Teetee ran up through the mass of knees and threw her arms around his hips. "I'm sorry, Fascinosa! I'm so sorry!" she sobbed.

He crouched down and picked up her chin. "Not to worry, Princess. We escaped with our lives and I'm alright. See? Not a scratch on me." He held up an arm and found it bloody where the fire had caught him. "Oh, well, maybe some scratches."

The first mate came by to deliver the bad news. "Caredor navy approaching off the portside, Captain. Any suggestions?"

An uneasy silence spread through the ranks.

The Captain smiled and gestured to Ena with a grand show of his arm. "Worry, not, Ginevra. We have Ngoltur to take care of that problem."

Ena brought the empty purple gulda back to her mouth and breathed in with an audible hiss.

"She's not-" Myrrel started.

"Friends." He put his arms around Myrrel and Ena. "Torno told me all about it."

They shot Torno a look. If he wasn't coughing up blood, they'd be inclined to kick him.

"Crew, we are not on a simple trip to sail to the faraway land of Leben Erde, but we are once again agents of prophecy!"

"Does this prophecy pay anything?" Ginevra grumbled.

"But of course." He held up three rainbow gulda. "Now, I believe everyone has tasks to jump to."

Captain Fascinosa's crew sprang into action. Myrrel pulled out another purple gulda and sucked it down. She went back to Torno.

The Captain, with his fancy red hat and vest, leaned against a mast like he was talking to Ena at a bar. "So, what do you need from us?"

"Look, I don't want to scare you." She got closer to whisper.

He leaned in to hear her. "What is it?"

"I'm not exactly great at being a hero. I have a lot of power, but you saw how bad I was out there."

Captain Fascinosa frowned. "Bad? You were stunning. Never before have I seen someone cast haste while bleeding and burned."

"Okay, yes, that was a pain, but I don't know what I'm going to do about those upcoming ships."

"You take out your wand and freeze the water. No ship can sail through an iceberg." He pat her on the back and turned to address his crew. "Make sure dinner is prepared in two hours. I will be in my quarters." And then he just walked into a door. He was that sure of Ena's ability. No doubt his confidence came from Torno talking her up.

Remembering Torno's confidence in her, she reached inside her pockets. Ena couldn't believe she'd forgotten about her wand during the fight. It was still there where she'd put it. Ena wasn't a hero of legend, she couldn't even stop a single Archmage. Yet, when she walked up to the front of the ship with her wand out, the entire crew of Endless Grace watched in awestruck anticipation.

Teetee was holding her cat in her arms. "Look, Butler, Ngoltur's going to cast magic now!"

Butler the Tabby didn't look impressed, but he didn't fight to get out of her arms.

Narla walked up beside Ena. "What's the holdup, Sweetness?"

"I can't do this," Ena whispered. "I don't know how to make an iceberg."

"Listen, you have the power. You might even have limitless power. Trust that power. That wand in your hand will direct your energy but don't channel all your ether through it. Use it to start freezing the ocean far away and then draw in the ether around where the strand hits. It should be easy." Narla offered her flask of whiskey.

Desperate for any help, Ena took a swig.

With a grin, Narla told the crew, "She needs a drink first."

They laughed. Narla and these sailors were treating all of this like a joke, but their lives were in Ena's hands.

She took a basic stance, one hand palm forward, and the battle wand right above her head. It was the first stance they taught casters at the chantry. With her body turned sideways she became a smaller target, though no one was aiming at her. She just needed to relax and fling the ethereal strands as far as she could. With a simple flick of her hand, she sent out a single, concentrated bolt of blue. It flew out into the ocean and didn't even make it halfway to the oncoming fleet. She couldn't see where it hit, but she could feel the cold on the tip of her index.

Reaching out, she grabbed that tiny fleck of cold like a snowflake. She pictured it suspended in her hand. Delicate and fragile, the little thing needed her will to sustain it. She attached ethereal threads to the points of the snowflake and drew on its moisture. She could feel the surrounding air chill and freeze, expanding the flake into something solid and unforgettable.

Ice spread into beautiful crystalline patterns very much resembling a snowflake. The sight of it was breathtaking and humbling, but Ena could feel the fragility in its form. Tossing the wand aside, she worked her hands through the evocation. Made small by perspective, she could believe the patch of ice was something to be tossed into a drink. She found it easy to pour the cold over the ground like a simple sheet of ice. It ran the length of the galleons, spreading from hull to hull. The larger spikes of ice sunk deep into the ocean and flipped the mass over. Water flew up in geysers from where the makeshift glacier turned over and broke apart.

Cheers went up.

A yanking on Ena's legs drew her eyes downward. Teetee gazed up with admiration as she offered Ena her battle wand. Ena took the wand with an appreciative nod, and the child of five or six pressed herself into her legs. Patting her on the back did nothing to make her let go, so Ena had to wobble her way back to Torno. Thankfully, the stairs extricated the child from her leg, but the kid followed her like a shadow.

"Any better?" Ena asked Myrrel.

Tears had turned her makeup into dark streaks on her cheeks. It was clearly an effort to lift her head and meet Ena's gaze. "He's not waking up."

BOOK 2
Voyage

THE FIFTEENTH CHAPTER

In Which Leadership is Discussed and A New Title is Bestowed

There was a lot of blame flying around but none of it from one person to the other. Visk felt responsible for having the fight break out in Sapphire Cove. Narla insisted that all the fighting would've been prevented if she properly scouted the area. Sal regretted that he delayed their exit by standing back to talk to Fascinosa. Ena had been the one to fail to stop the Mage's attack that hit Torno. Myrrel lacked the knowledge to continue healing Torno. The discussion had gone around in circles for over an hour, but only after everyone voiced their guilt for Torno's condition were any of them able to see their situation clearly.

A small saving grace was that they were alone to contemplate their failure. The crew of the ship was off doing the things that kept a ship sailing. Those that weren't working had been asked to leave them alone. Well, Ena asked Teetee three times and then First Mate Ginevra yanked the crying child away. Hultur was there too, watching the entrance to the mess while he scribbled in a book. He was there because he shared a quest with Ena, the others were there for her.

Myrrel was the first one to break the silence. "I think we all need to forgive ourselves."

"That's what all of you do," said Ena. "This my fault."
She'd already been crying for some time and now her voice
was strained.

"Ena, that isn't helping," grumbled Sal.

"I'm Ngoltur Reborn!" she shouted for the tenth time.
"You all saw what I did. I created a glacier large enough to
block off seven ships! I'm the Gods' chosen! But I didn't do
anything in the battle!"

"Stop it," Myrrel grumbled.

"I stopped a disk of fire forming over the mage's heads,
but I couldn't be bothered to throw an attack at them! I
blocked myself with a wall, but I didn't block the attack-"

"Ena!" Narla snapped.

She was angry at Ena. She wasn't angry at her for
fucking up the fight or getting Torno hurt, but the rage
was real enough. That little outburst satisfied enough of
Ena's guilt to let in her sorrow. Torno was bedridden and
unconscious and no one knew if he was going to survive. She
couldn't go back and stop herself from talking to Kalta. She
couldn't stop Kalta if she was following them. She was so
tired that she couldn't even cry. Impotent whimpers escaped
her lips.

Sal cupped Ena's back in his hand.

Narla passed her the pitcher of water. She waited for
Ena to take a drink before speaking. "I'm sorry."

Ena shook her head. "I deserve it."

"You choked, Ena, but you weren't alone. We're used to
fighting monsters from a distance with lots of preparation.
I was in the Liberation War while you were still in your
swaddling cloth and I did close to nothing once everything
fell apart. I was too drunk to keep my hands moving right,
for fuck's sake. We all fucked up because we weren't ready
for a battle, it's as simple as that." Narla paused to wait for
anyone to offer an alternate explanation.

Ena stayed quiet. Her guilt wasn't helping anyone.

"Starting today we're no longer a Band of Brokers, but

a Military Squad. I'm your Commander and all of you are my Corps," Narla declared very much like a Commander.

"Shouldn't we have a say in that?" Hultur asked from the other side of the mess.

"I'm not talking about you, Hultur. As far as I'm concerned you're an independent agent. Just keep writing in that little journal of yours," commanded Narla.

He adjusted his spectacles and went back to his book.

"I don't much like the idea of being in the military," Myrrel admitted.

"Tough. We're traitors and we're probably being hunted by that scary Archmage. Like it or not we're a military group and we now have all the same needs and responsibilities of one."

Narla was transformed by her declaration. She was serious and stern and her change in attitude was unnerving. It had been strange when she snapped at Torno back in Sothlen, but this was something different. She was sitting up straight, her eyes were focused like strands of ether, and the tone of her voice left no room for debate. With one decision, she'd made changed herself from the inside out.

Ena shifted forward to drink, but it brought everyone's attention to her. Clearing her throat, she said, "I support you as our leader, Narla. If you think we need to behave like a Corps, then I have no objections. I'll do whatever you think I need to."

Visk nodded. "I think Narla is correct. Torno never treated us like warriors and we were able to relax and enjoy ourselves, but the time for enjoyment is past. These are times for wand and spear, not words."

Myrrel sighed and looked to Sal to back up her position. Even outnumbered, the two of them might be able to convince the group.

Sal rubbed mud under his eyes where his tears broke apart his face. He rubbed at the patch of stones where his nose wasn't. "Our quest is one of peace. Once we find Muttur we'll be able to bring about an age of peace. I didn't think we would need to fight, but I think after everything that happened in Sothlen and our battle with that Archmage, I think Narla's right. We're going to need to fight. I know that I can't do much when the fighting breaks out, but if Narla thinks we can improve our abilities, then I'm willing to try.

"Yet, I don't know if Narla should be our leader. Ena is Ngoltur Reborn. There is no denying that anymore. It is her destiny to unite Gulambar and lead them in the Grand Dream. She needs experience calling the shots." He was looking at Ena.

She slinked out of his arm to better meet his eyes. "I appreciate that you'd be willing to follow me as a leader, Sal, but that's not me. Ngoltur from history was born in a castle. She was raised from birth with the skills to size up a situation and make a ruling. I can't do that. I don't have those skills. I can't even lead myself in battle. Narla has the experience, she's our elder, and most importantly she's ready to do it."

Sal took another look at Narla. He took in the change in her demeanor, the confidence in her stare, and the presence of her rigid back. And his lips wriggled around like a worm on a hook. "I wish we could ask Torno what he wants to do."

"He will return," Visk said with confidence. "I have complete confidence in Myrrel's healing abilities. When Torno wakes, he will support whatever decision we bring to him."

"How do you know that?" Ena asked.

"When we were on the monorail, Torno came to me for guidance."

Had it only been one day since they were on the monorail?

Visk continued. "I came upon Torno in one of his rare candid moods. He understood that his time as a leader had come to an end. Since I led warriors in my youth, he asked how I was able to step away from a position of leadership. I told him that a strong leader does not want a follower who denies power, but instead wields it for others."

They waited for Visk to say more on the matter but she was done.

Ena looked to Sal. "Does that make your decision to follow Narla any easier?"

Sal nodded. "It does but it still doesn't feel right. This entire journey feels wrong."

"It is wrong," said Hultur. He put his journal away and walked over to join the group by the bench. "The Gods demand that the Turall work like actors in their play. Now that we have gone off script we have challenged their authority."

"What do you mean?" Narla asked.

"Before, when I was alone in Ki'an, and even as I was trying to find Ngoltur, the Gods took no notice of me. Once I stepped up to talk to Ena, I felt the eyes of the Gods. It was like walking onto a great stage for the first time in my life. Though I can't see the audience, I know they're there. They're judging all of us, sizing us up to determine if our actions are moral or not, and I do not believe they like what they see." Hultur was growing surprisingly passionate.

"But we're working for peace," Ena protested. "How can you say that the Gods wouldn't support that decision?"

"I don't know. Maybe they're bored. Perhaps the Gods simply adore the sight of violence. We are on a quest for peace, but we arrive at Sothlen precisely as a mega monster is tearing apart the city. Torno is talked into being the spark for a revolution and against all logic he accepts. We were thrown into a warzone that manifested overnight. We succeeded in getting Ngoltur off Gulambar, but only by fighting for our life. The Gods have shown that they do not like peace.

"If the Gods truly are what is good, then to act against their will is evil. Thus our mission is evil. Since you were able to feel this, Sal, it could be an indicator that you are a spiritual guide."

Sal rubbed the back of his head-shoulders. "I'm not bread, you don't need to butter me up."

"Wait, are you saying that the Gods are working against us?" Ena asked.

Hultur shook his head. "I don't know. Ki'an's understanding of the Three Prime Gods is skewed towards Hultur and his role as Bloody Unifier. War brought our people strength and so we chase it with every generation. I was hoping to learn more about Gulambar's understanding of the Three Prime Gods, but sadly I never got the chance to discuss the matter with the Clerics and…" Hultur noticed eyes glossing over.

"I got a little off track, I apologize." Hultur cleared his throat. "What I'm saying is that we are acting against the will of the Gods. That does not guarantee that the Gods are working against us. All I can say for certain is that the Gods are watching us, and at times they are watching us closely."

"Creepy," Myrrel mumbled.

"Look, all that stuff is over my head," Narla admitted. "If it's true, fine. The Gods have never done me any favors. As far as I'm concerned they can all fuck off. Gods or not, we need to train to fight, and I know how to do that. Sal, you might think that Ena should be leading us because of some grand prophecy, but she's not going to do it."

Sal looked at Ena. "You really won't lead us?"

Ena shook her head. "I can't. I'm not the Ngoltur from the Grand Dream. I'm too different from the Ngolturs that came before me. Whatever's happening, we can't look to the past to determine what's next. I think our best chance of success comes by playing to our strengths. Narla was a Commander back in the Liberation War. She knows how to lead us."

Sal nodded. "I'm convinced. I support you, Narla."

It was all left to Myrrel, and she didn't look too happy

about all of them siding against her. "It isn't that I don't trust you, Narla."

"Oh, I know, Gorgeous. We've been friends for too long for any of this to hurt my feelings. I promise." Narla put a hand over her heart.

"We want to know your thoughts," Visk assured Myrrel.

"My hesitation doesn't have anything to do with Narla or even Ena. I don't like being a person in the military. I never wanted to serve in the military, not even to stitch up the injured. I'm not a fighter. I don't have the stomach for it. The thought of fighting, it..." Myrrel steeled herself, pushing her trepidations somewhere deep.

"We're all here to help Ena. If that means getting into fights, then fuck it. I'll stitch people up, but I'm not going to review my combat spells. I don't have any aptitude for it."

"I wasn't planning on putting a staff in your hand," Narla assured her.

"Alright then," with a sigh, she resigned herself to her new position. Myrrel stood. "I stand behind you, Commander Narla."

The others stood and voiced their official support.

"Thank you." Narla sniffed but kept her face stoic. "Before I accept command, there's one more thing I need to bring forward. No matter what, Torno can't be our leader moving forward. He had no right to drag us into a revolution without discussing it with us first. We need to know that we're all working together to achieve the same thing. If I fail you as a Commander, that's fine. I'll step down with grace and hide all of my bitching."

A few chuckled.

A smile spread over Narla's lips. "When Torno wakes up, I'm not just going to tell him that I'm in command. He needs to know that he can't assume command again. Are there any objections to this?"

There weren't.

"In that case." Narla stood and saluted. "I accept your support and once again take up the role of Commander. There are going to be a lot of changes in the group. First, I'm giving up drinking and I'm going to need your help recovering, Myrrel."

The healer nodded. "You should feel normal in three days."

"Drinking is strictly prohibited while training and when going into a planned battle. Failure to follow this order will be met with punitive actions in the form of physical exercise.

"Training up Ena will be our top priority. As a group, we will go through one hour of physical training and one hour of magical routines, each of us will then have ninety minutes to train Ena."

"Except for me, right?" Sal asked.

Commander Narla shook her head. "Sal, you might have the hardest job of all. Casters of Ngoltur's caliber have dedicated Councilors. Your job will be to not only manage her stress but to help her form quick paths to emotional nodes."

"I have no experience with that," he said with a self-depricating chuckle.

"None of us have," Narla pointed out. "But you're smart and empathetic, and I can't think of anyone better for the job."

Sal nodded. The boulba was already chewing on the idea.

"Visk, you are going to cover combat imbuing. Teach her everything you know about imbuing weapons with spells. In the short term, you'll be walking her through the basics of Ki'an magic. Your long-term goal is to work with Ena to get her to imbue an entire army's worth of swords. That was one of the things Ngoltur was capable of."

Visk scowled at the challenge rather than voice her objection to it being a waste of her time.

"Hultur, you need to teach her how to make that sphere of yours."

"It is not something that can be learned in a few weeks," he objected.

"The two of you are Turall, you'll figure something out. Myrrel, she needs to know anatomy and healing magic."

"I don't know if I'm comfortable with teaching her how to kill," Myrrel said with a sneer.

"Then don't. Teach her how to heal. Ngoltur was supposed to be able to heal an army by blowing a kiss into the wind. Besides, it wouldn't hurt to have another healer."

Myrrel nodded but she didn't look optimistic about the prospect.

"Narla, what am I going to be learning from you?" Ena asked.

"Nerves. You choked because you weren't ready when the fighting broke out. I'm going to break your habit of hesitation. By the time I'm done, you should be the first one to react, even before me," Narla said with a sadistic grin.

"Wait, that's almost ten hours of work," Ena calculated.

"Don't worry, we'll make it eleven once Torno wakes up." Narla patted her back.

"Making my job the hardest, are we?" Sal asked. He and Ena laughed, but it was a bitter laugh born of despair.

"I'll have the daily schedule ready by dinner time," Commander Narla assured them. "Until then everyone should be figuring out their first lesson for tomorrow. Ena, enjoy your R&R, because starting tomorrow, you're going to be a magical workhorse. We're going to make your time at the chantry look like a tea break."

Somehow, despite Commander Narla's promise of grueling work and being drained in every way possible, Ena was at peace. There was a plan now, and unlike a Torno plan, she actually knew what it was. Despite Narla's mock threats, she was looking forward to being tested. It brought a smile to her face. It made her want to fight Kalta again.

~ ~ ~

When Teetee found out about Ena's extensive magical training, she begged Commander Narla to let her join. In order for that matter to be resolved, she had to talk to Captain Fascinosa about it. When he heard about the training, he requested that the entire ship participate in the physical training. So First Mate Ginevra was volunteered to lead the physical training for the ship. As for Teetee, she could beg as much as she wanted, but there wasn't any point in giving her any magic training. Marinelds couldn't learn magic. They had an innate ability to master water, not the ability to manipulate water. Ena let the kid down as gently as she could, but Captain Fascinosa himself came to argue for Teetee's inclusion.

"She can learn magic," the Captain told Narla's Corps.

"But she's marineld," Narla grumbled. "No offense, but won't it all be one big waste of time?"

"Marineld are not like boulba. We are not made from magic but are of magic. Teetee was born Princess Titiarna. Though living in exile, she is descended from Marineld Queens. Many of them learn the ability to heal or to call upon the earth to shake and spill out deadly bubbles of heat. Some Queens have wielded the power to evoke lightning. She has the physical ability to learn magic, though I make no promises about her temperament as a student."

"So what you're saying is that the decision is ours to make?" Narla asked.

He nodded and the Commander looked to the instructors.

"No," Hultur said, immediately.

"I have to go through the basics anyway," said Myrrel. "But it's high magic. I've never heard of a five-year-old learning the art. I guess it wouldn't hurt to have her around until she gets bored."

"I'm five and a half," corrected Teetee. "And I won't get bored."

"Five and a half," Myrrel conceded. "You're going to have to do a lot of writing. Do you know your script?"

She nodded as seriously as if they were discussing funerals and succession. "I can read books written for bigger kids, too."

"How do you feel about it?" Visk asked Ena.

"It could be fun having her around when I learn magic." Ena smiled at the kid.

"Then I will accept her as a student." Visk crouched down to get in the child's face. "But be warned, I will not be going easy on you because of your age. If you cannot keep up with the lesson, then you will be removed."

Teetee took on a serious scowl and nodded.

"I'm sorry little one," Sal said with a condescending smile. "But I cannot have you with us."

"I'm not little!" the girl said with a pout.

"Sal, I'm going to need to teach you the basics of emotional resonance," Ena pointed out. "Would you have a problem if she was there with us for that?"

He considered it. "I suppose not."

Teetee smiled widely at Ena and took her hand.

"What about you, Narla?" Ena asked.

The Commander shook her head. "No can do. Sorry, Princess."

Teetee stuck her tongue out.

"Then it is settled," said Captain Fasci. "You will have access to our ship for an hour of physical exercise, which will be led by First Mate Ginevra. The deck will be used for another hour for basic magic forms which Teetee and I will join. And then Teetee will join three classes covering advanced magical theory; each one ninety minutes long. Congratulations, Teetee, you've just signed yourself up for six and half hours of training on top of your studies with the rest of the crew."

"What?!"

"You didn't think you'd have to stop learning about history, math, and writing, did you?"

Teetee crossed her arms and pouted.

"Are you sure you still want to do this, little princess?" She looked to Ena.

"It's a lot of hard work," Ena told her follower. "No one will tease you if you back out."

"I can do it," Teetee insisted. "I'm gonna learn magic and take back my mother's crown someday, even if nobody believes I can do it!"

Ena crouched down and smiled. "I believe you."

Teetee pulled Ena into an embrace.

Her moist skin was almost slimy at first touch, but once Ena got past the initial shock, she found her flesh subtle and responsive in a way that was pleasant and easy to sink into. It almost felt like hugging a bed soaked in water close to a boil. She hoped things would work out for this child. It couldn't be easy growing up on a boat without ever knowing her parents. In some ways, Ena admired this child's courage. Bad as things were, Teetee viewed the world with optimism and she didn't back down from a fight. Ena would need that courage if she was going to survive this training.

THE SIXTEENTH CHAPTER

Where Ngoltur Starts Her Training

Mornings began with a moment of quiet reflection for Ena. Commander Narla had scheduled her day down to the minute, but Ena could have a moment for herself if she woke up a little earlier. There was time to walk up to the deck, wave at the lookout, and gaze at the endless serenity of the ocean.

Life had been simple for them under Torno's leadership, but there was always something to do. Homes needed to be rebuilt, batteries needed to be powered, fields needed to be cleared of monsters, but all of it was manageable. After the first three months, Ena got used to the flow of endless tasks. When she needed to sleep days and work nights, she did. When she pretended to run out of ether, she helped Sal or Narla with their repairs. None of them had been surprised to learn that she was Ngoltur. If any of them had resented her choosing to stop working magic, they'd never let her feel that way. They always gave her the space to think and feel what she needed to.

Ena had been reflecting on her time as a Broker a lot. Maybe it was because that time was behind her, or the fact that she'd finally left Caredor. Maybe it was because she was safe. She was thinking about Haenir too.

She'd remember his timid smile, those shy stolen

glances, and the way all of that stopped the moment her lips touched his. She'd never known Haenir. There had been so much to him, so much more than she ever thought possible, and she learned more about him in one night than she'd learned in the three years prior. She'd watched him grow from a tall, awkward teen of seventeen into a handsome man of twenty, knowing the entire time that he wanted to kiss her. It had seemed like a mistake back then but it hadn't felt like a mistake. Of course, it hadn't felt like a mistake when she had sex with Ve'an, either.

That man at the bar only wanted to talk to her, she recognized that in him. But the more she thought about it, the more she wanted him to touch her. Now that their encounter was past them, she didn't feel regret for what they did. But she didn't dwell on her time with him except to wonder if it had been a betrayal to Haenir. She knew she didn't owe him anything just as he didn't owe her his exclusion, but she couldn't escape the feeling that she'd let him down.

She was letting a lot of people down lately.

The ship's crew gathered early. Ena learned too many names to remember and they were all so personable and warm to her. The ship's navigator, Norden, was particularly easygoing. The Leben man was frequently paired with Ena in the day's bouts. He was of a similar height to Ena, and similar stature. In his glasses, he looked uncertain or cold, but without them his face took on a brutish quality. Every time she had to match him in a sparing match, she found his sudden burst of strength and ferocity startling.

Norden had taken a fancy to Ena and that reminded her of Haenir as well. He tried to talk to her about her interests and find out about her life, but the two of them were never alone for long. All the sailors had plenty of scars, and every scar came with a bombastic story. Captain Fascinosa had traveled all over the world in his ship, Endless Grace, and they'd all joined up in one port or another. They were garbed in an eclectic assortment of clothes, spoke with thick accents, and had no end of stories to share.

Strange as it was to see the blue skin and pointed ears of a Leben, it was surreal to be walking around so many marineld. Ena had so little experience with the fish folk before this journey that she'd believed all of them to be born from one source, but such was not the case. On board Endless Grace were three races of marineld, and more species existed beyond that.

The Marineld that Ena was used-to--well, was aware of--lived in the Warring States inside the Ocean of Harmony. The Ocean of Harmony lay between the three continents, with End of the World blocking them off to the south. Among their people, marineld from the Warring States were known as Harmineld.

Harmineld were covered in fishlike scales running the gamut of arboreal hues. Spots small as freckles or larger than palms distinguished an individual Harmineld. Another fishlike thing about the Marineld from the Warring States was their conical teeth and lidless eyes. The fins on their forearms, ears, and tails tended to run the range of yellow to red. Their head-tails came in two variations, depending on if they originated from the East or the West. Western Harmineld could be identified by their tendency for scales mottled by pattern, if they existed at all, and a short stubby head-tail with a large fin that spread out from the back of their neck with the top of their head. They were also quickly identified by the substantial webbing between their clawed fingers. Eastern Harmineld had smaller spots covering their back, with some even having stripes. Their head-tails were thick as the base of their skull and were of a similar size to their forearm. These distinctive head-tails wiggled with excitement, especially when they ate.

Teetee hailed from the far north, under the Anzu Ocean. Marinelds born from that part of the world, Anzuneld, had almost no scales to speak of, instead their round flesh was unmarked save an occasional white patch. Their headtails were long as their forearms and stayed erect, wiggling parallel to the ground when they stood upright. The fins on their forearms, tail, and ears were long, wavy, and made of a semi-translucent material that was soft to the touch. Those fine-sand-soft fins resembled bubbles or the petals of a flower.

Teetee was counter-shaded, with her mouth, inner arms, and chest more white in appearance than the periwinkle along the rest of her body. The ends of her frilly fins were tipped with a vibrant magenta that made her fins look like they had been dipped in paint. Her lips and nails naturally shared the magenta hue of her fins. Possessing human-like teeth and nails, her features were soft compared to the Harmineld so common on the ship.

Marinelds of Squall Ocean were born with scales, but they were fine scales, so interwoven and close together that the naked eye failed to see them at a distance. Rather than thin membranous fins, Squanelds had fleshy shark-like fins protruding backwards to hug their triceps when they straightened their arms. Nails were thick and pointed, but still resembled a human's shape. Squaneld headtails varied in thickness and shape, either taking on the same dorsal fin shape or looking like a shark's tail.

Nearly half of the Marinelds on board were Squanelds, including First Mate Ginevra and Captain Fascinosa. Though only Fascinosa had three head-tails with tiger stripes along his green back. All squanelds were counter-shaded, sharing the same white mouth, neck, and chest as Teetee.

In short, there were three races of Marineld aboard the ship. The sharp-toothed, thick-scaled Harminelds who were distinguished by their pointed accordion fins. The smooth-bodied, bubble-finned Anzunelds, who had almost human-like features in their face and hands. And the streamlined, angular Squanelds whose pointed nails, teeth, and protruding brow gave their mostly human appearance a sinister edge. Ena had learned to distinguish them by physical characteristics but couldn't make sense of the differences in their homelands.

All marinelds, regardless of their background, were welcoming to Ena and the Corps. Every morning before physical training they were eager to share their stories with Ena. If ever she was feeling lonely she needed only to stand in one place, and the fish folk would engage her in conversation.

Ginevra started every morning by selecting a member of the crew to lead everyone through stretches. What followed largely depended on how sadistic the first mate felt. After a morning full of grumbles, Ginevra roped everyone to masts and chucked them overboard to swim. One day, when bodies moved without her orders, she had everyone climb rigging. By far the crew's favorite exercise was single combat. Whether it was wrestling, staffwork, or swordplay, they put odds on matchups. Ena had quickly developed a perfect record. No wins. Not a single one.

It wasn't that Ena wasn't trying, she simply couldn't overpower anyone physically. They'd started to make jokes about her wrestling Teetee, and Ena was horrified by the possibility that she might actually lose a fight with a child.

Even though everyone wanted to see a match between Hultur and Visk, the big man refused to participate in the physical training. He couldn't even be talked into going up to the deck to watch. Visk had been undefeated until she wrestled Ginevra. There were a lot of coins and gulda exchanged on that day. Visk took the loss with grace and seemed to be in a better mood following her defeat. She took her physical training seriously and vowed that she would defeat Ginevra before the end of the journey.

Magical warm-ups were nice, not just because they helped to correct Ena's forms, but because Teetee's enthusiasm was infectious. The girl of five and a half was deadly serious about the lessons. Narla led the first lessons with hand stretches, finger formations, wand stances, and full-body gestures. They were all new to Teetee, and the little girl kept asking which spells went with which hand symbol. Since there wasn't any time to explain the nuances of it, Narla decided to pick one spell a day, and everyone was called forth to cast the spell at the end of training. Though Teetee never successfully cast anything, she was happy to hold a wand, and happier still to shout an incantation.

Since Ena's heart rate was already up, and Narla had "shit to do," Narla's nerve training came next. Most of the training was quick draws and drills. Some of it was just Narla yelling at her, and the woman was well-practiced at the art of surprise. At first, the surprises came in the form of quick casts, but a few days in she'd figured out a way to make flash-bangs out of eel skin and supplies the ship had in abundance. After that, Ena was expected to grab and suppress the bombs before they exploded in her face. Then Narla just started throwing actual bombs at her. She'd come at her with knives, too, and Ena learned with some dismay that her first instinct was to get out of the way.

Only after her third activity in the day could Ena eat breakfast. The mess was always empty when she and Narla ate, and it gave them time to talk. Narla still wanted Ena to take charge, but she agreed that the woman of twenty wasn't ready for command. Commander Narla spent most of her days learning about Leben Erde, so she'd gotten to know Norden pretty well herself. She liked the man of twenty-five but he was too cautious for her to work with. They'd had some kind of discussion about math and mechanisms, and Narla lost all patience for working with someone "obsessed with measurements."

Ena's morning routine had her going to Sal next, and their progress had been complicated.

Their first day began with Ena teaching Sal and Teetee about the basics of emotional resonance. Since they were just talking, Ena decided to run through it all in the mess.

She found it intimidating to stand before a boulba and a marineld to tell them about magic. Boulba were created from magic, though whether they had been rocks turned into people or people turned into rocks, none could say for sure. Marineld, on the other hand were never fish nor men but had been created from ether itself to rid protect sailors from ocean monsters.

"Do either of you know the seven fundamental emotions?" she asked to start the lecture.

Sal and Teetee shared a look of bewilderment and shame.

Sal spoke up first. "There are far more than seven emotions. I think any who tried to categorize them all would live a life unfulfilled."

"I agree," Ena said, "but when it comes to magical theory, the obvious is frequently made complicated."

"Do they have something to do with babies?" Teetee asked.

"That's right. The Wizards of old looked to babies and saw seven traits that they all shared in common. When they traveled the world and studied all people, they found that the same emotions were all the ether-touched."

Ena took out seven candles, arranged in the order of the rainbow and sharing the same fundamental colors. She lit each candle as she listed the emotion the color was associated with.

"Anger." Red.

"Disgust." Orange.

"Contempt." Yellow.

"Happiness." Green.

"Fear." Blue.

"Sadness." Indigo.

"Surprise." Violet.

"These emotions have many names and many smaller emotions connected to them, but for the purposes of magic, it helps to visualize each element with an emotional resonance. For example, when I first heard about 'Contempt' I thought it was redundant. How is anger different from contempt? If someone is feeling contempt for someone, aren't they angry?

"But I was getting lost in the words. Contempt can also be thought of as discomfort. We all know what it's like to sleep in a bad place or to hear loud noises. Anger can be a response to discomfort, but it's not exactly the same. Contempt is closer to annoyance than outright anger. If someone gets a toy you were waiting for, you might be angry with them, but you might also just be annoyed that you can't have the thing you want. Language does a poor job of explaining emotions, and it does an equally poor job of explaining magic."

Sal raised a few arm-sized fingers and Ena gave him leave to ask a question. "Is there a reason the emotions are arranged in that order?"

Ena nodded. "Some magicians believe that the emotions mirror the spectrum of a rainbow because they can blend one to the other. They believe that it's easier to go from feeling anger to disgust than from anger to happiness."

"But you don't believe that."

Ena shook her head. "I've been sad and got angry quickly, and I've felt shock and disgust at the same time. Emotions are complex and they intermingle, and most magicians know this. There have been a lot of attempts to explain the way that magic resonates with emotions, but none of it is perfect."

Teetee looked annoyed. "Then why are we learning this?"

"Because even though the path from one emotion to another might not work like a road map, it does resonate with the seven basic elements of magic."

Sal pointed at each of the candles, guessing how each element was associated with those basic elements.

"Fire." Red and anger.

"Lightning." Orange and disgust.

"Earth." Yellow and contempt.

"Wind." Green and happiness.

"Ice." Blue and fear.

"Dark." Indigo and sorrow.

"Force." Violet and surprise.

Ena wasn't surprised that Sal had gotten it right in his first try. He'd seen every color from the ethereal threads cast by wands. "Exactly right, Sal."

Teetee's confusion grew into outright irritation. "But there are more than seven colors. There's no brown here!"

"And there's more than seven types of magic. The point of the rainbow of magic isn't to give us rigid magical rules, but to give us a place to start looking," Ena said, doing her best to keep her voice level. This might've all been too far above Teetee's understanding of the world.

"I don't understand why magic needs an emotional connection," said Sal. "Remember, I've never cast magic before."

"Yeah, me neither," Teetee pouted.

"Okay, so let's say you learn a spell to cast a gout of fire. You move your hands through the right gestures, you recite the incantations, you visualize glyphs, but when you finish…" Ena demonstrated the motions of her hands, if not the incantations.

"Nothing happened," Teetee said, crossing her arms.

"That's because I didn't put any will into it. Without will my ether can't flow from my soul into the world. Remember, the point of all the fancy stuff that casters do is to make it easier for ether to flow from inside ourselves to outside. Gestures, incantations, and even wands are designed to weaken the ethereal barrier of the world. It's like the act of casting is reaching out and shaking the hand of the world." She held out her hand.

Teetee shook it. "Hello."

"Hello, my name is Ether. Would you like a fireball?"

She threw her hand at Teetee's belly and tickled.

The kid giggled. When Ena let go, she slumped down into her seat to look at the floor.

"So emotions help to focus your will, they help your soul talk to your mind?" Sal asked. Despite having no connection to magic himself, he was doing a good job of following the ideas.

"Most magicians think it works that way. Emotions are the soul's way of communicating to the mind and the self. So if I'm able to grab onto a thought that holds one emotion, it's like I'm making a request of my soul. Can we feel sad, right now? Then maybe my soul says, 'Yes.'"

"But I wanna cast magic," Teetee complained, her eyes still examining the baseboards.

"I understand that, but if you can't control your thoughts then you're going to have a very hard time doing that. If you just think about magic to cast magic, it's exhausting. The brain struggles to hold onto those thoughts and you can't do anything. If you want to do a fire spell, it helps to be angry. Can you be angry, Teetee?"

Sitting up, she showed Ena a scowl. "I'm really good at that."

"Good, then you might become a powerful fire caster."

"I hear people talk about casters all the time, but what does 'caster' mean?" asked Sal.

"It's just a catch-all for people that cast spells or think about magic," Ena explained with a shrug.

"I'm mad at the candle, but the flame isn't getting any bigger," Teetee pouted.

"I know." Ena crouched down next to her. "You still need to learn incantations, gestures, glyphs..."

"That's too much," she grumbled.

"I'm sorry, but magic is really hard. Can you go play with Butler? Sal and I still need to talk."

"Okay." Teetee walked off with a deep scowl on her forehead.

"I think I'm getting all of this," said Sal. "So we need to form nodes so you can grab onto an emotion fast."

"Right. If I have a strong emotional memory that makes me feel something like fear, then I can call upon a lot of ice magic. I've got a few of them and I've recently added a few more: my parents laughing and Kalta lashing me with fire from all sides." Ena let out a growling sigh.

"How can we get you to connect with something like surprise, though? Force is a powerful magic, but I rarely see casters throwing out violet strands of ether."

"If you think about the moment that you get startled, there's a kind of tremor in your heart. If you hold onto that and keep holding onto that, it turns into something new."

"Anxiety!" Sal said with excitement. He looked to the candles and pointed at the orange one. "What about disgust?"

"I'm not sure. If I was, I wouldn't need your help. But remember that the emotion doesn't have to fit that feeling perfectly. Magic is like a conversation between your soul, your mind, and the world. In some ways your body is like the translator," she explained.

"Hmm." Sal thought on it. "Okay, I guess that makes sense. But how are we going to form nodes, we just find traumatic moments in your life?"

Ena nodded. "In theory, I don't think it needs to be a bad memory, but those tend to stick out in the mind. Well, in my mind at any rate."

"Isn't that going to put a lot of stress on your mind? If I spend all day thinking about bad things I don't really want to do much of anything."

She sighed. "You're starting to understand why it's so hard to form nodes. I've got a lot of strong memories from when my parents were shitty to me, but it's been getting harder to hold onto them."

"Why?"

"I don't know. I think it might be because life has been

getting better. Good thing I've picked up more reasons to feel miserable. I knew I wasn't going to like going to the capital."

Sal rubbed her back, like all of her back at once because each of his hands was big as her chest. "Don't worry about it, Ena. We've got a month or so to figure this stuff out. Maybe more. If we can get you even one or two more nodes to draw on, that'll help, right?"

"Oh yeah. It would be great to be able to use more than just ice magic."

"You will." Sal got out a massive scroll. It was the kind used for formal declarations, but in his hands, it was barely large enough for him to take any notes at all. "Now that I know what we're doing I think Narla was right. I won't need magic to help you, but I am gonna need your complete trust. No matter how dark your thoughts, you're gonna have to share them. Are you going to be able to do that?"

"I don't know," Ena admitted. If she had perfect control over her thoughts and emotions she wouldn't need Sal's help.

If her work with Sal was nothing but trying to find the most traumatizing moments of her life, she wouldn't be able to go on. Thankfully, as the caretaker of her mental well-being, he was also there to help her relax. They'd find Teetee and play with Butler, or play a game with sailors on a break. They'd sit and drink tea and reminisce about their lives as Brokers, and it would help ease the weight on her mind and shoulders. Sal always tried to make sure that Ena left her lessons with a smile on her face, and sometimes she managed to find one.

Her daily work went on jumping from one mentally draining activity to another. Ena got so exhausted towards the end of the day that the small bits of physical activity during Visk's training came as a relief. She practically begged Visk to have more hands-on training and so she gradually started to teach Ena Ki'an magic forms. Her time with Myrrel was so cerebral and monotonous that her first day with

Hultur ended with her falling asleep on the deck.

Day after day, she went through a routine that pushed her brain every which way. It made her absent-minded and robed her of the ability to form a coherent sentence. Each of her teachers adjusted, giving her less work and trying to engage her brain in a different way, but it was like an explosion of new information. She was simply too small for all the debris to hit her.

Dinner was as much about eating as it was about keeping up relations with the crew. She'd sing half-forgotten sailor songs, dance until people got tired of being kicked in the shins, and play tag until she could only lay on the deck panting. But at the end of the day, no matter how exhausted, she always returned to Torno's side.

The sound of his breathing pained Ena. It was wet and labored, and his chest rose out of sync as one lung filled faster than the other. She knew that she wasn't supposed to hold onto her guilt, but she'd tried to stop that mage's attack. She saw the blue threads of ether spiraling towards Torno and struck out at it with an ice spell. Ice against ice might've burst the spell out of their threads, but it had done nothing to stop the spell itself. Torno had maybe twenty feet of air to stop the spell, but spells moved fast as arrows.

Ena had never used magic against a living person. She didn't want to know what it did to the human body. She didn't want to know what kind of damage freezing cold did to blood and sinew, but Torno had to live with that pain. There was fluid in his lungs and tissue damage all over the afflicted side of his body. Muscle and ligaments had experienced rot, and skin had frozen so completely that Myrrel couldn't stop the necrosis from showing.

Ena didn't have any scars from their battle with Kalta. The only thing she lost was some hair, but the mostly shaved style suited her head anyway. Myrrel had been there to heal her from the moment she was on the boat. Torno used the last of his strength to insist that Ena was a priority.

Why?

Why did he keep putting her above everyone else? Because of love? He didn't really love her. He didn't really know her. Ena thought she loved Haenir when she kissed him, but she'd only known a fraction of him. Torno claimed to love Ena despite knowing so little about her past and secret thoughts. He had never known what he was to Ena or why she'd hated him before she ever met him. All he knew was that the novelty of her bone-white skin was striking. For that, he denied the advances of the women in those tiny villages. Torno had gone through three years of abstinence for her. It didn't make any sense.

Anger and sorrow were supposedly on opposite sides of the magical rainbow, but she could access both when she thought of Torno. She could clench her fist and cry. She could whimper and growl in the same breath because she hated him for sacrificing himself. She'd never asked him to forgo healing for her. She'd never wanted him to die because he had to make sure that she was up the gangplank first.

He took her fist in his hand.

"Torno?!"

He gave one of those unreadable smirks. The fucker probably thought it made him look sweet or handsome or something. She hated having to look in those eyes, especially after everything he'd suffered. His voice was ragged when he asked, "How did I hurt you now, Precious?"

THE SEVENTEENTH CHAPTER

When Ngoltur Envies a Child

The worst thing about Torno waking up was that he'd seen her crying. There was no denying it. She was at his bedside crying over him. The ego-maniac probably thought her entire life since his injury had been her waiting by his bed and crying over his wounds. Whatever she felt about him, it wasn't like that. Thankfully, Ena was able to run out of the room under the excuse of gathering the Corps. The change of leadership gave her a convenient way out, but she still felt like a coward to flee with such brazen haste. Which wasn't fair to her. Ena wasn't scared of Torno, she was merely being strategic. Really, it was a courtesy. All of their discussions only ever ended in an argument; that couldn't be good for his health.

Visk was the last to arrive. The woman looked more pink than red, so she'd probably been throwing up again. The summer winds had been kind according to the marineld crew, but any time the winds picked up Visk had a miserable time on the ship. Torno showed her concern at once, but she assured him that this had been an easy trip.

"So..." Torno let out a wheezing sigh. "I'm assuming I'm past the worst of it?"

Myrrel nodded. "You'll be okay now that I have a patient that can communicate."

"Most of my pain is in my chest. It feels like I'm sharing my lungs with a slime." He winced. "What have I missed?"

Narla stepped up. "Quite a lot."

The Commander explained Ena's training regiment, each of their roles in her training, a basic outline of her strategy once they landed in Leben Erde, and the change in leadership.

Torno nodded in agreement. "You're a good choice, Narla. I stand behind you, Commander."

Narla bowed her head, and Sal and Myrrel let out a sigh of relief.

"Once I'm able to walk-" Coughs wracked his body. He reached for a rag and coughed up blood and phlegm. "That looks bad."

Myrrel shook her head. "You're healing. This is good, believe me."

"I just coughed up blood and you didn't cast a thing. That's pretty bad last time I checked." He smiled and started to laugh, but pain stole his chuckles.

"Just get some rest, Champ," Narla told him. "We'll be stopping at a port in a day or two."

"Faigovaidon?" he asked, thinking they were heading into Doronel.

"A city in Baliku. It'll be my first time on Ki'an soil."

Torno looked to Visk and then reminded himself that he wasn't in charge. "I'll try to come up with a list of things that aren't cigars."

Myrrel slapped his arm. "No smoking!"

"Or what, you'll kill me?"

"Don't think I won't," she said, sweetly.

He tried to laugh again, but pain stopped the outburst.

The Corps said their goodbyes. Ena tried to slink out while they did.

"Ena," Torno called out.

He waited until she turned her head before saying what he was going to say. Everyone was looking at her, and he'd come back from the verge of death. The least she could do was look at him. Leave it to Torno to use a near death experience as a means for leverage.

"Can you stay behind?" His words came out weak. "I'd like to talk to you."

"I'd rather not."

"Maybe some other time, then."

Ena nodded and left.

He was back. He wasn't going to die, and that was all that mattered. Everything else was sugar sprinkled on sweetcream. She didn't have to spend any more time worrying about him. She could just focus on herself. Things had to get easier now.

~ ~ ~

In some ways, they did. Ena awoke feeling rested, and all her hard work was starting to show its progress. She even scored her first victory against Norden, striking him in the face when he rushed forward to grab her leg. She broke his nose, but it felt too damn satisfying for her to feel bad about it. Narla focused on building up Ena's reaction times, and after the nerve training was done she mentioned that she was going to throw a flash-bang when Ena's concentration slipped, but it never happened. Even her session with Sal was easy going. He suggested that they create one word associations with their nodes, but that ran the risk of a node activating at random. Ena threw out the idea of creating a house full of memories, but Sal thought that navigating a house in her mind's eye would take too long to access what she needed. In the end, the two of them just spent their time drawing pictures of the nodes Ena had identified.

Training with Visk had been very basic so far. Since the very beginning, Visk had just been laying out the foundation of Ki'an imbuing techniques. Ena loved the simplicity of it. Unlike so many other high magicks, Ki'an imbuing was more about precise control of the body rather than memorizing giant charts and page-long incantations.

The trouble with Ki'an magic was that Ena couldn't translate the magical forms into anything she could augment. Neither of them knew the first thing about remote imbuing. After about ten minutes of trying to surround a wooden sword with ethereal power, Visk switched to teaching Ena Ki'an combat forms.

Princess Teetee survived the first day of training with Visk, but only just. The next day Visk had them stand on one foot for ten minutes and then switch feet to do it again. Teetee threw a royal fit and Visk dismissed her. No matter how she apologized, no matter how she begged, Visk would not take Teetee back as a student. The kid still hovered around the deck to watch them though. They needed to be on the deck to see the swell of the ocean. Visk was confident that training on rolling waves would give Ena the balance she needed to shift between Ki'an forms. Though Visk was optimistic and supportive, the Ki'an forms and balance work burned her inner thigh, core, calfs, arm pits. Everything else was the normal kind of muscle pain--too much. After seeing Teetee booted, Ena kept her mouth shut. Visk made it clear that she would tolerate no complaints.

The day after Torno awoke, Ena finally got a breakthrough. The hanging sword was suspended before her, with the tip facing up. Visk went through the motion with her, activating an imbuing strike with an upwards stab. The idea was that since the motion ended with the sword in the same position as the hanging sword, Ena would be able to resonate with the blade, and extend her aura out to the object. On that day of breakthroughs, it finally worked on her first try. The wood came alive, cracking with lightning. The second Ena realized what she'd done, the spell dissipated.

"Did you see that?!" Ena asked, bouncing up and down on the balls of her feet. "I did it, Visk. I did it!"

"Do it again."

She nodded. The women found their center, rolled through the motions, and nothing happened. Visk even tried a few times to do it herself, but with no success.

"What happened? What were you doing differently?" Visk asked.

"I don't know. I wasn't even really thinking. I was just focusing on how my body felt and it just...happened. I did feel the ether flow, though."

"Was it any different?"

"No, it was the same kind of feeling as when I imbue something I'm holding. Maybe I'm just overthinking this. I'm not used to Ki'an magic. Everything I learned in the chantry told me that magic had a logic to it. I always thought there was a geometry and arithmetic to magic. I guess..." Ena thought better than to tell Visk the truth.

"Ena, you must share all your thoughts, no matter how shameful." The look on Visk's face was less rigid and formal than amused. She was implying something with her words, suggesting that outside distractions were somehow connected.

Ena thought of Torno and avoided her gaze. "I thought that since there wasn't any magical theory behind Ki'an techniques, they couldn't do what Gulambar magic can."

"Theory only exists to verify practice." It was Hultur.

Neither of them had seen or heard him approach, and they jumped when they heard the deep baritone of his voice. Teetee screamed so loud that Butler's tail went poof.

"You scared me so bad!" Teetee exclaimed.

Ena put her hand on her own chest. "How did you sneak up on us when you're so big?"

"It was not my intention to scare anyone." He bowed his head apologetically.

Visk sneered at him. "Why are you watching us?"

"Ena's lessons have been...sub-optimal. I was hoping to find an instructive technique to improve her retention."

"Never mind that." Ena waved the issue away. "What were you saying about theory?"

"I merely said that theories only exist to verify what

occurs in practice. A sailor may imagine an alternative geometry that explains the motion of waves, but they can only use the theory to improve their travel times if the waves can be modeled by those estimates."

"Fine, you've said your piece, now leave us to our discussion," Visk hissed.

Butler growled along with her.

"Visk, please. I think this is helpful." Ena tried to coax the woman.

She leaned against a mast, keeping murderous eyes on him.

"I don't understand what a sailor's calculations have to do with magical theory."

"Magic is indivisible from the world. Ether is a part of the world just as gravity and magnetism are. Any theory of spellcraft is an approximation for the actual behavior of magic. We will never have a perfect understanding of magic because magic is beyond the understanding of the human mind. We may feel gravity pull down when we jump, but we do not feel it when we are at rest. We understand so little about a fundamental reaction that makes all life possible.

"Ether has never been known to act upon people without influence from an agent. It has no will of its own but it resists the suggestions of the soul, so there must be some order to it. Comparing magic to water, casters do not hold ether in a cup and expel it when necessary. Ether responds to spells like water thrashing about a swimmer. Undercurrents or winds may exist, but we have no way of observing those changes."

"So you're saying that magical theory is incomplete, that it doesn't give any mastery over the elements?"

"I'm saying that mastery is an illusion. It is a dream of the thinking mind. Reality wakes us up."

"Okay, but imbuing is a high magic." Ena's voice was coming out curt. It always took so much work to understand him. "High magicks aren't something that come naturally to casters. Learning time magic took a lot out of me. I had to memorize charts, specialized glyphs, and incantations. Without that training, I couldn't use time magic at all. If all of that theory is meaningless, then why does it work? Why can't Teetee just will a spell to happen and have it work?"

"Yeah. Why not?" asked the petulant, if not mostly confused, child.

Visk had moved on to training trusts but kept her focus on Hultur.

He took off his hat. "Allow me to motivate your answer with a question of my own."

Ena waved her consent.

"If what you say is true, how was it that Gulambar magicians ever came to develop theories that explain time?"

"They observed the flow of time and learned its shape through ethereal explorations."

"But if time is so foreign and unnatural, wouldn't they need time magic simply to feel the flow of time? One cannot think a magical theory into existence. There is a reason love spells do not exist, magic cannot explain the workings of the mind. If theory preceded practice, then this wouldn't be an issue. Some powerful magician would've come up with an idea for a spell that reads thoughts as if they were words on a page, and yet there are no spells of telepathy."

Ena was dumbstruck. She had no rebuttal to his argument, though she was sure some must exist.

Pouting, Teetee voiced her own concern. "Why do I have to learn all of this?! Tell me how to do it!"

The tall Ki'an ignored her and bowed to Visk. "My apologies for intruding. If you wish, you may take her time from my lesson today."

Visk thrust her spear in his general direction. He returned his hat to his head. Once his back was turned, Teetee bared her teeth at him. He retreated below deck to his journals and books. Visk came over to survey the damage to Ena's brain.

Ena rubbed her forehead. "You can see why I'm having trouble learning from him."

"That man says many words and few of them are worth hearing."

"I disagree." Before Visk could protest, Ena continued, "I think you need to talk to him."

"Ena, that-"

"Visk, the language barrier is clearly a problem. I love you and I've never had a problem understanding you, but the things he's saying go beyond simple conversations. That man has a greater understanding of magic than anyone I've ever heard of. If we're going to figure out how to do remote imbuing reliably, we need his input."

Visk seethed.

"Visk."

"It is time for your lesson with Myrrel."

There was no point in arguing with Visk when she was silently fuming. Maybe her opinion would change with a little consideration.

Work with Myrrel was a slog. Memorizing and reciting anatomy charts was one thing, but going through the lengthy incantations was a complete nightmare. She'd learned the basics back in the chantry, but this was far worse.

Even though Myrrel had memorized what she needed, she didn't have any magical tomes on the basics. That meant that Myrrel was more or less forced to skip past the basics that Ena had forgotten and try to teach her whatever intermediate bits that Myrrel could remember. Of course, without Ena's foundational knowledge, she couldn't do anything. It was the opposite of training with Visk, all theory and no application.

Lessons with Hultur had been going worse than her time with Myrrel. She could feel his growing frustration for her as a student. By his own admission, he'd only tried to teach magic one time, and by the end of three months, his student was unable to cast any spells at all. He was trying a lighter approach this time around, and so Ena spent most of her time sculpting things with clay. Literally.

After dinner, Ena wandered around the ship looking for Teetee, but the Princess wasn't in any of her usual places. Lookout hadn't seen the child, nor most of the crew. Ena checked storage. It gave her time to greet the horses, but there wasn't any sign of the Princess. Teetee had to be somewhere she wasn't supposed to be. So Ena snuck into the kitchen stores and found Teetee hiding beside Butler and a half-eaten rat. The cat rushed out of the door, leaving behind his prize and prisonguard.

Ena crouched down to get closer. "Teetee, what are you doing in here?"

"Why do you care?" she asked.

"Because I care about you," she said through a smile.

The girl wasn't having it. "Stop lying to me. Everyone lies to me because I'm a kid. They think that I'm dumb! I know what people think about me. They all hate me. Even Butler, that's why he ran out of here so fast."

"Maybe he wanted to get away from his old lunch." Ena held up the dead rat and stuck out her tongue.

"Stop treating me like a kid!"

Ena sighed. She'd helped kids going through a hard time before, but Teetee was really struggling. She didn't have any brothers or sisters to play with or even any kids her own age. She didn't have any parents around to watch over her, just a ship full of strangers. They might care about her, but it would never feel like the same thing.

Ena stood up and offered her hand. "Let's get out of this rank cell. Come with me to my room and I promise not to treat you like a kid."

Teetee took her hand.

Ena took the remains of the rat out, explained the situation to the cook, and walked side by side with Teetee. When the fish-girl got to Ena's room she threw herself face-first into the pillow.

Ena sat beside her. "I don't hate you, but some of my friends do. They don't like that you get in the way of my lessons and think that we're wasting time having you in basic magic training."

"Fine, then I won't come anymore."

"I don't want that, Teetee. I like having you there. It helps me think about magic in a different way and it makes this easier."

"You're just saying that." Teetee kicked her shoes onto the bed.

"Teetee, look at me."

The girl of five and a half could see the serious expression on Ena's face and she put on one herself.

"Let's make a promise. As long as we're in this room, we can't lie to each other."

Teetee agreed.

"You're my friend, Teetee. I like spending time with you. Without you on this ship, I would've had to take a day off. I'm learning a lot of really difficult magic and I need a friend like you."

"Why, because I'm a kid?" she asked with a pout.

Ena nodded. "I never got to be a kid. When I was your age I moved around a lot. I spent all of my time in a carriage or hiding in a room where I wasn't allowed to make any noise. When I played with animals, Dad sent me a little shock. He'd flick his wand and send a bolt of electricity right into my bum."

Teetee laughed. "That sounds fun."

"It wasn't. It was like getting pinched really hard. I hated it, but I couldn't do anything about it because he was my dad and I had to love him."

"Is he dead?"

"He's not dead, but he's not my dad anymore. They left me behind to be rich and start a new family without me."

Teetee looked sad for Ena. "Do you still love them?"

Ena shook her head. "I don't know if I ever did. They only ever cared about money and having nice things because they were a King and a Queen."

"You're a Princess, too!" That got her excited.

"I am. And just like you I had to leave my home when I was very little."

"At least you got to live with your parents." Teetee looked like she was trying to decide which Princess had a harder life.

"My parents didn't like having me around. There was never anyone who loved me, and that's why I'm jealous of you."

"You can't be jealous of me. My life is horrible. I have the worst life on this boat," she pouted.

"I am jealous." Ena scooted onto the bed and took Teetee in her arms. Her large, fancy ear fins felt like rain-washed leaves against her skin. She stroked them along with the side of her head. "You live on a ship with Captain Fascinosa and First Mate Ginevra and all of these other kind, happy people, and I know they love you."

"You said you can't tell a lie."

"I'm not. I talk to them about you sometimes."

"What do they say? They don't like me, right?"

"No, they do. They like you very much, but sometimes you make them mad. They don't like it when you throw tantrums."

"I know. I don't want to, but no one ever listens to me."

"They will if you talk to them without screaming or pouting. And sometimes they're too busy to talk to you by that doesn't mean they don't care."

Teetee was suddenly so excited that she picked up her head. "I just thought of something! You could live with us! That way you wouldn't have to be jealous of me!"

"I wish I could."

"Then you should! Please, Ngoltur! You could live with us and it would be like I'm your sister!"

Pain shook Ena's heart. It sounded so nice. If they all just took off, would anyone even be able to find them? There'd always be work on the ship for Ena and she'd be surrounded by friends.

She was crying. She came into this room to cheer up a child, and she was crying. "I can't, Teetee. I have to save the world."

"Maybe you can after. After Muttur kills Hultur, you could come back and live with us." It was the most obvious thing in the world to Teetee.

Ena hugged Teetee tight and sobbed.

~ ~ ~

Waking up was hard the next morning. She wasn't sure when Teetee left her room. Ena had slept in fetal position on top of the covers. Her neck thanked her for the bad position with a pain bad enough to dull everything else. She leaned back and stretched, and that's when she saw it.

A love letter. Torno had written her a fucking love letter. She didn't know why she opened this one, but it was open before she even debated the ethics.

Except, this wasn't one of his usual apologies or love confessions. This was a poem. She bit her lip and read.

Rainbows are most beautiful from a distance
Would that you lived among the clouds
Then I wouldn't feel my heart ravaged by haste
Sleepless I beg for reprieve but it beats loud
Were I not in pain I could forget
How you entered my life perfect
Snow and surf
They melt down and pop
They don't hurt
The way your skin blinds
Since then I've lost sight of sense
And dream of a love that never relents
Toss and turn
Nightmares sooner stop

Sprouts from turf
I rise just to find
If your heart beats as loud
Let me grow not in askance
Or like a rose lost in shrouds
Ease these wounds and close this distance

There wasn't a signature, but there could be no doubt as to who it was. It had Torno written all over it. After everything he'd been through, she couldn't believe he had the strength to write her a love poem. Of all the immature things for Torno to try, this was pretty hopeless. It wasn't any good, not really. Okay, it was fine, but he was trying way too hard to win her over. As if a poem would change her mind after everything they'd been through. The first time she refused to talk to him, and he sent her this "anonymous" love poem.

The worst part about it was that if she walked over and talked to him about the poem, the madman would get exactly what he wanted. She'd rejected him at least six times by now and he was still trying. It would be flattering if he wasn't so gross. Torno must've thought Ena was a grand fool to fall for cheap theatrics like this. She read it one or two more times just to make sure he wasn't trying to send her some kind of hidden message.

THE EIGHTEENTH CHAPTER

Where Ngoltur Exposes Herself

C oming to port in Baliku meant Ena's lessons were on pause for the day. Sunrise didn't wake Ena from her slumber and even the sound of some spellcraft only made her toss and turn. Spells sizzled, combatants screamed, and the battle was over before Ena pulled herself out of bed. Laughter and amiable comments marked the end of the danger. Realizing they didn't need her help, she fell back asleep without a second thought.

When she finally did stir again, the entire ship felt different. She jolted upright and scanned the floor for her jacket. Her panic didn't pause when she found it on a wall hook. Producing the wand from a pocket, she finally realized why the ship felt so strange. Endless Grace was anchored.

After having a good chuckle at herself, she read through the love poem again and started her day. It was a sweet silly thing, the love poem. If she got a chuckle or a grin out of reading it, what was the harm? It's not like she was rushing off to Torno's room to tell him how much she loved him back. She would take her time getting back to him, and if the two of them happened to interact she would act like she hadn't even seen the thing. Hopefully, that would teach him to stop trying to woo a woman that had rejected him six times!

Myrrel caught Ena on her way to the ship's shower. She'd picked up a black wig and blue toner. It wouldn't be perfect, but a stranger disguising herself as a Leben would draw less attention than Ngoltur reborn.

"Any luck finding magic-" Ena's own yawn cut herself off.

Myrrel shook her head. "They don't have any books on healing or time magic, and what they do have is in Kest and whatever they speak in Baliku. Qirshod is a beautiful city though. You should check it out."

Ena made a sound. It didn't sound like anything, but her throat vibrated and air came out her nose.

Myrrel chuckled. "But we'll be in port for at least another three hours, so there's no rush if you wanna keep sleeping."

"No, no...I wanna..." She fought a yawn. "I wanna..." It won.

Myrrel gave her a half hug and dropped the disguise in Ena's room.

The glorious Ngoltur, majestic and resplendent in her sleepiness, stumbled her way up to the deck. Myrrel hadn't exagerated, it was a beautiful city.

Spires of gold, bronze, and mythril defined the rooftops. One patch of the city was built with roofs like short, stout bulbs; elsewhere another district was defined by pyramid tops decorated with hanging flourishes and guard rails made of golden flames. Leaning towers supported each other with bridges and string-like ornaments tying them together like an art fixture. Everywhere the eye wandered it found a new bit of architecture to admire. Ena lacked the language to explain what she was seeing and smiled at the city teeming with creative vision.

Even so, the sights were nothing compared to the smells. The second she came on deck, Ena was treated to aromas of juicy meats, smokers, spices for cooking, incense for leisure, perfumes for love, and so much more. Every time she tilted her head another direction she smelled something new and enticing. The buildings and vendors didn't fight for space, they shared it. Looking from the stalls to the open doors, it was a magician's puzzle finding where one ended and the next began.

Qirshod welcomed her with a smile and a plate of tempting meals. So much of what the city offered was small bits of food skewered on sticks. For a gulda she could try any of it. By the time she got to the baths, Ena had tasted scorpion, pufferfish, dragonfly, and something crispy that seemed to be a sweet and salty fish fin. Which was to say nothing of the expertly cooked jeweled beef, tiger chicken, and butter prawn. She didn't know how these vendors came up with these simple eclectic names for their wares, but she couldn't get enough of it. It felt like the city was made especially for her. The second she wanted something starchy, her eyes caught the fluffiest baked potato she'd ever seen, or a conical wrap of spongy bread with a medley of fresh vegetables. Ena easily ate three meals worth of food before she finally found a place to wash herself.

It was the custom of Ki'an people to bathe in large communal baths. Ena had prepared herself for the stareds and unasked questions, but to her delight her search brought her to a welcoming tower with very little foot traffic. Ki'an workers spoke no word of Dorospek and argued a little about accepting gulda until they took a purple and handed Ena three coins of three very different designs. She was sent to ride a turbine lift up to the eighth floor and was greeted by women her own age. They were all very kind to her and one of the women was at least partially Gulambar and able to guide her through the soaps and oils. It was a more intimate bath, built for maybe eight people if they sat shoulder to shoulder. Soaking in the heated bath, Ena spread out and let her thoughts drift away like the lily petals on the water.

Fili, the maroon-skinned stranger who communicated in broken Dorospek, brought Ena out of her revelry with a tap on the shoulder. The tall woman offered to take turns rubbing oils on each other's backs. Ena suspected that she was interested in more than applying oils and made to leave. It wasn't that the woman wasn't beautiful, she was shapely in a way Ena had never seen before, and she had seen very much of it indeed! She simply found the gesture too off-putting given their setting. That sort of thing simply wasn't done in baths; at least not in Gulambar.

After her bath, she ran into Narla and half a dozen crew members. They wandered around for a bit before Narla got the notion of purchasing a luxury tent. It was a good idea, but Ena wasn't sure if she wanted to burn all their gulda so soon after leaving Caredor. Their funds needed to last them the entire trip, and after the cost of the baths, she felt quite the fool for burning so much of it. Besides, their lives could be saved by a purple gulda or two in the future, the same would never be true of gold.

"Hey." Narla was excited and pulling on Ena's arm in a way that she'd only done when she was drinking. "Do me a favor?"

"Sure," Ena was eager to see what had Narla so excited.

She pointed to Visk and Ginevra walking about and looking into baskets. "Play shield for me."

"Huh?"

"Go drag Visk off to do something else. I'm gonna try my charms on the First Mate. You've never heard of playing shield?"

"I never dated or courted, Narla." That blush crept up on her again. Besides which, Visk and Ginevra seemed to be having a lovely time. "Wait, Narla, what if something's going on between the two of them?"

"It's Visk." She chuckled. "Now help me out. Please don't make me beg." She primped her hair and adjusted her cuffs in the mirror of a nearby jewelry store.

"Alright. So how do I do this?"

"We walk together just the four of us, and then when

the moment is right, find an excuse to drag Visk away."

Ena wasn't sure how subtle she would be, but this was Narla. She deserved a little romance. Neither Visk nor Ginevra complained about the company. Ginevra had a relaxed air about her. Between the eyes of the Captain and her crew, she had a lot of coats to wear on the boat. In a more private setting, Ena could understand why Narla was interested. With an even tone and an easy smile, she talked about her life. She'd been born into a life as a tailor in the Squall Ocean. It was her pride that took her away from a simple life weaving textiles and shaping scales. Boasting about her abilities, she gained enough notoriety to grab the attention of petty Squaneld lordlings. Ena was so engrossed in Ginevra's stories that Narla had to kick her heel to get her mind back to the plan.

"Visk, can I pull you away for a bit? There's something personal I'd like to talk to you about."

Narla winced.

Visk didn't notice. "I will have to catch up with you later, Ginevra."

"See you on the ship," the First Mate said casually.

At first, Ena wasn't sure what to talk about, but then she remembered her encounter in the baths. It should've been an easy thing to talk about a little encounter like that, but there was this awkwardness between them. Ena had used a man at a bar to forget about everything and Visk had been there when she came back. She knew what kind of person Ena was. It was a part of herself that Ena would rather not have. Yet, Visk hadn't treated her any differently since they left Caredor. Well, she hadn't treated her with any kind of cruelty. Once Ena started talking, the short and ultimately innocent encounter was easy to tell. The warrior listened to Ena's story with death in her eyes, and then, when she finally understood what happened, she laughed.

"Hey, I'm not from Ki'an. I didn't know that women touched each other in baths. I'm not trying to speak poorly of your people, but I found the entire thing very rude," Ena pouted.

Visk composed herself. "I'm sorry. I did not mean for my laughter to sound so judgmental. I can't imagine a more comical way to enter a brothel."

"What?! No, that can't be. There were oils and soaps."

"Yes, and how were people leaving the baths? By themselves, or in pairs?"

Ena thought back on it. "It's not so strange to go to a bath yourself. I was there by myself." She was blushing so hard that she was starting to feel faint.

Visk only laughed harder.

"You're being very cruel!" Ena exaggerated her outrage.

"I'm sorry, I'm sorry." Visk composed herself. She took one look at Ena, blushing and pouting, and laughed again.

This time Ena joined in. It was funny, but it would definitely be funnier if it hadn't happened to her. "Oh, Torno wrote me again."

"Another love letter?"

"This time a poem." She sighed. "What do you think I should do about it?"

"Fuck him."

Ena stopped moving.

Visk had to physically grab her and pull her away from the flow of traffic. "Are you alright?"

"Are you determined to shock me today?!" She slapped Visk's arm. Her flesh felt solid.

Chuckling, she led Ena forward with her hand on her back. "What would be so bad about having sex with Torno?"

"He's in love with me! He's been in love with me for almost three years."

"Yes, and I imagine that would bring out a great deal of passion."

Ena frowned at her usually cautious friend.

"There is a good chance that many of us will die on this

trip. That Archmage almost killed both of you. We will meet her again, and when we do, I do not know if all of us will survive," Visk mused. "If Torno made love with you before you died, I think it would ease his loss. Can you honestly say the same wouldn't be true for you?"

Ena didn't know what to think. "Why the sudden change of heart, Visk? You always told me that kissing Torno would be a mistake."

"That was when we were Brokers and he was our Captain. If Torno's heart is broken, he might give up on this mission and sail somewhere else. That wouldn't be a bad thing."

Ena nodded. "True."

They could see the ship, so Visk led Ena away from the main flow of traffic. "Women feel a great deal of passion when they battle. There is a heat that comes with killing, and it is well quenched with sex. If something happens, do not apologize. Kiss him. Love him for what short time we may have left."

"But what if we survive, Visk? I can't do that to him. I can't just use him for sex! He'd be devastated!"

Visk was looking at her like only a woman of thirty-one could look at a woman of twenty.

"What?"

Visk looked somber, but whatever thoughts she had, she didn't voice them. Instead, she knelt and embraced the shorter Ena. She hated how she had to crouch down to hug her. It made Ena feel like a child. But at least her arms were warm and her heart was kind. "Listen to your heart, Ena."

"I always have."

"I am returning to the ship now. You?"

Ena shook her head. "I'm gonna wander some more."

Even keeping a tight knot on her purse, Ena had a pleasant time wandering the streets of Qirshod. A seller of crystals and herbs grabbed her attention. Stepping against the stall, she closed her eyes and took in the scents. She couldn't name the fragrances, but there was something familiar and sensual in the air. It reminded her of stolen dreams.

A strange thing happened. One of the bodies broke from the crowd. Ena felt it. She knew it was happening, but she didn't act on it. Though the moment was maybe a second long, it was long enough for her to feel the danger and deny that impulse inside. She might be powerful, but she couldn't feel when people were coming for her.

Yet a hand reached out from the crowd and gripped her.

THE NINETEENTH CHAPTER

In Which Ngoltur Battles Silence

When a hand touched her shoulder, an ounce of Narla's training kicked in. Ena reeled about, spinning her arm to try and break the grip. Shock, fear, and anger all bloomed in her heart, but habit brought an orb of cold into a single clawed hand. The assailant was taller than her; most people were. But this man was marineld, well dressed, and responded immediately to the threat. Hands raised in deference, Captain Fascinosa gave an apologetic smile.

It was Ena that apologized. "Sorry. I guess all of my training is working."

"I should've known better than to sneak up on you like that," he chuckled. "Are you busy? Was I interrupting-"

She answered with a smile and shook her head. "What were you doing?"

"I'm on a vital quest that requires your assistance," he said with vibrato.

Giggling, she said, "Okay."

"Will you help me pick out a gift?"

She shrugged and walked into the flow of traffic. "Sure. Who's it for?"

He walked about her to stay between her and the main thrust of foot traffic. "That I cannot say. Us Captains take pride in cultivating an air of mystery."

"And exiled Princes twice as much."

"Ah, you know a little about this."

"I happen to be the exiled offspring of a monarch."

"That's right. I won't be so crass as to try and pry the secrets out of you."

"How proper."

"We are monarchs. If we do not work to be noble, nobility becomes us."

Chuckling, she grumbled out. "Somehow I don't think that's the thing I'm becoming."

"Hmm? Is that the whiff of a secret I smell in the air?"

She chuckled. "Only my apprehensions. I don't know if anyone's told you this, but I'm by nature a fearful person."

"You?" He scoffed. "Not true. Without your bravery, I would be a pile of crispy meat picked over by the bottom feeders of Sapphire Cove."

"That's quite the image."

"It's your image that stays with me. I haven't forgotten the sight of you casting with both hands while your skin still smoked."

"Listen, you seem to have the wrong impression of me." She said more jovial than she expected to. "I'm not some heroic exiled Princess righting wrongs wherever she sails."

"Then tell me about you. Who have I agreed to transport?"

"Okay, well, first of all, I'm a mess. Everything from haircare to fashion is a mystery to me. I'm not even a monarch, not really. I was a Princess for one day before my parents signed away my claim to the throne."

"A technicality."

"Hardly! It's the technicality that makes me a Princess. Okay, you want to know how awkward I am?"

"I'll hold my breath until you do," he said with a warm smile.

"I tried to find a bathhouse. I saw people coming out of

this place with damp hair and so I went in. Two people were trying to push me out and tell me that I wasn't in the right place, but I kept on pushing money in their hands until they took it. Even after a woman offered to rub oils on my body I didn't figure out that I was in a brothel."

He laughed.

"I was so busy thinking like a woman of Caredor, that I didn't think about how strange it was for a woman to offer themselves to me. I had to have Visk tell me that I was in a brothel. That is not the kind of woman that should run a nation."

He ended his laughter with a sigh. "Being a monarch has nothing to do with that."

"And why's that?"

"I actually had a similar experience happen to me."

"Really?" she found herself blushing, but Ena was sure the flush was from recounting her own embarrassment.

"It was a casino. They don't have them in Caredor, right?"

"I'm aware of the basic construction of a casino. I've read about them in books."

"They teach exiled Princesses about casinos?"

"With lots of pretty pictures."

He chuckled. "Alright, so I was on the main gambling floor. The staff were all visions of beauty. I couldn't believe my eyes. They wore these really saucy numbers, things that just made you bug your eyes out and pat down your crotch."

"Can't relate."

"I'd hit a rough patch in my life. Bad breakup. I was feeling like the worst catch in a haul, but one of the men was giving me eyes. He'd stroke my finger while I took his drinks. So I did what everyone else was doing, I tipped him."

"Oh no," she said chuckling, knowing where this was going.

"Oh yes. All of the staff were prostitutes. I'd basically paid for sex three times over. So he stuck by me and kept getting more touchy. By the time he got me away from the gambling table, I was ready to go. So here I was, feeling down on myself, thinking that this was something it wasn't, and I brought him into the bathroom. We fucked in the stall when I had paid enough to sleep in a full bed."

Ena tried not to laugh. "I am...sorry that happened to you."

"You don't sound sorry."

"I'm not that sorry," she laughed.

"That was without a dought, the most expensive bathroom romp I've ever had."

"You've had a lot of bathroom romps?" she arched an eyebrow.

"Passion has a way of demanding immediacy."

Ena thought back on her walk back with Ve'an to his house. It had been a strange walk and one with far too many awkward pauses. Maybe things would've been easier if they had invaded a bathroom.

"Royal secrets?" he asked, leaning his face down.

"Yes, and they are mine."

"Fair," he said raising his hands. He pointed not just with his hand, but with his whole body. "A wand shop!"

"You're looking for a wand?"

"Do you think that makes for a bad gift?"

"For a caster?" She shook her head.

He took her hand and led her forward. "Come! Swim like a marineld, through the crowd."

It was less of a swim and more of a clash of limbs, but Ena got there.

Ena hadn't spent a lot of time in wand shops, but this one was surprisingly high quality. Each of the wands on display had sanded edges and expertly cut gemstones. Signs in Dorospek accompanied the labels in Ki'an script.

Fascinosa knelt down to whisper in her ear. "Should we try somewhere else?"

"Only if you're trying to save some coin," she muttered.

"These are beautiful."

"Excellent." Popping up, Fascinosa said something to the vendor.

The marooned-skinned man bowed his head in appreciation. He was so much taller than Fascinosa, but looked more docile than Merryl. Ki'an men were raised to be intellectual crafters. Ena thought about how Hultur's own attire hid his massive arms and solid chest.

"Can you ask him if I can touch them?" Ena said to Fascinosa.

"Feel free," said the vendor.

"You know Dorospek!"

"As my first tongue," he said with a bow. "Feel free to ask me any questions. Many of these are acquisitions from Doronel traders."

Ena was certain that they were more than likely the ill-gotten gains from pirates, but there was no point trying to question his sincerity. She moved from one wand to the next, trying to feel the elemental resonance within. Wands were a personal purchase. It made buying for someone else a difficult matter. Torno had purchased an ice wand for her because he knew her. He knew that she held back her power and so an amplifying hilt would be better suited than a strong core.

"Any winners?" Fascinosa asked.

"Huh?" She forced a smile. "They're all lovely. You can't tell me anything about the recipient?"

With a thoughtful smirk, he told her, "I think the gesture will be worth more than the item."

She gave some thought about who the recipient might be. His first mate Ginevra wasn't a caster and Teetee was too young to receive something like this. Besides, Ena knew her birthday was nearly half a year away. No, Ena was wasting her time considering marinelds. Wands were a gift given to Gulam.

There was a Gulam on the Endless Grace. She was

a plump beauty with the cutest dimples. Her name was Corina. Ena had a few conversations with her. She spoke with a Duan Si accent that reminded her of her time as a Broker. Corina was clearly interested in the Captain. Ena thought about how strange it was that a monarch would consider a lover that wouldn't produce an heir. Then again, this was a very expensive wand shop. Maybe this was more than a simple birthday gift, but something closer to a confession of love.

"Anything catching your eye?" asked the vendor.

Ena glanced over to dismiss him and saw three deathstaffs behind the counter. "Are those for sale?" she asked.

"Of course." He took them off the rack one at a time and laid them on the counter before him.

Ena didn't need to see all of them. The one in the middle with the red core was finer by far. The others were models used by academics or maybe even holdovers from the democratic revolution. The deathstaff that caught her eye was ornate and surrounded in bone or marble. Touching it, she was sure it was covered in whalebone. This would've been the treasure of some young lordling or Senator's offspring. The treasure had a phoenix engraved all the way to the core. A caster could touch skin to the core and channel a great deal of energy through it.

"This one?" Fascinosa asked.

Ena kept fingering it. The deathstaff was attuned to fire. She didn't know if Corina was a fire user, but out on the high seas, it would serve her well. She looked to Fascinosa and nodded. "This is it."

Fascinosa and the seller haggled, but only enough to go through the motions. He wasn't concerned with the cost, only that the gift would be well received. Whenever he looked to Ena with doubt, she nodded, assuring him that this was a treasure any caster would adore.

The trip back to Endless Grace was slow. Captain

Fascinosa seemed to be dragging his feet. When she asked him about it, he said he didn't want to leave Qirshod. They couldn't stay, though. Caredor ships might be on their trail, and even if they weren't, Kalta had probably issued a bounty for Torno.

It bothered Ena that Visk was so certain they would encounter Archmage Kalta again. The woman had torn apart her defenses and outclassed her. Ena had never seen spells that could appear so far from the caster without warning. There was still so much she didn't understand about magic.

"I wanted to thank you for looking after Teetee," the Captain said as they approached the new gangplank.

Ena shook her head. "It isn't a chore to me, really. I like her."

"That's precisely why I wanted to thank you. Teetee adores you. I could tell right away that she'd chosen you as a role model. I was sure she'd get hurt or that you'd yell at her. Most people don't like being around children."

Ena guffawed. "What? Who doesn't love kids?"

"Sailors."

They shared a chuckle.

Captain Fascinosa took off his hat with a wave and a bow. "Thank you for the company."

Ena chuckled. "It was a pleasure." She left before he righted himself, eager to get back to her room and think about all of the magic she and Narla's Corps hadn't been able to figure out.

~ ~ ~

Torno was getting better and, as much as Ena hated to admit it, he was helping out. First and foremost, he remembered the basics of healing magic. While Myrrel had learned through brute force, the rise of the academy formalized many mnemonic devices, including songs to go along with the gibberish of incantations. After that, Ena's healing magic lessons included Torno, but thankfully Myrrel stayed in the room with them. The three of them spent so much time singing basic healing incantations that they became earworms for the crew. While some knew the lyrics of old Doronel songs, many didn't. This culminated in the entire mess singing the incantation of decreased blood flow like it was a sea shanty, with plenty of liquor helping to slow their heart rate.

All Ena did was mention glyphs to Hultur and he switched his lessons over to teaching her about glyphspek.

In ancient times, when writing was first finding its way, most magic was performed through glyphs. Casters would spend hours or even days drawing large, artistic circles in the dirt. Glyphspek was developed as a way to keep track of what changes each line or curve did to a spell, but magicians soon found that by speaking the words aloud they could create the same effect as drawing the circle. In time, they switched to reciting incantations in glyphspek while they pictured the circles as glyphs. Some were able to be simplified, but others, the high magicks, were not.

While it was interesting for Ena to learn that the gibberish came from an old, forgotten language, it wasn't helping her learn magic any faster.

In Gulambar, high magic was mastered through the art of compression. Once Ena learned the three-minute song that was the incantation for decreased blood flow, she had to go through the incantation in a slow, deliberate manner. Through use of electric sense spells, Myrrel identified which parts of her brain became active while reciting the incantation. Myrrel used spells to alter Ena's brain while she talked her through a guided meditation. Within twenty minutes the incantation was compressed down into a single phrase with a corresponding image. One compression enabled another until Ena had an entire page of a spellbook compressed down into a single sentence. It was a slow exacting process that devoured her leisure time.

Compression was also the reason that Myrrel wasn't

able to help Ena get through the basics. She remembered an entire page of information as one word and working backwards was almost impossible, despite the fact that her brain actually flashed through all of the same parts when she spoke that single word. Incantations for intermediate spells were full of phrases that were in truth lesser spells compressed. So, even though Myrrel had an entire spell book of intermediate and a few advanced spells, they'd needed Torno there to recite the basic healing spells.

It was weird spending time with him without him telling her what to do or confessing his undying love for her. It was actually kind of nice. As a teacher, he was patient and knew when to talk slowly and when to shut up. Which was strange because the man so rarely kept his lips shut when he was their Captain. Still, Torno found a way to remind Ena that he was in love with her.

Torno never said it in words, but he would light up whenever she got excited or stare at her whenever she was trying to concentrate. The only saving grace was that he never brought up the love poem. Even though he was still trying to trick her into loving him, he actually had the tact to let her focus on her lessons.

Soon, Torno was walking about the ship. Myrrel was with him the entire time, but he all but ignored her. Torno wasn't a subtle man. Every time Ena looked at him, he was there looking right back at her. Something about his looks told her that he wanted to talk. So after dinner, Ena climbed the sails with Teetee until they passed out. In the end, she still got a love confession; from Teetee. Though those three words were spoken in sororal love. Ena stayed on the deck with her after that, just staring up at the stars and making up constellations.

Still, Torno had to find a way to ruin things. He sent her another love poem that very night. This one might've been more obvious than the first.

Yesterday

I thought I may
Tell you how you take my breath away

But today
To my dismay
My demonstration proved far too effective

Selective, I was
In picking, a love
That I knew would last a thousand sunsets

Protective, I doth
Observe in, your trust
But I beg that you give me the chance to earn it

Shallow you might think me
For praising your beauty
But know that my soul is smitten too

Kindness and courage are rarely found in earnest
Nor mercy and candor so abundant in their splendor
I find your presence more dazzling than moonlit snow
Forgive me for lacking the wit to express you so

If I could I'd kiss you
If I knew you I would lift you
Away from this dark world unfit for your grace

Tomorrow I might tell you
How sunlight makes you capable
of turning all my fantasies into foundations

If I do, don't dismay
It's just my way
To speak of beauty when my heart, mind, and soul
        are   far   far   away

With a word you can bring me back
With a touch, to a place of trust and promise
But know that I am willing, waiting, and able
To love a woman that makes me a fool today.

He was a fool every day, why would today be any different? She couldn't make sense of these poems. The first one he'd written to try to get her to talk to him. She got that. But this? It had to be his little passive-aggressive way of getting back at her for ignoring him. These poems were childish. Real men just walked up and admitted their feelings. Torno used to believe that. But maybe this was a side of Torno, too.

After all, he'd written love poems for Kalta, but considering how that turned out, Ena wasn't sure if she should be flattered. There was a small chance he was actually writing these poems because he was thinking about Kalta. Come to think of it, he'd gotten work as a Broker Captain a little after his breakup with Kalta. Well, after his disappearance. The great goss had put Torno in the Far Lands in the months following the airing of his infidelity, but Ena doubted that trip was anything more than examining brothels and bars.

The man was a lecher and a liar, but there she was, lying in bed thinking about him!

Once again, Ena was thinking about Torno instead of focusing on her studies or any of the other men on the ship. He had to know Norden was crushing on her. Maybe this little ploy was a jealous little fit, a desperate attempt to get her to think about him while refusing to get with anyone else. Ena wasn't going to fall for that. She needed to get better at battle magic. She didn't have time to worry about romance.

Ena hung up the rose that came with the love poem and froze it. She put it up on the wall so that anytime he'd walk by he'd know just how cold she could be. That put a smile on her face. She read through the poems, thinking about all the things she would tell him when he finally had the courage to try confessing again in person.

The next day, she didn't even look at him. She didn't look at anyone else, either. Ginevra paired her up with Corina, Captain Fascinosa's crush, for swordplay. And even though Ena scored a couple of good hits, she couldn't get the win. Corina had a wonderful time at Qirshod, but hadn't received any gifts. Maybe the Captain was waiting for a birthday, or for the two of them to have extended shore leave. There was also the possibility that Captain Fascinosa was shy. As a Captain and a friend, he was loud and bombastic, but maybe love was something he had trouble with. He'd mentioned that someone broke his heart, but how long ago was that? Ena wanted to ask Ginevra about him, but she wasn't exactly a sociable person.

The night after their trip to Qirshod, Narla made her move. Ginevra rejected her offer outright. No real explanations were given, just a simple, "I'm not interested." Commander Narla said it was good to feel the sting of rejection and laughed it off. She wore that brave face well, but Ena smelled liquor on her breath when they went through the day's nerve training. Ena kept giving her opportunities to talk about it, but she stayed silent.

It seemed like the only person in Ena's life that didn't keep quiet was Torno. Another ninety minutes of healing training went well. He was respectful, patient, and best of all quiet. He was so quiet that there were times that Ena even forgot he was in the room. She stood, thanked them for the help, left. Torno the Daft followed her out of the room and then all the way up to the deck.

"Ena, can we chat?"

"I don't really have any time. I have to study with Vamere." They'd been using Hultur's fake name for the crew of Endless Grace.

"I asked him if I could talk to you instead, and he didn't have any objection." He did that annoying thing where he walked in front of her. "And Narla okayed it too. We need to talk."

Ena turned around and walked back down the stairs. "Fine, let's break up. You and I are no longer a thing. Can you leave me alone now?"

Torno chuckled. "Cute. Didn't see that coming, especially not from you."

"Maybe I'm taking a page from your book and doing things preemptively. I guess if I'm really emulating you I should be talking to you in poetics." She raised her nose up and spoke in an austere, mocking tone. "In fairness, you are silenced. With my exit, we are balanced."

"Hey." Torno ran up to grab her elbow. "Hey!"

Mad as he was, Ena's glower still made him release her. She'd give him plenty to be mad about if he tried doing something like that again.

"That is not fair and it's not funny. I don't write poems. I never have, and I never will!"

Ena had no idea why he would lie about something that everyone knew was false. But he was serious enough for her to believe it. Maybe that was how liars convinced so many people because they were so good at tricking themselves.

Torno sighed to calm himself. "I'm sorry. I shouldn't have...Why are you so mad at me anyway?"

"Because I don't want to talk to you, Torno. Because we had a system that was working and even though you're not in charge anymore, you still managed to displace that system just to satisfy your petty desires."

"Hul-" Torno pinched the bridge of his nose while he tried to remember Hultur's alias.

"Vamere."

"Vamere said that your lessons were going nowhere. That's one of the things I need to talk to you about, Ena. I'm from the capital. I know that makes me a puffed up pile of shit unworthy to kiss your cheek, but it also means that I have the training that you have been trying to emulate. I was trained to create nodes. I was taught techniques to compress multiple high magicks. I had to learn healing, time, imbuing, empathy, and conjuring all at the same time." He listed them off on his fingers. He apparently had more achievements to boast about, but Ena didn't let him finish.

"Well, that's great for you, oh, master of magic, but some of us had to make do with our simple upbringing!" She walked around him to get to her room.

His suppressed scream came out as a groan through his teeth. Ena was at her door when he finally found the words to stop her. His delivery was somber, but a hint of desperation betrayed his true feelings. "I don't blame you."

It worked. He got her to pause at her opened door.

"For the dock...for what happened with the Archmage and what happened to me...I don't blame you. I'm not mad at you now and I wasn't mad at you then. I was just trying to tell you how to fight them, I swear."

"No, you weren't." She slammed the door and walked up to yell at Scruffy Face. "No, you fucking weren't! Not only were you ordering me around, you were chiding me! Once again, I wasn't doing what you wanted me to do and it almost got you killed. You..." She hadn't meant to say that. She was planning to say something else entirely. Her lip quivered. Her cheeks were hot.

Torno reached out to her, that fucking look of pity on his arrogant face. "Ena..."

She slapped his hand away. "I told you not to touch me! I told you so many fucking times! But you never listen to me! You say that you love me but you don't give a fuck what I have to say or why I say it! You want to come over here and tell me that it's not my fault so you can be this big hero that takes away my pain? Well, fuck you! I've had it with your lies!

"I know I fucked up! I know everything that happened,

happened because I wasn't strong enough! They won't say it. They try to blame themselves and make it seem like it's only natural to blame yourself when something goes wrong, but they're not the same as me. None of you have the responsibility of the entire world on your shoulders. When one of us dies, it's not gonna be because Myrrel didn't learn an obscure healing spell or because Sal had a really bad day. When someone dies, it's going to be because of me. And you of all fucking people should know that I deserve to feel like shit when I fuck up!

"So don't you fucking lie to me about whose fault it is!"

Tears were rolling down her cheeks in rivers. SheHarsh breaths shook her chest, but she wouldn't give in to the sobs that needed to come out. Torno, clammy and shocked, looked past her. Sal, Narla, Myrrel, and Visk were all standing in the hallway. They were staring at her with pity.

"Fuck." She ran into her room and slammed the door closed.

THE TWENTIETH CHAPTER

Where Ngoltur Chooses Solitude

With all the power of Ngoltur, Ena couldn't be dragged out to face her shame. Her friends didn't even try. They let her stay in her room and sulk. The brooding didn't help and neither did the sobs. She hadn't meant for her words to come out as they had, but they were honest. This journey was Ena and Hultur's.

When a few hours had passed and she'd finished chewing on her guilt, she found them all chatting in the mess. They were worried about her; every one of them. Narla talked about adjusting her schedule, but that only felt like a defeat. The schedule was one of the only things keeping her together. Sure, the training had been grueling at first, but she was finally starting to get a handle on things. Even with the threat of Torno teaching her something, Ena wasn't afraid of the additional lesson. Knowledge and physical challenges were things that she could handle. It was everything inside that terrified her.

One of the biggest problems with Ena's big speech about blame was that she wasn't in any position to tell Sal that he hadn't failed. His job was to help Ena manage her stress and he was the first and last to admit that he wasn't doing his job. But instead of falling into one of his downward spirals, he gave a somber, if overly formal, apology. Sal requested a reprieve from his responsibilities and vowed to come back with a real plan to help Ena manage her stress. In the interim, Torno would be taking over his time slot, but not his task.

Instead, Torno was going to take Ena through weapons training. The idea sounded foolish to Ena, but she was hardly in a position to argue. Ena had wronged them. No matter how many times she apologized, despite all of the sensible things her friends told her, nothing made her feel any better.

She didn't sleep that night.

Neither the rise of the sun nor the sound of footsteps gave her the motivation to get up. The promise of an hour or two of sleep kept her in bed, but a tightness in her chest made that impossible. Torn between a need to sleep and a futile desire to conceptualize a solution, time dragged on.

Norden ended up being the first to knock at her door. Commander Narla shooed him off, saying, "Give her some space."

Space wouldn't change anything. Neither would time. Ena needed to wake up and act like the hero they thought she was. Sympathetic eyes and lulled tones welcomed her. She tried to smile and play off her embarrassment, but those looks of sympathy were omnipresent.

It was bad enough getting the soft touch from her friends, but everyone on Endless Grace knew what had happened. Between stretches and bouts, crewmembers offered condolences and solutions. Norden the Navigator took on forced casual airs while he happened to mention how reading and journaling helped to clear his head. Others were more direct, and offered to join her quest in the hopes that additional support might relieve some pressure. First Mate Ginevra, though still brusque and impersonal, offered to slow down their trip with additional shore leave.

Thoughts of Kalta catching up gave Ena's head a vigorous shake.

At least Captain Fascinosa tried a different tactic. He acted like nothing had happened and went out of his way to join her for lunch. She tried to imagine his stories working as a musician under the employment of a Ki'an pain merchant, but her own pain was too distracting.

Training with Torno came without ceremony. The handsome bastard waited on deck with a stoicism so unlike him that it woke up Ena's survival instincts. He was just waiting on deck in his old Broker's outfit. The Magus' blood still stained the sleeves.

"Why the fuck are you wearing that?" Ena asked.

"Name every weapon and explain why magicians need them." He was stiffer than Commander Narla.

"Umm..." His attitude caught her off guard. Ena swallowed. "We don't. Magic comes from inside. Weapons change how we interact with the world."

Torno turned about to leer at her response. "Then all Mages are fools? When the Archmage reached for a staff she was wasting her time. Do you think she should've continued her attack?"

"I didn't say that. Kalta switched to a staff because she wanted to cast different spells. It obviously worked, since she burnt most of my hair and skin off."

Torno gave her the strangest look. A mixture of confusion and doubt pinched his eyes. For a moment, it was like he was seeing her for the first time. Something she said made him reconsider who she was, but it all seemed innocuous to her.

Ena answered his question; anything to get away from that look. "Rings, amulets, and bracelets are for close range. Wands, staffs, and deathstaffs are used for long range."

"What?" A flabbergasted Torno shook his head. "No. I mean, kind of." Then he was back to being Instructor Hardass. "Tell me what magical weapons do. How do they help magicians?"

"Rings loosen the ether-net around the user, making it

easier to gesticulate some effects.

"Wands take a spell and fling them forward so the effect won't weaken over the distance.

"Staffs make the surrounding ether-net resonate, magnifying your ether output instead of easing the effort it takes to cast.

"Deathstaffs are like wands except they use the effect of a staff to power up a spell.

"Bracelets manipulate ongoing effects.

"Amulets...pinch ether?" She shrugged.

Torno blinked. Once again his hardass composure slipped. "Pinch?" He thought about that definition. It wasn't exactly wrong.

Ena furrowed her brow. "It focuses like a magnifying glass, concentrating a magical effect into a single point of power."

"Why didn't you mention spellbooks and scrolls?"

"Because no one uses them anymore."

"Why not?"

"They're too slow."

"And what do they do?"

"Seriously, Torno? Magical scrolls? I thought you were going to teach me how to use weapons, not waste my time with pure theory." She was in his face again. Amazing how fast he dragged that anger out of her.

"At this point I'd be happy if-" He stepped back and sighed. "You're my student, Ena. This isn't going to work if you spend the entire time questioning my methods."

"Fine! No one uses scrolls because they're useless," she snapped.

"Useless isn't descriptive," he snapped back. "Tell me why scrolls are useless. Talk to me like I've never used magic."

"It's a picture on a piece of paper. It's slow. It's situational. You have to unroll the scroll and lay it on the ground or surface of intent before you can even start casting."

"Good." Torno sighed, remembering that he was supposed to be composed. "Good."

"This isn't going to work," Ena muttered.

"What weapon should you be using?"

She didn't have an answer. She didn't even know if any were better to use with time magic. "Wands?"

Torno shook his head. "Rings. Right now you're relying on your hands too much to use anything else."

"Oh, real mature."

"Yesterday, you yelled at me for trying to comfort you. Now you're mad at me for calling out your behavior in an actual fight. Narla said you've gotten better at reacting to threats, but you have to play to your strengths and your weaknesses. We only have ten to fifteen days before we reach Leben Erde. After that, it could be a day before we run into Archmage Kalta again."

"If we do, we'll run."

"And what are we going to do about Hultur?" he shouted. "Have you ever considered that?"

Ena looked to the crew of Endless Grace listening in on her training. *Was that question for their benefit or did he actually not trust Hultur?*

She shook her head. "What does it matter? He'll capture me and propose to me everyday until Muttur saves me. Good thing I have so much experience turning the same man down."

Torno ran his hands over his face. He laughed at nothing as if gripped by a spirit and then clapped his hands and steadied. "You're going to train with rings. You're going to relearn all of the gestures of high magic with them on, and then you're going to learn stronger evocations for everything else."

"We don't have time for that."

"You think I don't know that?" he snapped back. "We don't have a lot of options and you're too busy reminding me why you hate me to listen to any of my ideas."

"Fine, what are your ideas?"

Torno rolled his eyes.

"I'm serious. I want to know. Unless this is another one of your secret plans. Which, by the way, you don't need to do. Everyone knows you don't know how to lead."

Some of the crew giggled. Ena and Torno bent their necks to leer at the gawkers. Suddenly the crew's work on the sails was a matter of life and death, despite a horrizon free of storm clouds.

Torno was the first to jump back into it. "You need to master every weapon. Beyond that, you need to learn how to drift, snap-cast, split, pop, and bleed."

"I'm not going to bleed my spells," she scoffed. "And what's a pop?"

"Popping is when you throw a spell deep into the ethereal net and let it take shape without your guidance."

"You're talking about what Kalta did! Can you really teach me how to do that?"

"I've never learned how to do it myself, but I did learn how to defend against it. That's why she didn't bother using it against me."

That was the closest he'd ever come to admitting that he knew who Kalta was. If he could teach her how to defend against a popped spell they might actually have a chance against her. "Alright, so what's drifting?"

"Drifting is basically fighting blindfolded. You drift from one spell to the next." With a pause, he frowned at something he saw in Ena's eyes, and jumped into a explaination of everything else.

"Snap-casting is where you over-cast an effect, but you put it all into a single moment. By shoving a bunch of ether into a spell in a single moment, you create what's called net-drag. It casts the spell at a delay. The idea is that a snap-cast can overwhelm a target's defenses by being able to hit them from multiple angles at the same time.

"Splitting is-"

"I know what splitting is." Anyone who'd ever seen a Mage split a wand cast into several strands knew what splitting was. She didn't see the point of snap-casting if she could split.

"That's the plan. Alright, Precious? You want to know what we're doing, we're doing all of that. I need to attune you to rings so that you can break the habit of casting everything by hand. I need to bulk up your low magic to keep your rhythm consistent when you switch from high magic to innate. I don't care what you think, you're going to bleed your spells. Believe it or not, Ena, I actually know what I'm talking about."

More chuckles, and more turned heads when Ena and Torno looked to find the source.

"Says the man telling me to bleed ether." Bleeding was what happened when children started to use magical weapons, but then they stopped holding onto the effect. Without proper guidance, all spells would be powered only by their personal ether. It was a large part of why untrained practitioners cast spells that were so weak, because most of their power bled into the ether-net.

Torno brought a fist to his brow and sighed. "Do you remember what happened when you used the deathstaff?"

Ena pointed to scars on her hands and arm.

"That's why you need to bleed. Without bleeding, your power output will destroy every single weapon you use. You're going to have to unlearn proper casting and learn a whole bunch of advanced techniques. No one in the world would be able to fight like that, but you don't have a choice."

Ena thought back on their escape from Caredor, when she made that massive glacier. "Wait, bleeding was Narla's idea!"

Torno nodded. "We wanted to discuss magical strategy with you, but we couldn't because you hate my guts."

The seagulls chuckled again.

"Fine, I'll admit it, you have a decent plan. But this is too much. How am I supposed to learn all of this in a week or two?"

"Maybe your mystic destiny will activate and you'll just start mastering everything the second I teach it to you." He shrugged. "Until then, we get to work and see what we can accomplish."

Ena was done trying to fight him. As much as he might make her blood boil, he actually did know a little bit about magic. These were the kind of advanced techniques she should've been learning from the beginning.

Learning how to bleed her spells was like learning how to walk backwards while standing on top of her shoes. It went against every instinct she had as a caster, but it was something small she could do while going about her day. The problem was that Torno was also making her relearn gestures and postures. So she'd have to go through the motion of three-step hand positions while holding onto the cast before she could bleed. It was a hassle, but at least she could practice it on her own.

That same day, Hultur was optimistic to start his lessons. It put Ena at ease until she saw that creepy white smile. He wasn't waiting with clay for sculpting or parchment for glyph work. They were finally going to work with magic, or so Ena thought. Instead, Hultur led her down to storage. A full-sized loom was bolted into the floorboards beside a few barrels of fresh thread. Gesturing at the machine, he regarded her with that too big smile of his.

"You've got to be kidding me," Ena grumbled.

"You're going to make a rug with the time glyph stitched into it."

"Fuck. You."

Hultur laughed, but he wasn't joking. He was seriously going to make her construct an entire rug instead of teaching her how to defend herself, and he wouldn't be talked out of it. Ena had it. She called in a big meeting with the Commander and all the Corps, but he wouldn't relent. He insisted that this was the only way she was going to learn how to create a sphere of pure ethereal energy, and he got his way. Lessons with Hultur had Ena working on a loom while he burried his nose in books and wrote in his journal.

~ ~ ~

A few days into the new routine, they had another stop at a port city, Situ. It was the last one before the final trip to Leben Erde, so they went all out. Captain Fascinosa gave them all a day and night of shoreleave. People could visit brothels, get pass-out drunk, or sleep in a bed of down. Ena didn't do any of it. She was in too foul a mood to drink, party, or fuck. After she'd taken a hot bath in view of a hundred Ki'an eyes, she snuck back onto the ship to be alone.

She spent the night going through all of her training, and when she'd sweated too much to think, she worked on that damn loom. The simple repetitive motion with slight changes helped her zone out, and that led her to reflect on her past. She hated reflection. It was one of the things she loved about the busy seasons as a Broker. The work never stopped, so her memories could never start. But that was back when Ena believed she was a victim of her upbringing, that deep down inside she was actually a good person.

Ena didn't entertain those delusions anymore. She used people and hated them for never being able to give enough. Torno was like that. He used Kalta and then went around the world to drink whatever didn't kill him and fuck whatever didn't scorn him. He was nineteen when he was caught cheating on Kalta. Ena was twenty when she met that man at a bar. Maybe she hated Torno because he was a reflection of what she really was.

If the Gods were kind, they would've let Ena fall into a routine of training to get past these thoughts. Instead, the ship left Situ and entered a storm.

THE TWENTY-FIRST CHAPTER

In Which Ngoltur Resists Reflection

Seasoned sailors saw the storm coming even when the sky was pristine blue. Favorable winds were pushing them away from Situ and the continent of Ki'an. Puffs of white came in with a haze and then on the second day out, the morning fog only got thicker. When the first drops of rain fell, they came down fat and thick and showed no sign of letting up. Narla, stern and relentless, continued the lesson for the time she had. Ena couldn't hear Narla. Without a flow of ether, she couldn't sense her, and Narla pelted Ena's body with bruises. After lunch, Narla's corps were told to avoid the deck.

Training in the mess meant that most of the crew could hear all of Ena's failures. It meant that she didn't have anywhere to hide from Torno. It also meant that Visk's sea sickness was taking Myrrel's attention. Ena spent her time with the healer trying to pick up hydration spells. Torno invened in that annoying helpful way that gave her no reasonable excuse to be angry at him, but eventually the sound of his singing was too much. Pushed past the point of patience, she panicked and pushed past onlookers to retreat to the loom.

Hultur wasn't there. No one was. It gave Ena a reprieve

from the eyes of the crew and all of Torno's well-meaning
condescensions. Things were simpler with the loom. Even
with the erratic shaking of the boat in the storm, she could
shut her mind off and focus on the shifting threads.

"Are you okay?" asked Sal.

"Fine," she snapped. Sighing, she looked back at Sal to
apologize.

Her old friend seemed to see the words on her face and
waved them away. "I'm not here as...Whatever I'm supposed
to be doing. I just wanted to talk to you as a friend."

"You mind if I keep working?" she asked.

"Go ahead."

She did, falling into the rhythm as she traced the
design of the time circle drawn down on map parchment.
It was a huge design and unbelievably complex. This was
the kind of spell casters used scrolls for because it was too
much to remember. That had been her first impression. Now
that she was closer to done than not, each individual glyph
fit like a children's puzzle. She understood how the glyphs
controlled the space of the effect or enhanced the intensity
of the haste spell. The entire spell was taking on a new
meaning to her, being something intuitive.

"I know that you and Torno haven't always got
along..."

"Because I can't," she muttered.

"What do you mean by that?"

She sighed. "I do try to get along with him, you know?
I do so much to put things behind us and just coexist with
him, but he's always pushing me. He thinks..." She sighed
again. "You know about his confessions, right?"

Sal chuckled. "I don't think there were any secrets in
that wagon of ours."

"So he's talked to you about it."

Sal didn't confirm this. It didn't really matter if Torno
told Sal. He could've heard it from Myrrel or Visk. Narla
probably knew about Torno's obsession with her too. He

wasn't a subtle person. Except, apparently, when he was planning revolutions.

"I know that he means good, Sal. I know that he's your best friend, but he doesn't listen to me."

"Is that what happened right now?"

"No," she admitted. "I guess I don't like being cramped up down below deck. Fuck this storm."

"It's not all bad."

"What do you mean?"

"When things get truly difficult, they can tie me to the hull and use me as an anchor."

"Sal..."

"At least then I'll have a use on this ship."

Ena didn't know what to say to that. It was impossible to talk him out of his pity parades. She thought he was getting better. Maybe he was, but now he didn't have anything to do. He hadn't been helping Ena manage her stress and she wasn't managing it herself.

"Sorry," he said.

"I wish you wouldn't talk about yourself like that. We need you, Sal."

"I'm not building homes and fixing wagons," he said with a chuckle. "That fight with the Archmage was scary. If I wasn't hiding on the ship, one geomancy shot could've killed me."

Ena's mind put an image to those words. His rocky exterior cracked off like an egg shell, the loamy soil underneath innert, and the crystaline core of his heart glistening like a glass thrown to the floor.

"That probably isn't helping you manage your stress."

She chuckled away the sting of tears starting to well up. "You think?"

"Ugh! Lemme try again."

"No problem, big guy."

"How are you?" he asked.

"Annoyed." She shook her head. "Frustrated, I guess. I

want to just be able to work. I wish I was on deck right now. I want to be up there to practice my balance. Visk thought it would make it easier for me to manage Ki'an dance magic."

"So, do it."

"They told us to stay below deck."

"Yeah, but you're Ngoltur reborn. The crew loves you, Ena. They'd let you get away with murder."

"You're doing a really poor job of talking me out of killing Torno."

He laughed. "Well, he's not that good of a friend."

She joined him in laughter until the thought of him lying unconscious in bed returned. "I do...care about him. I know that he doesn't try to be difficult. He's just a capital fuck boy."

Sal didn't answer that. When Ena looked back to get a sense of his emotions, the rock-man shrugged or raised his brows. The gesture was identical on his compact frame.

"I'll try to be nicer to him."

His head and belly shook in tandem. "He wouldn't want that. He just wants you to be happy. We all do."

"I'm not like before. I promise. I couldn't do this without you; without any of you."

He nodded.

Ena turned her attention back to the loom.

"I'll tell Myrrel and Torno that you're mulling everything over."

"Thanks, Sal."

"Can I have a hug?"

"Yeah." She got up. "Of course."

Mud-pattered rocks pressed against her skin. Fingers long as her forearm came across her back and pressed in. It couldn't be a lot from him. He ground rocks down to powder for every meal. He had a raw strength forty times that of a human. It was only by living a life with humans that he could give a hug with the perfect amount of strength to mimic a human's embrace. It was comforting to feel his solid body against her. Chest against his cheek, she hugged as tight as her weak arms could manage.

"I'll always be here for you, Ena," he promised.

"I know." Ending the embrace, Ena found him still hugging. "I'll try to come to you more."

He let go and gave another shrug that raised his brows. "Only when you need to. Anchors are pretty valuable."

She rolled her eyes. "Sal..."

Chuckling, he left her.

~ ~ ~

Sal was right, Captain Fascinosa didn't have a problem with Ena using the deck to work on Ki'an magic dances. Visk wasn't around to watch her form and Hultur wouldn't talk to her about the theory. The big guy didn't give a reason, he just said, "No," and kept his nose in his book. So far Hultur had been anything but helpful, but that would change once they were on Leben Erde. Ena could feel his dedication when he talked about a peaceful resolution to the Grand Dream.

Illuminators were on deck shooting light bursts deep into the waves. Corina still didn't have the deathstaff from Captain Fascinosa. Ena had to have been wrong about Corina being the recipient of the gift. She looked around at the other casters to see who caught the Captain's fancy, but her eyes wouldn't move past Torno. It was nice of him to help illuminate the waters. He might've been born into the aristocracy, but he wasn't above doing tedious work. It had made him a good Broker.

Ena decided to let her guard down. He was doing good here and Ena said she was gonna try to be nicer to him. She took two steps towards Torno before the call went up.

"Monsters port side," bellowed the lookout.

Torno flicked out his wand, one strand split to six. They sailed deep into the choppy waves and exploded. Three silhouettes, all serpentine and large.

"Drummondar!" Firstmate Ginevra called out and other voices echoed it.

Marinelds shouted, slamming fists and weapons together to rally their fighting spirit. The fish folk sounded more excited than scared. Getting into groups of five, they dove into the monster-infested waves with zeal. Marineld were created to remove sea monsters wherever they found them. Many still saw fighting sea monsters as a great honor.

Captain Fascinosa ran out of his quarters with a blade in hand. Orders came out fast and louder than his natural voice should carry over the howl of the wind. Oration magic, a true sign of his noble upbringing. A glance to Norden and the blue-skinned man was given command. With Ginevra at his side, Fascinosa jumped off the ship.

Chaos had brought Narla and the others on deck. Even a pale Visk had dragged herself onto the rocking planks like an old woman missing a leg. Fear flickered behind those tired wet eyes, but something inside her wouldn't let her cower at the threat of a monster. Inspired to heroism, Ena threw off her soaked jacket and untied the laces on her shoes.

Torno, who had been in such a favorable light not even ten minutes earlier, grabbed her fucking arm. "What are you doing?!"

"I'm Ngoltur Reborn, remember?" she shouted. "They need my help."

"What's the incantation for breathing underwater?" he asked.

When blush crept up her neck, he let her go. "We have to help them somehow."

"Relax, Sweetness," slurred Narla. "They got it covered." She thrust a thumb back towards Norden or maybe the crew as a whole. It was a little hard to tell with her swaying against the waves. She'd been drinking again.

"Vessel portside," shouted the lookout.

A wand shot went out to draw the eye. The ship was smaller than Endless Grace by two masts. Two masts long, the vessel should be on its side from the force of the waves, but by luck or divine will it was keeping steady.

Torno watched it from his spyglass. "Sails are down."

"Gimme that," Narla slurred.

He opened his mouth but obliged.

Norden shouted orders to adjust course. Moving slant against the waves, Endless Grace adjusted course to intercept the stranded vessel. Chatter went back and forth filling Ena's head with nonsense. She couldn't keep track of it all. Somewhere below Marinelds were fighting for their lives and they were moving towards a ship without sails. Ena's spells wouldn't reach the other ship and she couldn't see into the waters below. The only bolts of light fired were following their course instead of looking for coming threats.

"Teetee's in the Captain's quarters," Myrrel told Ena.

She hadn't even thought of the girl. Guilt grabbed hold of her heart and squeezed.

"There's no rain," Narla muttered. She put down the spyglass and shouted at Norden. "Turn aside. We're heading into a slime."

"What?"

"Where?"

"Around the ship," Narla told everyone. "That boat is being carried. We're sailing into a lighting slime."

Once Narla had pointed it out, the deception was comically obvious. In the middle of the abandoned vessel was a flat surface in the middle of the ocean. It bobbed up and down along with the current, but only enough to keep up the illusion. Swells evened out when they came in contact with the slime and were too short to be from the same source on the other side. As for the rain, no drops were pelting the surface along that mostly flat plane. Even sloshed Narla was the only one who'd seen the slime.

"How did I miss that?" Torno muttered.

"It's too late," Norden shouted from the helm. "I can't turn us about."

"Come on, Sweetness." Narla pulled Ena's arm. "It's time to put all that new magic to use."

"Lightning slimes are weak against geomancy, aren't they?"

"Just freeze it!" said Narla and the crew of the ship echoed her sentiment.

They were hungry for a spectacle, and she was Ngoltur Reborn. With a roll of her free hand, she prepped the rings. She took a duelist's stance, waved her battle wand slowly over her head, and snap-cast a concentrated bolt of ice near the base of the ship. Ether lit up her battle wand like a beacon. The shaft glowed bright blue, but it didn't break.

Ice magic came out in a ball and spread out over the water like a handful of salt. The slime took on the look of being frozen, but it continued to slide toward Endless Grace. Ena's second cast was a simple flick of blue ether. It hit the slime close to the ship, and the translucent monster parted from the freezing water. Three gestures gave her control of the spreading ice and the ether-filled cold. She bled into the spell, releasing her hold on the rings and pouring pure power into the spell to spread it out over the water.

Spikes of ice caught the slime, and once they did, she sent power into those tendrils; spreading it like lightning. The slime tried to split and spread out, but trapped on the surface it had nowhere to go. It broke apart smaller and smaller until its form rose into the air as thick motes of yellow-tinged smoke. Above them, the dark storm clouds let out the rain that the slime had held back.

Endless Grace sailed up next to the old, wrecked ship, and though the crew threw lines across to pull it closer, it was starting to sink before it got close enough for any to jump aboard. The lightning slime had been holding onto the wrecked ship for weeks, maybe even months. Those that came close were taken apart by the Drummondar. The slime got a fresh meal, a fresh ship, and their hunt continued. Countless ships had been destroyed by this partnership of destruction.

Captain Fascinosa and the other marineld came up

not long after they let the damaged ship sink to the ocean floor. Several had to be helped up the side of the ship, and five hadn't come back at all. There were three Drummondar below the waves, and from the look on the crew's dour faces, it had been a tough fight.

Funeral rights were overseen by the Captain. Over the roar of the wind, he delivered the somber news and spoke an informal version of last rights. Kind words were said. Tears were shed. For all her sympathy Ena couldn't put a face to their names. She was guilty to feel so relieved.

They got through the storm a little before dinner time. Only Captain Fascinosa stayed on deck, looking back at the clouds that claimed the lives of his crew. Ena lingered there. She didn't know why she imposed on his mourning, except that she felt a profound sense of guilt.

"It was a nice service," she praised, impotently.

"Thank you." Captain Fascinosa didn't take his eyes off the waves.

"I'm sorry for your loss, Captain."

"Don't be. They fought bravely to the end. All Marineld who die fighting monsters, die fulfilled." He waited a long time to say anything else, and tears flowed slow and true. When at last he brought his hat from his heart back to his head, he turned his attention to Ena. "It isn't my crew that I mourn, not truly, but the spirit of my people. Along the seas of the Ocean of Harmony, sea monsters swim the waters unchecked by the Harmineld. Their kings are too concerned with titles and treasure to be bothered with doing their sacred duty."

"Is it better where you're from?"

He shook his head. "Worse by far. The practice of culling monsters is seen as a waste of resources. My uncle, the King Who-Sits-the-Throne, sees it as a way to add to the treasury of the land and celebrates the death of every ship. He is an embarrassment to all marineld. Even warlords live with more honor. He dishonors every marineld that gives their life for the safety of the waves."

Ena took his hand. The fishman acknowledged her kindness with a smile. "Things will get better," she assured him.

"How can you say that with such certainty?"

"Because the Gods have sent me. Change is coming, Fascinosa, and even though I can't join you in those underwater kingdoms, change has a way of spreading. As long as there are brave warriors like your fallen friends, the future will improve."

He raised her fingers to his lips and kissed them soft as surf. "Thank you."

Ena bowed her head slowly and made her way below deck.

Narla was at the tables with the grieving soldiers, a mug in her hand. Between drinks, they found reason to smile and cry. Ena felt the camaraderie between them, but couldn't still her urge to interrupt them. Torno reached out but stopped just short of her arm.

He shook his head.

"She said she would stop drinking, Torno," she whispered. "One of us should say something."

"Fine. Let me be the voice of bad news, but do not interrupt them."

Ena watched Narla take another drink and let out a hearty laugh. "She was drunk before the fighting started."

"I know," he whispered. "But you have no right to interrupt them now."

"Why not now? Why let Narla slide deeper?" Ena's voice was carrying enough to draw looks from the mourners.

Torno walked over to the wall and she followed. "Drinking to honor the dead is a tradition as old as drink itself. Breaking that up doesn't just bring shame to Narla, it dishonors those that fought. I'll be here to make sure she doesn't hurt herself. If you must talk to her, do it tomorrow."

Ena couldn't find the spirit to argue with him; strange

how seeing compassion from him quelled her wrath. "You're not in charge anymore, Torno. You shouldn't be the one doing this."

"Are you saying that you're finally ready to lead?"

She showed him a rude gesture and left.

That man always had a way of getting what he wanted. If he was dragged bloody to an interrogation chamber, he'd find a way to get a pillow and ale before the night was done. Ena went back to her room and refroze the rose on her wall. Torno's love poems were hidden deep in her packs, but she was able to retrieve them in no time at all. There was no reason for him to lie about writing these poems. He'd not only lied about this shy gesture, but about writing poems at all. He had to know that Ena knew about his history with Kalta, or at least suspect that from her. Maybe his lie had less to do with these poems and more to do with trying to wipe the guilt off his hands.

Something slid under her door.

It was another letter. It had to be another love poem. She ran out and opened the door, but saw no one. Her room was closest to the hall's entrance. No one looked her way. The sender could've walked up the stairs or gotten lost in the crowd. She'd never be able to find out who gave her this letter, but maybe there was another clue inside.

Lost in a storm without a cloud in the sky
I am not too proud to cry.
These tears flood like a monsoon
and my screams deafen like a hurricane.
But I will no longer wallow in pain.

If I must drown to feel your lips
And I lay gasping at your feet
Leave me to die
Better to end the ache in my heart
Then to know your kiss without love

I am above but below stars.
I wait close but feel so far
Away you may send my intent
Worry nothing for that sear of regret
I will still cherish the day we met
And live on to find merriment

Simply tell me, oh, come to me and
Reward me with your candor
Love or hate
Pity or spite
This storm of anguish needs that truthful light.

This read less like a profession of love than words of goodbye. It pained Ena to think that these poems of surprise would come to an end. But there was more to the poem than Torno lamenting the end of what could never be. The poem said the author was above. Could they mean now? Was the author waiting above to hear how she felt about him? Surely that's what this poem had to mean. Biting her lip, she threw her coat back on and went up deck.

It was empty there, quiet except for the sound of drinking and stories from down below. Ena glanced up at the lookout and they pointed to the ship's bow. She ran up to find her secret admirer and found him holding a fresh rose in his hand.

THE TWENTY-SECOND CHAPTER

In Which Ngoltur Feels
Her Cage of Stress

Before that night, Ena hadn't seen the way stars danced in his eyes. She hadn't noticed how his toothy grin was slanted not only to show swagger but because he held so much uncertainty. Responsibility pulled at his shoulders and he fought that pull with smiles and laughter. But that night all of his bravado was gone. He wasn't a great leader who must fight for a better future, but a man who was lonely because none could share the weight of his destiny. Ena was learning that feeling, and it was still new enough for chains to chafe. Captain Fascinosa had been living with it for years, and when he was faced with his heart's desire, that selfishness made him shy as a boy.

Again, she knew nothing about a man until he approached her with the honesty of love. There was so much he'd hidden from her because he couldn't show it to his crew. Maybe in order to lead, he also needed to hide it from himself. That rose in his hand wasn't just to earn her favor. He held onto hope. It was the hope that he wouldn't have to be alone as he forged his destiny; the hope that his life could be measured not by the toils of harsh suns and cold nights, but by glorious burst of color and life that came with a sunset; and the hope that his future of war and death could also contain love.

Ena saw all of that and more in his eyes and in the way he waited on a slant. Surely, he must've seen the disappointment that Ena felt when she realized that Torno hadn't been writing her those poems. Everyone always saw what was on Ena's mind. Her pale skin exposed more than veins but her every intention. She hoped he didn't know why she was disappointed, or why that disappointment made her so angry. She only hoped that Fascinosa saw how touched she was and that she finally understood that this man was going through much of what Ena was just starting to struggle with. Seeing that in him gave her hope too, because he had lived with this responsibility for years, and he could still laugh.

He had seen her disappointment and the same feeling swept through him. That rose in his hand seemed to wilt in time with his shoulders. There wasn't any bitterness in those cunning eyes, only pained acceptance. Yet like a wave finding the peak of its crest, he churned up that mask of confidence. A grin. A tilt of his head and the cavalier captain was ready to greet her. There was something truly disheartening to watch his honesty fade so fast.

"You've come at last to put an end to my sleepless nights," he said with bravado.

Ena tried to match his smile. "I have. I hope your nights haven't been as painful as everything you wrote."

"They've probably been worse than you might imagine." He twirled the rose in his fingers.

"Is that for me?" She reached for it.

"It's for My Love," he said, seriously.

It stilled her heart to see that wounded honesty return.

"Take it if you wish to take my hand, only if you would swim to the depths of my heart and feel our bodies meet in sensual surrender."

That made her smile more genuine, but more because

it tickled her sense of humor. "That sounds like a lot for a first date."

"I am a passionate man, moreso for you." He honestly sounded sweet, and that made it harder to make sense of his swashing smirk.

Ena had to look away to gather her thoughts. "Why moreso for me?"

"It's not enough to know that your beauty is unrivaled in the eight oceans and the fourteen seas?"

"Not even slightly."

He took a half step forward. "What about to know that your courage inspires me and makes me stand taller?"

"That's a sweet sentiment, but still hard for me to believe."

He stepped closer still, close enough for her to smell the salt of his scales and a musk unlike any human's, one full of rich, stony herbs. "Would you believe that I heard Teetee ask you to live with us and knew then that I wanted the same?"

That she could believe. Her wit failed her and she thought of the sweet Marineld princess smiling.

He didn't take her hand, or brush her cheek, or grab at her head to keep her eyes from straying. Instead, he brought that rose up to eye level, letting purple petals dance between them. "I pictured us together, giving her the life that neither of us had ever known, and I wept tears of joy. I imagined waking up beside you and felt a life without wants. I heard how you cared for someone I loved so much, and knew that I couldn't let you walk out of my life without trying."

Ena took his wrist. His shoulders eased, his breath relaxed, and he relented to her grip. When she brought the rose down to the level of their hips she could feel a sway altogether separate from the motion of the boat. "We hardly know each other, Fascinosa. But you're talking about marriage and the rest of our lives. Doesn't that feel strange to you?"

"Love is strange. It can't be reasoned with. All we can do is close our eyes and feel."

"You want me to close my eyes?" she whispered.

"Would you?"

It was a simple request, but clenched teeth and a pinch in her shoulders fought it. They wanted her to go back to her toiling, to sleep and forget the inconvenience this man held in his hand. But she would not be a slave to her body, nor the demands the Gods gave her. Her heart was her own and she would let it beat.

Even after making the decision to acquiesce to his request, her eyelids fought to close. A breath made it easier, but they only blinked. There were so many things that she needed to do, not just on this ship, but in the many days that came after. Fear had her by the spine, where her shoulders met her neck. She felt like she was being hung by a hook. Swallowing, she sunk into that pain and her eyes closed.

Thoughts flowed through her faster than the river of time and with more momentum. She thought of death, failure, responsibility, magic, weapons, conversations, hands, lips, eyes, and of ether, gold, and blood, but she could not think of herself. Trapped in this cage of stress, she could not feel her heart or hear a single word of what it wanted.

She reached down to grab the rose by the bud, just below where the petals grew. He let go of the rose. She tossed it onto the ground. She ran her hand over the flesh between his thumb and index and then across the back. Every knuckle was attached to his wrist, and she could feel every tremor underneath a skin soft and subtle as the finest sand. She placed a hand on his arm and stroked up. With motion, the friction of his skin brought a sharp focus. It felt uncomfortable and harsh. As long as her hand stayed still she could feel the warmth underneath and a softness that was too welcoming for her to trust. She laid a hand where his arm connected to the shoulder and felt the tension of his responsibilities.

She held on to kept herself vertical. His shoulder announced that he was going to touch her. Breath held, she anticipated pain from a man whose intentions were anything but malicious. It took an effort to let go of that breath and her lungs fought to hold on once again. But she was in control of her body. Stray thoughts and worst-case scenarios tried to pull her out of the moment but she stayed firm and worked to empty her mind. When she finally steadied, only then did his hand meet her hip.

He did not hold her but felt her body, sensing where she would move and following along the drift of her breathing. She slid her fingers back to receive him and he took her hand slowly. There was no push or pull on how they held hands, no give or take. It was nothing more than two hearts meeting.

There was a sway about them. It wasn't the rocking of the boat, but the motion of their bodies. Hips in lust wanted to pivot and grind, so too did legs in love want to sway from side to side. Her own impulses were hard to discern. She felt the motion obeyed. He followed without a word and when the gentle bellow of a crooning sailor broke the silence of the night it felt as natural as the beating of her heart. Gentle harmony came in low and high, soft as Fascinosa's skin.

A guitar added to the music and drifted along the timber of the two men and one woman in song. Each note was delicate and soft, easy to lose under the creak of the boat or the surf bubbling against the wood of the hull.

So it was that they found themselves dancing on the deck of the ship. The sweet serenade of the crew led their steps into gentle twists and turns, and as the music swelled and she felt a tinge in her heart, she opened her eyes. Gone was the bravado, or the smile of a man eager to please all in his company, or even the rigid shape of his trapezius. Serenity had hold of him. The sway of the dance captivated him. With a gentle stroke against his shoulder, she brought his eyes open.

At the meeting of their eyes, he remembered purpose and protocol and his face twisted to find an apology. A soft blink silenced him. A gentle squeeze of his hand asked for forgiveness again, and she squeezed back to let it rest. She moved her hand down and his up, switching to the proper stance of a man dancing with a woman. She sunk into his waiting arm, pressing her chest against his, and her cheek upon his bare heart. She could feel the excited pounding of a mind filled with dreams and listened as his heart settled back to a calm rhythm.

Five songs passed before they came apart. By that time, many couples had joined them. Among them were Visk and Ginevra. Visk was well over a head taller than her partner and Ginevra looked off balance to be made to dance meekly, with both hands on the Ki'an's hips. Teetee had partnered up with Torno, and the man danced on his knees. Sal danced with Myrrel, with most of her resting against the boulba's cheek. Narla danced with Corina, the crush Fascinosa never had. And everyone was having a pleasant time if not a romantic one. Everyone except for Hultur, who read his books somewhere out of sight.

Fascinosa waited for the end of the song and pulled back to clap. Cheers broke out among the crew. People were clearly looking for some kind of an explanation for what was going on between the Captain and Ngoltur Reborn, but he sent them off without offering a single word. They grumbled in disappointment but shuffled back to their quarters.

"Thank you for a lovely dance." Fascinosa escorted her over to the stairs.

Ena nodded. "It's nice to take things a little slow sometimes, isn't it?"

He chuckled and made his way down the stairs off the back. "Maybe I was too scared that I wouldn't have the time to do anything more."

She leaned in and kissed him on the cheek. "I am, too."

He stood there speechless and watched as she glided

around him. She went to bed with a smile on her face. She hoped that he slept well that night. Ena did.

~ ~ ~

Of all aboard Endless Grace, none were more eager than Teetee to know what was going on between Ena and Fascinosa. Ena was coy, smiling and being vague to drive the child frenetic with curiosity. As much as she took joy in watching the child bounce with enthusiasm, it wouldn't be right to tell her anything at that point. Ena didn't know what was going on herself. She didn't know what she felt for him or anyone. All she knew for sure was that she was stressed and suffocating from secrets.

Torno hadn't brought up the dance during his lessons and he didn't ask her about Fascinosa. He didn't even seem mad. He was just acting cool about the entire thing and that made her more confused than ever about him. Jealousy was a natural reaction when someone you loved shared a slow dance like that, but he was calm. Maybe he was finally giving up on her. Instead of bringing her happiness, it only added to her confusion.

Visk was in a sour mood and after some prodding, she relayed her night's encounter with Ginevra. Visk had spent the trip convincing herself that she had no interest in Ginevra. That had changed after shore leave in Situ. They'd finally had their wrestling rematch, and this time Visk was on solid ground. It was her turn to show Ginevra just how powerful she was. Ginevra won again. Visk had finally met someone who could best her in a contest of physical strength and with that loss, she had another new experience.

"You got drunk?!" Ena asked Visk. The woman had never tasted a drop of liquor in all the time she'd known her.

Visk gave a grim nod. The pair had escaped to Visk's room under the guise of "training through meditation."

"I can't believe it. I thought that you didn't want to drink because you were worried about a surprise attack."

"That is a small truth. I used to drink after every battle

and sometimes before. The last time I drank I was in Mu. I'd achieved my greatest victory. Geshuri challenged me to games of drinking and my pride kept me from refusing. I awoke in a prison, covered in my own vomit. I wore that vomit for almost two weeks as my beloved was defiled. I swore that I would never drink again.

"I blamed the drink for my own failings. I have blamed myself for many things since I lost her.

"When I left Caredor, I asked Duli if I was still honoring her. I asked her spirit what she wanted of me. She wants me to keep her in my heart but to release enough of her to let another in."

"Wow." Ena sat up and inched forward, eager to hear more. "So you were going to make something happen with Ginevra?"

Visk let out a long sigh. "I..."

There was a knock on the door. Myrrel crack opened the door, "Can I come in?"

"Always. Has my time with Ena come to an end?"

"Close the door," Ena said, waving her inside. "Visk got drunk in Situ!"

"Oh, is that what you were up to? That was quite a night," Myrrel chuckled.

"And what trouble did you pursue?"

Myrrel waved it away, she didn't seem to think it was more important than Visk breaking a promise over four years old. "What made you decide to drink again?"

"It is a story that comes from deep inside. On the outside, I am ready to love again." She swallowed. There wasn't any blush on her red skin though. There never was.

Ena scooted over to let Myrrel sit beside her.

"Ginevra and I fought on solid land. She gave me a true defeat. When she choked the breath out of me, I knew my time as a Broker had made me soft. I found I enjoyed that feeling of being soft. I wanted this woman to teach me more."

Ena and Myrrel chuckled, shaking her as they voiced their eagerness.

"So I decided to get drunk and see what would happen. Though I drank a great deal and sang many songs, she did not try to kiss me. She didn't even sit with me. I was ready to put the matter behind me, but last night while we were watching Ena dance with the Captain, she asked me to join her."

"And you did." Myrrel was grinning ear to ear.

Visk gave a bashful smile. "And I did. I don't like Gulam dances, but having done it with a true woman, I understand the appeal. She was much softer when she wasn't trying to hurt me. After the crew went to bed, she invited me to her quarters for drinks. We talked about war, death, and loss. I felt the warmth of the drink and I told her that I wanted to kiss her."

Ena and Myrrel were hanging on every word.

Torno barged in. "Hey, we training or what?"

"Torno!" Ena screamed.

Myrrel threw a pillow at him. "Get out of here!"

He hid behind the door. "Wow. Rip my head off, why don't you?"

He grumbled something about being out of the loop and walked off. They waited until they could hear his footsteps wandering into the mess. Visk's head hung low.

"Oh, I'm sorry." Myrrel rubbed her arm.

Visk picked herself up. "It was her right to refuse me. But I wonder if this wasn't a sign of something greater. The distance between the spirits and the living is vast. Perhaps I misheard Duli's wishes and I've brought her shame."

"Visk, it's been four years," Myrrel reminded her.

"You told me before that she was looking over you with sorrow. She wants you to live your life, Visk, and that means-"

Another knock on the door.

"Lemme talk to him," Myrrel said.

"No, let me," Ena scrambled off the bed and flung the door open. "Don't you know when to fuck off?!"

Hultur stood there. "Yes, and it is not now. I have called a meeting. The others are already waiting."

He was serious, but then again, he was always serious. They followed him into the mess. There were a few members of the crew chatting and playing cards and Hultur personally shooed them out of the space. Torno had just finished saying something to Narla but stood up straight when he spotted Ena. Narla had been sober and professional earlier in the day, but the guilty look on her face let Ena know she'd been drinking. As for Sal, he was more worried than usual.

Sitting on the table between them, was the rug that Ena had been working on. She'd needed maybe three more hours to finish it, but there it was completed. Hultur finished it without her and that sucked. The man had no right to take that small joy from her. It was her rug.

"Whatever your dramas, you may return to them after you make a decision on this." Hultur pointed to the rug. "This is a living scroll. I've imbued it with a considerable amount of ether and once the proper incantation is recited, it should hold slowed time indefinitely."

"How fast-" Narla burped. "What's the rate?"

"Time inside will be roughly sixty times slower. My exact calculations put the sedation factor at about sixty-three point four, but I've never worked with this medium."

Narla and Torno looked at the thing with awe.

"You can enchant and you didn't think we needed to know that?!" Myrrel asked with venom.

He nodded. "I did not want to be taken from my research to work on petty improvements."

"Petty improvements?!" Myrrel stood up and Sal put a hand on her back.

"Yes, petty improvements. Whatever tasks you would put me to, it would inundate my mind with temporary matters instead of focusing on the future. Ours is the weight of the world, yours the weight of lovers and friends. While I can appreciate the severity of your feelings, I do not have the luxury of weighing them heavier than the needs of the world."

"Hey!" Torno snapped. "Myrrel does a lot of fucking work for us! If something happens to you, she's gonna be the only thing keeping you from ending up in a grave."

"Impossible. Destiny will not allow me to die before it is my time."

The table was fuming at Hultur and he looked harder than Sal.

"Listen." Ena held up her hands to get their attention. "Vamere has spent this trip in solitude. Not for lack of trying by anyone, but let's face it, he has no reason to think of anyone here as his friend. We've been cramped on this boat for six weeks and he has a lot of pressure on his shoulders. Let's listen to what he has to say and then we can have a nice long debate about love and the best way for us to spend our time. Does that sound fair to everyone?"

Ena made sure each of them nodded before waving for Hultur to continue.

"I had Ena construct this for two reasons, the first is to memorize the glyphs. She must have an intimate knowledge of its shape and function. Now that she does, she'll be able to sit inside and do the real work of learning how to shape ether to her will. We have almost a week left on the trip so-"

"A year," Torno gasped. He snarled at the giant Ki'an. "She'd be in there for a year!"

He nodded. "I've kept careful records of her rate of consumption and we have adequate supplies in the ship's storage to provide for her. There should be no problem with her living inside the circle for a year."

THE TWENTY-THIRD CHAPTER

In Which Hultur Demands a Sacrifice

The mess exploded with shouts. Everyone but Sal and Ena screamed at Hultur, cursing him for treating the act of isolation as a trivial matter. Visk was angrier by far and yelled at him in her native Kest. Whatever she'd said, the stoic Hultur took notice, but he replied to none of it. He sat and waited for their outbursts to cease.

Sal stepped between the tables and *clapped*. When boulbas clapped it wasn't a soft thing that made people feel appreciated. It was a meeting of boulders, two massive slabs of stone connecting with force and purpose. It sounded like the coming of death, and it brought out a deep, instinctive reaction. All eyes shot to him and none spoke.

"I don't think Hultur understands what he's asking of her. He spends every day alone in his thoughts. He doesn't know what it's like for other people to be alone, and he has come forward to talk to us about this. Maybe we should try to be civil before we start condemning one of the three Turall."

Hultur adjusted his glasses. "That would be preferable."

"Okay, it's a terrible idea." Torno pointed at the rug. "That circle is what, six feet in diameter? She barely has enough room to sleep in it. If her foot came out of the bubble, her body would experience temporal dissonance so severe that it could send a blood clotting right to her heart."

"Hey, Commander here. Remember, Torno?" Narla asked.

He sneered but sat.

"She needs to exercise. She needs to move around and talk to people, and she can't do that if she's living in sped-up time. And it's too fucking small!"

"All of her daily exercises can be done within that space, I have checked myself. I have thought about the problem with the foot as well. I will be close by to magic a barrier around the edge while she sleeps. I could also pass her food, and remove waste when she defecates. However, in order to guide her studies in ethereal manipulation, I will need the entire ship to know that I am Hultur Reborn. As this is a decision that could potentially turn the crew against us, I felt it prudent to get all of your opinions on the matter."

There was something about his tone that unsettled Ena.

Myrrel raised a hand. "Yeah, I have a question. How do we even know this thing works?"

"Because I've already tested it," he said calmly.

"For how long?" Ena asked.

"One night. I spent approximately one month inside the circle. Contrary to your objections, I found the experience relaxing, and was able to complete a great deal of work."

They all looked at him with shock.

"How did you get all the shit out?" Narla waved the matter away. "Nevermind. I don't want to know. Listen, this is umm...an idea, but we're not going to do it, for several reasons. Not the least of which is our relationship with the people of this boat. If they learn that we've been harboring Hultur, the Master of Evil, on their ship, they're going to think we've lost our minds. And frankly after listening to your plan, I'm starting to wonder if we have."

"I want to try it," said Ena.

"No, Ena," snapped Torno.

Myrrel tried a more delicate approach. "Ena, listen-"

"It's my life!" she yelled back. "It's my body and my mind that all of you are trying to protect! This entire trip you've all been trying to tell me what to do, when to do it, and how to think. It's exhausting! I know that I'm not ready to fight and that I need to get better, and I'm grateful for the sacrifice that all of you have made to help me. But I'm the only person inside my head. I need to be able to have the final say on what happens to me.

"Everyone has been complaining about how we don't have enough time to train me to fight an Archmage, let alone whatever's waiting for us in Leben Erde. Hultur has come up with a way for us to squeeze a little more time out of this journey and we're all looking at it like it's madness, but there's nothing rational about three people deciding the fate of the world. We are working against the Gods. We are trying to unravel the design of beings that may have created everything we see. What if the only way to do that is to try something unconventional? If doing this will give me the ability to protect myself from all incoming damage, then I have to at least try it."

No one had any objections. No one could even raise their heads to look at her. The weight of their journey still hadn't sunk in. This quest demanded so much of them, and only Hultur kept that perspective. They were all there because they trusted what he said, it was time to prove it with actions. She just hoped it wouldn't snap her mind.

~ ~ ~

Captain Fascinosa took the news rather well, but when they asked if they should tell the entire crew what they were doing, he urged them to keep Hultur's identity a secret. Many had seen him create an unbreakable sphere of magic. They already knew that he was a powerful practitioner. There was no sense in worrying anyone with talks of the Grand Dream, the Turall, and altering prophecy. Fascinosa would be the one to tell members of his crew about Hultur and only if he thought they needed to know. That was the entirety of their discussion.

Ena wanted to stay behind and talk to him. She thought about sneaking into his chambers that night, but there would be no sneaking around. His room was accessed through the deck and there was always a lookout. Besides, there was very little she actually wanted to say. Whatever was coming for her in that circle, only she could face it. She needed to learn how to handle her anguish alone.

The day leading up to her first attempt in the circle was filled with dread. She'd never been imprisoned. The broker's wagon had been the only small space she spent a lot of time in, and she usually tried to sleep through the rides. Part of her knew that she wasn't prepared for what was coming. Trying to act normal, Ena found herself copying Captain Fascinosa's smile if not his attitude. He made his crew believe that everything was under control and that he was proud of them. If she was going to be a good leader, she'd need that skill.

For her ninety minutes with Hultur, she was going to try sitting in the circle of haste. The Corps all came up to the deck to wish her luck. She was going to be in a sphere of slowed time for almost four days, and the sun was approaching the horizon. It was strange how their well wishes annoyed her. She understood they were worried about her, but she just wanted to get it over with.

Hultur had been right about working the glyph into the loom, she knew the design. She was able to recite the incantation with confidence, and the intricate glyph was clear as the sun in her mind's eye. The circle activated and the boat stopped. She knew it was only an illusion, that the relative motion of the boat was reduced to almost nothing, but it was a dizzying experience. Feeling the slant of the ship was odd, and it took her at least a full minute to stop pressing her foot down on the rug.

Adjusting to the outside was hard, too. All her friends looked like statues. Hultur was working through the hand positions for a ball of light. He'd always cast it in seconds, so she had minutes to prepare. They were speaking, Ena could hear that from the way the air sounded like it was singing. Hearing the timber of their voices stretched out was pleasant for a second, but it quickly resembled a forest of trees falling one after another. It reminded her of the sound of Sothlen while the city was tearing itself apart. She tried to put her hands over her ears to get them to back up, but unless she stayed there for minutes, they wouldn't understand what she wanted. So she sat and prepared to catch Hutlur's ball of light. When it finally formed, the light threatened to blind her. Even wearing dark glasses, enduring the glare robbed her of her concentration. But she had hours to learn how to focus.

The magical attack was kept suspended outside the field of slowed time. Even with Hultur's limitless patience and power, he couldn't have kept the sphere of activated ether going for this long. She threw ether against the sphere for a hour, maybe three. Fatigue and hunger started to set in. She pulled in a parcel of food with kinetics, ate, drank, and then that other embarrassing bodily function came up. Ena had to shit in a bucket in front of half the ship. There was just no getting around it.

After that embarrassment, she felt dirty. She grabbed her arms and tried to hide, but there was nowhere to go. It didn't matter that people were trying not to look at her, every glance lasted far longer in her time. Their expressions looked skewed and exaggerated. It made them feel like monsters, not like bad people, but actual monsters. It was triggering that broker instinct in her to cast and kill. She had to stop looking at them. The longer she closed her eyes, the more she realized she was tired. She magicked the pillow and mattress into the circle and slept.

Her sleep was dreamless and stiff. She kept waking up feeling her foot pressing against something unpleasant. It was rigid and unforgiving. She'd pull off her sleep mask and glance down at her foot pressing against the edge of slowed time. Hultur was protecting her while she slept. If she was getting eight hours of sleep, that would mean eight minutes of continued evocation. Before meeting Hultur, she would've balked at such an impressive display of magical power. Now it seemed like a trivial matter. She rolled over the other way and went back to sleep.

Ena started the day dazed and annoyed. She could leave the circle at any time. The thought tempted her. She already felt so cut off from the world. It would've been nice if people could hop inside and talk to her, but she couldn't risk it. Stepping through the circle would expose their bodies to different rates of time. Blood would pile up against the edge of altered time. Their flesh would be denied a fresh supply of blood, which was to say nothing of what it could do to the heart. Death by temporal dissonance was a well-documented phenomenon, and it was one of the first things time magicians were taught.

Hultur was crossing his hands over his chest and she couldn't figure out why. Then she realized his hands were going to his lungs. Air. Ena cast a wind spell to cycle in fresh air from outside the sphere. She was sure to take from the sides of the circle, otherwise she'd draw in stale air from above and choke herself. Eventually the patch above might even become visible. Strange as it was to admit it to herself, she was intrigued by the possibility.

Morning stretches were nice, but the second she went through them, she knew she'd have to go through the routine more than once a day. When she sat down to receive Hultur's attack, it struck her how she hadn't spent any real time thinking. One of the things she'd been dreading was spending too much time in her head, but that hadn't happened yet. Maybe she'd be okay as long as she just focused on forming ether.

When Hultur finally got around to explaining why he'd made Ena "waste" her time with sculpting and working the loom, it actually made a lot of sense. He'd explained it the day before.

"For other casters, ether is the first thing to give out. Unless they're weaving tiny strands of ether together to make gulda, people simply don't have enough ether to continue magical effects. Mages can only spend a minute or two pouring out a flame spell. Alerathon, the strongest magician in the time before your democratic revolution, could sustain bolts of lighting for eleven minutes. The first time I attempted to outdo Alerathon, I could only keep the spell going for about seven minutes myself.

"For the Turall, our true challenge comes with boredom and patience. While it might not seem like it, the act of casting spells is mentally tedious. When a spell starts, the high of creating the effect can last a minute but not much longer. Casting spells is like thinking about one word without replacement. It doesn't matter how interesting that word is, in time the word will lose all meaning in the mind.

"Shape casting was formed to keep spellcasters from losing interest in the middle of long battles. By turning a burst of flame into a lion, the image extends the excitement. Pouring a flame over trenches is boring, but the act of having this creature walk extends the temporal understanding of the action. If the lion is personified, it can scoop into trenches like a cat hunting mice, and it can clash against a shield of ether with an irritation that matches the caster.

"The problem with this approach to extended magic is that it's trading interest for mental processing. Creativity comes with a mental cost. Thus the act of visualizing must be something intuitive to the conscious mind if it is able to maintain spells. You were made to craft shapes out of clay because you need to be able to make spells out of a medium that doesn't hold forms but resists them.

"The act of shaping ether is laborious at first, but with experience it becomes tedious. Interweaving strands of ether must become something of a second nature to you. You must let go of the flow of ether and focus only on the shape. By threading the ether slowly and repetitively, your mind will intuitively understand the way for strands to take up any shape. You will think 'falcon,' and ether will take the image without needing to orient strands.

"This is not something that can be learned in weeks or even months, because the process must be written into your mind. Your casting has already taken shapes, though you may not be aware of it. When confronted with danger, you shape ether into a wall of ice. Strictly speaking, shaping ether wastes mental energy. Your walls have divots and texture but you create them because they are familiar.

"You also have taken to casting attack spells with a claw. This is because the clawed hand is the last gesture in your cold spell. After casting the same spell for three years and never learning anything new, you were able to simplify the cast into a single outstretched claw, but that meant that you were sending out strands of ethereal nails. Yes, when those slashing marks came together they formed a directed ball of cold, but no novice performing the same spell has that effect. You created it because you've come to associate the two actions as one.

"I am able to form a sphere of ethereal protection because I believe it is always there. From the moment I wake up, to the moment I fall asleep, I believe the sphere is around me. I do not think about turning it on, I make the decision to turn it off. When you are training inside the circle, you will see me sitting further away than I need to be. This is because I need to keep that bubble from touching the edge of your temporal spell.

"Only by shaping ether tens of thousands of times can you shape spells without concentrating on the flow of the strands. Only by visualizing objects constantly can you switch from one image to the next without straining the mind. Only by practicing the same spell over and over does it take shape in the mind as a habit. Only by walking every day does the mind no longer think about how to step. This is the level of mastery you need to create something like my sphere.

"I was not lying when I said you did not have time to learn how to form my defensive sphere."

So it was that Ena had to engage in the shaping of ethereal strands. By pressing them against Hultur's ball of light she could know that the strands were holding. As spell met spell Ena would reshape his ball against the inside of her construction, but it struggled to take the forms Ena thought about because she was not used to consciously moving ether around. Sometimes even when she got the shape right, destructive light would seep out of the holes in her construction. She had to focus on the flow of ether and pull and pinch and swipe it into the forms she demanded. It was a frustrating and thankless task. To make matters worse, she would have to stop every five minutes or so because maintaining the spell was simply too annoying.

There was only her, that ball of light, and her command over the ether. The day moved along at a snail's pace, but her ether reserves never drained. She never once felt the fatigue and shakiness that others talked about. After lunch, she didn't want to go back to the work. She tried making a simple cube, but it was just like Hultur had said, it was hard to keep her focus when she could barely shape the ether into the proper form. She had to be experimental and playful, or she'd lose her concentration before a single side could take shape. The hours went by against a sun that was always setting.

Then she had to do the same day all over again.

On the third day, Ena was starting to feel gross, but she still refused to bathe with a bucket and a washcloth. She wanted to keep an eyelash of privacy and a whiff of dignity.

Ena kept thinking about Torno standing outside the circle watching her. He wasn't around, but it felt like he could just pop in and gawk without her knowing. But the opposite was true. Why couldn't she get that thought out of her head?

In the end, Ena was able to make it through the four days without washing.

First thing after leaving the circle, Ena scaled the sails. The rope felt good on her hands, the act of physically pulling at something was a welcome contrast to flicking unresponsive ether. She could kick at the sail and it moved without her thinking. She pushed hanging pulleys and they danced back and forth. This was a world of cause and effect, where every action created an immediate response. In there, it felt like she was pushing against a world of stone.

When she finally did get around to taking a shower, she puked. She didn't know why, but it came as a relief. She leaned against the wall and cried. Puke and tears all washed away. Maybe it was the cleanliness of it. Maybe it was the simple act of watching drops fall, but she didn't want to leave the shower.

The corps were waiting for her at the mess. There was a full meal before her, a glass of whiskey, a mug of ale, and a bottle of wine. Ena drank from the whiskey. It stung. It felt good to hurt a little. Someone poured her another glass, all the way to the brim.

"You don't have to-"

"I know!" Ena snapped at Myrrel.

She was staring at the table. The threads of the wood were calming in their consistency and welcoming in their rigidity. She hadn't thought about what it would be like staring at a ball of light all day. The long surface contrasted the ball of light burning the center of her vision. Some instinct made her want to mash her face against the table and fill her eyes with the pattern of the woodgrain.

"Do you want to be left alone?" Sal asked.

"I do."

They stood.

"But I don't think I should. This is the last time I'm going to have to talk to you. It doesn't make any sense. Why don't I want to talk to any of you? I don't even want to look at your faces." She rubbed her own face. "My eyes hurt."

"Looking at the ball of light was unpleasant?" Hultur asked.

Torno left and Myrrel followed him.

"It was like a nightmare, Hultur. The glasses helped. I could stare at it all day without it burning my eyes, but something about staring at the same thing hour after hour just wore me down. When I close my eyes I can still see the ball, pressing and shaping against my walls." Ena took another drink. She tasted something. That had never happened before when she drank whiskey. It tasted like wheat and stew left over the fire.

"I could try shaping a ball of darkness, but it will be difficult for me," Hultur grumbled.

"As hard as it is for you it's sixty-three times harder for me, I guarantee it."

Narla rubbed her back. "We can put different things out there. Maybe we could bring you a deck of cards or you could play a game of chess with Hultur."

As bad as it sounded to repeatedly lose to Hultur, it sounded better than doing nothing but staring at that fucking light. "Yeah. Okay. I don't think I want to be on the deck. I couldn't feel the breeze and there were too many people talking."

"You didn't like to hear voices?" Sal asked.

Ena shook her head frantically. "It was like a wall of sound, but the pitch was all wrong for music. There wasn't enough...stuff." She was finding it hard to grasp the words. Four sets of eyes were all melted with worry. Well, except for Hultur's. This was just another puzzle for him to figure out. Find the right combination of environmental stimuli to keep Ena going.

"We could try having every day like this," Narla suggested.

Ena shook her head. "I think it'll be better if I'm just in a corner somewhere. Going in and out will make it harder to adjust to everything slower inside. I don't want people to see me. I don't even really want Hultur to see me."

"We could put a curtain between us. I could alternate the element of the orb I used. If you don't press ether against it in five seconds, I won't cast the spell again." Hultur sounded positive, but that would still mean five minutes of that light burning her fucking eyes.

Ena nodded. "Yeah. That would be better. It sounds a lot better. We need to keep the room closed. I don't want people coming in and out asking about me. Any time someone showed up it was like a band of assholes was showing up to play for the whole village."

"Hultur, would you leave us?" Visk asked.

He frowned but bowed his head and walked off. "I have some writing to do anyway."

Ena took another drink. Past the alcohol, the drink was actually kind of pleasant. She could see why Narla liked it.

"I have been considering our events up to this point and I worry that we may not be as free as we thought," Visk whispered.

"Why, because I'm choosing to walk into a circle of time?"

She nodded slowly. "Gods do not like to lose. If we will not play a game of violence, then we must fight Hultur in another way."

"He's been peaceful," Sal said in his defense. "He may have different values, but I don't believe he's done anything out of malice."

"That's not what I mean."

They stared at Visk.

"Truly. I no longer think he will hurt us. You were

right about him, Ena. He means to work with you. However, I don't think this means he is harmless. Regardless of his past, he is a man. There is nothing a man sees that he does not consider a tool. Should he wish to build a tower, he will erect it with bones if he must."

They considered that for a long time.

Ena ate from the stew and found herself sinking into the delicious broth.

"I see what you're saying," said Sal. "This is all in the Grand Dream. Hultur united Ki'an and then traveled to Gulambar to ravage its lands."

"None of that's happened," said Narla.

"It has when we consider knowledge. He might have a hundred books and they include some of the greatest tomes of Doronel. I wouldn't be surprised if he owns books written by every magical theorist in Ki'an. He did unite Ki'an, only not their military. He united their knowledge. He ransacked the libraries of Doronel, and then he imprisoned us with ideas.

"Let me get this straight," said Narla. "You're telling me that the Gods are still trying to do the Grand Dream, but things are playing out like a metaphor. Instead of having a big battle, everything is going to come down to a polite conversation."

"Which is why we should reject Hultur's ideas," Visk whispered. "He has never once changed his position about anything. The man is agreeable because he is getting everything he wants. When we oppose him, his violent nature will reveal itself."

"This is horrible and all." Ena wiped her mouth. "But I don't want to think about it. If everything is settled with talking, then I don't need to learn how to fight. You heard Hultur, the Gods don't like peace. You can say that I'm imprisoned by ideas or whatever, but I don't care. If the profecy is fulfilled through a metaphor, Muttur will save me, but I can't count on that.

"More troubles are coming and I need to be ready for them. I'm going back into that circle."

They left her to her meal. With the meeting over, the crew shuffled in to sing songs and talk. Some tried to strike up a conversation with Ena, but her continual one-word responses eventually got the message across that she wasn't interested in talking. She just wanted to zone out and take in their atmosphere of camaraderie. The drink was hitting her, too. It felt nice to sway with the boat again.

THE TWENTY-FOURTH CHAPTER

When Ngoltur Enters Torment

Wood planks, the temporal rug, a hanging rug, and a lantern shining ambient light on one side of the front; this was to be Ena's world for close to a year. Hultur would need to take at least one rest in that time, and the plan was for her to continue on without him. Someone on the ship would be by once an hour to remove three days of refuse and place three more days of food. The kitchen staff would be able to cook meals, but there were no guarantees about the variety. Each meal might be the same stew from the same stock for close to two weeks. All of these were inconveniences Ena was prepared to live with.

Or so she thought.

If the greatest enemy to extended magic was indeed boredom, then Ena was going to master it. She had a deck of cards, journals, finger paints, and a guitar to keep her interest. Art and music were known for their ability to inspire and express the ineffable and with any luck they'd keep her from losing her effing mind. The little book on the basics of guitar was for Daun Si children, and though she couldn't speak the language, the diagrams were clear enough for her to follow. It helped to have a lesson plan for her to follow. But as days turned into weeks their very existence was a reminder of how little she'd learned.

Orbs of power popped into view without any warning. Her response to Hultur's little balls of magic were varied, and she soon came to personify each of them. She'd grow tired of one collected ball of power and then come to miss them when she hadn't seen one in weeks. They'd show up while she was taking a shit, and she'd get so excited that her bowel movements would stop or so angry that she struck out at the orb with a bolt of power to dismiss it. They'd pull her out of her journal writing and she'd stare at the old friend and cry for caring so much about the tiny little thing. She started having one-sided conversations with them as she bound them in ethereal cages or slapped them around.

Training was her everything and she attempted to stick to a schedule with rigid severity. Her choice of manifestation was diliberate and began with the same five simple geometric shapes, ten animals, and five man-made objects. She would construct them slowly, one thread at a time, unravel them, and then try to do it again as fast as she could. By the second week, she cycled through the compositions of ether quickly and gave up on manifesting the same ideas. After the sixth week, shapes were constructed without any purpose or direction. One day she'd play around with a wedge shape, the next she'd fuck around with tetrahedrons, scrunching and stretching them to follow her arbitrary whims. But that was about the time the troubles started.

From day one, her eyes strained to keep staring at the orbs of power Hultur constructed. She had to squint and strain her eyes to make out darkness. The crackle of lightning turned into a source of fear, and she had more than one nightmare of Hultur roasting her alive with it. Fire was calming, alluring, and at times seductive. Ice made her squint and growl and reminded her of her many failures. Light remained elusive and reminded her that she wasn't worthy of its shine.

Ena thought that her worst times would be when she

had to concentrate to make the shapes slowly, but once she got past the needs of the limitless patience required to bring them into form, her mind started to wander. It happened so gradually.

First, she'd find herself considering what shapes she'd do the next day or how to advance her art or guitar lessons. These practical questions gave her no pause. It was the memories that hunted her. They came for her, circling the depths of her psyche to probe for weaknesses. Keeping them at bay when she exercised or played music was hard. Keeping them back when she constructed ethereal shapes was impossible.

Memories were always annoyances for Ena. They sucked the bliss out of pleasant moments, turned deep conversations with friends into discussions about herself, and made her fail to carry out the tasks of her job. Here, they were monsters. There was simply no other way to describe how they haunted her. The first time her memories grabbed hold of her, she didn't respect their power. Gripped by their torment, she thrashed with such rapid ferocity that she came inches from swinging her fingers out of the sphere. Sobs twisted her over the floor like a fish out of water. They took control of her emotions, and through the intense overwhelming feelings, she took no note of her body or why it moved. One thing saved her, a crude circle of wood with a sun painted on one side and a moon on the other. Torno had put it up some time during the second week. It allowed Ena to signal to Hultur when she needed him to construct the barrier.

Pushing back the memories became a priority. She created extremely complicated shapes, ones that should be too much for her to think about anything else. They gave her mere minutes of reprieve. Hultur had been right about the creation of shapes becoming an automatic task, something that failed to keep her attention. Animal or abstraction, she could move them about like puppets or comically distort their proportions into absurd representations, but it wouldn't keep her memories back. They'd found a way past her defenses, and now that they had, she had to fight to keep them from dominating her mind.

She knew them all with deep intimacy. Her listless childhood as an inconvenience that needed to hide in rooms. Her time as a pariah hidden away in a small village where she named every animal and bug. Her teen years as a whipping post for student and teacher alike to work out their frustrations. Her falling into the fly trap of the Great Generation. Going to be a Broker. Falling in love with Haenir. Losing her virginity. Seeing her brother. Letting a stranger touch her. Dancing with Fascinosa.

The story of her life was full of moments of pain, fear, guilt, regret, shame, and scorn. If the seven base emotions did exist, happiness surely was the most elusive. Rarely did she look back on her life through a positive lens. Seen through the scope of her life, her night with Haenir had been one of lies. His love was little more than a tool to get off. Ena was incapable of feeling anything for the people in her life. She was using her friends to pamper her because she was too useless to cope by herself.

Ena tried so many things to keep the memories from gnawing her psyche. She tried to catalog them and identify the emotions they evoked. Using memories as nodes became a delightful lie but their terror wouldn't abate. Her memories would come at her from another angle, and yesterday's source of guilt would turn into today's fuel for anger.

Her mind had become a puzzle, and the solution to it was Ena's fundamental nature and her immutable flaws. Knowing she was a creature motivated by selfishness, she planned the best way to relinquish her friends from their responsibilities. But she couldn't commit to a life of loneliness for long. She liked them. Beyond that, they seemed to like her. Cutting herself off from the world was another form of selfishness and one that would hurt them.

Try as she might to convince herself that their pain would be less after their separation, she was either too selfish or too compassionate to hold onto that idea forever.

Ena needed to escape these foul loops of hypotheticals. She needed a way to combat these transformative reframings of her experiences and this desire to create a single, unifying narrative of her life. So she took to writing out the larger memories in her journal. Buildings like Haenir's farm and the Chantry were sketched out as crude scribbles. Profiles were written about her bullies at Lirond Chantry, trying to understand them from a place of empathy rather than unwavering rage. Ena cried tears of sympathy for her abusers and their sad, miserable, competitive lives. She manifested her parents into effigies of pure ether and yelled at them. She returned to lustful thoughts of Torno again and pleasured herself while she pushed against a cage of wind that kept sound from traveling. She imagined marrying Hultur, killing Hultur, and leaving him behind to try and change destiny himself.

The memories became easier to handle. Their wrath became familiar. The sorrow they evoked was a song she could hum along with. Her guilt became a simple statement of fact. Still, some matters required a deeper level of understanding.

The first was Torno.

He'd been popular when Ena was growing up in the chantry. The great gossip was fascinated with Kaltor. By listening to the weekly updates about the Great Generation, Ena became enamored with him. She imagined herself as Kalta, a beautiful, respected woman of Caredor. She'd enter a room and all would turn and whisper about her grace, power, and beauty. Though the voice gems hadn't given an exact image of Torno, she had constructed a mental image of him as a man of high society and genuine class. Taking from a well-to-do man from her childhood and a kind delivery man that frequented Lirond Chantry, she constructed an image of Torno. They danced until they laughed and talked until they kissed.

Then dreamcasts of him started being passed around the chantry dorm. Even though Ena was an outcast, she overheard enough conversations to figure out that they had images of Torno dancing with his beloved Kalta. The girls of the dorm had friends to talk to, games to play, and relatives to visit. Their full lives gave Ena ample time to be alone in the dorms. She found forgotten corners to breathe in a pilfered dreamcast and saw him. His beauty surprised her. He was classy and better dressed than she'd imagined, but there was this sweetness in his eyes, a compassion that was so deep it pained him.

One of the dreamcasts was from the perspective of a woman tripping off a flight of stairs. The stiletto of her heel broke and she tore her dress and scraped her arm in the fall. As a woman of only seventeen walking into high society, the scandal of an revealed leg and underclothes could ruin her. Torno found her half exposed on the floor. She crawled into the bushes to hide herself, but he reached her first. With tenderness, he healed her arm and only spoke to ease her nerves. Kalta was outraged by the sight of them, but once she understood the situation, she fetched a wagon to come around the back of the manor. Kaltor stayed and talked with this lady and wished her well as she was taken away from the ball. Ena had watched that dreamcast a hundred times and knew every sensation better than any memory.

She longed to be that girl and have a chance encounter with this handsome man. Dreams came to her of Torno attending the Chantry with her. He'd show up and heal the bruises she'd gotten from a punitive slap from an angry teacher. While she sucked back tears in bathroom stalls, Ena imagined Torno healing her body with magic and her soul with a kiss.

The moment Ena found a romantic escape she stopped sucking in the memory at once. She only wanted to experience a stolen memory of bliss with Torno. Finding herself in a bedroom staring at Kalta's body in a mirror was itself one of the most exciting memories in Ena's sad life. Breathing in a romantic escape with Torno was as close as she'd ever come to true bliss. For the first time in her life, she had reason to touch herself. The feel of his skin, the smell of his musk, the shape of his muscles, and the taste of his lips all drove her to the height of ecstasy. She had to breathe in the dreamcast twenty times before she even lasted to the satisfying act of penetration.

Ena stole the romantic escape with Torno and kept it as her own. Whenever she lusted, she imagined Torno in her bed, whispering her ear. But he wasn't with her. He loved Kalta and remained loyal to her. Anytime Kalta looked down at her body and saw Torno licking her rich chocolate skin, Ena was reminded that it wasn't hers. Still, it wasn't that hard to imagine that she was beautiful and dark--she'd been doing it her entire life.

Ena hadn't just been a fan of Torno's, she'd been in love with him. After loving Haenir, she was sure that her love for Torno had been genuine. Even though he'd never met her and even though he loved another woman, Ena loved him in her own sad, lonely, pathetic way. The more she indulged in her fantasies, the more the Torno in her mind and the Torno that danced with Kalta bled together. She came to think of herself as Kalta. The announcement of Torno and Kalta's first break up shook her, but it also filled her with a dangerous hope. When Torno cheated on Kalta, that hope was gone. She destroyed the romantic escape. Her fantasies of their love were replaced with daydreams of revenge. She imagined freezing him with a snap; his look of pained shock suspended for all of the Great Generation to laugh at.

Going to work with him had been surreal.

The Torno she'd fallen in love with had been a clean vision of elegance. This was a sad, broken man who reeked of tobacco and sweat. He was an unshaven mongrel that flirted with every woman in every village. It meant nothing that he flirted with Ena, too. She was clearly just another conquest to him. But Ena had already been taken in by his charms once, and she wouldn't be swayed again. It took her almost a full year to stop thinking of him as Torno of the Great Generation, and instead as the bossy asshole she came to call Captain.

Now, she knew that he never slept with any of those women in the villages, that he'd rebuked them all to try and earn her favor. Still, he had suspected she was Ngoltur Reborn from the first moment they met. A selfish knave like Torno would see her power and birthright as tools for his ambition. All these details made it difficult for Ena to form a solid image of the man. There were three conflicting visions of him that lay in her heart. He was the perfect gentleman, the handsome, charming, kind man that cared for her wounds and said "I love you" with every kiss. He was a selfish scoundrel, a horny manipulator that saw every woman as a prize. He was a pained revolutionary, so desperate to free the people from the chains of the Supreme Magus' society that he'd put his own life at risk. The only way for Ena to come to terms with these conflicting images of the man was to forget them all. She needed to let go of his past and figure out who he was with her own eyes.

Strange as it was to admit, Ena had more important things to consider.

The Gods had a plan for Ena. Each of the Three Prime Gods governed one of the Turall and picked them out of a continent of millions, or from a royal lineage of centuries. They chose Ena to be born with albinism and take on the role of Ngoltur Reborn. There was a chance that her past had been constructed to fit their new design for this Grand Dream.

If the Gods could be judged by what happened to her as Hultur suggested, then they not only craved violence but suffering. From birth, her life had been a stream of nonstop tragedies. She'd known loneliness, been denied the loving caress of her father or the supportive words of her mother. She'd been an object of pity, disgust, and rage for teachers and students alike. Perhaps all of her suffering growing up was nothing more than practice for her time imprisoned by Hultur.

It was impossible to know the will of the Gods, but she could draw conclusions about what they weren't. They weren't kind and they weren't merciful. Ena had finally found happiness with the Brokers. Her twentieth birthday marked a life full of possibilities, but she was made to go on a quest where she and everyone she knew might die. Sure, there was the illusion of choice, but maybe that was all part of the joke the Gods were telling.

The final matter Ena needed to figure out was her role as leader.

It wasn't enough for her to simply choose to be a leader. Narla and Torno had very different approaches to leading, and so did Captain Fascinosa. Each of them expected different things from the people under them and demanded their time in different ways. Torno saw every conversation as a dialogue serving a larger purpose; that with every action people revealed their intent and ambitions. To Narla the life of a soldier began when they agreed to serve and ended when Commander or Country fell; every member needed to be vigilant in their service. Fascinosa looked to his crew to support him without question. He trusted them to handle their personal problems on their own.

Ena didn't know what she believed about leadership, or even what she believed about the nature of the mind. There seemed to be no answers to the hardest questions. One hundred people might lead in a hundred different ways. So however Ena would lead, someone would disagree with her decisions. There would always be disagreements and there would always be people fighting to seize power. Yet she didn't want to rule like the Supreme Magus or any other leaders she'd seen in her lifetime. None of it felt right. Ruling felt like a lie to her. It was a thing that was supposedly necessary, but there was no way to do it right.

This final, great challenge in her mind seemed like a tower of unbroken stone. She could push at it, but it would not wobble. She ran the length of its base but found no entrance. Ena imagined ruling Narla's Corps or Torno's Band. She constructed entire conversations and felt no more certain that she should take up the mantle of leader.

Ultimately, Ena had to accept the simple truth that only she could rule. Torno had lost their trust. Narla couldn't handle the pressure. Sal was too uncertain of himself. Visk lacked the language and the empathy. That only left Myrrel. She could probably lead for a time, and she might actually be a good ruler of a nation. But they weren't a nation. They didn't need the decisions of policies but those of strategies and tactics. As a group, they could only move forward and confront impossible challenges if their spirits were kept high. Myrrel was best when things were going well, but when things took a turn for the worst she lost herself in the care of others. She was doing that with Torno now. She'd been hovering around him for most of the trip. Ena had to lead, and the fact that she understood that meant that she was ready.

She came to these three great conclusions and felt confident in her ability to work through problems. She wrote them down so she wouldn't forget them, even constructing dialogues with a reticent version of herself. But she was still in the circle. By her calculations, she needed to stay inside for another nine months.

Ena tried to stay stalwart, but without the challenge of internal issues to process, true boredom dismantled her resolve. Living in that circle left no room for doubt and made balancing all the right mentalities a dream. One after another she'd lose sight of the right mindset about her past or how to view herself. The same problems returned with the same level of intensity as if she'd never considered them. Ena spent most of the day convincing herself that she wasn't to blame for what happened to Haenir, that he knew she wasn't going to stay. She reminded herself that he was smiling when she left him. Whatever fate awaited Haenir, it wasn't her fault. This gave her a momentary bit of relief until she realized that she'd worked through that exact issue a dozen times before.

Everything clenched. Her fingers wrapped in on themselves. Shoulders came as close together as they would slide. Legs buckled and toes curled. Her stomach churned. Her brow furrowed into pain, anger, sorrow, confusion, and everything bleeding together. Every muscle in her face shook. Emotions forced out a wordless, primal yell. She ended the scream fast and snapped the time bubble with a swipe of her hand.

Growling and hissing, she walked up to the wall of the ship and punched it until her skin broke. Pulling back the curtain, she took in Hultur with a seething sound hissing through her teeth. He dropped his book and raised his hands in surrender. Words failed her. It had been so long since she'd said anything to anyone. His face didn't look right. It was simultaneously too expressive and too waxy. He was a puppet of flesh and skin and cloth. An impulse urged her to sink her fingers into his eyes and tear away his facade of a calm, unfeeling being. Phrases of hatred, contempt, disgust and bitterness hopped into her mind, but she couldn't breathe them to life.

"Maybe it's time for you to take a break," he said as calmly as he could. He stood and brought his hands forward an inch to touch her.

She pushed back with magical force.

He flew back into the wall and his defensive sphere popped into existence. It shook and rattled against the force of her spell, but it held. The sheer power of her casting against that barrier rotated the boat and strained the wooden planks of the ship. Cracks in the wood stopped her spell. She tried to breathe, but she only seemed capable of exhaling. The boat swayed to correct itself and that motion lurched her stomach. She retched on her feet.

Staring at her puke pulled her out of whatever was happening. She was alive. She was free of that prison. Ena stomped out of the hold. She marched right past all the onlookers. None said a thing. She got to the showers and immolated her clothes off. Bits of ash floated down to the bottom of the shower. Closing her pained eyes, she pressed on the water crystal. She saw the wood grain of the walls. The marks of age on the wood moved like worms. Words in her book and the ongoing inner monologue she'd developed continued. Already she was assessing herself, trying to figure out the best way to process this trauma as it was happening.

Washed, Ena got out of the shower and marched past her friends naked. She didn't even bother closing her door. She rummaged through her belongings but couldn't find anything to wear.

"Ena...?" asked a very worried Myrrel.

"Where the fuck are my clothes?!" she screamed at the woman.

A flash illuminated Myrrel's face. She reeled back in terror.

Ena took in the room. Sparks were flying about. Crackles of lightning set fire to her bed and the wood. She collected the light and flame into a man and woman of their respective elements, and they bowed in apology.

One of the crew came to the threshold and tossed a fresh set of clothes into her room. Ena used to remember her name. She knew that. She had known who that woman was. Now she was just a lump of flesh giving her what she wanted. *Good. Go away, flesh thing.*

She got dressed and walked out to greet the gawkers. Her friends were pressed against the wall. Only Torno

stood tall, a wand and bracelet at the ready. A sad waste
of ether whirled before him. It was an inefficient shield, a
pathetic attempt to block any attack by pushing the ethereal
forces outward. She reworked the design, correcting it not
as individual threads, but as solid planes of power. She
reshaped it, pulling the barrier towards her to let the convex
shield redirect incoming power back toward the caster.

Torno dismissed the spell, a look of terror in those
arrogant eyes of his. He could be scared. That made her feel
better. He'd never shown that to her. Maybe that meant he
wasn't as cocky as she had assumed. Ena still had the shield
in her mind, suspending it without a second thought. It was
there to stop her attack, wasn't it? Was it her turn to cast a
spell? That didn't feel right.

She looked into the mess. People had gathered to see
what had rocked the ship, but their curiosity had loosened
its grip. They were afraid. Fear was a good source of ice. She
hoped they remembered this moment well. It was important
to hold onto strong emotions so they could handle big
problems when they came. They needed to be ready to fight
the archmage. But this was the crew of Endless Grace. They
didn't have to fight the Archmage. That wasn't their destiny.

Teetee walked up. Someone pulled her back, and put
their hand over her mouth. Why were they doing that?

Ena wouldn't hurt Teetee.

They were looking at her feet. She'd created a fractal
pattern of ice on the wooden floor. Sweat or lingering beads
of water from her shower had frozen onto her skin. She'd
thought about ice magic. She must've surrounded herself
with an aura of power. Strange that she hadn't noticed that
before. With a blink, the frost and ice returned to water.

The deck called her. Outside after three months of
isolation, the breeze welcomed her. She could breathe deep,
full breaths. There were stars above her and waves out before
her. Strange that she'd looked at the water and thought it
inert before. It was a thing of pure life. She was alive again,

she just had to remember how to be alive. Language would return. She'd stop thinking of things in terms of magical utility and shape.

"Ena, I'm a friend," said Sal.

She meant to smirk, but the emotion bubbled up like boiling water. Laughter shook her from the gut up. She had to lean against the side of the ship to steady herself. She laughed so long and so hard that Sal joined in without knowing why.

"I know that, Sal. I know who you are."

He held up his hands again, taking the posture of something that was harmless. "Where are you?"

"Endless Grace. We're heading to Leben Erde." She shook her head. "I wasn't trying to hurt anyone. I just forgot...I got a little confused about why we use magic."

"You're okay?" That came from Teetee. She was peeking up from the stairs at the back of the ship.

Ena smiled. "I'm okay."

Teetee ran up to hug her. Ena received her on bent knees. The Marineld child was crying.

"It's okay. I'm not gonna hurt you. I just forgot that magic was scary. I forgot it could hurt people. That's all."

Teetee sobbed. "You scared me."

"I know. I'm sorry. I'm okay now, really."

With a child crying into her shoulder, she looked up at her friends. When she'd come out before they'd been worried, now they were scared. They were scared not for her but for themselves. She could kill them without even realizing it. She had summoned power without consciously thinking about it, without even putting in the effort to move her hands or consider an incantation. She'd gotten through the first three of Hultur's benchmarks.

There were only two more to go.

THE TWENTY-FIFTH CHAPTER

In Which Ngoltur Offers Herself

After spending so long confined to a sphere of existence, Ena was filled with frenetic energy. She moved over the ship like a cat chasing ghosts. All of the movement felt stilted and draining, but she pushed on, climbing up sails and running back and forth with a mixture of sobs and exhaustion robbing her breath. When her body finally gave out, she collapsed and let the ocean blow away her sweat. It felt good to be free of that rug of slowed time. Ena needed a break. There wasn't anything wrong with taking a small break.

One night means one month.

This break was a waste of time. She needed to go back to the rug where they weren't afraid of her, where she could gain power without anything getting in her way.

She passed Hultur going back to his chambers. The man was rarely surprised, but he stopped in his tracks when he saw her. Without a word, they returned to the laundry room. The crack in the wood was waiting for her. It couldn't have been three hours since she almost broke the ship open. She hadn't been trying to hurt Hultur, she'd just been. With more time inside, she could learn to keep that from happening.

"Have you finished your break?" Hultur asked.

"I feel like I might sleep now. There's no sense in wasting eight hours, that's about twenty days of training."

He nodded. "I'm surprised you agree."

"I just need to learn more control now. That's all. I wasn't trying to hurt you, Hultur. Really."

He didn't react to her apology. He didn't doff his hat or grimace or demand an apology, he just looked at her.

Ena was tired of looking at him. She went back to the rug and activated the circle. Well, she meant to, but she found her mind blank. She'd forgotten how to work through incantations. The songs came back to her like distant memories of a story she'd read. But what were the words again? Wasn't she supposed to do something with her hands?

Hultur peeked around the curtain. She could feel his eyes on her body before she even looked up to glower at him. Scowling, she brushed him aside, gesturing for him to go to his chair. She couldn't remember the incantation, that's all. Ena brought out her journal and flipped through the pages. It wasn't in there. She had a time spellbook back in her room, but she didn't need that. She was Ngoltur, wasn't she? Couldn't she just make the flow of time move how she willed it? Wasn't she that powerful?

She out with her senses. She felt the surge of time, raw and unforgiving. She and all who lived were pushed along its flow. Raising a finger she tried to touch it, but felt nothing. It would not reach to her hand, nor shape to her will. Thinking about the river of time was about as useful as thinking about sex with Torno.

Then she remembered that the incantation was very close indeed. She was sitting on it. She'd not only forgotten the words, but she'd forgotten that she'd woven the rug itself. Ena stood up, looked upon the glyph, and froze. Her hands were in the first position, the glyph shined in her mind's eye, the incantation lay on her lips. She remembered how to cast the spell. She remembered it like she'd cast the spell yesterday. Maybe she had. It had to have been close to two days on the outside. All of that was two days and she had six more to get through.

Ena grit her teeth and forced the motion. Ngoltur Reborn would not be weakened so easily. Three hand positions, one incantation, and she was back in her prison. It welcomed her like the maw of a monster. Its teeth sank into her like there were grooves. Perhaps there were. She had been in there for so long, she was so familiar with the pain of sitting in this circle. Sleep would help her resettle. She flipped the marker of day and night and laid down.

Her heart wouldn't slow. Her eyes wouldn't close. There was a heat inside, a shaking of her shoulders, and a grinding of her teeth that wouldn't settle. Her fingers were working her nails into the threads of the rug, pulling at the tapestry to rip it apart a little at a time. Ena slashed the air, popping the bubble of slowed time. Crawling out on all fours, Ena the feral animal scrambled out of the room. Pulling herself up by the door frame, she picked up her pace so Hultur wouldn't follow.

The mess was clear. Most of the ship had fallen asleep. Good. She didn't want to see that look in their eyes again.

Ena went straight to the Captain's quarters and knocked. No one but the lookout was outside. She bounced up and down, she itched at these new clothes that fit her so poorly. Knocking again, she found air and Fascinosa's inquisitive eyes.

"Is Teetee inside?" she asked.

"She's sleeping with Ginevra and Butler. Do you want me to get her?" He grabbed the door to close it on the way out.

She put a hand on his bare chest and pushed him back inside.

They were alone in his room. Surf smacked the side of the ship. Parchment and ink added to the smell of salt, and here and there his small rose garden sent floral aromas onto the breeze. Fascinosa smelled stronger. That stony musk of his mixed with something creamy she'd never caught a whiff of before. A desire to taste him parted her lips.

"Do you still want me?"

Fascinosa nodded slowly, a deep swallow bobbed up and down the length of his neck.

She stepped before him, putting herself within his grasp. Her lips were close enough for him to lick. "I'm yours to take."

He tilted his head ever so slightly to meet her advance. He tried to speak.

She took him by the back of the neck and pulled him down. Lips met like waves slapping against the cliffs; she the waves, he the rigid stone wall. He relented on the second crash, parting to let her fill him. He tasted of cooking herbs and spice; his tongue a smoother dancing partner than his legs had ever been. He softened in her grasp, flowing with every press of her tongue and gyrating against her eager hips. She pushed on him, pressing him back to the bed where she would take him if he would not.

His legs hit the bed and he stopped. Gasps and winces broke through his nose. Any attempt for him to talk she silenced with a kiss. Her hands spread over his chest and worked their way down to his crotch. But he wasn't responding. She desired his affection. Her body demanded his attention but he'd grasped her forearms not with want but to still her. Even his savory kisses stopped. Unreadable eyes met her own, demanding a different kind of reaction.

She kissed his neck and pressed into him. She didn't want to see anything but lust, she didn't want to feel anything but sex.

"Ena, stop."

Her lips kept exploring his skin.

"Please."

She rested her head against his shoulder.

"I've been where you are."

"I sincerely doubt that." She doubted anyone in the world had even survived what she'd done to herself.

"Ena, I know it feels like sex will fix what you're feeling right now, but it won't. It will just push it all back like the surf recoiling, but it will come back to crash on you again."

"Then give me that escape. Give me that release." Ena pushed him down to the bed. She took his head in her hands and showed him how bright her yearning burned. "I want you to fuck me."

He took one of her wrists and lowered it from his face. "I don't. Ena, it pains me to see you like this."

"Then help me. Save me with that overwhelming love you wrote so poetically about." Her lips found his cheek.

"I asked you before not to kiss me without love," he reminded her.

That finally stopped her. She leaned back onto her knees, half sitting up on the bed.

"Ena, I'm here for you, but I will not be a handle for you to pull when you need to get off." He sounded firm. Not upset, but he was making it clear that he wasn't going to relent.

She wanted to disappear. She wanted to run out of the room, jump into the waves, and swim to Leben Erde. Vaguely, she knew that Torno was on deck. If she came to him, he wouldn't tell her no. He wasn't that kind of man. She stood.

"Ena, please don't leave."

"You're hardly making me feel welcome."

"You're always welcome." He touched her hand, and she allowed him to move it onto his chest. "In here." He touched his head. "And up here. But I am not a young man who will let himself be used. I tried that once and I couldn't keep being a giver who never asked for anything. I need love, Ena. I need to know that what we have isn't about tonight."

"It isn't," Ena was quick to say, but when he paused to give her a chance to elaborate, she couldn't find the words.

"Then leave your lust behind. Sit with me and share the pain in your heart. Tell me why you're hurt."

She shook her head frantically. "I can't..." Tears burned to be let out. "I can't go back."

He hugged her tight, bringing her face onto his chest.

Her thoughts strayed like leaves on the wind. The feel of the circle's edge pressed against her heels, her forearm, and the back of her head. The sight of the wood grain, paneled walls, rugs, pages, and floors returned the second she closed her eyes. Orbs of magic judged her, demanding more effort and faster progress. She squirmed in Fascinosa's arms and the feel of his smooth, warm skin grounded her to the now. She squeezed him and cried onto his chest.

Fascinosa brought her down to the bed and stroked her head. She retold the harrowing experience in the circle of slowed time. The more she described the feel of the prison, the less she feared it. Because all of that was behind her. She spoke of it in the past tense because she was past it. That made it easier for her to talk about the Archmage, her fear of failure, and the weight of the world.

"I can't do this," she admitted to him. "It's not just being Ngoltur. I know I can't be the Queen of a nation. I don't even want that, but even this...Even traveling to another continent to talk to one kid is too much for me. I don't have the skills that I need. I've only ever fought monsters. I'm not a leader. I'm not a strong caster. I'm not even a good person."

The admission pained her but not half as much as the knowledge that she and all her friends were headed toward their doom. Thoughts of the future flooded in. She closed her eyes. Tears forced out, but her chest was still; unable to breathe. They'd already given up their jobs and their country for her. It wasn't right of her to ask them to risk their lives for her. It wasn't right! Everything she was doing was nothing short of selfish.

Fascinosa stroked her cheek. It brought her eyes open, but couldn't move her lungs. They felt gummed up inside. Swallowing didn't help; not when her thoughts kept reminding her that she was too weak.

"Bad people don't think about their own morality," Fascinosa told her. "They simply act in their own interests."

"That's what I'm doing. That's exactly what I'm doing."

He shook his head gently. With the two of them horizontal on the bed, he was actually moving his chin up and down as if acknowledging her words as true. "Why do you say that?"

"I..." Tears made it hard to speak. "I need to go back onto that rug and master magic."

"Ena, you almost broke the ship."

"I know."

"You...look terrible."

She chuckled. "How romantic."

He smiled a genuine smile full of mirth, it looked so much warmer than the crooked grin he gave to the crew of his ship.

"They're all so brave."

"Your friends?" Fascinosa asked.

"They gave up everything to go with me. Torno almost died and he's still coming with. All of them are willing to die for me, and I...I can't even sit on a rug for a year." Ena rose into a half crouch.

"Please don't go." He didn't reach out to her. He didn't try to contain her. He simply asked her to stay and hoped that she would.

"I have to. They need me to do this. I can't be a coward about this. I have to be willing to sacrifice everything just like they are."

"Ena, that's their choice. That guilt that you're feeling, it's normal."

"Normal?"

He gave a gentle nod. "I've been in exile since I was ten. My father was killed. Hundreds died to get me out of the palace. The same thing happened to Titiarna. She watched her mother and father die when she was four years old. Nearly three thousand marineld died to get her to the shores of Mannachuu.

"We are royalty. There will always be those who sacrifice their lives for us. There is no repaying their sacrifice. All we can do is remember why they fought and be inspired. There is a temptation to let their sacrifice sink into your heart and make you bitter. Don't give in to that. Repay their loss with kindness and grace."

"Endless grace..." she muttered the name of the ship.

Rising to a sit, he nodded. "That is what we owe those that serve us. They deserve our grace and dignity because they are willing to give so much. If we give in to despair, we squander what they bought us."

"I don't..." she gestured at his handsome face and noble visage. "Have what you have. I'm not graceful."

"You're wrong."

She looked away.

He scooted forward and put his hand on her shoulder. When she turned to look at him, he took her cheek once again. There was an earnestness in his eyes. He believed that she was graceful, that she somehow embodied the same noble bearing that he possessed.

"You are worth fighting for. Your prosperity is worth dying for."

It was all too much. Inside, she knew his words for falsehoods. She knew exactly how easy it was to despise her. Even as a child her parents couldn't love her. Hers was a voice that evoked revulsion not admiration. She wasn't worth anything.

He kissed her cheek, catching a tear sliding down her cheek. Eyes open, she took in his tender worries. This was a man who cared for her, who truly wanted to share her pain. She leaned in to find his passions in his kiss, and just barely managed to stop herself. He'd already told her not to kiss him. She needed to remember that he wasn't here for that.

Then he finished the motion and kissed her. It was tender, slow, and long. It was a kiss that asked for nothing and simply cherished the kiss for what it was. She was stilted, transfixed by his offering. A kiss wasn't nothing. A kiss meant something to her and it meant more from him.

The moment the kiss ended, she went in for another. Their lips touched quick, parting in the same breath. He'd meant to end the kiss, to keep things formal or civil rr something. She came apart feeling shame and he...Well, he looked to her with desire and need.

They came together not like waves and cliffs, but in unison. He took her into his arms and fell back to embrace her. He met her kisses with the same level of intensity and passion. Every breath she fought for, he chased. The more she touched him, the more he pressed down on her back to keep her in his strong arms. He wanted her in his life, not just for a night, but for the rest of his life.

She would give him everything she could. Everything else could come later. There was an urgency in her that needed to be filled. She could feel the shape of his desire forming between his legs and it promised to quench that heat she felt. Hands brought her shirt up. She took it off, exposing a brassier so tight it pinched her flesh.

She went to remove it and something sobered him. Whatever had made him decide to do this had gone. He looked guilty and ashamed. They each tried to form words of concern or permission, but there wasn't any need. He wasn't ready for this.

She picked up her shirt and kept it in her hands. The fabric was scratchy against her palms. They were soft hands now. All of her callouses from working wood and fixing homes were gone. Her hands looked thin; the skin around her wrist was recessed, sinking into the too-visible flesh and veins underneath.

"I'm sorry," he said at last.

"Someone really hurt you, didn't they?"

"How much did Torno tell you?"

Hearing his name made her look out to the door. If he'd ever been outside on the deck, he was likely gone now. "Nothing. He told us you were a good sea captain, that's it. We haven't been talking except when we need to. You don't have to tell me anything."

He reached for her hand and looked relieved to intertwine his fingers with hers. "I need to. If you're willing to listen."

"Of course." She got closer and touched his face.

A small measure of anguish eased at her touch. With a long sigh, he tried to let go of the past and landed somewhere contemplative. "Things happened pretty fast. It was just sex at first. That's all it was supposed to be, something to fight the boredom while we were at sea. I...feel in love so fast. I tried to deny it but, well, he figured things out." He noticed something on her face. "What?"

"You said you were with a man when you went to a brothel. Do you prefer them?"

He considered this. "Beauty comes easily to women."

"So my beauty is common?"

"Yours is rarer than diamonds."

"Graceful save."

Smiling, he continued, "When a man is handsome it's something special. I'm not typically drawn to men, but when I am, it can be hard for me to pull my eyes away."

Ena thought back on the man from the bar and even Haenir. As much as they were nice and trustworthy, they didn't have that sex appeal Torno had. "I think I see what you're saying."

"You still haven't put on your shirt," he observed.

She looked from the shirt in her hands to his bare chest. "Can I take everything off?"

He gave her a conspiratorial smirk. "Up to no good?"

"I told you I was a bad person," she joked.

He winced at that.

"I'm not, I'm not," she said quickly, more out of a reflex. "I just...I don't want to be alone."

"We could sleep together." He was earnest in saying this and a glance at the pillows added to his candor. "In each other's arms."

"Could I..." she scooted up until their arms were touching. "Kiss you."

He leaned in close and gave her a soft peck. "Maybe once."

"Or twice?" She kissed the side of his mouth and he tilted his head to meet her lips.

"As much as you want," he promised.

She kissed him back and their tongues met, tenderly, assuring the other that they weren't alone. She made no effort to get him undressed again and he only ever touched her to comfort her or show his love. They kissed and hugged and talked, and she fell asleep in his arms.

THE TWENTY-SIXTH CHAPTER

In Which Ngoltur Must Wake

Gentle kisses roused Ena from her sleep. Fascinosa slipped out of her grasp. Some sound of want rumbled in her throat and he kissed her cheek. Stroking her head, she settled into the pillow. The feel him rising filled her with a momentary dread, but her eyes wouldn't open and her throat wouldn't work. Sleep had already claimed her and there was no reason to fight it.

Teetee jumped onto the bed. She crawled into the covers and wiggled herself into Ena's arms. Alarm gave way to a smile, and Ena embraced the young princess. Not thinking, she kissed Teetee where her stubby head-tail met the base of her skull. She smoothed the sheet-soft fin of her head back and kissed her head again. Teetee said something but Ena fell asleep before she could process the words.

Ena awoke to someone standing in the Captain's threshold. Teetee was gone. Butler the tuxedo cat was curled up beside's Ena head. The motion roused the cat awake. A short purr died and he got up to wash Ena's filth off his fur. Ginevra stayed by the door, studying Ena.

"I'm awake," Ena told her.

The First Mate entered. "Are you hungry? Do you need anything?" There was something cross about her tone.

"Did I break anything?"

"You may have fractured the keel, but there's nothing we can do about it until we dock," the woman explained with a removed tone.

"I'm sorry."

Ginevra let out a long sigh. "The Captain says you went on a spirit journey and brought something evil back with you. He says that the wickedness has been excised."

Clever. Best of all the story wasn't that far from the truth. Except of course for Ena's evil being removed. That part of her was still very much alive.

"What's it like out there?" Ena cleared her throat. "How do the crew feel about me?"

"They're scared. I won't lie to you about that. They used to wonder if your friend Vamere was Hultur Reborn, now they're wondering if that's what you are. The Captain is keeping everyone focused on their duties." Ginevra poured Ena a cup of water from a nearby pitcher.

"Thank you." Ena rose to take the cup and Butler put some distance between him and the human.

"The Captain's had a lot of lovers come into his life, but you're special to him. Teetee's like a daughter to him. When he sees you with her it makes him think about the three of you as a family. I know he's a handsome man, but for him this isn't about making a long trip pleasant. He wants to marry you."

"I know." Ena's throat was tight. And she had to pee. "I'm not going to...nothing's happened. I'm not trying to hurt him and I don't want to use him. I'll talk to him about it."

Ginevra gave a small, stiff nod of approval.

"I didn't mean to damage the ship. It just kind of happened."

"That only makes what you did worse."

Ngoltur Reborn was strong enough to destroy a fleet, but not strong enough to give this woman a proper apology. She could only impotently mutter the words, "I'm sorry."

Butler sauntered over to the door and Ginevra left with the cat.

~ ~ ~

It was close to sunset when Ena was finally ready to face the world. Her fatigue surprised her. She'd slept a short time before leaving the rug of haste. The isolation had taken a larger toll on her than she'd realized. She lost weight, she lost sleep, and very nearly lost her mind.

The crew wasn't antagonistic with Ena, but they were hardly forgiving. Everyone on the ship kept their distance. When she returned to her room, she saw all of her clothes washed and folded. On it was a note from Hultur.

I have returned your possessions.
Please don't disturb me for two days.

Ena could relate. She hadn't thought about how taxing caring for Ena must've been. He did it all without complaining. Though Ena had been annoyed that he wouldn't fight, Hultur had proven himself time and time again. He was committed to their mission. Maybe he was so committed to peace that it made him a total pacifist.

Small rapid-fire knocks preceded a chuckle from the other side of the door.

Fascinosa's rose was still hanging on the wall of her room. Ena took it down and stuffed it into a drawer before opening the door a crack. Myrrel and Teetee stood on the other side. Myrrel waited with patience and a hand on Teetee's shoulder. Teetee was bouncing up and down, her eyes widened to maximize their cuteness. This Princess of six-and-a-half had already learned a few tricks.

"She wanted me to check on you," Myrrel explained with a bit of a smirk.

Ena opened the door and crouched down. "Worried about me, are you?"

She leaned in to give Ena a hug. "You slept for a long time."

Ena returned it with a smile. "It's all Butler's fault."

Teetee pulled back from the hug with a scowl on her face. "You said you wouldn't lie."

Ena looked at her position relative to the door. She was definitely inside. She nodded. "You're right, I'm sorry."

"Should we come back tomorrow?" Myrrel asked diplomatically.

Ena retreated back to the bed. "I cast a diagnosis spell every morning. I didn't see anything wrong at the time."

"Self-diagnosis is unreliable at best," she muttered. "Especially when it comes to small problems. Your arm."

Ena held it out for Myrrel to touch.

Teetee jumped up onto the bed. "Can I touch her?"

"Only if the patient wants."

Ena brought Teetee in with her free arm. The child hugged her tight enough for something in her spine to pop.

Myrrel didn't respond to the sound. "How is the patient?"

"Groggy. It's probably just from sleeping all day."

"I was worried about you," said Teetee.

"Because I slept all day?"

"You were gone for two whole days."

"I was supposed to be gone for the rest of the trip."

Teetee pulled away from the embrace. The first signs of a sulk were showing.

"Teetee, why don't you let me talk to Ena alone?"

She looked to Myrrel with a rather imperial mein of defiance. "Is she alright?"

"There's nothing seriously wrong."

"Come on, Teetee. We need to talk. I'll play with you after we're done."

"You promise?"

Ena nodded.

Teetee kissed Ena's cheek and hopped off the bed. She bound out of the room like a lizard on the hunt. After slamming the door, she scampered up the steps to the deck.

"I'm sorry for attacking you," Ena said immediately.

She nodded. "You don't need to say that."

"I do."

Myrrel chuckled and shook her head. "Well. The ether's settled now."

"I really didn't know what I was doing. It was like emotions and magic had mixed up in my head."

"But you're better now."

She nodded. "Did I hurt myself?"

"Physically? I don't think so. There's some minor tissue damage around your hips and your tendons are worn down, but you should be able to treat it using what you know."

"I'll look out for it. Thanks."

A weight dropped Myrrel's shoulders and her eyes followed them down to the sheets.

"I'm sorry for putting you through that. I didn't want to hurt anyone."

"I know, Ena. I know." She got up and made for the door. "You don't have to keep apologizing."

She said that, but Myrrel wasn't looking at her the same way. There was something between them now. It kept Ena from speaking up to ask about Narla and the Corps. She wanted Myrrel's advice about Fascinosa and about how to talk to Narla about taking over as leader. She couldn't. Not when she seemed so scared to share a room with Ena.

"Just rest up," Myrrel told her.

"I will. Thanks."

She went to leave.

"Myrrel."

There was a strange expression on Myrrel's face.

Ena was pretty sure it was fear, but she couldn't be sure. "I'm glad you came to see me."

"Yeah. Of course. I'll let everyone know that you'll be better with bed rest. We'll talk later." Myrrel left her, leaving something unsaid between them.

Ena remembered the promise she made to Teetee, that neither of them would lie when they were in her room. Lies were rarely the problem when talking to people. It was the silence that hurt more. At times what wasn't said could be deafening. Maybe if Ena had been raised to be a Queen she would've found the right way to apologize to Myrrel.

~ ~ ~

Teetee was with Fascinosa when Ena came to find her. Fascinosa looked to be scolding the child. At the sight of Ena, she ran away from Fascinosa and her responsibilities. She threw her arms around Ena's legs and squeezed.

"Ena! Let's go play."

"Wasn't Fascinosa talking to you?"

Teetee pouted, avoiding the gaze of all.

"It's okay," said Fascinosa with an even tone. "Just behave and stay out of the way of the crew."

Quick as that Teetee was back to smiling and pulling at Ena's arm. "Come on, let's play."

"What's going on?" Ena asked. There were far too many people on deck for simple sailing maneuvers.

"Another storm," he explained. "I'll need everyone to stay below deck."

"Can I..." Blushed robbed her voice.

"I'm sorry, Ena. I have a lot to do," he said to dismiss her. "I'll visit when I have a moment."

"Oh, umm..." She tried to find the words to give him leave or approve of the sentiment, but he was already talking to his crew.

"Come on," Teetee whined. Pulling at her again, Ena followed the child down below to get into some kind of mischief.

~ ~ ~

After being well and truly rebuked, Ena found it hard to sleep. Her mind was full of thoughts of the Captain. She wanted to sleep with Fascinosa or at least spend more time with him. She'd been so bold before, so why had she been so nervous to ask him about their night together? Teetee knew she'd slept in Fascinosa's bed. She didn't even seem to care about it. Fascinosa was a Captain, she knew that, but it still hurt to have him dismiss her like that.

Voices from down the hall pulled Ena's head off the pillow.

"It really isn't a problem, Cap," said Torno.

"I know that, Tor. I do. Things are just a little tense right now. This is something that the crew needs to handle on our own."

"Understood."

There was a pause in their conversation. That or they were leaning in to whisper. Ena got up to get closer. She inched over the floor and put her ear to the door. That door swung open, leaving Ena flailing about to catch her balance.

"Ah! Don't come in here without knocking!" Ena swung at the intruder.

The flat of her palm smacked Fascinosa's chest. "Sorry." He took a step back. "I thought..." He shook the thought away. "I'm sorry." He did a half bow and moved to leave.

"No, Fascinosa. Come in. I'm sorry. I thought you were someone else."

Fascinosa looked back at the hall.

"Come in." She beckoned him and closed the door behind them. With a wave, she cast a silence spell around the door and all the walls. With Torno, there was no such thing as being too careful.

"Does Torno barge into your room at night?" he asked more offended than she would've thought.

The thought of him dueling Torno to protect her honor flashed into her mind. "No, he just has a problem with personal space. I'm sorry for reacting like that. I don't want people seeing me in my night shift."

With a smirk, he gave her a once-over. "It has a certain allure."

Leaning back onto the bed, she smiled back at him. "Yeah?"

Giggling, he looked away. "Sorry. I'm probably giving you a lot of mixed signals."

"They don't feel mixed to me. They feel like they are going in the right direction."

He sighed.

She hated the sound of that sigh. He wasn't supposed to sigh when she was giving all of these opportunities to tear that loose fabric off and explore every curve and crevice on her body. All of her enthusiasm was replaced with a gnawing feeling of guilt. "You kissed me, Fascinosa."

"I did."

"You took my shirt off."

His cheeks turned red. She'd never seen a man blush before. It was sweet and more than a little vulnerable. She liked how the color made his eyes pop.

"I'm sorry about last night, Ena."

"I don't think you have anything to apologize for. Is this because of Ginevra?"

"Did she say something to you?" His tone was far too serious.

Ena looked away to keep from lying.

"It's not about her." He went to sit on the bed and turned around instead. "It's about me. I like you, Ena. I like you a lot."

"I like you too. Isn't that why you're here?"

"I came here to apologize. In five days we reach Leben Erde. You have this huge journey in front of you and I...can't go with you. I have a responsibility to Teetee, to my crew, to my Kingdom. I can't leave all of that behind to be with you and protect you from all the threats that you'll face on Leben Erde."

"I'm not asking you to do that."

He turned about and showed her eyes on the verge of tears. "I'm thinking about it. I care a great deal about you,

Ena. I meant what I said. You are not a bad person, you are wonderful. I would spend all of my remaining days with you if I could."

"What are you saying? Since we can't have forever, you don't want to have sex?"

And he nodded.

It hurt to see his head shake up and down even as his eyes were close to tears.

"It would be so much more than the physical act for me. I'm falling for you, Ena. I have a bad habit of falling in love with people before I really know who they are."

"I'm falling for you too. I want to sleep with you again." She got up and tried to take his head in her hands, but he was so much taller than she was.

"I can't. It's worse with you, Ena. The more I know about you, the more I love you. You almost destroyed my ship and I lied to my crew to protect them. I told myself I'd never do that. I don't want to rule with lies."

That stopped Ena. It was more than his feelings for her that was making him cry. He was a deeply compassionate man. He cared a great deal for his crew. Leaving them to be with her would be more than a dereliction of duty, it would be a betrayal of everything he believed.

"You love them," Ena said, finally understanding.

"I do. As much as I care for you, I can't leave them behind to help you."

"I understand." She said it and she meant it. Reaching out, he gave her his hand without hesitation. She squeezed his palm and his fingers wrapped around her. "I won't come to you again."

He opened his mouth but killed the thought with a nod. Serious eyes took her in. With dedication and maturity, he told her, "Thank you."

She wanted to kiss him goodbye. She wanted to pull him in and hug him and let him know just how much he'd come to mean to her. Instead, she let him leave like a stranger. The only sign that they ever knew each other was a single stolen glance. It didn't do her any favors that it was a look of somber regret.

THE TWENTY-SEVENTH CHAPTER

In Which Ngoltur Takes Power

During the storm, Ena spent a lot of time in bed and even more time plucking out songs on her guitar. Corina heard her playing and came down to check on Ena when she'd depleted her ether. She corrected her form, gave some pointers, and taught her some sea shanties. Ena couldn't carry much of a tune, which didn't surprise her. Corina had grown up singing in a Duan Si Church. Ena grew up getting smacked for carrying a note.

Teetee came by Ena's room frequently, asking if she could help her find Butler or play hide and seek in the mess. Outside meant having to look at the crew and her friends and deal with the shame of endangering their lives. Ena's vow of honesty compelled her to admit to Teetee that she simply didn't want to leave her room. Eventually, she stopped trying to get her to come out at all.

The fourth day after Ena almost broke the ship, they'd passed through the storm. It had been a rather mellow weather pattern compared to the last. Yet when Ena went out to the mess, the crew looked exhausted. Every marineld with a sliver of watercraft used up their ether protecting the hull. to say nothing of the physical labors the storm demanded of them. It was Ena's fault that they'd had to push themselves so hard to keep the boat afloat, but none so much as glanced at her with scorn.

Sal picked up his belly-chin when he saw Ena. He, at least, wasn't afraid of Ena. If anything the boulba looked happy to see her out among the crew.

"Morning. It's good to see you," he said.

A smile came easy. That surprised her. "Thanks, Sal. I think it's time we had a meeting."

"Now?"

She looked about the crew, they were already giving her and Sal a wide birth. "Yeah. Can you get everyone?"

"Sure. They'll be happy to hear from you, believe me."

She didn't.

One by one Narla's Corps came out to join Ena at a table in the corner. Tension held everyone's tongues as they waited for everyone to join them. Torno sat besides Narla and the commander gave him an amiable shoulder bump. He smirked and gave her a half hug, relieved that whatever had passed between them was passed. Hultur sat on the far end and Ena waved him over to sit beside her. He returned his nose to his journal and went back to his scrawl. Myrrel offered to help a wobbling Visk to the table, but she walked with her head held high. Visk looked worse than before. Her normally cherry-red skin was now closer to wind-washed bricks. She regarded Ena with a tilt of inquiry. Ena tried to smile to let her know she was okay. Finding a seat on her own, the meeting could finally begin.

The crew had already cleared out on their own. There was no more putting this off.

"Obviously apologies are necessary. Everyone warned me that what I was doing was dangerous and I didn't listen. I thought I could handle it. I was wrong. I know that now."

"We're just glad you're alright," Sal assured her.

Narla silenced him with a single shake of her head.

"The good news is that I've obviously gained a lot more mastery over my ether. I can craft ethereal shapes with almost no thought. I don't know how useful that will be on our journey, but it certainly won't hurt. I did what I could to work on the other skills and think about what everyone else taught me, but honestly I may have forgotten more than I gained. My progress with the nodes is almost completely wiped clear. I'll do what I can to work on new nodes, but it's something that I'm gonna have to do on my own. I know that I was...strange when I came out, but I already feel a lot better.

"I had a lot of time to think and I came to a lot of conclusions about my life and my role in the world. I'm Ngoltur Reborn. I'm done denying that. It's my destiny to lead, so it's probably best if I start by leading the group." Ena paused. She waited for someone to argue that she wasn't fit to lead the group. No one did.

"No objections?" she scoffed. "Why?"

"We're here for you, Ena," Torno pointed out. "We've always been on this mission to support you. If you're ready to accept your destiny, I won't question your command. But we're all here as a resource. If you need us to plan out a battle or handle supplies when we're coming into a village, we can take care of that for you. You don't have to do this alone."

"I second that," said Narla. "I never wanted to be the leader, but you needed me to take charge. I know I made some mistakes, but I did the best I could. That's all any of us can do. You trusted my experience and value my judgment, and your confidence in me really helped me turn my life around. I...well, I can wait for everyone else to talk."

At that, everyone anxiously waited for Narla to finish her thought. But she wouldn't.

Sal hemmed and hawed into he found the words to go next. "I wanted to know what you'd been through in the slowed time. So I asked Torno and Hultur to help me into the circle. It was a miserable experience. By the end of the third day, I was getting ready to tear that rug apart. If anyone questions your dedication, I'll be the first to jump to your defense."

"Right after me, buddy," Torno pipped in with a smile.

"What about you, Myrrel?" Ena asked. "I always thought you would be next in line to lead."

"Yeah, fucking right?" Myrrel scoffed. "I don't want to lead. I'm a healer. I'm needed the most when shit goes down. The last thing I wanna do is make calls about who should be doing what when I'm elbow deep in someone's bowels. Even if I would take charge, I don't want to fight you for it, Ena. You're intelligent, compassionate, and you understand the big picture. You've always been thinking about us as a group. There's never been any doubt in my mind that you were going to be a great leader, Ena, prophecy or not."

All eyes went to Visk. "I had my fill of command in Asutura. I was best giving orders in the thick of a battle. Everything else just gave me a headache." Visk shook her head at the memory. "That being said, I will only follow commands I don't like when there is no time to debate the matter."

"Good," Ena said. "I expect loyalty but not blind obedience. What about you, Hultur?"

That caught everyone off guard, including the stoic man. He picked up his eyes from his book and took off his hat. "Excuse me?"

"You're part of this team, Hultur. If we are going to keep traveling together, I need to know you'll follow my orders without a fight."

"I cannot agree to those terms. If people know what I am, that could compromise our mission."

"You think I don't know that? Have you seen the way the crew of this ship has been looking at me? I'm not eager to announce the coming of Ngoltur, believe me. But I need you to trust me. We won't be able to find Muttur without some people knowing who and what we are."

Hultur grimaced. "You seem to be forgetting that I came to you. The Gods have chosen you to be a leader, so be it. If you need an entourage of followers that is not my concern. Your assistance is little more than an adendum to my designs. Should the need arise, I will be more than willing to make this quest a solitary one."

"Fine by me. Three men have proposed to me since our quest began. I'd be happy to live a quiet life with one of them. You want to play hardball with me? Fine, but I'm not going to follow your lead. You have no clue how other people think. I don't trust you to make decisions about the group and I don't think you could convince Muttur of anything. When we meet him I'm going to be doing the talking, and you'll be doing that as my aid."

Hultur was taken aback by her zeal. He considered her words, seemed to formulate an argument in his head, and then bowed his head in acquiesence. "Very well, Ngoltur. We will try to succeed in our mission of diplomacy under your leadership."

"Good."

Narla and Torno were impressed by Ena making the man finally concede to something.

"Is that what we're called, your aids?" Sal asked.

"That was my idea." She shrugged. "I'm not really crazy about any names or titles, to be honest. According to the Grand Dream, Ngoltur is accompanied by her Aids, so it feels appropriate."

Sal said the word over and over again, occasionally adding his own name into the mix.

"Formal doctrine being what they were, I'm pretty sure we would've been called your Retainers and collectively known as your Retinue." Narla had a bit of her old lackadaisical attitude back already. "And I'm realizing that all of you are too young to care about Doronel titles. So instead, I'll share the big news."

Narla could be theatrical, but this wasn't a pause made intentionally. She was struggling to find the words.

Ena was certain that she new what this was about. Given how hard the trip had been for her, it only made sense that Narla wanted to leave. They all had a right to abandon

Ena and start a new life far from her. Narla's departure would come as a relief to Ena.

Narla's first attempt to tell them came out as a squeak. So she cleared her throat and tried again. "I'm pregnant."

"What?!" voiced several at once.

"Congratulations," Hultur muttered. He opened his book in preparation to ignore the coming conversation.

"Do you...who's...but it..." Torno's brain had fried.

"Yeah, I uh...thought that I couldn't conceive, so I just...didn't keep it from happening. I am forty-one," she chuckled. "I guess I've got a few reasons to quit drinking now."

The room erupted in pandemonium and soon the crew of Endless Grace were filing in to join in the celebrations. Talk of a child brought out kegs and bottles. They teased Narla by bringing alcohol close to her nose and touched her belly until she started punching arms. Ena apologized endlessly and the crew made a show of cowering before her. Ginevra was the first to share a drink with Ena, and her thick arm weighed heavy on her shoulders. They celebrated well past lunch, the crew of Endless Grace and Ngoltur's Aids joined together in song and laughter.

~ ~ ~

Excitement and sorrow mixed together when the first gulls were spotted. Land was close. Land. After all this time at sea, they were finally reaching Leben Erde. They'd be able to go to bars and spend some time apart. They could buy supplies and care for the horses. There would be a new wagon and plenty of room for everyone to stretch their legs. But this also meant that their time on Endless Grace was coming to an end. Ena couldn't take her eyes off the horizon and Teetee spent a lot of time watching with her.

The fish-girl usually had a lot to talk about but she was quiet in the hours leading up to the end of the trip. When the port city finally came into view, Teetee started to cry. Ena tried to comfort her, but she ran off to hide her tears. Ginevra had been watching them for some time and came over to join Ena beside the deck.

"I'm sorry if I was too hard on you earlier," the First Mate said.

"It's fine."

Sunset cast long shadows over the port city of Vergebaum Heff, lamps and fires lit throughout the city casting an eerie yellow and orange glow over a tree stump hundreds of feet tall. The felled tree had once stood at the center of a city ruled by handshakes and promises. It had been thousands of feet tall then, providing ether for any who reached for it. When Hultur's forces had landed many generations back, they cut the tree down and used its lumber to craft a navy to bring back Leben slaves to the Ki'an homeland. Cast in the light of so many buildings, the stump looked ablaze.

"There's a colosseum in there." Ginevra pointed at the massive stump when Ena looked over for clarification. "Ki'an and Leben warriors fight to the cheers of tens of thousands. It's a great place to earn gold on bets and a better place to lose gold."

"I'll be sure to avoid it. You think we need to worry about all these Caredor ships I see in the harbor?"

She shook her head. "We'll be pulling into the west port, away from Dorospek districts. You'll still find some people who speak the tongue, but you'll have to look for them."

Ena nodded. She straightened her back and offered her hand. "Thank you for all your help on this trip."

Ginevra took her leave. "Just doing my job."

Ena knew she'd done more than that. The fish-woman had led them through physical training almost every morning for five weeks. Humble to the point of being aloof, she was a complete mystery to Ena. Two of her Aids had expressed their romantic interest in her and she turned them both down. She never knew why, and didn't feel close enough to ask.

The crew crowded onto the deck as they approached open ports far from the heart of the city. Gale and Li'at, Hultur's expensive horses, were saddled and ready to ride off in a gallop if needed. Their belongings were laid out in a stack. All the delays behind them, the goodbyes began.

Norden, the Leben navigator with glasses, gifted Ena a collection of maps to find her way through Leben Erde. The man took his time hugging her goodbye. He'd never admitted his feelings for Ena, and it came as a relief that he didn't do it then. Corina offered Ena her guitar and she refused the gift. The women shared an embrace. Corina whispered, "I'm sorry," before kissing her on the cheek. Then the plump woman from Daun Si ran off to hide from Ena.

Teetee was dragged out to say goodbye. The crew kept asking if she wanted to say goodbye to Ena and she kept shaking her head. Ena came to kneel before the Princess. "I had a good time with you, Teetee."

"I don't care."

"I do," Ena told her. "No matter what happens, you'll still be my friend, Teetee." She leaned in and kissed her forehead.

Ena turned around to leave and the girl threw herself around Ena's legs. Picking her up, she gave Teetee a tight embrace.

"Everyone always leaves me," Teetee said between sobs.

"I know. I'm sorry."

"You can't leave me. We're both Princesses. You have to come with me and help me win back my crown. You have to!"

"I can't promise that, Teetee."

"Yes, you can, just say it." She smacked Ena's back. "Say it!"

Ena put her down.

Through her pouting and tears, she hissed her outrage. "Why did you spend time with me if you weren't going to stay behind? I hate you!"

"I love you."

Teetee hugged her again and they shared a long embrace, adult and child taking turns crying. Someone touched her shoulder and Ena ended the hug. Ginevra took the child from Ena, rubbing her back as she continued to sob.

Captain Fascinosa was already down on the docks, saying his last goodbyes to Ngoltur's Aids and a chubby Leben man. The Leben was definitely a member of Endless Grace's crew, but Ena couldn't remember his name, nor even his position on the ship. The blue-skinned man had a familiar look about him, but beyond that, he could be anyone.

Fascinosa turned to see Ena off. He took off his tricorner hat and placed it on his chest. "It is with a heavy heart that I must say goodbye."

"How about you just shut up and kiss me goodbye instead?" She grabbed him by the belt strap and pulled him in close.

With one hand on her back and the other on the back of her neck, he dipped her. Suspended, she floated on a sea of love. Their lips met with haste and stayed together with sorrow. She told herself again and again to let go of his back or end the kiss. But she was being carried off on a current, and if he'd taken her back to the boat, Ena wouldn't have noticed. She wasn't even sure if she would complain.

He ended the kiss first and Ena whimpered for it to go on. Tender eyes took her in. Something had been left unsaid, she could see it in his eyes. Still, he swallowed and smiled that swaggering smile of a man who didn't have the luxury of being vulnerable. Ena pulled him in for another kiss and he met her lips with a slow, soft, closed-mouth kiss. He righted her, pecked her cheek, and took a single step back.

"Ena, if fate pulls me back to your port, should I dock or keep sailing?"

"Of course I want to see you again."

"No matter what?"

"No matter what," she chuckled.

Blushing, he nodded. "Then I hope you will forgive me for this."

Captain Fascinosa walked up to Torno, probably to settle some matter of accounting. Torno's eyes were hazy, his hands shaky. Fascinosa took him by the hips and Torno grabbed the sides of the Marineld's face. They whispered something to each other and kissed.

This was not a kiss of momentary passion or a kiss of two people who'd shared a single night in bed together. This was a kiss of lovers. It was deep, slow, passionate, and intimate in a way that made Ena more than a little jealous. They kept pulling back and whispering something to each other and then leaning in to find their lips again. It lasted long enough for Ena to get over her shock and gather up all of her things.

The crew of Endless Grace were shouting and hollering at their less-than-graceful Captain. Torno wiped his lips, picked up his stuff, and mumbled something about finding a hotel.

"Oh and Ena," Fascinosa called out. "Do take care of Zukoch."

Ena and her Aids looked at the chubby Leben man. He was all smiles and had his hands full of his own gear. Everyone from Torno to Hultur took turns looking at each other to figure out who had asked the man of nineteen to join the group. After walking a few blocks they came to realize, no one knew this Leben sailor.

BOOK 3
Gold

THE TWENTY-EIGHTH CHAPTER

Where Ngoltur Learns of Violence

For millennia, the Grand Dream began with the strongest woman in Ki'an becoming a man of unrivaled power: Hultur. Men of Ki'an were not made for combat and strenuous exertions, and yet the Bringer of War took the form of a man. Under his leadership, men weak and small joined the ranks of his army. The Bloody Unifier brought together all the nations and clans of Ki'an and sent them across the oceans. Hultur himself oversaw the sacking of Gulambar, to force the proud Ngoltur to surrender, but this was never his only goal.

Since the time of the second Hultur, Ki'an warships sailed to Leben Erde to kill the heroic Muttur. Hultur's western campaign began with the conquest of Vergebaum Heff. A port city of incredible resilience, Vergebaum Heff changed hands with the phases of the Grand Dream. Through conquest, subjugation, and uprisings, the Ki'an people mixed with Leben. Not all were children born of assault and not all Ki'an on Leben Erde lusted for glory. On the eve of liberation, in every iteration of the Grand Dream, there were Ki'an who rose up against the the Geshuri and joined in the celebration when Hultur's armies fell.

So it was that Fieta slowly came to be a nation of two races. The Ki'an of Fieta looked to combat as an expression of personal success. They saw to the development of their art as a duty near divine, their ultimate purpose to oppose Hultur and his warriors of death. Generation after generation, the people of Fieta fought. They fought to take the country for Hultur, they fought to take it back, they fought to prove their strength, they fought to show their beauty, and they fought to determine who would take out the trash.

Wandering the streets of Vergebaum Heff, it was impossible to not encounter one fight or another. Friends greeted each other with a slap and screamed insults with a smile. Children appeared in gangs thirty strong and warred with rivals with sticks. Adults watched with glee, betting on the outcome as children fell. Large men in spangled uniforms and oiled muscles heckled pedestrians to pay for the honor of defeating them in a "game" of trading blows to the face. Fencers danced in a circle of spectators and struck at each other with blunted foils or sharpened blades. When one bested the other, the pair collected coins from a hat as casually as any street performer, even as fresh blood trailed down their arms.

Ngoltur and her Aides wandered this land of casual violence as a team of mixed minds. Visk and Narla watched every slug fest with great interest. Sal winced when people injured themselves and gawked at every feat of strength. Torno fell behind to watch street performers, dropped vital coin, and rushed forward to catch up before finding himself distracted all over again. Myrrel preferred to avoid the sight altogether, actively blocking her vision with a raised hand. Hultur couldn't go two steps without some strong man challenging him to a free bout. Still recovering from her months of isolation, Ena was simply overwhelmed. Thankfully, the latest addition to their crew had no trouble navigating the city.

A chubby Leben with an especially round belly, Zukoch looked like the last person who would've been found on a ship and yet he'd come from Endless Grace. Zukoch didn't have any wands and didn't have the body for the manual labor needed to work the sails. As far as Ena could tell, the only thing good about Zukoch was his mastery of Fietspek. For the better part of an hour, Zukoch had been talking to locals. He'd spent coin from his own purse to hire a group of wide-shouldered men and women to carry their belongings. The short-termed mercenaries pushed aside brawls even as they exploded out of a bar.

Zukoch lead them to the grand entrance of a hotel. The building was a landmark location with a great deal of artistry invested into the four story tall pillars. Long colored banners hung over recesses in the walls but a furling wind revealed a headless Ngoltur and a one armed Muttur made in some forgotten age. It was the kind of place that people used as a natural gathering point.

Zukoch placed coins in the hands of their six guards but the imposing figures stayed at attention by the steps. Cupping his hands over his mouth, Zukoch shouted something in Fietspek. Not a soul reacted to his shout, not even to gaze at him with ire, yet the mercenaries were at last satisfied and swung their arms like cudgels as they sauntered off.

"Why did you waste money buying guards?" Narla asked. "Between Hultur, Visk, and Sal, I don't think anyone would mess with us."

"Oh, it's not about the protection," Zukoch said with enthusiasm. "If I didn't pay guides, we wouldn't have been able to walk a block without another group stopping us. You can't get anywhere in this rashy armpit without a guide." Last inside, he leaned back to take in the engravings on the wall and the paintings on the ceiling. He gave a long whistle of admiration.

Again Ngoltur's Aides looked at each other to see which of them knew this Leben man. From their years of traveling the road, the former Brokers could say a great deal with just their eyes, but no one knew why Zukoch was there.

Confused to the point of being worried, they all looked at the newcomer.

Like all Leben, Zukoch had a rich sky-blue skin tone and soft orange eyes. Ena knew better than to use his short height as a marker of his age, he was the same height as she was, but he still looked like a teenager. He had a face full of enthusiasm that wasn't made any more mature by his puffy jowls. To make matters worse, there wasn't a scar on him. The eager adult looked back at them with a smile.

Torno walked up to ask the tactless question on everyone's lips. "Who are you?"

He laughed and slapped Torno on the back. "Oh, that's good. Classic, Torno." He waved someone down and hired them to take the horses out back. He then handled the purchasing of five rooms.

"Um, I should really be doing that," Ena said when he reached for his purse.

"It's fine, the real fees won't come up until we're buying a wagon. We'll be lucky if we can get a few more horses," Zukoch said with another chuckle.

"Who is this guy?" Narla asked Myrrel well above a whisper.

"I'm just happy to be inside. This city is a healer's nightmare. I saw a man waving around a compound fracture like he'd just won a medal." She shivered.

Bellhops gathered their things and brought every suitcase and garment bag to a windmill lift. The non-magical construction was constantly in motion and required people to jump in to a cabin to get to their floor. Zukoch finally noticed that everyone was staring at him. Still jovial, Zukoch cracked a smile.

"Can you guys believe that Captain Fascinosa kissed Torno? I didn't even know they had history. I bet you were a little jealous, huh, Ena?" He nudged an elbow affectionately into her side.

The gesture was strange and forceful, but Ena smirked

to make him stop.

"Again, I must ask," Sal said, stepping forward. "Who are you?"

"Wait, are you two…" Incredulous eyes took in the faces around him. "Do you really not know who I am?"

They all nodded in unison.

Disappointment flashed over his face, but he carried on with a smile. "Myrrel, I brought your meals while Torno was laid up in bed."

"I was probably too focused on Torno to notice," she admitted.

"Narla, you gotta remember me. I was there after Ginevra turned you down. We drank three mugs of ale together. You're the one who suggested that I should join in the first place."

Narla winced. "Yeah, that could've happened. I don't remember much of that night."

"Hultur, I was caring for the horses. You told me every single one of their dietary needs."

"I may have." Hultur shrugged and kept his eyes on the tome in his hands.

"What about you, Visk? You don't remember when I was taking care of you after you puked in Situ? We had an entire conversation about Ki'an poetry!"

Visk lowered her head.

"Okay, but Ena, you weren't drunk when I was on deck singing. I was the first to start singing when you and the Captain started dancing! Or all those times I cleaned out the chamber pots from your journey into slow time!"

Ena shook her head apologetically.

"Torno, you really don't remember me going back inside that woman's house after you had to jump out the window? How could you forget that?"

"Honestly, I've been trying to forget that entire trip to Situ."

"Did we have some grand adventure too?" Sal asked. "I

feel like I would've remembered talking to you."

Zukoch shook his head. "I didn't talk to you much, Sal. But I did bring you rocks from storage sometimes." The weight of what had happened was finally starting to sink in and he sank into a nearby couch. "I don't believe this. First my dad dies and then I'm surrounded by people I thought were my friends, only to discover that none of them remember me."

Ena sat beside him and put her arm on his shoulder. "I know this must hurt, Zukoch, but we obviously must have had some connection to you if we invited you to come with us."

"How much of a connection could it have been if none of you remember me?"

"But they liked you when they were drunk. Just because this is a fresh start for us, that doesn't mean that we can't still be friends, right?" Ena rubbed his back.

"Yeah, I guess." He was dazed. His sad eyes traced patterns on the ornate tiled floor.

The bellhops returned and they were escorted them to their rooms. Zukoch had purchased two private rooms for Ena and Hultur. He was sharing a room with Torno and volunteered to switch with someone else. But Torno agreed to share a room with the friend they'd all forgotten. Visk and Myrrel had no problems sharing a room, nor did Sal and Narla. Two for a room was better than squeezing into a wagon.

Ena took in the lay of her suite, wandering from bedroom, to washroom, to the small study with fresh parchment and a quill at the ready. The place was a palace compared to the small inns she was used to. Paintings hung on every wall, live plants filled up corners, and strange fragrant piles of wax sat on every table. The semi-sweet floral scent drew Ena in until she was sniffing at a bit of thin rope like a flower pistil. Flushed with embarrassment, she realized she was inches from a candle. It was a common thing in Leben Erde, she knew, but she'd never actually seen one.

"Hey, Ena," came the dour voice of Zukoch. He was standing in the threshold, but didn't walk through her open door. "I'm gathering gulda for the money changer. I'm warning you now, the exchange rate isn't going to be great, but it's only gonna get worse as we move inland."

"Oh." Ena took out her personal bag and handed over all the smaller valued crystals and a few twenty-gulda purples.

He took the gulda and handed her some a few coins. "For tonight."

She glanced at the strange looking pieces of silver and gold. "Thanks."

He went to leave with his head hung low.

"Oh, and Zukoch."

"Yeah, yeah, you're sorry, and it's nothing personal." The kid knocked on the next door over.

She felt bad for him, but there really wasn't anything to be done about it. Somehow coincidences lined up to omit this boy of nineteen from all their memories. It might not have been fair to think of him as a boy. Ena was only twenty herself, and just as short besides. But then again, plenty of people called her kid. Ena could probably be in her forties and old lady Narla would still be calling her "kid" and "little girl." Of course, she would be doing that with a son or daughter to take care of her. It made Ena smile to think about Narla being a mother. Hard as she was, the woman had never shown much affection for babies. Hopefully, being a mother would change the woman, but they'd all be there to help her.

Assuming they all survived.

That was a somber thought. Ena was still thinking about them like they all had a future and that their future would be shared. After everything that happened, they couldn't go back to Caredor. That was, unless Ena wanted to have Ngoltur publicly support a revolution. She remembered

Sothlen in chaos and pictured Caredor City in flames. The thought churned her stomach and she had to close her eyes to settle it.

"Ena," it was Sal at the threshold. "Visk, Narla, and I are gonna try to find this colosseum we've heard about. You wanna come?"

Her head was shaking before she had a reason for it. "I'll think I'll find something a little more low key. You three have fun though."

Ena tried to settle in and caught a glimpse of herself in the mirror. She looked thin, sickly. Her months in the rug hadn't exactly gone as plan. She was supposed to have a lean body ready for combat, not a frail physique. Of course, her white skin always looked wrong. That's why the teenagers of the chantry spit on her and called her bone bitch.

Torno marched past her open door. He didn't wave or nod or even look at her. *Great. The silent treatment.*

Ena shook the dread away. They were going to be on the road sharing a wagon for months. She couldn't let this hang between them, whatever this was. Running out to catch him, she had to sprint and shout to get his attention before he stepped into the windmill lift.

"Torno!"

Hard eyes met hers, but he stopped.

She gasped from the short run over. It was embarrassing to be out of breath so fast. Well, at least the run gave her a reason to blush.

"Did you need something, Precious?"

"Um..." She swallowed, glanced over at the empty lifts and then stepped forward to speak for his ears only. "I'm sorry."

He fingered a cigarette. "Hmm, a free apology. Maybe I should make you earn my forgiveness."

She scowled at him. "That's not gonna happen."

"So magnanimous." With a snap, he conjured a flame on his finger and lit the smoke. Ignoring her continued glare, he asked, "What are you apologizing for?"

"I..." She stepped closer still and caught a whiff of his body, it was acrid and cloying in a way that hung about her lungs and wouldn't let her breathe. "Fascinosa."

"Oh." Smoke blew out his nose. "It's fine, Ena. All that's behind us."

"Yeah, but-"

He walked away. "I've been on the ship for too long. We can talk tomorrow if it's still bothering you."

Then the knave stepped into the lift and sank under the floor. Once again, he didn't even look at her. She thought about stepping into the lift and chasing him down in the hotel lobby, but Torno made it clear he wasn't in a mood to talk. He wasn't even smiling when he teased her. Sighing, Ena gave up on Torno and went back to her suite.

Myrrel was hanging on the threshold of Hultur's room. By the looks of her swaying figure, she might even be trying to flirt with the bookworm. The woman was smiling an awful lot for talking to Hultur. It seemed like a waste of effort to Ena, but if anyone could get that man to open up, it would be Myrrel.

Ena searched her stuff for a hat and found a gold and purple head wrap. Then she remembered the Leben disguise Myrrel had got her. This might be a chance for her to try it out, but if she did, everyone would just talk to her in Fietspek. Ena needed to talk to people if she was ever going to get back to something resembling normal. She wrapped her head and debated leaving a strand of hair out.

Growing up, she'd always tried to hide her hair. It looked like burnt rice and felt like sun-dried wheat. But men liked her. They threw themselves at her and proposed without so much as a kiss. When her time at the chantry ended, Ena dressed to hide as much of her skin as she could. It took her about a year of tears and support from the Brokers to wear casual clothes. Dressing with a little flare hadn't hurt her back in Sothlen. She'd felt so beautiful and sexy that night. Maybe she could find something like that in the marketplaces here.

Ena peeked her head out to see if she could borrow some makeup from Myrrel, but she had vanished. Hultur's door was closed, and as she crept closer she could hear the two of them chatting. Hultur didn't sound any warmer and Ena couldn't walk around with her natural skin showing. Mentally apologizing, she knocked.

Myrrel answered the door with a smile and a tilt of her head. When she saw it was Ena she scowled and glanced back. "Hey, Ena, you going somewhere?"

Ena could take a hint. Luckily Hultur wasn't in direct line of sight, or he would've noticed Ena snickering at her friend. "I need a coat of brown before I hit the town. Do you still have some skin creams?"

"Yeah, lemme show you where I keep it. I'll be back soon," she called back to Hultur.

"Give me no concern. I have plenty of reading that needs to be done."

Myrrel closed the door and muttered in conspiratorial tones. "You see what I have to work with."

Ena followed close to keep up the whisper. "Why the sudden interest in him?"

"The man is seven-and-a-half feet tall and has a literal magic penis. I owe it to the prosperity of all women to see how well it works."

Ena was laughing too hard to think of anything witty to say to that. "Aren't we in a city full of men?"

Myrrel closed the door behind them. "Those men?" She shook her head and got out her makeup, placing each and every container onto a nearby vanity. "I mean, they're fit, but at what cost? I've heard men literally fight over women in this country. I don't know about you, but watching a man get beat unconscious isn't going to put me in the mood. From what I've seen of Vergebaum Heff, I don't think I'm gonna like Fieta."

Ena approached the mirror and grimaced. There were so many powders and creams and all of them looked as useful as the other. Myrrel had been helping her beautify for the past two years and she was still helpless without her.

"You want some help?"

Ena pouted. "Sorry. You should dress up too. Maybe it'll help Hultur see you in a different light."

Myrrel went to work, applying products that she so rarely applied to the light patches on her own skin. "No, if I'm too obvious he's gonna know something's up. I literally had to tell him, 'Social bonds help keep morale high,' to get him to talk to me. This man's never had a romantic thought in his life. Well, I guess he was a woman at some point. How do you think that's changed his perspective?"

"You could ask him."

She scoffed.

"What if I asked him?"

"You would?"

"Yeah, why not. I mean, he is my subordinate now, so that might make him more inclined to share details about his life," Ena suggested.

"Abusing your power for personal reasons. Torno would be proud."

Ena scowled and ruined Myrrel's work around the eyes.

Myrrel chuckled, soaking up her victory. She made Ena soften her face and fixed the mess of colors. "Speaking of the knave, did you know about Torno and Fascinosa?"

"No. I assumed he knew Fascinosa since he hired him to take us from one end of the world to the other. But I never would've guessed that Torno was hiring his ex. They had to be lovers, right? That goodbye was..." Ena had to stop talking as Myrrel worked on her lips.

"The kiss? Yeah. Wow, that was something else. There was definitely history there. Do you want me to add some gold lines to your cheeks? I only know how to do spirals and pedals, but I don't think they work on your face."

"Yeah, don't bother. I wish I could look like how I looked back in Sothlen. I felt so sexy."

"Camellia, you always look sexy." She looked over her.

Ena tilted sideways and struck a little pose.

"That's it, girl. Just like that. See that man, give him that look, and he'll be yours."

Ena giggled. "Are you going to ask Torno about him and Fascinosa?"

"Fuck, no. You?" Myrrel held the door open.

"I tried to apologize. He acted like he didn't care, but I can't help but feel like I'm ruining Torno's love life."

Myrrel gave her a weighted look.

"What?"

"Why all this interest in Torno all of a sudden?"

"He's my subordinate now. Isn't it my responsibility to know what's going on with everyone?"

"Why, so you can lead like Torno?"

The comment sat ill with Ena. Even though she'd given Torno crap for sticking his nose in their lives, she didn't want to grow apart from her friends. There had to be a way for them to communicate their feelings without Ena overstepping her authority.

Done with touching up Ena, Myrrel went back to Hultur's private room. She gave him two knocks of warning before opening the door. She led the way in and showed off Ena like a project. "What do you think?"

Hultur only picked his eyes out of his book for one second. "Well applied. I saw no smudges."

"You barely looked at her."

He glanced again. "No smudges."

"Hey," Ena said to grab his attention, before sitting on the couch next to his office. "You were born a woman, weren't you? Don't you have any opinions on any of this?"

He sighed, put a bookmark between the pages, and twisted his chair around so he could face her. "I do not. My time as a woman was unpleasant for a variety of reasons. I had an aversion to makeup and an allergy to a very common ingredient found in cosmetic powders. When I was dressed up in *ibbi tan* for my sixth birthday, my face was bumpier than flatbread. It displeased my father and shamed my father's mother."

Myrrel sat on the bed beside Hultur. "Why did it upset them so much?"

"Every woman is raised to learn the spear, but when she must lay it down, she is expected to do so to take in the spear of the flesh."

Ena visibly cringed at the mention of "spear of the flesh."

"Quite the disgusting term, is it not?" he asked with something resembling enthusiasm.

Ena nodded. "I'm sorry. I know it's part of your people's culture-"

"I despised it. I despised the term and the expectations. Though I am born Ki'an, I find it difficult to relate to them," he grumbled.

"Is that why you dislike Visk?" Myrrel pried.

Hultur blinked but betrayed no emotions. "I know nothing of her character, but I have a hatred for her reputation; and her legacy."

"You knew about Visk before meeting her?" Ena leaned forward with interest.

After fraught deliberation, he nodded. "I was raised in Libesh; the Bleeding Sands. Our clans were deathsworn. Every victory she won, shamed my people, but tales of Viskursang were some more. I was ten when she began winning skulls. She became the standard that all other women were measured against. Even in my lands, the geshuri spoke of her and her urahatu as an example for young girls to strive for."

"You don't sound like you enjoyed that."

He shook his head. "I hated combat."

Myrrel reached out and grabbed his massive biceps. "Really? With these bad boys?"

"It was my hate that gave me strength. The better I was at breaking my opponent, the quicker I could return to my studies. I grew powerful only so that I could avoid accusations of negligence. My father and uncle cherished their time with me, and whenever one was busy, I could learn the trade of the other." He smiled as warm memories returned, but darkness soon devoured that mirth.

Myrrel tried to soften the conversation. "At least it wasn't all bad."

"Those happy moments were cloaked in secrecy and shame. My mother opposed my studies in every way she could. She hated me as only a mother can hate her daughter. Every victory of mine was too slow or too sloppy. I spent every free moment of my adolescence learning about spells, history, machines, philosophy, and other masculine pursuits. My behavior dishonored the women of my family. Were familial shame non-existent in our culture, she would've whipped me in the streets and encouraged all to throw stones at me." A snarl broke through his grimace. "I do not like to reflect on this."

"Okay, well, what if we talked about something a little lighter?" Ena asked with a smile. "Did you have a girlfriend growing up? You must've had an Urahatu, right? Or was that only a custom practiced in the Diamond Sands?"

"Wherever the geshuri are welcome, Ki'an women bleed for each other. I had no Urahatu. My first menstruation was a full year after all of my peers. The women of my age cut me with their rejection and when I was made to ask those younger, the wound grew infected. My mother and sisters wouldn't accept my isolation and demanded that I look to girls two years younger. In my first real act of rebellion, I dishonored my family and cut my own arm." He pulled at the fabric of his sleeve, but it was too tight to be rolled back and so he ripped it clean to show the scar. It was deep and spread out in tendrils; scarified to be so much more than a simple cut.

Myrrel and Ena shared a look of shock.

"As I said, I do not have pleasant memories from my time as a girl, nor a woman. Though that time was thankfully short." He breathed out a long, slow breath to calm himself.

"Then let's move past that," Ena said with a smile. "You're just a man named Vamere."

"I actually prefer to be called Hultur."

Ena didn't want to relent on that point, but he needed to be relaxed if this conversation was going to go anywhere. "Okay, you're Hultur, the man. Not Hultur, the Master of Evil and all of that, but just a man. Have you ever been aroused? Have you ever wanted someone to touch you?"

He considered her question in expressionless silence before answering with a simple, "Yes."

His delayed answers gave Ena hope, but after everything Hultur had said, Myrrel was guarded.

"We don't have to talk about this if you don't want to."

"I want to. There was wisdom in your words, Myrrel. Companionship is an important part of any group. If I am to be a member of your team, I will need to share a little of myself." He seemed to dread this, grimacing like the memories had to be extracted out of him with blades and pliers.

"My feelings of lust are strong as any man I've read about, but they are corrupting."

"Corrupting?" Ena asked before seeing Myrrel's raised hand intending to silence her.

"My first encounter with lust sapped me of concentration for days. I was only able to dispel this distraction by beating a tested warrior half to death. Since then I've endeavored to keep lust as nothing more than a passing thought."

Ena looked to Myrrel, who asked, "What's it like now?"

"Lust is a dark memory now, nothing more."

"Umm..." Myrrel tried several times to improve her own mood in hopes of changing the atmosphere.

"If you'll excuse me, I have a great deal of serious research I was hoping to work on tonight. Our talk will stay in my memory. I will endeavor to find a more pleasing story about my life without love when we next bond."

The women had no choice but to agree and left him. Having soured the mood for both of them, Myrrel decided to try her luck at the hotel bar, and Ena went to buy new clothes.

THE TWENTY-NINTH CHAPTER

In Which Ngoltur Takes Matters Into Her Own Hands

Lively as the streets were, Ena found the markets of Vergebaum Heff subdued by comparison. Vendors didn't hawk their wares until anyone's eyes lingered too much on any object. It wasn't until she found a man with familiar brown skin that she realized they were talking about the history of the object, their manufacturer, and the great skill required to craft the object. The man spitting Dorospek bragged about the accomplishments of the designer like he was a personal friend of the merchant's.

Finding something to wear had its own set of problems. For one thing, women's fashion seemed to arise out of traditional Ki'an garb, but favored the aesthetic of violence rather than any military application. Scalemail was woven onto leather bikini straps with smooth undersides. Cloth shirts gave the illusion of brigandine patterning, even though the fabric was cut off at the ribs to let a woman show off her stomach. Ornamental chains with blunt-tip spikes dangled between shoulder pads and bracelets to create the illusion of an arm guard. Massive spiked pauldrons of linen attached to a matching top that looked closer to a brazier for the skin it showed. Hip to shin velvet skirts were made to look like faulds of steel, opened enough on the side, back, and front to ride anything a woman desired.

Though Ena thought these were perhaps novelty items, all but the poorest women were walking around with this look. They held their heads held high, proudly exposing hairless thighs, oiled abs, and cleavage made shiny from skin creams. It was all very daring and Ena was enticed to make a purchase, only the costs rivaled the gown she bought in Sothlen; which offended her sensibilities as a shopper, as she was hardly buying any fabric at all!

Nearby, more sensible styles could be purchased from less pricey competitors. Ena purchased a shoulder cape decorated with a faux chain-mail pattern made from gray threads, a proper jacket with aluminum scalemail pattern woven against the ribs, pants with a knee to calf faux-armor made from some flexible, smooth substance that was shinier than wax, long boots with a steel armor plate sticking up from the toe, and a necklace with the glyphs for a second-tier blizzard spell hanging like a meaningless trinket.

That was another interesting thing about the people of Vergebaum Heff. Despite the fact that there seemed to be no actual magic, they'd taken to displaying magical glyphs as bits of stylistic flare. Men walked around with fire spell glyphs tattooed on their chest, women had lightning glyphs drawn on their cheek, children wore capes with glyphs to summon clouds of decaying darkness, and none found it strange.

Back at her suite, the garment bags found a home on lounge chair and Ena was too anxious to sit. She'd accomplished the one thing she'd set out to do and now, she had intended to go back to her training. Only, she couldn't take a step into the small study. The mere sight of her bags gave her pause. Inside was her journal where she'd written notes about Torno's advanced magicks and Ki'an battle dances and a whole lot of her ramblings from inside the rug of haste. It was still there, the rug. It would be an easy matter to unroll it and accomplish days of training and yet, she couldn't even take the damn thing out.

Sighing, she paced and chastised herself for being so craven. This wasn't a boat. She'd have plenty of time to focus on her studies inside the rug and no one would be there to watch her change. She wouldn't have to deal with Hultur's orbs or Torno's questions or Fascinosa's rejections. She missed him. Looking at the mirror, she saw a beautiful Gulam woman.

It wasn't just Myrrel's skin creams that made her look beautiful. Men had fallen in love with her, they had proposed to her. Denying that truth didn't make her any more humble, it only reinforced the cruelty she endured as a child. She felt sexy and she wasn't about to pass the time alone in her room.

There were no shortage of bars in the area, though it was hard to tell what made one stand out. Strangely, fist fights seemed to draw ever larger crowds. A pair of Leben women giggled at the sight of a man tossed out bloody and they primped their hair on their way inside. One tavern had a sign on the window in Dorospek, "Live Music! Live Spirits! Dead Magic!" Ena chuckled, walked past, and came back around to try it out.

String instruments and dim lanterns created an instantly calm atmosphere. Patrons were a mix of people too old or too poor to adorn themselves in the flashy, aggressive styles she'd seen in the marketplace, and there were several brown-skinned patrons who looked too tired to be anything but locals. The bartender was a Leben-Gulam mixed woman with dazzling ring of indigo surrounding otherwise brown eyes. The woman must've been something breath-taking in her twenties because she was gorgeous in her forties, if not a little worn down by the hardships she'd survived.

She asked something in Fietspek before quickly switching to Dorospek. "What are you looking to drink?"

"Do you have a whiskey that's light on the tongue?"

She nodded and poured a glass. The woman then

scooped out water with a specialized spoon. It was an ice spoon just like back home. Ena smiled and watched the woman cast an ice spell, turned it around, and smacked the ice out with a practiced motion that chained naturally with the spell. The bartender took her fee and was on to the next patron.

When a man did finally approach Ena, she found him energetic, but obnoxious. She tried to engage the Leben man about his job and he used that as an excuse to flex his bicep. Her attempts to talk about the world only made him go on about his own journey to the Far Lands, where he'd snuck his way into the male harem of some wealthy woman. It wasn't that the man was physically off putting, he had the same engorged muscles as every other man in that city, but there was nothing interesting about him. He didn't have any tattoos or jewelry and he told her nothing about his interests, save that he did in fact have a penis, and had even used it on occasion.

Five men walked in with a presence that commanded the attention of all in the forty person bar.

They were warriors of some kind. Battle-tested steel lay oiled, stained, and scratched atop leather and thick cloth. Swords rested in sheathes on their belts, and all wore the symbol of a two-headed bird on their breastplates. The man in the lead was Ki'an and his face was clean shaven. His orange-gold eyes were cunning, and looked over every person before he nodded to his fellows and chatted up the bartender.

Like most Ki'an men, he was shorter than the women but was still an imposing six-and-a-half feet tall. He had wide shoulders, which was very unlike male Ki'an, and his chin length hair was unbraided and unoiled. He seemed to have quite a bit of rapport with the bartender, and she made him crack a smile several times. He had a good smile, it was warm and inviting. Eventually, he glanced over at Ena and the bartender said something that made him laugh.

When the big man approached, Ena remembered her drink and then remembered the Leben man who had been going on about something for a good minute or ten. The man in armor met her eyes. What Ena might've once confused for disgust, was very clearly interest. He looked to her like Torno gazing upon Kalta and closed the distance between them. There was nothing intimidating in the way this beefy man stepped between Ena and the man chewing her ear. He wanted to be there, and so that's where he stood.

"I'm Obi. Tell me your name."

"Excuse me," came the Leben man. He'd mentioned his name at some point, but Ena didn't bother to remember it. The slighted man stood up and puffed out his chest and he almost came up to Obi's shoulder. "I was talking to her."

Obi barked a question. "You're lovers?"

"No, but-"

"Did she promise to go home with you tonight?"

"No, but that's hardly-"

Obi stepped forward and the man retreated, pushing his hip into the edge of the bar. "Are you going to make Izild clean up any blood?"

He glanced at the bartender, Izild.

She was cleaning a glass. "I don't like cleaning up blood. These are new floors too."

The Leben man slinked off.

Obi turned his attention to Ena and sat where the Leben man had been. "Name?"

She supposed that a proper lady would refuse to give her name. None of his behavior was civil in Caredor and she should expect to be treated with certain measure of respect. But then again, she liked how he looked at her. There it was more than that. She was enticed by the depth of his voice and even the way he bullied the shorter man. Ena wasn't like Myrrel. When faced with this casual violence, some of it excited her.

"Ena." She offered her hand.

The man cared nothing for formalities and didn't take her hand. "Your beauty excites me. I wish to take you to my room and fuck you."

Whether it was a language barrier or just this man's way, Ena didn't mind. The brusque tone compelled her. She could only obey or fight him, and Ena was tired of fighting. The longer she stared into those deep eyes, the longer she wanted to see the shape of his muscles underneath all that armor. "I want that too."

~ ~ ~

Nothing held any reverence in Obi's compact flat, be it a map, his collection of swords, or the small gold statues collecting dust. Everything had a place simply because the item was placed there. A desk sat in a corner collecting dust, boxes kept the chair from being usable. The floors were clean as they could be, with the man's possessions taking up more real estate then the flat could reasonably accommodate. He used the place to change clothes, store his stuff, and fuck. At a glance, Ena wasn't even sure if he slept there.

But she wasn't there to sip tea.

For all the disarray and neglect the room suffered from, the bed was clean, the blankets were fresh, and the mattress was soft as the one in her hotel--as a cloud. Her shoes were kicked to one side and she sat on the bed to watch him undress. Armor could not be flung off like a shirt, the man had to work off those worn-down plates of steel. Knicks and dents marred the metal. Red stains spotted the aketon that separated metal from flesh, and they were folded and placed in the bare corner assigned for his return.

With the threads of everything that could be called armor gone, she got to see the man underneath. She expected a man indented by the curves of highly defined muscles, but saw a body as practical as armor. He was solid. Arms, abs, and chest were leaner than she expected. These weren't oiled objects of display, but weapons of war. Thick scars of failed death marked his body like crevices. Along his belly, three mismatched shapes came close to ending him. Flesh had burned into jagged patterns, forever marking where lightning had struck the man. He pulled off a shirt damp with sweat and exposed a section of raised flesh on his chest that had taken off a nipple and surely came close to puncturing his heart. Thick black hairs mottled that scarlet skin of his.

She bit her lip.

With a nod, he beckoned her.

She slid off her pants and stood to let them fall to the floor. His glimmering, orange-gold eyes studied the bare flesh of her legs and lingered on the damp mark where her vagina had stained her panties. He scowled. Not out of anger, but from a hunger he willed to wait. His chest rose and fell as deep breaths fought shallow ones. He flicked at the buckle of his sword belt, and it fell to the ground with a clunk.

Her head naturally came up to his large, hairy chest, and so her hands found his taught stomach effortlessly. Every time he breathed she could feel the shape of his abs underneath. Scarred bits of skin danced under hairs that thickened as they spread down. Oh, she shouldn't have looked down. Her lungs weren't ready for a bulge like that, nor the way it strained against the cloth.

Breaking whatever seductive dance they were performing, she touched his cock. It was bent against his pants, promising to be larger still once freed. Her hands worked the straps, his caressed her arms before gripping her with a sense of urgency. A grunt brought her eyes to his. They glowed like a bonfire. Restraint kept his hands on her clothes, but they were tightening. Flexing pectorals and biceps promised to tear the cloth free. The time had come to bare herself to him and she did so without any thought to his shock.

When she took sight of him again, he was naked, still standing in a hump of clothes that hid a man crafted by pain. That gorgeous cock of his was more spear than sword, in not only the pronounced swell of its helmet, but the thick length of its swelling shaft. Long and erect as it was, she found the flesh still subtle, giving where she squeezed him. It pumped like a heart and was slow to consolidate its power.

He took her hips. Another brief glance of permission and she went from being eye level with his sternum to having that smooth face of crimson staring fire at her. She wrapped her arms around those solid shoulders, her legs half on his ribs and caressing those hips. He kissed her, his lips half open already, and she wasted no time bringing her tongue into his mouth. And it curled her toes the way his tongue smoothed against hers. He held her body with his large hands on her thighs and ass, but she dictated how their kiss went. And her tongue was moving faster. Her hands couldn't get enough of his surprisingly soft hair that grew damper by the second.

Sweat collected between them where chest met chest. The pounding of his heart shook her. She slid down along the length of his body, and her wet panties came to rest against the rigid flesh of a now fully erect cock. A grunt of need from him was all the warning she had before he'd laid her down onto the bed. A final glance of permission, she answered by jerking the panties half off herself. His thick arms snapped the threads as easily as the man could surely snap a neck.

Fuck, she wasn't ready for that massive penis. The helmet, swollen as it was, spread her apart like the first time all over. She had to work her legs to take in the thickness of him. He assisted with care, parting her at the thighs. She worked the lips of her vagina and positioned him perfectly, and still he cleaved her. She was made taught around him, and it took so little work from his hips to bring that cock into her depths. If she wasn't so fucking wet, he never would've made it. There was so much of him and so little of her.

Just holding it inside her, she could feel the heat of her lust burning. Small pivots in her hips brought him back enough to give her relief or position him against the yearning walls inside. He pulled back slowly and she shivered with relief and a need to have him fill her again. But he couldn't thrust. His balls never touched her. A single, solid thrust might actually tear her.

She realized with some shame that she'd been screaming. Whether it had been from pain or pleasure hadn't mattered. There was pain--there was indeed pain. He pulled back slowly until the base of his head spread her lips further and then he looked at her.

"Say when."

What does he mean? He slid back in, deeper and deeper. Her hands slapped onto his back, but there was nothing to grab. That back was wet and thick, but she curled her fingers in. Nails met skin. *Fuck it, what's ten scars to him?* Then the pleasure was replaced with a sensation like falling. Panic. He was too deep. He'd hit something inside. She thrashed not in pleasure, but like a rabbit in the jaws of a wolf. This beast could finish her.

"Less, less," she panicked.

He slid back.

Fear brought her hands down. She found herself pressing against him, but he was holding tight. It was okay. This was fine. He could just kill her with his fucking penis. No big deal. He kissed her cheek. His lips smacked to pull air back.

She was covered in sweat. So was he. She ran her hands over that glorious chest, her fingers lingering over that scar on his heart. He kissed her cheek again. She kissed his lips. He was warm and hungry. There was passion in that kiss. His tongue almost flicked against hers, he was so eager to feel her flesh. He was so horny, desperate to fuck, but he held his cock deep inside, waiting for her signal.

She pulled back, nodded and watched. From one extreme to the other he worked slowly, mapping the path of her with precision. He barely saw her. Those burning eyes closed and concentrated on the thrust of his cock. And he did thrust. He thrust deep, fast, hard, and stopped just shy of the end of pleasure. His gasps, his grunts, his every moan and hiss wasn't for her. This was for him. He wanted her to satisfy his needs.

"Do it," she told him. "Fuck me."

He grunted louder. He was panting, gasping as his hips failed to meet their edge, but surged from the insatiable hunger of a man who couldn't fuck her with everything he had. She knew that feeling, of being denied more than she was. That had been her fucking life-one of hiding and fear. No more of that. She would take the pain with the pleasure.

"Do it, you sexy man," she grunted. "Fuck me."

His thrusts came frantically. His thick, leathery hands grabbed her body and kept her steady with a pressure that promised to bruise. Then he pounded into her. Far past flames, past the point of being hot, her body crackled. She grabbed him, needing to feel his flesh. It was inside her, so deep, so fucking thick and hard. And she came before she even knew it. She screamed into his ear, shouting obscenities. She steadied him. Gripping him with her legs. She pulled back, found that perfect spot, and flicked at her clit as the orgasm continued to wrack her body. She shook and cracked and shattered.

Breathing.

That was all she could do then. Fuck, if he wasn't far more than she could handle. He was still so thick and ready to keep going. She just wanted to pass out. If someone tossed her into a coffin and buried her, she would the mistake. He was breathing hard too, more grunts than wheezes. There was still so much need in this gorgeous lump of flesh called man.

She took him by the cheeks and kissed his lips, as he strained to stay still, she pulled back to look him in the eyes. "You need it, sexy?"

He gave an affirming grunt.

Licking her hand in a single obscene gesture, she could

feel him pulsing with anticipation inside her. With a hand wet and ready, she guided his cock out, pushing against his hips until her head slammed against the wall. She grabbed the base of his cock and the sound of that man's satisfaction threatened to quake her innards all over again. Tenderly, she cradled his balls. She could feel the churn of them as they pressed deeper into his body.

"You poor, sexy man. You don't get to really fuck, do you?"

Another grunt. Shock and elation softened hard features on his face. He kissed her sloppy and full of need. She tilted her head, directing his lips to her cheek and neck. Her hand worked him from the base to not even half the length of that huge cock. His hips shivered, and he pushed into her. She could take him like this. She wanted to. She wanted this sexy man to get what he needed.

"That's right, sexy. Move those hips."

He didn't so much grunt as he screamed. He was lost to lust. He was pushing into her now, shoving his abs against her arm. Whenever he slowed to linger on that feeling of satisfaction she rolled her fingers along his testicles and it spurred him back into action. And fuck, that massive cock felt glorious in her hand. He was so thick and hard, harder then he'd been when he was entering her. This was his pleasure they worked towards and he was holding little back as he fucked her hand.

Lips left her skin. He pressed a hand against the wall for leverage. She scooted up to suck at his neck. He fucked harder, moving as fast as those deadly hips would go.

Taken by this need to pleasure him she spurred him on with a growl. "That's right. Do it! Cum, you sexy bastard. Cum. Cum. Cum!"

Something slapped her cheek. It was wet, and full of heat. More of it followed. He spurted onto her tits and all over her belly. She was drenched in him, covered in the fresh orgasm of a man at last satisfied. And her hand left those quivering balls and shaking cock and found her clit. She rubbed herself and pressed up, mashing her smothered belly into that still surging cock. She came, screaming into his ear. He kissed her to silence her and the orgasm flared back to full, illuminating her like a fireball.

They lay like that with all sense of urgency faded. Gasping was the only option for her. She had thought she wasn't ready for a fight, but that had been a fight. She took on the challenge, and he kissed at her cheek with gratitude. Oh, she smiled to feel those lips and hear that coo of pleasure. He sounded like a tiger purring. She liked that sound. Pride swelled in her chest and she realized with no small elation that her anxieties had given her a reprieve. There was a confidence that filled her and she had the sense that any challenge that came to her, she would be ready for it.

They made out for a little bit. He ran his hands over the liquids of their sex on her belly, hers tenderly stroking along that slowly ebbing cock and into the short hairs on his chest and pelvis. He liked to kiss her slowly, and she was happy to accommodate. She found she liked to grab his wet hair, even pulled it back a little to move his chin into the range of her lips. Satisfying as these acts of casual pleasure were, he didn't swell again in her hand, and she knew she couldn't take another ravaging.

Obi tossed her a towel and got into the shower. Getting dry was a more daunting task then she would've thought. They'd been lying there for so long, their sweat and sex mingled together like an estuary. With a little bit of shame, she pulled back the curtain of the shower. Obi was already lathered up from neck to knees. His hands were working his way down to the toes.

"Sorry, it's too small to share."

So she leaned into the wall and enjoyed the view. "That's alright. I'll find another way to amuse myself."

He smiled at her like a man finding religion. "You're something else, you know that?"

So, his brusque attitude hadn't been the result of language after all. Ena was finding the man more appealing by the minute. The sight of his awestruck eyes made her heart flutter.

"I'm glad you found me pleasing." She giggled.

He nodded emphatically. "So much more than that. Are you staying in the city?" He rinsed off, running those large hands over his solid body. He caught her staring and laughed with pride.

"Staying? No, I don't think so. There's a lot of traveling I need to do. I might have to go from one end of Leben Erde to the other."

"You need some protection?"

They traded places in the shower.

"I'm a mercenary," he told her.

Ena made sure to leave the curtain open. She liked the way those orange-gold eyes watched her move. "Hiring you after that would feel like paying a prostitute."

He chuckled. "It's more than just me and my boys from the bar. I'm the leader of a mercenary company. We're a hundred strong on a good month, but more affordable than you might think. I'm open to negotiating a lower rate, provided we get a percentage of wealth obtained on the road."

"Wealth obtained...?" Ena wasn't sure what he meant by that or why he was being so pushy about this. Her eyes followed his to the dark skin creams bleeding off her forearms and a few facts came together. Ngoltur. He knew she was Ngoltur and knew that she didn't have any reason to be on Leben Erde before the end of the Grand Dream. He could be talking about the percentages of a city treasury.

Obi spoke with a measured tone for addressing a Turall. "Guard work comes with the spoils of war. Brigands end up with a few valuable things they have no way to hock, things like that. Even if you only travel to the edge of Fieta, you should seriously consider hiring a mercenary company.

There's lots of Reptears out there, especially with fall coming around."

Reptear were created to kill the monsters of the continent in the same way Marinelds made the oceans safer. It had been the idea of one of Ngoltur's sons, King Olaur III. He used Leben Erde as a staging ground to test out the viability of an autonomous monster hunter race. Within a generation, the Reptears had learned to work with monsters. The lizard-men were not only a blight on Leben Erde, but a key argument against supporting monarchies.

Hiring this man might be a great way to defend against the unknown threats of Leben Erde, but his protection would come with complications. Obi might keep her identity a secret at first, but sooner or later there'd be a subordinate that needed to know, and then the whole of Leben Erde would know that Ena was Ngoltur Reborn.

Ena anticipated a long drawn out argument. "I'm part of a team and all of us know how to handle ourselves. We should be fine."

Expecting a perturbed mien, she was relieved to find him staring at her hands running lather over her breasts.

"Lemme guess," Ena mused. "I'm fine and know how to handle myself?"

"Huh? No, I was just going to say you have a sexy body."

Ena laughed.

"I don't like word games. I like things to be simple, direct. That's why I prefer guard work; there's rarely drama."

By his tone, she could guess that Obi had been a part of sieges and played weapon in some politician's armory. Yet, his expression was relaxed and was more interested in the sight of her body than the shadows of his past. When Ena stepped out of the shower, he was dressed in finery fit for any merchant. He handed her another fresh towel.

"If you change your mind about hiring us, send word to any fort in Fieta that you want to hire the Twin Eagles and we will find you."

"It's a nice name," she said conversationally. "How'd you choose it?"

"My wife and I picked it out."

Ena burned with shame. Had she just fucked a married man?!

He chuckled at her shock. "We're divorced."

Ena leaned against him to catch her breath.

Laughter shook his chest. When it died in his lungs, he leaned down and kissed her. It was soft, tender, and a way of saying goodbye. "It's been great. If you're ever in the city again, look for me. Izild usually knows where I am."

Great. After making him come so hard that it turned his permanent frown into a smile, Obi described their sex as "great." The man was no poet. "Oh, okay. Are you waiting for me to leave?"

He nodded in haste. "I'm running late."

There was clearly more to say about that, but the man showed no intention of explaining. Ena got back into her drab clothes and walked out. He showed her down to the stairs, locked the front door of his apartment building and marched off like he didn't even know her. Maybe it was best that he was acting so removed. This was goodbye and even if Ena came back to Fieta, she wasn't sure she'd look for the "great" man.

THE THIRTIETH CHAPTER

In Which Ngoltur Argues
with a Fool

F un as her encounter with Obi had been, Ena hadn't expected to wake up with so much pain. Outside of her entire downstairs being out of commission and the feeling that she couldn't walk or ride saddle, her wrist was killing her. There was even some pain in her shoulders and hips. She'd been a little disappointed that Obi left her so suddenly, but all things considered, it was for the best. Healing magic took care of the worst of her problems, but she wasn't sure what to use on her nether regions. Myrrel probably knew a spell, but Ena wasn't about to ask for the incantation. There were parts of her life that she didn't want her friends to know about.

There were a lot of things on Ena's mind, but she wasn't in a circle of haste. She needed to keep active or she would fall into lethargy. So she went through the long process of dressing like a Fieta native. The blue skin creams did a decent job of making her look like a Leben, but her own natural paleness kept her looking untanned and sheltered. Well, maybe it would mean the locals wouldn't look twice at her.

Candle flames became useless with the rise of the sun. A wave of her hand put out the scented oddities and she made her way into the hall. It was quiet. She couldn't hear Sal grinding his teeth or Myrrel's snoring. Somewhere in the rooms Visk was probably thrashing in her sleep and Narla was muttering from her night terrors. Any of them would be happy to help her, but they would standout. There was only one person Ena could take with her.

Ena knocked on the door to Torno's room.

Maybe he wouldn't answer. Maybe he was out sleeping with some sexy beau, or a marineld that reminded him of Fascinosa. She needed to get that kiss out of her head.

Thankfully, Zukoch answered the door. He was already dressed and flushed indigo. "Morning, Ena. You here for Torno?"

She shook her head. "I'm going out for some supplies. Do you have my coin?"

"Yeah, hold on."

He closed the door but left it open a crack. Leaning forward, she listened for the sound Torno's nocturnal murmurs, but only heard Zukoch moving coins. He was out with someone. It made her feel feint, but she was supposed to be relieved.

Zukoch came back with a bag of coin. "I was able to get 7 gold and 4 silver for each gulda." He was about to pull them out and count them back to her, but she swiped it.

"That's fine. Listen, I'm gonna need your help with the bartering. Can you come with me?"

"Sure. Is it close by?"

"No, I'm gonna need to go to the Gulam district."

"Oh, uh, that might be a problem. We-"

The door was flung open. A mostly naked Torno stood with his hand on the door. She'd seen him naked and "in action" when she experienced Kalta's memories, but seeing him in person was something else. He was older. His lithe compact frame had filled out with impressive muscles. Obi had been build for war, but Torno seemed to have been crafted for Ena. The sight of his abs popping in and out with his breath drew her eyes down and that made her glance down at his boxers. She didn't see anything, which was a shame because he had a gorgeous body below the hemline.

Blushing, she brought up a hand to block him from her view.

"You're not going," Torno barked.

"You're not in charge anymore, remember, Torno? And you're not even dressed."

"I'm in my boxers," he grumbled.

"What's the problem?" Zukoch asked.

"She's going there to look for Kalta."

"What?" she scoffed. "You think I'm going to look for Kalta to try and get revenge?"

"I wouldn't put it past you. It's honestly not a bad idea, but she'd rip the ether out of your half-spells."

"So what? I'm not going there to fight her. I just need some supplies. Maybe a set of rings since you keep telling me that's the only way my poorly trained ass can fight, and can you put some clothes on?"

Rolling his eyes he picked up a bed sheet and draped it over his chest. "Better?"

"Zukoch, puts your boots on and let's go. It takes this dandy twenty minutes to get dressed."

"As I was trying to tell you, I really don't think that's a good idea. We won't be able to check out without talking to the hotel staff and grooms."

Ena had no idea what a groom was, but focused on the major point. "Hultur can help them with that."

"He doesn't speak Gwos." Zukoch saw the confusion and clarified. "Fietspek."

Ena groaned.

Torno dropped the sheet and jumped the bed. Clothes were flying over his head. "Save your breath, Zukoch. She's going."

"I'm not going if it's going to be an inconvenience."

Torno guffawed. "I know that look in your eye. You

won't be talked out of it, so I've got no choice but to come with you."

"No choice?! You can sit there in your boxers and cry for all I care. I'm not going out into the city and I wouldn't need your help even if I was."

Torno was already dressed and he patted Zukoch's back on the way out. "Make sure our stuff is packed when we return. Chances are good that we'll have to leave here in a hurry."

"How long are you gonna be gone?"

"How long does it take to walk to the Gulam district?"

"Assuming there aren't any zeck potich? An hour."

"Then give us three hours."

Zukoch looked at the clock and repressed an explotive.

Torno thanked him and walked out into the hall, his quick pace all but forcing Ena to fall into step.

"No, you don't. Torno, you're not welcome to accompany me on my trip."

"Then why are you following me?" He asked with that cock-sure grin of his.

"To tell you to go back into your room." She followed him into the perpetually revolving windmill lift, stepping into the same box. "You're not even wearing a disguise."

"Oh, you're right, I should've worn a dark cloak and a pitch-black mask that reads, 'not a spy.'"

"Kalta will notice you," she growled.

"So you are searching for Kalta." And that fucker glowered at her like he'd won some argument Ena never agreed to start.

Jabbing a finger into his not-that-impressive chest, she castigated him. "You are not the boss of me, even if you were still the Broker Captain. What I am doing with my free time is my business and you coming along doesn't help me, it only makes my mission that much harder."

"By walking around looking like a local? What are you going to do if Kalta knows Fietspek or if one of her Mages does? Do you even have a plan of attack?"

"I'm not planning to get into a fight with her."

"Then you're more gullible than I thought you were."

Reaching the bottom, Torno and Ena stepped off in unison. Torno, the master of disguise, put on a hat. Outside of hiding his ostentatious quaff of hair, it did nothing to obscure his features. Ena rolled her eyes and walked out into the city with Torno at her side. The streets looked calm.

"What do you think that zeck potich thing is?" Ena asked.

"I'm pretty sure zecks are those gangs of kids that hit each other with sticks."

Ena glanced at the sky and tried to make her way north. She tried to ignore Torno and not give him the satisfaction of dragging her into one of his arguments, but he'd gone for her character and she wasn't about to let her subordinate think that he could talk to her like that.

"Kalta said that she only wanted you. She was willing to let everyone else go if I gave you to her."

He scoffed. "And you believed her."

"Of course I believed her. What reason would she have to lie?"

"Listen, I don't know how much of the Great Goss you were infected with, but you don't know Kalta like I do. You can't trust her."

"She's an Archmage. You're an exile that had to beg for a job, who does that place in a more trustworthy position?"

"Wow," he said with a condescending laugh.

"What? What is so stupid about what I just said?"

"Kalta got that job because Urson trusted her. Think about that. The Supreme Magus, the monster that breaks apart families and sends soldiers off on suicide missions, trusts her. Now I know I'm still on the outs for siding with a coup-"

"Without telling anyone!"

"Without telling anyone," he conceded without any

genuine humility. "But I wasn't under the impression that anyone had a problem with me actually murdering Magus Yersen. It was the logistics of it, the-"

"Deception and utter disregard for our feelings?!"

"Right. That." He pointed at Ena and continued on gesticulating as they walked. "You can't tell me that you actually believe that Urson's plans are good for Caredor."

"No, of course I don't."

"So why is it you're so eager to trust Kalta? The woman almost killed you."

"Maybe it's because she has good reason not to trust you. Did you ever think of that? As far as she knows we're sucked into your bullshit."

"And what a vortex of feces it is," he said dripping with sarcasm if not literal filth.

"Shut up," she snapped. "Kalta is an Archmage. It's her job to ensure that Caredor has order and follows the rule of law. I'm not about to condemn her to death simply because you had a bad breakup."

"It was more than just a bad breakup," he said through his teeth.

"I don't wanna hear about it, Torno." Growling, she turned her eyes back to the road and focused on her argument. "You are a traitor. She had every reason not to trust you or me. I can't believe that every Archmage is perfectly fine with Urson and the Great Generation and all of the evil that he's committed in the name of his damn thaumocracy. If we find her, you're going to hide, and let me do all the talking."

"You really don't know the first thing about Kalta."

Ena rolled her eyes at his ignorance. Oh, she knew the first thing about her alright. She knew what she looked like naked, how she felt about Torno, and his cock, and the kind of sounds she made when she was having an orgasm. It was all pretty embarrassing. Beyond that mess, she knew that Torno was the one who wronged her by cheating. He deserved to be dragged by the Great Goss and his exile was self imposed, besides.

"What do you think it means if Kalta is here on Leben Erde?"

"That she's diligent. That she wants to take you back to Caredor for retribution. Maybe she figures that executing you will quench the flames of rebellion. Your death could be the catalyst that saves thousands of lives."

Torno points. "My neck is right here, executioner."

"From her perspective! You fucking baby."

"Sothlen was in open rebellion when we left it. Did you have a look around my promotion ceremony? Most of the top brass in the city were there. The revolution had momentum and surprise on their side and even if they survived that first night, the leadership was going to be fractured in petty disputes about succession. Our rebellion in Sothlen was a success."

"Oh wow, Torno. You are such a genius, and so handsome too."

"The point is that Caredor is in real danger. They need Archmages like Kalta now more than ever. Those Junior Mages had to have told her about Magus Yersen's death. She's smart enough to know that any one target isn't worth weakening the defenses of Caredor City. If she's here in Leben Erde, that means she doesn't care."

"Or maybe she doesn't know the extent of the rebellion in Sothlen. She likely only got second hand information anyway. Have you thought of that? If we explain this to her, maybe we can get her to go back home."

"Empty handed?" he laughed. "You really don't understand the politics of command if you think she would return with nothing to gain."

"You are such a condescending prick, you know that?!"

"Yeah and you're the Princess of Sincerity."

"I told you not to call me princess."

"Or what, you'll offer me up to Kalta as a token of

peace?"

She forced a laugh. "Don't give me any ideas."

"It won't work." He was suddenly serious, his tone hard as rock. "You could roast me over a spit and it wouldn't do you any good."

"What do you mean?"

"You still haven't figured out how I know Kalta is following us, how I knew she was going to try to attack you."

"You broke her heart, Torno. I don't think this requires empathy magic to understand."

"Your parents live in the Capital."

"And?"

"They live in the Capital within walking distance of Urson's palace, the Chamber of Dreams. Urson put them there to keep an eye on them. Do you think that it's some oversight that he hasn't used his tricks to make them remarry? He's watching them, Ena. He knows about you."

"Bullshit! If he knows..." She looked around at the crowd. Even now, before the Grand Dream was known to be active, merchandise with Muttur's symbol could be seen in every clothing boutique and tattooed on men's biceps. Ena lowered her voice and stepped closer to the knave with an ego problem. "If Urson knows about me, then why did he let me waste away at a third rate Chantry?"

"Why not? Either you were lying and it's good to keep you ignorant of true spellcraft or you were actually that weak and he thought he could control prophecy by keeping you away from any thrones."

Ena hated how intelligent that sounded. "Only a sinful man would conjure up such demented ideas."

"Which is why you need me," he said with a self deprecating smirk.

The weight of Torno's words were sinking in and it drove Ena silent brooding.

"If Kalta is here, she's here for you. My death might be satisfying, but it wouldn't be worth an impromptu trip a quarter of the way around the world. At best, Kalta would come home to a dishonorable discharge from a very public hearing. Kalta will be here because she wants to be the woman that kills Ngoltur."

~ ~ ~

The only thing worse than petulant condescending asshole Torno, was smug I-told-you-so Torno. Kalta was in Vergebaum Heff. Ena knew it from the first Caredor Mage they saw roaming the streets. Spotting them was no great feat. The peacekeepers were instantly recognizable by their crisp crimson uniforms. Every officer bore the square inscribed into a circle, the symbol of the thaumocracy, on their chest. Around the decorated officers, scores of Acolytes fanned out in well-pressed black, the red trim keeping their silhouette in plain view. Kalta's search part was so noticeable, that Torno and Ena were able to stay well out of view just by watching the eyes of the pedestrians.

"Well, Caredor definitely sent someone," Ena grumbled to Torno.

"Our scouting party was a success, now let's get out of here."

"Hey, asshole. I'm in charge, remember? We came all this way, so we might as well buy me a set of rings and bracelets."

He wanted to argue, but the subordinate finally learned to keep his mouth shut and nod. "Just...don't do anything to make a scene."

"You don't make a scene. You're the one that likes to start revolutions!" Ena spotted a arcane emporium with Dorospek on the door. "You know any Fietspek?"

He said a phrase and then clarified, "It means, 'I don't speak Gwos.'"

"Wonderful."

Torno rushed forward to open the door for him.

The motion gave her pause.

Torno glanced out at the crowd. "Fieta men hold the

door open for women."

Conceding with a nod, she walked inside. "You do the talking," she whispered.

"Obviously."

The clerk was a gulam woman with a blackened triangle scaring the top quarter of her face. She brought her one good eye to glower at Ena, but smiled when Torno came in. The damn flirt was smiling back. She spoke honeyed Gwos and ended the phrase with a Dorospek, "Welcome."

"Thank you," Torno said with a smile. He took his time removing his hat. "You speak the Queen's Tongue?"

The clerk smiled crooked. "Uh, I speak Dorospek. I'm not sure what the Queen's Tongue is."

"Queen Ngoltur's tongue," he said with a laugh. He jumped right into small talk and soon she was volunteering information about where she grew up, how many family members she had, how she got her scar, and the stability of her employment as an arcanum dealer. It was all pointless to Ena, but the man made the conversation feel natural. His lie about Ena being his protege was indistinguishable from the things he said with truth.

While he flirted or manipulated the shopkeep, Ena investigated the rings and bracelets. There wasn't anything remarkable about the selection. They all looked like second-hand acquisitions, with a few bearing marks from Caredor chantries. About the only thing to distinguish the weapons were elemental bonds, which would be any help to her since she needed to bleed after initial casting.

Torno handed her a silver bracelet with a band of green hued metal on the inside. The band was mythass, a tarnished alloy of brass made to look like mythril. It wasn't even a good forgery. Ena held it up and clinked the mythass with her finger and he shoved it back into her hands, his focus completely on this middle-aged woman with a rancorous laugh.

Torno grabbed a matching set of rings placed it onto

the table. Then at long last began the haggling and it was a rather dull affair that wasn't going Torno's way. Then midway through, Torno broke into a tangent about breeding kikaas that lasted several minutes. When things got back around to talking about the rings and bracelets, the clerk agreed to Torno's price. It didn't make any sense to Ena, but she still thought Torno overpaid.

When they were outside Ena said, "These bracelets are fake."

"No, they're just not mythril. Brass still makes a decent conductor of ether." The second she started to argue, he interrupted her, "Relax, Precious. I'll buy you the genuine article if we're needed at a ball."

"It's not about appearances and you know that. This cheap brass could shatter or melt if I put too much power into it. We could've spent some extra coin to get a bracelet with quartz."

"We're stranded on another continent. Even if we're only going to be here for a few weeks, we need our coin to last."

Ena wasn't listening. She double backed and craned her neck around a corner to confirm her sighting.

"Is it her?" Torno asked stepping up behind her.

She shook her head. It hadn't been peacekeepers from Caredor that had gotten her attention, but Fieta mercenaries in full armor. They were carrying the banner of their company, the two headed eagle. If the twin eagle with marching down the street in formation, they had to be on a job nearby. This was Obi's mercenary company and they were talking to the acolytes and mages from Caredor.

"Looks like Kalta's hired mercenaries," Torno grumbled.

"I don't know why she would bother," said Ena. "Men with swords aren't much use against wands."

"Their worth jumps tenfold once a side is drained of ether."

Ena chuckled. "That hasn't been an issue so far."

"For you. Those of us untouched by the Gods, have a lot to worry about."

Ena rolled her eyes. "It didn't take you long to tell me how to lead."

He grumbled and stepped around a corner to explain with his big serious voice how the inexperienced Ena should think. "Kalta and I are almost equal, but her spellwork is at least three years ahead of mine. If it comes down to a battle of attrition, she's going to have a spell or two more than me. Visk is capable of forty-two ether a day, but she double casts so she has the combat effectiveness of twenty. Myrrel's vigorous but she won't be casting on the front lines. Narla is wicked efficient, but she was outputting twenty-one before her pregnancy. Now it's probably closer to seventeen."

"Those are caps!" Ena reeled on him. "You know our fucking stats?!"

"It was my job. They gave me your ether caps, efficacy, and quotients when I took the job." He at least had the humility to sound ashamed of it.

Ena took a step back and crossed her arms. "For someone who hates the Magi, you think just like them, you know that?!"

"That's how I was trained," he snapped. "The figures they gave me were off anyway."

"So you used your obsessive nerd brain to calculate the exact numbers, is that what you're telling me?!"

Torno looked away, shame lowering his chin.

"Did you give them reports about us?"

"I didn't have a choice," he muttered.

It would've been satisfying to char him to ash, but it wasn't going to change anything now. The damage was already done. He was their friend and behind their backs he was writing up reports on their stats. Ena's teeth were gnashing together. She turned around and rubbed her temples, but it didn't help.

"Ena..." He reached out for her shoulder.

She reeled about. "Don't touch me!"

His hands were already up. "Sorry."

"No, don't you fucking apologize. I told you not to touch me and-"

Narla's training got Ena's attention, but by the time she saw the Ki'an in armor, she was already yanking Torno back by the coat. In two shift motions, the towering woman had Torno pressed against the wall. One hand twisted Torno's hand at an angle that made grabbing his sidewand impossible and the other was choking the life out of him. Ena had her own concerns.

Another body was headed straight for her. He was tall, imposing, and staggering her breathing. Obi was standing before her in his battle proven cuirass, mail, and leathers. His expression was neutral and his eyes remained hard when they met hers.

Obi was calm when he asked, "Is he causing you trouble?"

Ena couldn't tell if he could see through her disguise, so she stalled. "What do you want with me?"

"I have found gainful employment," Obi explained in an overly impersonal manner. "Archmage Kalta would like to have a word with you. Is this man giving you trouble?"

Fuck. Ena glanced back at Torno.

Torno made his eyes manic and crazed. She nodded, understanding his deception in an instant.

"He's a stranger," Ena lied.

The Ki'an warrior tossed him to the side. Torno rolled on the ground twice over. He seethed and then laughed through his fit of coughing. "You're not my type sweety," he mocked the mercenaries and she returned the sentiment with a swift kick in the gut.

"Are you alright?" Obi asked as he placed a gentle hand on her shoulder.

Her attention hung on Torno's double-over form for

too long. She had to close her eyes to keep up the ruse. "Yes. He startled me, that's all."

"Come along then. If we hurry, the Archmage might still be enjoying breakfast."

THE THIRTY-
FIRST CHAPTER

In Which Ngoltur is Courted

Not twenty-four hours back, she was pushing him to the limits of pleasure but now Obi was about as detached as a man could be. If things got tense with Kalta, Ena knew she couldn't rely on him to come to her aid. Still, there was a short walk to Kalta's location. Maybe she could soften his heart the way Torno had done with the arcanum clerk.

"It sounds like you had a good night." Ena swallowed when his hard eyes looked back at her with worry. "Finding an employer."

"Ah." He cleared his throat and turned his attention back to the street. "Luck was with me."

"So, how much did she spend to employ you?" Ena asked as casually as she could.

"Mercenaries are forbidden to divulge costs to anyone but clients," said the woman behind her. She was about the size of Obi, nothing short, but over a head shorter than Visk.

Ena flashed her a smile. "Sorry." An awkward pause stretched out. "Obi, is this your-"

He cleared his throat loud to silence her. "She is what you might call a scribe or teacher."

"Oh, so you're like the brains." Ena turned around to offer her hand. "I'm Ena."

She shook it. "Parliz."

Ena smiled.

"I killed my brother."

"What?!" Ena stammered.

Parliz pushed her back in step. "I have no problems killing a friend to satisfy a contract."

"Contract is blood," Obi said.

Ena held her arms. "Good to know." Maybe small talk wasn't going to get her anywhere.

~ ~ ~

Casual signs of wealth lined the entrance to the fort. Oh, the tapestries, rugs, and plants all did a great job of elevating the building's pragmatic origins, but the solid stone walls were clearly constructed to withstand attacks. The proprietors would have to take the candles out of the murder holes and lay down a curtain of stone chains on the outside to get it combat worthy, but the location was defensible.

Past the winding entrance, a staging area was filled with colorful vendor stalls selling Ki'an curios. Down one path uniformed bellhops ran back and forth with goods, while another opened up to a cafe and water garden. Ena was directed to move behind the vendors where the space opened further to a terraced dining area.

Along one side workers scrambled to fill orders and the other drew the eye to a marineld singer. She was a soft featured azuneld colored a vibrant purple. Though her words were foreign to Ena, she clearly sang of hope in the darkest of times. Parliz knuckled Ena forward.

Kalta was on a private balcony big enough for twenty people. Three uniformed Mages faked a relaxed posture that their guests performed effortlessly. The Gulam and Leben locals laughed freely, enjoying the splendor of the Caredor's fortune. Obi's entrance made the Mages stiffen at attention.

"She's here," he said in his deep baritone.

Several eyes looked past Ena to try and find the

opalescent princess in the crowd. Only Kalta saw through Ena's disguise at once and her features softened into a warm smile.

"Leave us."

Bodies shifted and twisted past the short Ena, not a one of them understanding who she was. Ena faked a look of confidence and sat by the railing. If Ena turned her head about, she got a serene view of the boats, the docks, the ocean, and her only hope for escape. Obi closed the double doors on his way out. Kalta gestured the air into silence using arm and hand motions Ena didn't recognize.

The Archmage was a vision of Gulam beauty. Though clearly a great deal of work had been put into making the Archmage look regal, they were simple affectations when compared to the woman herself. Hers was an effortless grace made all the more alluring by her beauty-marked chin and discerning eyes. Whereas the years had been humbling for Torno, replacing flawless angles with rugged charm, Kalta had always been an elegant woman that cultivated adoration with envy and time had polished the jewel of her physique.

Beneath her finery, Ena knew she was only more gorgeous than those layers of wealth. She'd seen her naked, viewing the work of a lifetime of dedication in the mirror. Ena had longed for her body, but not simply because she was a perfect obsidian hue. Kalta was fit, toned from ankle to chin. Her breasts were a gravity defying round that never obstructed her movement. Her belly was a taut muscular tapestry that rippled with power when she orgasmed.

Pushing back those images wasn't easy for Ena. She'd been an admirer of hers and in all her time in the rug she'd neglected to realize just how much she still longed to be her. Seeing her smile with warmth, free from the stress of her friends watching, Ena was forced to grapple with the knowledge that she even wanted her sexually. Thankfully, the pain between her legs kept her grounded.

"Thank you for meeting with me, Ena."

Ena declined her head in the same gesture she gave her abusive teachers. "You're welcome."

"I'm glad you came alone. Things were...tense, last time. Wouldn't you agree?"

She nodded.

"You were trying to discuss matters of state and I wasn't receptive to hearing your perspective. I see now that there's some merit to your arguments. The Supreme Magus may have overstepped his bounds. You're right to be critical of him, but you must understand, I wasn't in a position to agree with you."

Ena relaxed. "What do you mean?"

"We were in Caredor City, the very center of Ursen's power. If a spy was reading lips, then I may as well have forfeited my life."

"But you're a figurehead in the Great Generation! You're..." Ena searched for the phrase to exemplify how important she was.

"I'm Kalta Minquet?"

Ena nodded realizing that said more than any title.

"I'm not as free as you might think. Ursen promoted me to keep an eye on me. These underlings make privacy come at a premium. Behind this veil of silence, I can tell you that I'm sympathetic to your cause. You want to bring about an era of peace." Her smile melted Ena's insides. "I can't think of a nobler end."

"So..." Ena had to swallow to find her voice. "You'll help me."

Kalta declined her head. A figure outside the double doors waved to get her attention. "Can I get you anything to eat?"

Ena was starving but she shook her head. Torno wasn't above poisoning Magus Yersen to start a revolution. Kalta could just as easily poison Ena's food and put an end to the Grand Dream before it had truly began. The thought shook her out of Kalta's charms. This woman had already tried to kill her once.

"What about Torno?"

Kalta urged her to continue.

"Torno's a traitor. He killed a Magus and helped start a revolution."

"The man's in Leben Erde. I can hardly be held accountable if a traitor found asylum on another continent." Kalta tried to sound detached, but she couldn't even meet Ena's gaze and his name was carefully avoided.

Ena pressed the issue. "So you're not here to get back at Torno for cheating on you?"

"He broke my heart, that is no trifling difference. I gave myself to him in heart, body, and soul. I believed in him when everyone told me that he was a self absorbed wretch. I begged my parents to accept his marriage proposal and it meant nothing to him! I gave him everything I could and he lied to my face to pursue carnal pleasures." Kalta was starting to seethe. Even through her dark skin, a flush rose to her cheeks.

Closing her eyes, she clasped her hands tight and breathed a harsh, calming, sigh. "I'm sorry. He has that effect on me."

Ena could relate. Maybe not in the same way, but Torno pulled anger out of her.

Kalta continued with a subdued countenance. "I have had many opportunities to destroy Torno, both politically and physically. When Torno returned from his...sabbatical, I was consulted about his potential reform. Ursen would've killed him if I had asked for it, but I urged him to consider mercy. Torno had already been disgraced. I believed that he posed no threat to me or the thaumocracy. I won't make that mistake again."

"That's why you wanted him in custody."

Kalta gave a reserved nod. "He is a man of dangerous ambitions who is willing to lie and murder to get what he wants. His betrayal is the reason I became a peacekeeper."

Ena watched ships from three continents compete for

space between the docks.

"I know that he has been a leader and a mentor to you these past three years. I know full well how charming and convincing he can be, but he cannot be trusted. Everything that comes out of his mouth is a lie. For us to work together, you must cut ties with Torno. I'm not saying this as a lovesick woman that never got over her heartbreak, but as a peacekeeper who has seen the depths that amoral men will sink to."

"What about the others? Did you mean what you said about granting us clemency?"

"Full pardons," she confirmed with a wave of her hand. "I can have the paperwork drafted within an hour."

Ena searched Kalta's for some sign of deception, but could only feel good intentions from her.

Taking on an air of professionalism, Kalta sat tall and scooted forward. "Bring them to me and we can put that mess at the docks behind us."

"You really don't care if Torno escapes."

She lets out an incredulous, mirthless laugh. "He can run off and impregnate every Leben harlot on the east coast. I've put his betrayal behind me, but I will no longer be his fool. Tell Torno to run and hide. As long as he never sets foot on Gulambar again, I'll consider him dead. This isn't about him. It's about you and the future of this world. Bring your friends to me. They can sign their pardons and then we can plan our next steps. I have a variety of resources that I know will be helpful on your quest. Gulda, gold, wands, spellbooks, tombs on military history and foreign policies...They're all at your disposal."

"That's very generous of you." Ena said, far too meek.

"Of course. I told you I'm willing to help you. Consider yourself my beneficiary. I've rented out this hotel for several days. We can take our time planning while your friends enjoy the pleasures of the city. I think it'll be nice to get to know each other." She smiled in such a way that Ena couldn't tell if it was a look of sororal love or seduction.

This was the kind of neutral response that tested the waters. Had Ena any history with such flirtations and veiled suggestions, she'd be able to return the smile and make a comment that let her own intentions known. Unfortunately for Ena, she'd only seen these kind of exchanges from a distance. Afraid of saying the wrong thing, she bowed her head and mumbled, "That would be nice."

"Are your friends far?"

Panic set in. She could be asking the question casually or she could be trying to set up an ambush. Again, Ena didn't have the experience to play the situation with grace and so she half stood. "Yes. I mean, not so far as we couldn't meet for lunch."

She flashed another cryptic smile. "That would be marvelous."

Ena finished standing. "If it's alright with you, I'd like to go talk to them so I can bring them back here."

"'Alright with me?'" Kalta laughed at Ena's choice of words. "You're Ngoltur Reborn. It's your decision to make."

Ena castigated herself, but declined her head. "Good. I'll get them as soon as I can. Don't wait for lunch on my behalf." She forced a smile. "Torno will probably throw a fit. It could take an hour or two to get him to see to reason."

Kalta shared in Ena's smile, but no mirth colored her words. "As long as it's done."

Ena smiled and nodded. "I'll see you by sunset at the latest."

"Oh my!" She leaned forward with a familiar warmth. "If you take that long I may have to plan for dinner."

A nervous chuckle seized Ena and Kalta joined in with a throaty laugh. Ena went for the double doors. Her hand connected with the wall of silence. The air was heavy, pressing against the force of motion. A second attempt and it was gone.

Kalta called out to Obi behind her. "That will be all,

Commander. Thanks again for finding her."

He placed a fist to one of the eagle heads on his breastplate. "Your will is my pact."

Ena looked to Obi for some sign of remembrance or at least a goodbye, but he was stoic in his duties. She rolled her fingers in parting and fast walked to the exit. Obi, his scholar, and all the mages in the dinning hall didn't move to stop her. She was free to go.

Kalta had kept her word.

Back on the street, near twenty Twin Eagle mercenaries were patronizing the bazaar. None of them looked her way. Ena kept her head down and walked fast, but she had no delusions that she wasn't being followed. Of course, that kind of said more about her than Kalta or Obi. Kalta had been nothing but decent and seemed to be on her side. She didn't ask Ena to trust her, she expected her to. Maybe her hard exterior was a mask that she needed to survive while living among the Great Generation and she was really a sweet caring person underneath.

A figure loomed behind Ena. She turned to get a glance from over her shoulder and they pushed her forward. It was Torno. Ena could tell from his voice. "Keep walking."

She tried to match his quick steps but he was more than a foot taller than her. "What are you doing here?"

"Making sure you're still alive, for starters."

"You should've retreated back to the hotel," Ena hissed.

He ignored her, moving around crowds gathered to admire street performers. Out here, Ena expected the Gulam mixed population to be casting spells, but they were engaged in the same acts of displaying physical strength.

"How did it go?" Torno asked.

"She's offered to assist me in my goal."

He growled. Maybe it was supposed to sound like an impressive rumble of masculine drive, but it was far closer to a teenager being petulant. "I suppose her support is unconditional, provided of course that you bring Hultur back to her."

"Actually, there was a different condition." She met his skeptical eyes. "We abandon you."

He rolled his eyes. "Sounds like you're getting everything you want."

"You know, it might benefit you to be nice to me here and there. Especially since I'm not sure if I can trust you."

"Me? You're the one listening to Kalta. I told you that she's a liar and a manipulator." A scoff pushed out his lips. "I'll have you know I have a long history of trying to be nice. Trying is the operative word here since you have a habit of biting my head off for no fucking reason." There he was, trying to get her to talk about their past again.

"I have good reasons to mistrust you, especially since you've been keeping secrets from us for as long as we've known you." Her comment brought a look of genuine confusion from him. "You were sending reports about us to the Magi."

He stopped and held a hand in front of Ena's chest. Two figures flew out of a bar, one after another. Laughter followed them out and the two nearly identical Leben men collided with headlocks and punches. Torno sidestepped them and continued forward. "I had to."

"You could've told them 'no.'"

He bellowed a bitter guffaw. "I could've, and I'm sure my replacement would've had no problems telling the Magi every little detail about your personal lives."

"You were doing that anyway!"

"I was keeping track of your lives because you're my friends. No one's personal life was ever in my reports. I'll have you know-"

Ena mocked his self righteous phrase with half her tongue hanging out. "'I'll have you know.'"

"I never gave them your actual stats! Any of them. My quarter reports were full of lies; especially about you."

That silenced Ena, if only for a moment. Not that

Torno respected that silence.

"Your reservoir ranged for two gulda of ether a day to well over twenty. You weren't as good at lying about ether fatigue as you thought you were. If someone loyal came to replace me, they would've had you shipped back to the capital within a season."

She took on a tone of mock appreciation. "Oh, Torno! I never knew! You've always been so sweet to me! Whatever would I do without you?"

He didn't yell at her mockery. She'd actually hurt him and his glower turned into a rather dim sulk rather than a raging inferno. "If you tell me to fuck off, I'll go. I won't make a fuss about it. All I ask is that you don't go with Kalta. She can't be trusted."

"I know that."

Disarmed, Torno looked to her with worry.

"I knew a lot of women like her growing up and they all spit on my face and pushed me down stairs. Kalta isn't interested in principles or ethics, but power. Now that she's seen me create glaciers the size of galleons she wants to use me like a weapon. My best bet is that she wants me to use my power to kill Ursen and make her the de facto ruler of Caredor while I'm out doing stuff for the Grand Dream. She didn't even ask about Muttur, not once."

He gave a long sigh of relief. "I'm glad. I was sure she'd convince you not to trust me."

"Well, luckily for you it takes more than a pretty face and flattery to get me to trust them."

He didn't say anything about Ena admitting that she finds Kalta pretty. Then again, it was hardly a controversial statement.

The pair approached an intersection. Torno craned his neck up and about, spotting something Ena had no way of viewing through the crowd. He reached for Ena's arm but met eyes instead. With one nod she was following him. He ducked down low to push through bodies. Torno led them into an alley resting between two apartments buildings. There was a pile of rubbish and half destroyed pieces of furniture resting against the wall.

Torno held back a mangled bedframe creating a gap between the wall. "Get in."

It wasn't comfortable lodging herself between a brick wall and a pile of garbage, but she easily fit. Torno crouched down deep beside her and gestured quick and erratic as a squirrel's tail. Before them, less than two feet from the ruined bedframe's outer edge, a circular mirror manifested with a burst of white light.

The mirror was small, barely larger than Torno's head. It showed Ena and Torno crouching within the refuse. While most of their bodies were obscured by shadows and objects, their faces were easy to spot. Then faces rippled and bent into shadows and continuations of brick patterning. Torno was massaging the image, bending the light with a pinch and rub that almost resembled placing spices into a stew. Soon there was no sign of Ena or Torno in the disk.

Three Acolytes in subservient black walked into the alley. They looked right at the pile of garbage, staring at the mirror even as it angled to catch their eye. None of them reacted to the sight.

"Shit!"

"We lost her. We fucking lost her!"

"That was Torno. It had to be," said the hardest of three. He pointed to the driest of the bunch, a short Gulam with a near-permanent scowl. "You take the main road. Come on. They probably went through here."

They split up, with two of the Acolytes running through the alley to the other side. Torno's disk of illusion continued to levitate before them until the last of the Acolytes had left. Then the warping light dimmed out of existence.

Ena didn't even bother to hide her awe. "Was that invisibility?"

"About a foot and a half in diameter and only in one direction, but yeah, it's an invisibility spell." He tried to grab her arm but gestured instead.

They double-backed, going the way they came until they were squeezing past the same bodies of the intersection that first caught Torno's attention. In a few minutes he'd managed to give their shadows the slip. He kept looking out behind them, but eventually he gave his head a shake. "I don't think Kalta had time to set up a second shadow."

"Why would she set up a second shadow?"

"To make sure I think we're not being followed. She knows how I think."

"So...invisibility, huh? You've been holding out on us."

He shrugged. "It's honestly more of a parlor trick than anything useful. You wanna know why I don't take any pride in my art skills? Well, now you know. Every skill I possess is nothing more than training to perform spells."

"And the music?"

"That's kind of for everything. You wanna juggle spells? It helps to be good with music. Mnemonic devices can be pushed a lot farther than you might think." He glanced at Ena and rolled his eyes when he found her glaring.

"Why didn't you tell me any of this when we were on the ship?"

"What was I supposed to do, teach you how to paint a still life in three weeks?!"

Eyes forward, Ena picked up the pace.

"What?"

"You've always got more secrets."

He got in close so she could see his grin. "Yeah, but you trust me."

"Shut up!"

~ ~ ~

Ngoltur's Aids were gathered around outside the hotel's stable. They'd been there for some time judging by the bored looks on their faces, but they perked up the second they saw Torno. Sal had to do a double take before he recognized Ena in her Leben disguise. Hultur snapped a book closed and went to work helping Zukoch ready the horses.

"We bringing one of your paramours, Torno?" Narla ostensibly was asking him, but she stuck her laughing face in front of Ena.

Ena punched her on the arm, while failing to suppress a smile.

"Well?" Myrrel asked with her hands held wide.

"Our fearless leader talked to Kalta," Torno explained.

Ena got into the wagon. It felt sturdy enough but they had a long journey ahead of them. Expectant eyes were eagerly awaiting an explanation. She scooted deeper into the wagon and they all piled in. Soon the old band was knee-to-knee and shoulder-to-shoulder.

"She offered all non-Torno people a pardon and unconditional use of her resources." Ena explained talking on affectations of lofty magnanimity.

"So, she's lying," confirmed Narla.

"Naturally," said Torno.

"Yeah, but why bother?" asked Sal. "Kalta almost killed us last time. Ena's gotten a lot stronger, but she couldn't have known that."

"'A stolen wand is worth more than a pile of tinder,'" quoted Narla. "It's tactics, pure and simple."

"It's still a risk. Why bother with fake diplomacy unless she has some reason to think that she could convince you?" Leaning forward, Myrrel looked at Ena. "Were you convinced?"

Ena ignored Myrrel and poked her head out the front of the wagon. "We ready?"

Hultur was finishing up with the horses.

"Yep. We're all ready to go," said Zukoch. "What did Saqru say?"

"Saqru?" Ena looked back into the wagon, but nobody else knew who or what that was.

"The contact at the colosseum?" asked Zukoch. Seeing blank faces, he groaned. "Didn't Ginevra tell you about Saqru? I saw you talking to her."

"Umm..." Ena had thought Ginevra had just been making conversion and she'd cut the First Mate off instead of listening to what she had to say about the colosseum. "No, she didn't mention it. Any ideas on where we could find Muttur?"

"The closest sanctuary is in Taulge." Zukoch had more to say, but recognized the look of exhaustion on her face and turned his attention to the horses.

"Alright, enough about Kalta and the Grand Dream." Ena stopped to smile at her friends. "I wanna know what you did last night."

They broke into stories about a trip to the colosseum. Sal was especially excited about seeing bulba combatants. One of them, a spiky terror named Vlance, was disqualified for breaking a Ki'an's arm. Torno had joined them at the colosseum but had little to say on the night. He was looking at Ena with poorly veiled fascination. She'd learned one of his dark secrets but now that she had the opportunity to tell their friends about his reports, she kept the secret to herself. Maybe that made her just as bad as Torno.

Narla and Visk went to a brothel but insisted that they spent the entire time watching the local talent dance. Everyone in the wagon balked at such an obvious lie. Ena figured it was probably true, but she joined in on the jeering. It was too much fun watching Visk defend herself.

Myrrel ended up meeting a group of women magicians who called themselves Glirfs. They were a kind of activist group who were trying to unite with the city's large population of Doronel immigrants to bring magic into the culture of the city at large. Apparently, these Glirfs took great offense to the use of magical glyphs being used as fashion, and were rallying for magical exhibitions in the colosseum.

The outskirts of the city were marked with quarries

and vast sections of felled forests. The trees were mostly chopped down, save a few trees with a spattering of red leaves. A population of mostly boulba workers were pulling the stumps out of the ground, roots and all. Leben foremen sat on cranes and high wagons.

Sal waved high at some younger boulba waiting outside the gate.

"Ava, ava," the youths called out, twisting their hands into strange symbols.

"A-vlance!" Sal called back, making the same gesture.

He was smiling in a way Ena had never seen him smile. It wasn't paternal exactly, but there was a deep empathy in his stare. His humor was tempered by a sorrow.

The careful cultivation of lumber harvesting had an abrupt stop, marked by a wall of stone nearly thirty feet high. Two watchtowers marked the edge of the battlements and supported an interlocking gate wide enough to allow four wagons to pass at once. Past the gate the road went straight into a thick copse of trees. Once the wagon passed the guardpost, the wall was a gruesome sight. Reptear corpses were attached to spikes and hung up on chains like decoration. Many of the lizard-people were sharp edged skeletons, while a few still had enough flesh to lure carrion birds.

Zukoch pointed to the rotting display. "This is how Fieta is handling its Reptear problem. They can't spare the manpower to eliminate a rash of Reptear and continue its never ending war with Versweil. These walls help them run with the narrative that Reptear infected lands aren't Fieta soil. It keeps them from having to take responsibility for the deaths of their people."

"The Reptear use the road as bait," Narla said with certainty.

"That's right. It's a bit of a risk, but the fastest way to Taulge is through Black Tooth Woods."

"Maybe we should go around," suggested Sal.

"Not an option." Torno was bringing bad news as usual. Maybe for once it wouldn't be his fault.

Behind them, the gates into civilization were closing. Guards were taking up archery position in the watchtowers. Two figures were waving banners from one of the watchtowers. They were Gulam soldiers in black uniforms, their shoulders and chests adorned with white armor.

"It's the Junior Mages!" Ena seethed. "How the fuck did they follow us?!"

THE THIRTY-SECOND CHAPTER

When Ngoltur Must Decide Between Risking her Aides or Killing a Child

Indigo strands of ether ascended above the watchtower. Darkness spread from the lines of power, the shadow more smoke than impenetrable black. White strands followed, split to fourth from a single wand. The ether popped, fracturing beams of pure rainbow hues against the backdrop of indigo-tinted smoke. The Junior Mages had cast a sky writing spell and the message was clear: "She's here!"

Torno went for a long ornamental box and pulled out an expensive new deathstaff with a phoenix pattern inlaid onto the hand hold--the same Captain Fascinosa had purchased with Ena's assistance. Red ether collected at the tip of the death staff, sizzling as the power built. He was taking aim for the watchtower and a blast of that size might blow off the top.

"Torno, no!" Ena dashed forward and pushed the deathstaff aside, but he hadn't taken the shot.

He actually listened to her. "What?"

"Don't kill them!"

"Those are the Junior Mages from Sothlen, Ena. If they're here, Kalta can't be far behind." Torno liked stating obvious facts like they were new pieces of information. Surely it made him feel important.

"But they're not from Fieta! They have no authority over those guards and they haven't even opened fire on us!" She pointed and he took another look.

"She's right," Narla said. She was watching them from the spyglass. "From the looks of it, Fieta's military has realized who they are."

"What is your command?" Visk asked with authority, reminding Ena that she was in charge and they needed to make a decision.

"Follow the road."

Hultur snapped the reins and they proceeded with haste.

Ena watched the tower with the Junior Mages. Two figures in black with bright white armor were thrown off the perch of the lookout. They stuck the landing by falling into a bed of air. The pair of them looked like they were having a hard time getting up. Torno thought it would be best to kill the Junior Mages, but Ena didn't think they were worth the effort. It was Kalta who was the real threat.

"Archmage Kalta…" Sal murmured. "Why does that name sound familiar?"

No one told him why. Neither Ena nor Torno wanted to reveal how they knew anything about her.

~ ~ ~

Inside the Black Tooth Woods, light barely passed through the canopy. Darkness made a natural shelter for forest critters, but an eerie silence waited beyond the road. The leaves didn't rustle from birds in escape, the branches didn't shake from critters gathering food, and barely an insect could be seen. Creepier still, the road was clean as tiled floor. Every bit of debris had been meticulously swept clear.

They'd been riding for a little over an hour without any sign of trouble when Hultur called out, "Something's on the road."

Myrrel poked her head in the wagon from the jockey box. "It's a little girl."

Zukoch squeezed past bodies to have a look. He took one look at the child and shouted, "Kill her. Quickly!"

Myrrel snapped at him. "We're not going to kill a child!"

Ena snuck out the back, hanging off the side to get a better look at her. She was Leben by the dark blue of her skin, but it was hard to say when the girl looked so disheveled. Leaves and sticks were stuck in her hair and her long dress was torn at the knees and fit awkwardly besides. It had been a woman's dress, but was frayed at the bottom for this child of eight or nine to use. Even seeing her walk pulled at Ena's heart, the child could barely stand.

"Stop the wagon," Ena commanded and Hultur obeyed. She could get used to people obeying her. She jumped off the back the child immediately approached.

She came at Ena with her arms out and her cheeks wet with tears. In a broken meter, she repeated "help" in dorospek and probably the same in another tongue.

"No, Ena!" Zukoch shouted. "Stay back!"

Ena didn't listen to Zukoch nor her Aides telling him off. She ran up, crouched and hugged the poor girl. Her body shook so violently she could barely find her breath. "It's okay now. You're alright."

"My parents...my parents..." Was all the sobbing girl could get out.

"You're safe. We'll help you," Ena assured her.

The girl sniffed hard, whimpering as she fought through the pain to breathe.

"I think she got separated from her parents," Ena told them.

Myrrel crouched beside them and laid a hand on the child's back. "Don't worry. We'll help you out, okay?"

The little girl nodded.

Ena brushed the hair and tears off her face. Her breath

smelled terrible, like a pig pen when the sows had diarrhea. She swallowed back the revulsion. "What's your name?"

"Ki."

"I'm Ena. We're going to find your parents, Ki. We've got plenty of room in the wagon and we'll get you to safety."

"No, we won't!" Zukoch jumped off the wagon. He went for Ki's arm.

Torno grabbed his wrist, swung him into the wagon, and pressed his face into the wagon's body all in one practiced motion. He had Zukoch's arm wrenched behind is back as he applied additional pressure. "I think it's time for you to settle down."

"She's trouble, dammit! Why isn't anyone listening to me?"

"The little one's obviously been through a lot," said Sal. "She needs our help."

"Are you kidding me?" Zukoch winced from the pain in his elbow. "Alright, alright! I won't touch her. Just lemme explain."

Torno released him.

"Ow."

Ena was holding the girl close, keeping Ki's head on her shoulder so she wouldn't have to smell her breath. The stench of her hair and dress wasn't much better.

"I can take her," Myrrel said.

Ena let her have the child and joined her Aides on the other side of the wagon.

"She's a Cannegurin," Zukoch whispered. "Wicked people who follow Reptear. No matter what you tell her, she's going to convince us to put her in the wagon. From there, she'll lead us into a Reptear trap."

"Why would she want to get into our wagon?" Sal asked.

"To disable our weapons," Hultur surmised. "It wouldn't take much to ruin a wand or amulet and it would be a simple matter for her to swipe rings and bracelets."

Zukoch nodded. "That's right. Please tell me you've heard of Cannegurin."

He shook his head. "It is simply the best way to use a child to dismantle a group of travelers."

"Even if she is this Cannegurin," Torno said. "What are you recommending we do?"

"Kill her."

"No," Ena snapped. "We are not killing a little girl."

"Why, because she knows how to cry to lure people to their death?!" he snapped back.

Torno loomed over Zukoch.

The shorter Leben held up his hands and retreated. "Listen to me. She eats human flesh. There's no saving her. Whatever's happened to her can't be undone. Even Ngoltur couldn't save her."

They all looked at Ena, who was staring daggers at Zukoch.

"I mean the other Ngolturs, the ones who came before you."

"Why would a child side with Reptears?" Narla asked. She didn't like the sound of any of this.

"Reptears aren't like monsters, they think, they feel, and they can trick people. Sometimes they take prisoners and devour them over days, sometimes they steal children and raise them as their own, and sometimes they let people live and use the injured to set up a trap. It doesn't matter why that girl is here or how she came to be in their hands, she's a Cannegurin. She must be killed. If we don't kill her, she will live to lure another and kill them," Zukoch explained.

"I find all of this suspicious," said Visk. "You are far too eager to kill this child, when your words sound hollow. Their traps wouldn't work if Cannegurin are common knowledge."

"They're not," Zukoch sighed. "I know about them because...Listen, I don't have time to explain my sad lonely childhood, but it wasn't easy growing up as a fat kid in a city where people think punching each other is the height of human achievement. I read a lot. I liked reading about the Grand Dream. The reason I know Ngoltur couldn't save a Cannegurin, is the same reason I know what they are."

"He's a scholar of the Grand Dream," Narla said in shock. "Fucking shit, kid, why didn't you mention this earlier?"

"I did! But you all forgot about it!" He looked from Narla to Ena. "Please, listen to me. She has to die."

"No."

"I am inclined-"

Ena cut off Hultur. "I said, no. You all swore to follow my lead, and I'm making the decision here."

"Then make a decision founded on reasoned. This child weaves a farcical tale. There is no believable explanation for her presence in these woods," Hutlur tried.

"Kids can be resourceful," said Ena. "Maybe most kids wouldn't be able to survive here, but she clearly has. Judging by the look of her, she's been hiding in these woods for days. Whether or not she's being used as bait isn't the issue. I need to know if she is a co-conspirator or a victim. Sal, you're with me."

"Me?" Sal looked to Hultur.

"Whatever might hurt me can just as easily hurt Hultur. You can't be poisoned, you can hold your breath for as long as you need to, you're extremely tough in a fight, and your geosenses can locate things we can't see. You and I will escort this girl back to her parents. No one else."

Sal lifted his shoulder-brows with pride.

"Ena, I don't like this," Torno grumbled.

"Good, that means you still have a heart." Ena glowered at Hultur.

Ki was happy to be back with Ena and quick to mention how much she hated Zukoch. Her cloudy eyes lit when Ena explained that they'd be going on a trip alone. Ki clung tight to Ena's leg. When Ena offered her hand she grasped it tight and smiled. The rancid smell only got worse when she opened her mouth. Her hands were meaty to the point of being plump and held Ena's hand with confidence.

Ki confirmed Ena's suspicions, explaining that her parents had been attacked and that they ran into the woods to escape a roadside ambush. She was happy to show Ena where she'd last seen her parents, but she wanted nothing to do with Sal. Every time the boulba got close she shrieked and threw herself into Ena's arms.

Ena didn't relent. "He has to come with us, Ki. Do you understand?"

She shook her head. "No. I don't like him. He's a monster! He's gonna eat me!"

While no one knew where boulba came from, they were most plentiful on the continent of Leben Erde. This girl must've been extremely sheltered to have never seen a boulba before.

Ena thought of Teetee and smiled. "Ki, he's going to help us find your parents. You can trust him."

She frowned, but got beside Ena. She pressed into her legs and hugged. Ena held onto that wonderful memory of Teetee sleeping with her and did her best not to smell.

The path into the woods was wide enough for a small wagon to get through the trees, but a low hanging canopy would've torn any tarp. Looking around, Ena saw no signs of tattered fabric, broken wainwrights, or dropped supplies. But she did hear the gentle rustle of leaves dancing in the trees.

Ki traveled through a dizzying path of trees, pulling at Ena's hand to make her go faster. There wasn't any visible path for them to follow, but the child had no problem navigating the brush covered floor. They came to the edge of a small cliff and the trees opened up before them.

"It's down this way." Ki continued to pull, urging Ena to climb down the drop.

As far as cliffsides went, it was hardly a danger. The cleaning was only six or seven feet down and there looked to be plenty of footholds and roots to grab onto. For a seasoned hiker, the climb would be a trivial thing, but for a girl as small as Ki it made more sense to find another way down.

"Are you sure there isn't a way around?" Ena asked, sweet as honey.

Ki shook her head. "I don't know. I always use this way. Can we please hurry?"

Ena kissed the top of her oily head, the faint whiff of charcoal danced among the leaves. "Okay."

"I'll go first," she volunteered. "You stay there rock monster. You're too heavy."

Sal looked to Ena and she nodded.

Ki had no trouble descending. She hopped down on a patch of muddy dirt and matted leaves. She was smiling, urging Ena to follow. Ena did what she could to follow her foot holds and steps. It really wasn't that far down. Soon, she was at the edge.

"You're there, drop down!" The kid said, brimming with excitement.

Ena let go, her feet landed in the dead leaves and they crunched through. The dirt of the floor broke apart. Roots slithered about Ena's legs on her way down. She caught the lip of the pit, her fingers digging into the dirt beside Ki's feet. What happened next was very clever and very subtle. While getting down to help Ena, Ki dropped with her knees first, using them to hit the edge of the pit, dislodging the dirt Ena hung onto.

Fresh, sticky webs slid over Ena's form, covering her up to the chest all the way down until her legs crumpled against hard dirt. Older strands flew into her mouth with every inhale, but were easily pulled free. The rest only got more tangled as Ena tried to pull them free. One of the roots moved. The webs were dancing, shaking against her body as spider-like Ekeets approached.

Ekeets were three or four feet wide and had a four segment body laid out like a clover. In the center of the bulbous monster, venom-filled fangs hung below. A single bite from an Ekeet could turning a horse into a desecrated sack of dehydrated flesh. Ena would die in seconds.

Fear powered a cloud of ice that spiraled around Ena like a whirlwind. Ice crystals formed along Ekeet carapaces, turning flexible skin into rigid crystal. Ena held onto the thought of cold, frigid air, and summoned a gust of wind. Ekeets slammed against the crumbling walls of the pit, shattering their exoskeletons to break them down into mottle. With the monsters destroyed, their sticky webs rose up like smoke, the small black bits collecting with larger clumps of mottle as it dissipated into the wind.

Free from the monster's trap, Ena pressed her feet into the ground and evoked a geomancy spell to jump out of the pit. She flew out of the pit's entrance, up above the lip of the cliff, and soared to the lower canopy. Sal was surrounded by Reptear, being harried by the lizard-folk with spears. Metal bit into Sal's rocky exterior, lacerating him between the hard plates of stone. Pebbles poured out his sides, exposing the rich soil within.

Grabbing a branch to keep herself aloft, Ena had a bird's eye view of their attack on Sal, and it didn't last long. Flames spread out of Ena's palm and took the shape of five herons. The conjured predators of fire went to work immediately, striking out at their natural lizard prey. Concentrated beaks of flame cut through armor, skin, flesh, and bone. They scorched the rash of Reptear faster than they could scream.

Ena dropped not to the ground, but onto wings of solid force. Channeling magic through her rings, she pulled at the ether-net with three gestures. Dark decay came out in a spiral and on their edges they took on the shaped of a heron's talons. Black claws raked branches to withered husks ravaged by blight. Leaves of green shrank to brown bits smaller than ash. Reptears once lying in wait, were sheered down to their flesh. Her five heron heads of flame made a meal of the bodies.

Ena landed by Sal, her face consumed with rage and her cheeks wet with fresh tears. For a moment, she tried to work geomancy to restore Sal's skin, but found the wounds beyond her skills.

All of Sal's worry was on her. "Ena, are you hurt?"

"Where is she, Sal?" Ena asked with fury.

"Ena..." his voice came out weak.

Fire lashed at her heart and shook her wrists. "Where?!"

Lowering his face in defeat, he pointed to where the Cannegurin had run off to. Ena pushed off the ground and sprinted after her, the very earth aiding in her hunt.

THE THIRTY-THIRD CHAPTER

In Which Tears are Cried Over Lost Children

Earth tremors and thunder led Ngoltur's Aides to Sal. Myrrel was caring for the boulba when Ena returned. Some of his soft inner soil still lay on the ground. Loam, as the boulba called it, was their life's blood. It was what connected them to the cycle of life and what the ancient magicians had drawn on to construct them in the time before words. Stuffing the same dirt back inside could kill him, but then again, so could taking him alone into a trap. Myrrel was there, so he would survive. Torno had always said she was a fixer of mistakes, and for the first time Ena understood how that felt. Gratitude helped to ease her shame and to quench the last embers of betrayal that burned in her heart.

"What happened?" asked Visk.

"It's taken care of." Ena's voice sounded grim, even to her. She walked beside Myrrel, watching her work clay onto Sal's split sides.

Sal looked pained, but not because of his injuries. He could see something in Ena's eyes that worried him. There he lay broken, cracked on both sides from a savage thrashing, and his only worry was for the choice Ena made. It was the kind of thing that sickened Ena. He was important to them but always acted like his life was nothing better than expendable.

"I can get up now," Sal grumbled.

"No, you can't," Myrrel insisted. "This clay needs some hardening."

"Got it," said Narla.

Ena almost ordered Narla to stand aside and let her take care of it. The simple evocation of fire took so much of Narla's ether. It would be hours before she got that ether back, maybe even half the day. But if Ena kept them from doing anything, it would only be a matter of time before they felt useless. She knew this without having to ask them. Maybe they were communicating this in the way they were handling Sal's injury.

Reptear corpses littered the floor around them. Some of their insides had been burnt away into a perfect hole. Others had been split in half where the flaming herons had struck. Where the darkness had taken them, they could be mistaken for human, their flesh was so raw and bloody. The headless bodies made Ena wonder if a human had been among the dead.

Visk put her hand over Ena's fist.

She looked down at her cradled hand with horror. Again, her body was moving and reacting without her knowledge. Ena rubbed her eyes.

"Are you okay?"

"I will be. I think throwing all that magic around did something to my head. It was like being in *that circle* again. Let's get back to the boys. How's Zukoch?"

"Your guess is as good as any," Myrrel grumbled. From the sound of her voice, she was still sour about him rushing to the conclusion that they needed to kill a child.

"Visk, gimme a hand?" asked Narla.

They helped Sal to his feet and made their way back to the wagon.

Ena didn't tell them what happened and they didn't

ask. She sat in the jockey box and their journey continued. Now the woods were alive with sound. Birds whistled, strange mammals chittered, and leaves rustled as things followed them for a time. But all of those sounds came from Reptear. There would be no relaxation as long as they were in the Reptear's domain.

At night, Ena took watch. Her body was balled up, hunched over her knees as she stared into the flames. Fire didn't look the same to her anymore. Nothing was the same. Being in that circle hadn't just given her power. It had taken something. Life was dimmer now.

She dreamt of burning down the woods. When Torno tried to stop her, she decapitated him with a blade of magical kinetics. When Myrrel work her magic to heal Torno Ena laughed. She reached down, touched the bloody stump where his head used to be, and restored it in an instant. They were nothing to her. They couldn't compare to her power, and it was funny to watch them try.

Visk woke her with a tap on the shoulder. "We're ready to go."

Ena was cold, but the air was only crisp. She nodded and went back to the wagon. To occupy her mind, she had Myrrel walk her through some healing magic for boulbas. Ena could barely hear the words, she was so transfixed on the cadence of her voice and the life in her face as she emoted. Myrrel was so alive. Everything felt so strong for her. Every decision was important. Ena threw her arms around Myrrel and squeezed. No one asked why she cried, but she could tell by the looks in their eyes that they didn't understand.

~ ~ ~

There were no more attacks in Black Tooth Woods, but the sounds never stopped following them. The Reptears must've been spreading the word about Ena and her destructive power. Some part of her wished they attacked again.

Fieta welcomed them back with curiosity. A group

of guards came down from the watchtower and wanted to know all about their journey. Sensing Ena's split from socialization, Torno made the good-talks. He was bombastic and lively while he warned them about Cannegurin. The guards were curious about how many Reptears they'd killed and how they'd done it. They kept looking to Hultur, Visk, and Sal with awe. To these people, power only came with muscles and bulk.

They knew nothing of power.

The road through Black Tooth Woods came out in a small village the people there called a fort. The outer walls were made from two layers of moss covered logs and guards outnumbered civilians three-to-one, but it seemed a primitive showing when compared to Caredor defenses. Every business was provided vital service to the guards and that included not only a brothel, but a small casino.

The local population was far too curios about Ena and her Aides, but the language barrier meant that only Zukoch was harassed. She did, however, find common Fieta garb, which was far more utilitarian than the outlandish gear she'd acquired in Vergebaum Heff. Still, it was difficult to find a shirt that covered her stomach, and they simply didn't carry shirts with long sleeves. She ended up leaving the fort with wave-stripe shirts and pants that supposedly made it harder to see her in the woods. They called the patterning *rejt*, and every child and elder wore it on some part of their body.

Fieta looked more wild past the fort. Much of the terrain was shaded with trees, but the local population had been vigilant in keeping the trees spread apart. Flauschatz, cat-like mammals, hunted the land in huge prowls of forty or fifty. They were differentiated by their long pointed ears and tails that ended in fluffs big as a guinea pig. Zukoch said the things were harmless to humans, but they would sneak into farms and kill entire pig pens or kikaa coops.

A day or two into the wilderness, they came upon a

lone kikaa on the road. The knee-high avian was different from its Gulambar cousins by three long thin head feathers that poked up a few inches before trailing back over the length of its body. The poor lost creature wasn't even running away. It stayed beside the road even as their wagon approached.

"Can we stop?" Zukoch asked. "I want to save it."

"How do you know it isn't a trap?" Myrrel asked with venom.

He ignored her and looked to Ena. "Can I go get it?"

She couldn't think of a reason to tell him "no."

The moment he got out of the wagon, the little Kikaa came running up to him, its silly head feathers bobbing and swaying in the wind. Zukoch knelt down with open arms and the thing jumped into his embrace.

"Aww, he's shivering. The poor thing is so scared!"

"Better get back in the wagon," Ena told him. "We gotta keep moving."

He did, and named the little bird "Wulg," which apparently meant "lucky." Zukoch insisted that it was lucky for having survived on its own for so long. About an hour down the road, they saw how accurate that name was. There was an overturned cart just off the side of the road. Three dead Lebens lay mangled and stripped of flesh. Kikaa lay dead in cages or scattered about the wreckage as feathers and bone.

Torno took the lead on the investigation. He was used to playing tracker and had the best set of eyes in the crew. "Could be Vurnglek, but I think it was Chonchas."

Neither of the monsters had been a problem for them back in their broker days, but Chonchas in particular were scourges on little farming villages. Chonchas resembled ostriches with alligator heads, but were roughly half the size of both. They could outrun a horse at gallop and targeted travelers more than homes. There was no sign of the Chonchas or the horses the cart had been attached to. Torno found some marks in the dirt and figured the horses had probably run to the other side of a nearby hill. Most likely, the Chonchas had gone after the horses.

"Good work," Ena told him. "But we're not going to follow."

Torno objected, "Ena, those Chonchas-"

She raised a hand to silence him. "I know how dangerous they are, but it isn't our job and we can't risk the time. Those people have been dead for maybe two days. We need to keep moving."

She could see the Broker Captain inside Torno fighting to get out and scream at Ena. This kind of scenario was his to handle. He'd made the call for close to four years with no one questioning him. Now it was his place to nod and get back in the wagon. Ena stared at him until he did. Several eyes stayed on the carnage as the rode off and an uncomfortable silence went with them.

Close to sunset, a handful of riders approached on schistrau. Schistrau were built like ostriches but had thick legs with a double layer of scales. The birds were known for their friendly demeanor, beautifully bright feathers, and quick land speed, though over long distances the stamina of horses let them travel farther. The riders themselves were a militia by the look of them. One of them had a fancy hat that could've been mistaken for an officer's and the others wore worker coveralls with that *rejt* pattern.

They were a search party looking for the dead found on the road. Apparently, the riders were a family coming back from the fort with a fresh batch of Kikaa to bring life into a clutch suffering from inbreeding. Ena explained what they saw and where the Chonchas had likely gone. The young men looked eager for the fight, but their elders balked at the possibility of fighting a pack of monsters. Good news was, Taulge was half a day's ride from their village.

The militia thanked Ena for their help and they continued on their separate paths.

Torno and the others relaxed after that encounter, but only slightly. Talk of a proper village urged them forward, but even by the last light of day there was still no sign of civilization. They let Zukoch cook and his cooking was good as a meal from any tavern. Truthfully his skill could get him a job at a restaurant. Spirits rose as they praised the Leben's cooking, and soon they were telling Zukoch stories about their days as Brokers.

~ ~ ~

Taulge was a city older than Fieta, but unlike Vergebaum Heff, its giant tree still stood. There was a large splitting scar down one side of the tree, but its branches were thick and the canopy spread over most of the city. Its lush green leaves were just starting to turn colors, giving the leaves a look of being covered in a golden veil.

The trip into the city's heart kindled curiosity in the travelers. They'd arrived on the eve of a local festival of some kind. Everywhere they looked, vendors were hawking wines, grapes, and raisins. Gangs of children, instead of hitting each other with sticks, were throwing rotten grapes at each other. Adults were taking sips from chest-sized vases in between punching each other in the face. And their journey was cut short as one street after another denied their wagon access.

"I'll find a place to keep the wagon," Zukoch offered. When Hultur tried to stay behind as well, the Leben waved him off. "I'll meet you all at the base of Mawnah."

"Mawnah are the big trees," Sal informed the group.

"They're going to need to know who I am," Ena guessed.

Zukoch nodded. "There's going to be a walled off community around the trunk, that's the sanctuary. It's the sacred duty of every sanctuary to offer shelter to those in need. I say we skip renting a hotel until we've met with the Dreamers. They're trained to speak Dorospek and Kest, so you shouldn't have any problems communicating." A gathering crowd started pawing at the wagon and horses.

"Don't wait for me." He waved goodbye and directed the locals to help him turn around.

Ngoltur's Aides kept on, pushing deeper into the crowd. Once they reached a street corner they understood why it was impossible to get through. They'd set up grape mashes. Hundreds of people were all jumping into barrels to squish the fruit with their feet. Wine was flowing so freely that perfect strangers offered each of them a drink.

"Yeah, we couldn't have entered sobriety city," Narla grumbled. "This is torture."

Torno took a big gulp from an oversized vase. "The worst," Torno agreed, wine and sarcasm spilling out his mouth.

"Is everyone drinking the same juice they're stepping on?" Sal asked.

They all giggled at a question only Sal could ask.

"It's last year's batch," Narla explained. "Last year...when I could still drink."

"Just focus on something else," Myrrel suggested. "Like, look at that tree. It's very big."

"Yeah, and it's raining ether." Ena could feel the ether flowing through her like drops, but the sense of it wasn't anything like rain or even the raw ether transported down Caredor's ether-chains. There was something warm about it, like soaking up the heat of the day from a sun-baked boulder.

"Is it?" Myrrel asked. "I can't feel it."

"It's faint, but it's there," Torno agreed. "Maybe after a few more drinks, it'll all come into focus."

Ena smacked him mid drink, spilling wine over his chest and choking him. She glanced at Narla.

"It's fine, Boss Lady," said Narla. "Don't nobody hold back on my account."

"Only Torno and Myrrel will be drinking," said Sal. Then he looked to Ena, remembering that she'd been growing more accustomed to alcohol.

"Yeah, I'll be opting out too," she agreed. "I'll need my

wits about me. Anyone know anything about the Dreamers?"

"Only that they are religious leaders in Leben Erde," said Visk. "It was considered an act of great service for to kill the Dreamers while in service to Hultur. Many leaders still decorate their clan rooms with their three eyed masks."

"Was it like that for you?" Ena asked Hultur, but he wasn't interested. He was staring up at the impressive sight of the mawnah tree.

Looking up, it was easy to get mesmerized by the canopy far above the buildings. The sight of a million shifting leaves created an illusion that the city was of a size with ground mushrooms and they were tall as ants. Under the vast canopy of the mawnah, the city's population grew sparse, even on that day of celebration. Buildings showed sign of neglect. Piles of refuse three people high filled the space between buildings like motor to their bricks. Wide streets that held the potential for expansive markets, now gave uninterrupted sightlines to the mawnah's root system.

Four stories tall from ground to tip, the roots had burrowed its way through buildings so ancient, their designs seemed lifted out of history books. The growth of the millennia old tree had toppled watchtowers, apartments, civic centers, marketplaces, and lesser trees. Everything from support beams to stone had been pilfered to some degree, but many of the structures were still occupied. The lights of campfires burning through the glassless windows of long abandoned buildings.

Traveling through these ruins of civilization was both humbling and exhilarating. There was a sense that order had abandoned these streets a long time ago and with that isolation came a kind of freedom, like bathing in an empty lake hours from any homes.

Finding an entrance to the sanctuary was a nightmare. The street they'd gone down had ended in a wall of overlapping metal plates. Trying to follow the wall down to a gatehouse, only lead them to the large physical barrier of the root of the mawnah tree. So with some back tracking and a lot of turns, they happened upon a guard station. It took another ten minutes or so to get around to the sanctuary's entrance and there was Zukoch, talking to the guards with an annoyed expression.

"Oh, hey. There you are."

"How? How did you beat us here?!" Sal exclaimed.

"I went in a straight line?" Zukoch shrugged. "The guards say that they can't let anyone in during the festival. Supposedly, the Dreamers are in deep meditation."

"Meaning they're drunk," Narla guessed.

"It's my order as Captain of the Brokers, that we join the Dreams in their sacred meditation!" Declared an already drunk Torno.

Myrrel snorted. "You're not Captain anymore."

"I'm drunk! Drunkards are whatever they want to be!"

Smiling, Ena asked Zukoch, "Did you find a hotel on the way?"

"I did. It's not too far from the stables, come on."

Somehow Zukoch's path back through the city avoided every grape mash, rowdy brawl, and street converted into a marketplace. Ena couldn't have followed it back if she tried, but damn was it efficient. She gave everyone leave for the night. As tempted as she was to go out and have a drink, she thought it best to get some rest. The rowdiness in the streets had spread into the halls of the hotel, but as long as the doors were closed and the curtains were drawn, she could keep her mind off the flowing liquor. Still, once Ena settled in to sleep, Narla came over to knock on her door.

"Hey, umm...this is gonna sound childish, but...can I sleep with you tonight?"

"Narla! I'm a little young for you," she teased but showed her in.

"Yeah, and you're a little too cheeky for me." Narla walked in and immediately started pacing. "You think this is easy for me to admit? Myrrel came into my room with Visk and they each had a bottle in their hands. They wanted me to sing with them. If I started singing I was going to start drinking, I know I would!"

"It's fine, Narla. I promise to only tease you when it's funny."

"Yeah, good thing I haven't spent the last three years teasing everyone for every little thing." Her nerves were so frayed that she was physically shaking.

"Just come to bed and it'll be okay, I promise." Ena crawled into the covers and Narla joined her. She wrapped her arms around the veteran and smelled the wine lingering in the woman's hair. "Can I ask you something personal?"

"Of course."

"Why are you keeping the child? You can't be so old that you forgot how to move the eggs along."

"I actually have, but that's not the reason. The thing is..." Narla cut herself off to give a preemptory snap. "You have to promise not to tell anyone, especially Torno!"

"Hey, I'm not telling him anything he doesn't need to know," Ena grumbled. "I swear to keep this secret."

"I think it's fate. Hultur said that the Gods are watching us and maybe they are. I had a chance to be a mother once and it didn't work out. This was kind of like a second chance, and maybe the Gods want that for me. Maybe they want you to be the kid's aunt."

That thought made Ena hug her tighter. "I do feel that way sometimes, like you're all my family. I'm glad you think of me like a sister."

"Honestly, most of the time I think of you as my daughter." She sounded so serious.

"Really?"

"You remember how you were when you first joined up. You were so young and afraid. We all wanted to protect you." Her breathing became labored. "Now you're protecting me."

"I'm happy to, Narla. I'd do anything I could to keep

you safe. I don't even like drinking that much," Ena assured her, but tonight had been the first time she smelled liquor and *wanted* to drink.

Narla was crying. She dug her fingers into Ena's arm.

Ena hugged her tight. She wanted to tell Narla that she'd be a great mother or that it was okay to be tempted to drink, but she didn't think it would help. All she could do was hold her and let her cry.

"I'm scared. I always drink to get these thoughts away and now I can't." She tried to sniffed back tears but her sorrow only made her sigh. "Oh, this is gonna be harder than I thought it would."

"It's okay, Narla. You don't have to say anything."

"I need to talk about what I've been running from," she whimpered. "Now that I can't drink, I have to face this. I need to get this out, but you can't repeat this to anyone, not even to me! I'm not ready to think about it unless I choose to, do you understand? I'm going to talk, you're not going to ask any questions, and then you're going to act like you never heard a word of this."

Ena nodded.

Narla took a long time composing herself. She went back and forth between leaning into the tears and steadying her breathing like a soldier. Then, somewhere in the middle, the words finally came. "He hit me. I'd killed...two...maybe three thousand people. Dozens with my knife and my bare hands, and he just hit me. I knew it was coming. I knew he was gonna fucking do it and I let him. I let him hit me because I deserved it. He was my husband. She...she was our daughter and I lost her.

"I lost our daughter because I hadn't taken the pregnancy seriously. Someone was drowning, I went in after them, but I was too late. I saw him die. I saw the life leave that kid's eyes as he sunk deeper into those waters. I couldn't get him out, but I tried. I tried too fucking long to bring that kid out and give his parents some closure and I lost our daughter. I killed her, Ena. I…"

She cried some more. She cried a lot more. Ena could only hold her and cry tears of sympathetic pain. Narla tried to keep going, to add voice to some detail or moment that kept scraping at her mind. It wasn't a story. It wasn't even the words of one friend talking to another, it was just Narla breathing voice to a pain that refused to let go.

"He hit me, and I think the first time he did it, he thought that he'd surprised me. He was always a coward. I was more mystical, I had experience with the military, and contacts all over Caredor City, and he couldn't stand it. He hated me from the first moment his dick wouldn't get hard and I had to finish our marital duties.

"He was a bitter, miserable fucker, and I put up with him for so long. I don't even know why. I was just tired of fighting. I wanted a life where I could be weak. Every time I saw him get angry at my strength I felt shame. I didn't even want that power anymore. I hated myself for what I'd done. He and I wanted the same thing, we wanted me to be weak. But that kid was going to die and when I needed to be strong again it wasn't there. It cost me my daughter. When I came home and he hit me I thought, 'you can do better than that.' I guess he must've thought the same thing, because he kept going until he broke three teeth and cracked two ribs.

"Afterwards he hid and I wouldn't leave the bedroom. I wanted to see my blood. I wanted to feel every bit of that pain. When, uh…when I finally got patched up, I apologized to him. I tried to make love but he wouldn't even have me; not after I'd killed her. I drank to make the nights go away and then I started drinking at work. After I lost my job, they approved my husband's motion for divorce.

"He only hit me that one time, but it was for every moment I'd been stronger than him. Something inside him knew this might be the only time to hit me, and so he hit me with every bit of rage that limp-dicked coward could find. And I was right there with him, swinging those fists and kicking those legs, because I wanted myself to hurt. When he stopped, I was sad. I wanted him to kill me."

The tears had ceased. She was done crying and maybe done feeling sorry for herself. Ena hated that she could find gratitude for anything then, but she could. She was grateful that Narla wanted her to stay silent. Ena wasn't the kind of person who could help a woman on the edge of suicide.

Narla took her hand. "I don't want to die anymore. I want this. I want to have this child and be a mother."

And she stopped, and Ena had the words. They were screaming at her from the bottom of Ena's heart. She wanted to turn Narla around and beg her to leave Ena's side. There had to be a way to get Narla to come to the conclusion to stay here or any other village, but Ena had no right.

Narla had fought for five years to liberate the duchy of Caredor from an incompetent monarch, only to help bring about the rise of a different kind of dictator. She and her platoon had been absorbed into the country of Caredor so fast that none of them even knew what was happening. She'd been arranged to marry a stranger of high magic, to spawn the next Great Generation, and only after she'd come to the brink of suicide did she finally find a way to love life again. So many people had decided what was best for her. Ena refused to be another interloper.

THE THIRTY-FOURTH CHAPTER

In Which the Sanctuary Honors the Arrival of the Turall

Narla woke Ena on the cusp of dawn. She was going for a run and Ena was happy to join her. It was interesting seeing the entire city in a state of hangover, especially before the sun had properly risen. Piles of puke were a common sight, as were the people passed out on the street. Volunteer cleaners came by with massive barrels of water to wash the wine, urine, and garbage. Without the use of magic, the Leben workers had to push at the water with brooms and mops, their bodies covered with soap suds up to their waists.

When they got back from their run, Torno and Zukoch were in the dining hall sharing eggs and manly hangover grunts. The pair had been out drinking and seemed to have a lot to talk about. Torno was looking at the younger Zukoch with paternal affection. It reminded Ena of when he used to come in to check on her. Even though she'd hated him, he had been kind and patient, and had a way of giving her gifts that Ena actually liked. He spotted Ena creeping on them and waved her over.

Narla gave a sweaty hug goodbye and left to shower.

With a foot, Torno pushed out a chair for Ena, and she was relieved to know that he was still incapable of doing things like a normal person. She listened to them talk about wines and answered any question Zukoch had about their time as Brokers. It was strange how many arguments with Torno were funny or even sweet in hindsight. She'd forgotten that she snapped his birthday cigars in half for buying her a fancy Doronel style dress, but she'd been furious with him at the time. She'd specifically told him to stop buying her gifts. Now she regretted that she soaked the dress, froze it, and smashed it into pieces. It had been the finest thing she'd ever owned.

~ ~ ~

When Ngoltur and her Aides came upon the guard house, the Dreamers were waiting for them. Adorned in scalp to chin masks of wood, the Dreamers put off an unsettling presence. The three stylized eyes on their masks made no effort line up with the position of a person's, but the two lower pictures laid on where the cheeks might be. Each of the eyes sat on the vertex of an equilateral triangle and were surrounded by three more triangles making a mockery of eyelashes. Their tabards fell down nearly to the calf and were decorated not with patches or dyes, but with designs brocaded into the fabric one thread at a time. They were obviously hand woven, and the bright red, blue, and green stood out on the mostly white fabric. Each of the Dreamers favored one color, elsewise they made no effort to distinguish themselves from the other. At their side, the trio was accompanied by eight Leben with heads shaved bald that wore the long undergarments of the Dreamers, save the accents of color. There were also twenty guards with glaives standing erect. It was quite the welcoming.

The trio of Dreamers walked straight to Ena. "You will come with me," said the one in the middle with the blue trim. It was hard to tell the gender of the speaker.

"Wait," Ena told Blue. "Can I talk to you privately for a second?"

"That is why you must follow me."

She sighed. There wasn't going to be any way of doing this without scaring them. "As you have suspected, I am Ngoltur. These are my Aides and they must accompany me. The tall one is Hultur."

All of the Dreamer's stoic assistants backed up. Red actually jumped back. The guards brought their glaives to bear. Green looked to Red and they righted themselves.

Red stepped forward and cleared their throat. They sounded younger than thirty. "Raise your arms. We do not…" their voice squeaked. Maybe they are *much* younger than thirty. "We accept you, Hultur, and offer you our hospitality. Please follow me."

Hultur put his hat over his chest. "It would be my pleasure."

Green stepped past Red and Blue. "The rest will wait follow me into the sanctum." Green sounded older, maybe in their sixties and undeniably female from the vibrato.

Ena followed Blue into the sanctum. This place looked like so many pictures of Leben Erde that she'd seen in books. Old buildings made entirely from interlocked wood. Three-corner roofs covered hexagonal bases, and every door and window was warded with a hanging bits of string and bells. Leben children played in the streets in traditional garb and looked to Ena with a mixture awe, horror, and sorrow.

They came to a large statue of four tetrahedrons. The fourth was suspended in air with water pouring from its bottom. Nothing fed water into the topmost tetrahedron. The fountain underneath drained into two waterways split but flowing out towards the city. The other three paths of the hexagonal center lead towards the tree. Blue took the right path and Red led Hultur down the left.

"Come along," encouraged Blue.

Ena followed but found herself very worried about Hultur. He was taking in every detail, oblivious that these sanctuaries were meant for Muttur, not for either of them. Blue opened the door to a short, hexagonal hut and bowed to see Ngoltur in.

Ena walked inside to find a dark room full of dust and the smell of mildew, except for a lingering odor of sweat and...sex? Her eyes shot over to a Leben woman without hair pulling clothes over her exposed chest. A wiry Leben man with a full head of hair was quickly working on his pants.

Blue cursed at them in words Ena understood without knowing.

The youths bowed their heads and left with their clothes in their hands. They looked to be about Ena's age.

Blue snapped. Two light crystals, two lanterns, and two candles all flicked on. There were three rugs arranged over the center of the room. Well, they were meant to be, but the horny visitors had made a mess of one. Blue fixed it and muttered under their breath. They took a seat where none of the rugs touched and gestured for Ena to sit in the middle of the opposite rug. Ena couldn't tell if the glyph on the rug were imbued, but they were writ in the same Doronel style that Ena had studied.

The sight of a glyph covered rug filled her with nausea. Power swelled in her. Lightning surrounded one hand and the ground trembled from her pulling at the earth below.

Blue clapped.

Everything disappeared. The rugs, the lights, and even the floor and walls. It was all black except for Blue and Ena. That was a very powerful use of light magic. Ena was impressed.

"Better?" they asked.

Ena nodded quickly. Her damn cheeks were turning pink. "Sorry."

Blue pointed to the floor and the glyph on the rug illuminated again. Yet there was no rug, just the glyphs.

Ena sat, tucking her toes under her legs as Blue had done. "What's your name?"

"I forfeited my name when I became a Dreamer. I am a humble guide, Ngoltur. If you wish, you may call me

Wisdom."

"Do you know why I'm here, Wisdom?"

"I have received no dreams, Ngoltur. Neither have any Sages come to us. Your coming has taken us by surprise. We do not know why you have strayed from prophecy." Wisdom made no effort to hide their disappointment and rage.

"You erected a hut to welcome Ngoltur and now you resent that you have to use it?" Ena snapped back.

That shook them.

It surprised Ena as well. The thought hadn't occurred to her until the words were coming out of her mouth.

Wisdom bowed low, placing the eyes of their mask against the floor. "Forgive me, Ngoltur. Forgive us all. We are your servants."

"I'm sorry," Ena sighed. "Maybe this would be easier for me if I could see your face."

Ena was expecting there to be a long explanation about their traditions, but they complied. "As you wish."

Wisdom was a comely sort of fellow by the look of them. Yet it was hard to tell if they were indeed a man with all their hairs removed.

"What was your name before?"

The answer pained them. "Sontet, Wise Ruler."

Ena put a few things together at once. "You don't want me to use your given name, but you have to answer my questions."

"That is correct." Wisdom bowed slightly.

"Why did you remove your name? Why do you wear that mask?"

"Dreamers are meant to be the Eyes of the Gods. We can hold no name, own no objects, and possess no gender."

"You're a eunuch?"

"I am, Wise Ruler." They bowed. "If you wish, I will disrobe for you to verify my conviction."

"No," she snapped, the horror coming out in her voice. "No. I'm sorry. I wasn't trained to be Ngoltur. I don't know your customs and they unsettle me. I apologize. Please go on. Tell me about the mask."

"It is believed that whatever the eyes of our vestments observe, the Gods observe. That is why I have laid my mask upon my legs. I did not wish to blind Precise Seep."

"Precise Seep?"

"*Sengenladur*?" When Ena responded with a vapid stare, Wisdom went on. "Precise Seep is an approximate translation for the name of the God of Wisdom, Ether, and Mercy. The one you know as Poive."

Poive was mostly part of Duan Si superstition in Caredor. She was one of the divine triumvirate that laid the path for humanity to tread. Though Wisdom spoke of Poive as a genderless "one," Gulambar named her Goddess and prayed to her to favor female fertility. It took Ena an embarrassingly long time to remember that Poive was the Goddess Who Speaks Through Ngoltur. It was her role in the Grand Dream to govern Gulambar into obedience and fill Ngoltur with wisdom.

The people of Leben Erde called Poive, Precise Seep, and seemed to think that this "one" was watching over her through the wooden mask. If that was true, not only Poive was watching her, but Caisse and Varn were observing through that same cut of wood. Ena remembered Caisse was the God Who Guides Muttur's Hand and that Varn was the Dualdiety Who Weeps For Hultur's Blood, but other than that, few details remained. She only ever thought of the old religion on Uri'tyel, which supposedly honored the death of the first Hultur thousands of years ago.

The sound of Hultur's distant scream broke Ena from her failed attempts at recollection. Of course Hultur would be having trouble. He had said that the Gods had been watching them before that, since he'd met her on the night of her birthday. It didn't make any difference to Ena, she wasn't interested in walking the path the Gods laid.

Ena turned her attention to Wisdom. "You can put

your mask back on."

"As it pleases the Wise Ruler." They first worked the cloth back onto their bare head and then took a long time bringing the mask to bear.

"What's going on?" Ena waved the light evocation away, bringing the room into focus. "Are we allowed to go outside?"

"You are Ngoltur, and we are you humble servants," Wisdom told her.

She walked outside. Hultur was stomping towards her, rage on his brow. She'd never seen him like this. Well, she saw hints of this once before. She thought it best to meet him at the hexagonal center where the tetrahedrons stood.

"What is it?" Ena asked.

"They're set up on a hierarchy," he snapped. "They sent me a mutilated teen of fifteen to guide me! They've barely recovered from having their womb excised. How old is yours?"

Ena shook her head. "I don't know. Maybe thirty."

Each examined the conditions of their chosen huts. Outside of one being blue and the other red, they were identical hexagonal huts with plain three-sided roofs. Then in unison, Hultur and Ena checked out the middle path. It led to a palace of wooden structures adorned from the base to the roof with intricate script and glyphs.

"You thinking what I'm thinking?" Ena asked him.

Hultur glanced back at Red. The mask was in their hands. Their tabard was torn, probably from where Hultur had picked them up and thrown them across the room. The bald teenager's face was covered in tears and urine stained the front of their robes.

Hultur growled at his guide. "Bring the green one to us!"

THE THIRTY-FIFTH CHAPTER

Where Prophecies Clash
with Realities

G reen wasn't happy to accommodate the demands of Hultur and Ngoltur, but they didn't have a choice. The role of the Dreamers was to serve the will of the Turall, but Green did nothing to hide her resentment. Ena couldn't be bothered to care. She demanded that her friends be let in, and the three Dreamers were compelled to lead them all inside.

Each went to a task according to their hierarchical purpose. Green sat on a very fancy chair, Blue went to fetch Disciples to bring accommodations, and Red went to wash the urine out of their three month old vestments. Truly, these were fitting purposes for the Dreamers.

Upon deeming that all the pomp had been followed, Hultur barked the first of his questions. "Why is my emissary an untrained child?!"

"The Sanctuaries were designed to welcome the Turall, but in every cycle of the Grand Dream only Muttur has ever had need of them. In the thousands of years of our operation, the Sanctuaries have served two purposes: to identify and protect Sages and to council Muttur on his predetermined quest."

"Isn't that three purposes?" Narla asked. She raised

up her fingers. "Identify, protect, and council. I mean you…" She looked to the blank stares and waved her hands. "Nevermind."

"What you're saying is that you've never had to receive Hultur or Ngoltur," Hultur put together.

"That is true. The rooms were only built to silence the complaints of Ki'an and Gulambar of political influence that had the distinguished honor of visiting us. We had no reason to think that you would ever come. We have not had a visitor come to share a dream in five years."

"Five years?" Ena thought about where she was and where Hultur might've been at that time. "That could've been important. Who came to you? What did they say?"

"We don't need to know that," Zukoch said with a self conscious tone. "It probably wasn't important."

"Of course it might be important," Myrrel snapped.

"The last visitor sits before you." Green pointed to Zukoch.

"What did he dream?" Hultur asked.

"He dreamt-"

"Do we really need to go through this? Can't we just tell them that I'm not a Sage and move on?" Zukoch was blushing a deep indigo.

"No," Hultur insisted. "At this point, I have little faith in their ability to sort prophecy from banality."

"Oh, here we go," Zukoch muttered into his hand.

"He dreamt he had a romantic encounter with Ngoltur. Since he had spent the last three months reading about her, and studying pictures of her, we deemed the vision the act of a boy's imagination."

"What were the specifics of this encounter?" Hultur pried further, dragging a snort out of Narla.

"As I recall, he was studying in his room and she manifested out of the light. She opened a window and brought snow onto Vergebaum Heff—which is too far north to receive snow. She then climbed onto the lip of the window and offered her hand. He took it and she flew into the air with him. She whispered sweet things into his ear and they embraced like lovers," Green said with their same austere airs.

Ena smirked at Zukoch. "We had sex in the sky, huh?"

"We just kissed!" he shouted, desperately trying to defend himself. "And it wasn't you. She looked like a different Ngoltur."

"Bigger boobs, huh?" Narla asked.

"Why didn't it go to sex?" Torno added on. "Did you wake up when she started grinding?"

"When she started taking off my shirt," he grumbled. "I was fourteen, and you're all terrible for making me relive this!"

"I disagree," said Hultur. "Every word Ngoltur said could've come directly from the Gods."

"We have them written down somewhere," Green admitted. "But I would think our time would be better spent elsewhere. Such as telling me why the two of you have willfully gone against prophecy." Their ire flared up once more, promising only to die down to a simmer if they cooperated.

"You wish me to unite Ki'an through war?" Hultur growled. "You would have me kill millions of people to fulfill prophecy?!"

"Yes, and die from Muttur shoving Magoloiherdir into your flesh. That is the way of things. That is why the Gods chose you," they snapped.

"I choose peace! I choose to maintain the flow of progress!" He slapped his chest. He was getting more heated by the second, and was barely able to sit.

"We didn't come here for a lecture!" Ena had to shout to be heard. She stood up and held out her hands to silence them. "Nor did we come here to explain ourselves to you. We have come to find Muttur. That's it. With the three of us united, the Grand Dream won't need to play out like a nightmare. For a scholar of the endless process, living in a land that suffers every time Hultur arrives, I would've thought you'd be more sympathetic for our desire to end a cycle of death."

"You are the agent of peace," Green reminded Ena. "Never Hultur. If he sells a message of peace, it is the wrapping for a gift of war. You should know this. You are the Wise Ruler! It is your destiny to await Muttur's salvation!"

"Fuck that!" Ena hissed. "I won't order soldiers to surrender to invaders and be tortured in a tower so that I can fulfill prophecy!"

"She already told you that we're not here to listen to your lectures," Torno growled. He was just as furious as she. "Do you know have any idea where Muttur is?"

Green was silent.

Torno stood up. "There's nothing for us here, Ena."

Ena nodded. "Let's go."

Hultur scrunched up his face, but rose and followed. Everyone else went for the door, Zukoch faster than the rest.

"Please, listen. You are damning the world by doing this," Green said through tears. "You must know that this is not right."

Ena looked back at the broken Leben. They'd taken off their mask. They were on their hands and knees, begging for her to see reason. They looked up. Their bald head was full of wrinkles. Sorrow and defeat twisted their face into a direction the happy, self assured person wasn't used to. This was a person who'd given up everything to help Muttur save the world. Everything. For Muttur to be coaxed like a child playing with a stick broke not only their faith, nor their life, but the lives of every person they knew. There were desperate to find the value in their life's work.

"Go on without me," Ena told them, being sure to put her hand on Hultur.

"Ena, you can't let-" Torno saw the conviction in her eyes and shook himself of his nasty habits. "We'll be at the statue."

Hultur stayed with his hand on the door. Behind those tiny glasses he was glowering at Ena. He didn't trust her to speak to Green without him. Finally, he grunted assent, and closed the door.

Ena silenced the room, pulling at the air to keep sound from traveling. She knelt before Green and put a kind hand on their shoulder. "If Hultur is lying, how would I know?"

"I don't know," Green admitted. They shook their head. They looked so tired and bewildered. "Hultur comes to Ngoltur with power. Ngoltur surrenders because his power would break the world. It would kill all to continue fighting. If the Gods are still at work, then this is that fight. You must see the dangers that come from his lies."

Ena nodded. She wasn't sure she'd be able to, given the man's intellect and command of language. "What about Muttur? If I was him, what is it you would tell me?"

"I..." They looked sickly, like at any moment they could simply pass out and die. Their skin was cold to the touch and growing more white than blue.

"Please, Green. You must know that much. This was what you trained to do. You can still help destiny along, but you must pass on the information to different people."

"Courage. You are to call me Courage."

"Courage?" Ena asked. That was hardly something comparable to wisdom. "Fine, Courage. Where would you send Muttur? Would you give him a sack of coins and tell him to sail to Doronel?"

"No, he would not be ready for the fight." Courage found their namesake, remembering their life's work and grabbing on that experience to compose themself. "The Sanctuaries were created to guide Muttur to the Relics of the Hero. Only the Grand Dreamer knows their exact locations. They are in Schlabaum, a city in Erchritt. It is on the other side of Toberg Monte."

Toberg Monte was an active volcano and the capital

of the boulba country of Karzak. It was known all over the world as the mountain of death.

Ena gave a long sigh. "That's it? No treasure or army or secrets to unlocking my dreams?"

"I'm sorry, Wise Ruler. Our purpose is a humble one. I can only beg for you to leave Hultur's side. Please, return to your throne and await the coming war," Courage whimpered.

Ena left the old Dreamer. She couldn't stand to look at them anymore nor to hear them cry for a life wasted.

Her friends and Hultur were outside. Most were in good spirits, laughing at the failings of these people. Hultur had never looked so angry, and most of that anger was directed at her. She didn't say anything and they followed behind.

Narla was laughing. "I can't believe this place." She sensed Ena was off and ran up to look at her. "Hey, what's the problem? You didn't let her get to you, did you?"

"My problem is that there was a person behind that mask!" she shouted. "They devoted their life to thinking that one day an unimportant Leben boy would walk up and need their guidance. We took that from them, the other Dreamers, and every person who lives here. We may not be able to kill the Gods, but we might've killed someone today."

Ena stormed off. "Forgive me if I'm not ready to laugh about that."

They lingered behind, the shock of her words holding their tongues.

All except for Torno. "Here I thought I was a killjoy."

~ ~ ~

Ena had been quiet on the ride out of Taulge. She wasn't looking forward to riding through mountainous lands ravaged by a volcano, nor was she pleased about her conversation with the Dreamers. Wisdom had seemed kind enough, but they were just another piece in that tapestry. With any luck, the Grand Dreamer would be more helpful.

Hultur sat beside her in the jockey box. "You do not trust me."

"No," Ena admitted, immediately.

"I have sworn to follow you. It was I who came to you with horses and coin to fund our trip. I walked away from a life in Ki'an to bring about an age of peace."

"Yes, but you've also kept things from us, and not just about your personal life. No one knows what you've done or what you're capable of. The first time I met you, I knew you were dangerous and unbelievably powerful. That hasn't changed. I don't know how powerful you are or what spells you can cast," she explained through a sulk.

"The same is true of you. There are no records to suggest the limits of your power, should they even exist. Need I remind you, that of the two of us, it is you who has tested the limits of my defense. What little I do know about you suggests that you are volatile. Beyond these mortal concerns, the Gods appear to be keeping a careful eye on you. Given the historical relationship between Hultur and Ngoltur, all of these facts together makes me very nervous indeed."

Ena hadn't thought about it that way. She'd never considered the possibility that a buff man standing seven and a half feet tall and wielding the power to level buildings would be nervous about her.

"Trouble," said Torno from the back. "Trouble!" He was pointing askew from the city, just outside the edge of the outskirts. A distant cloud of dust lay on the horizon.

Hultur waved a hand and conjured an enlarged circle of enhanced sight. It was an army of maybe five hundred. They were waving banners of red and black, the square and circle of Caredor on most, the winged helm of the Mages on others. A few waved a smaller, simpler banner, a black heraldic eagle with two heads against a field of yellow. Obi and the Twin Eagles mercenary company was still serving Archmage Kalta. This massive military force was marching straight for Ena and her tiny wagon of eight people.

Trouble didn't begin to describe the shit that was headed for them.

THE THIRTY-SIXTH CHAPTER

In Which the Lion Bites the Ice

Every emotion is an asset. That was point one of Narla's training. Panic was a form of surprise and worked as a great fuel for raw magical force. Surroundings are the key to survival; point two. They were on the road more or less in the middle of an open field. A small collection of buildings sat around the edge of some nearby woods. There was a small lake there, Ena had seen it on the map when she checked two hours earlier. Some travelers were nearby, but none of them were making a move to attack. There were no geographic features between Ena and Kalta's army. Their dust cloud was growing darker; that meant they were using geomancy to aid in their travel. She could spot trebuchets in the ranks, so they'd be able to attack before Ena could strike back. Their wagon was on a well paved road, giving them a momentary speed advantage, but that would also mean that Ena would be unable to counterattack for longer.

Point three? *Allies are always available, even if they aren't present.* Visk and Narla were better than fine. Myrrel was panicked, but had faith in Ena. Torno's deathstaff was at the ready and he had ideas. Sal looked nervous, but not about the coming fight. Hultur was ready to cast. Zukoch was holding his kikaa. Okay, no help from him. Still, Ngoltur Reborn should be able to handle this.

"We could retreat to Taulge," Myrrel suggested.

"Four hundred Caredor warriors might be enough to take a Fieta city," Narla told her. "With an Archmage in charge, they could even maintain a siege. We'd be trapped and have an entire city turned against us."

"Torno and Narla, I need you to speed us up," Ena said.

They did. They started pushing their magic into wind and earth instead of saving it for the fight to come. They actually trusted her.

The same couldn't be said for Hultur. "I disagree. We should turn around. We can beat them into the city limits."

"Didn't you hear what I just said?!" Narla snapped.

"Angry or not, the fighting would thin out their numbers," Hultur argued. This was just another logic puzzle to him. None of this was causing him the slightest hint of panic.

"No!" Ena snapped. "We're not risking the city or any of the people inside! We're going to do everything we can to minimize casualties. I'm not about to put five hundred lives on my hands!"

Hultur took off his hat and stood up to hang off the side of the wagon.

"Sal, warn those people," Ena said of the travelers on the road. "Myrrel, do you think you can switch off with Torno?"

"It'll be a little hard to hold onto warm happy feelings, but yeah, I can try."

"Do it. Torno, I want you to bend the light between us and them."

"I can't work an invisibility spell on an entire wagon, even if it wasn't moving," he grumbled.

"Do what you can. If any of their shots miss or their eyes strain, that helps us. Zukoch, get all our gulda and keep them fed."

"Your money? How do I do that?" Zukoch sounded scared as his kikaa.

"You hold it up to our mouths," Myrrel said like the sweet, matronly woman she was. "It'll be alright. Trust Ena."

That was good. Myrrel could keep calm if she was focused on reducing Zukoch's fear.

"Hultur, I need you to solve a math problem." She ignored the outbursts of surprise. "We need to get as close to that lake as possible while staying on this road. You need to know when to leave the road, and what angle to take."

This was actually sounding possible. Ena had a plan and everything was going to work as long as there weren't any snags. She kept checking the progress of the army. They were definitely gaining on them and they were moving their trebuchets up the ranks. Sal was back from clearing the road of travelers.

She passed the spyglass over to Sal. "Keep me informed about their actions."

"You're intending to take us close to the lake, and then move back to the main road?" Hultur asked to clarify.

"Naturally."

"Then I believe I know when to turn and what angle to take."

"Switch with me." Ena handed him the reins. "When the time comes, give us a warning and turn. Narla, if shit gets bad and we have to stay and fight, you're taking over as strategist. I need you to come up with a backup plan. Myrrel, if we have to take refuge in those buildings, you, Sal, and Zukoch are going to gather all the people into one building. I can cover it in ice, but I won't be able to do anything more than that."

Narla and Myrrel nodded. They were taking all of this in rather well. So why did it feel like everything was about to go terribly wrong?

"Trebuchets launching!" Sal called.

Thrown rocks flew up high and then each were hit by dozens of strands of force. The rocks stayed intact, the kinetic spell pushing them farther than the catapults alone.

Ena couldn't make sense of how they'd managed such a nuanced spell. The rocks came down short or askew. With both parties moving at a constant speed, they'd be able to calculate the exact angle of attack soon.

"Ena, who's shooting the boulbas?" Narla asked.

The thrown rocks were moving, rolling towards the wagon with haste. They weren't just launching rocks, but boulbas. The rock-men must've been wearing some kind of magical armor that reduced incoming kinetics to their bodies without reducing the motion the force granted. Great, magical enigma solved and the solution was more bad news.

"I'll get rid of the boulbas," said Ena. "Visk, cover my blind spot."

One hand held onto the side of the wagon, and the other should be more than enough. She flung her arm out and the bracelet clinked into place. Three gestures for everything, the rings saw to that. The motion of her casting was awkward, but something Torno had drilled into her on the boat. She ran ether through the rings, timed the switch to power the bracelet, and then bled raw power to expand the form. Torno had been right about her switching to rings and bracelets. It gave her all the control she needed without having to sacrifice any mobility.

No interesting shapes leapt to Ena's mind, so she constructed a thirty foot long arm of purple kinetics. It took the shape of Ena's arm gripping the wagon. The ethereal hand was large enough to grab boulbas like rocks and chuck them back towards the attackers. They flew about sixty to a hundred feet out, but they were out of the way. Some avoided Ena's grasp and she had to smack them away with a backhand. Gone for now had to be good enough.

"Flame clods incoming!" Sal announced.

Flame clods worked like stones but they were thrown high into the air. When they broke apart, phosphorus reacted with the air and ignited the falling debris. Too close above them, fire fell. Ena ended her gestures in a two fingered point, wings of cold unfurled above them. She slapped the flaming pieces back towards the attackers and rebounded boulba, but they landed harmlessly a few dozen feet away.

"More volleys. More boulbas."

Ena thought he meant boulbas in the sky and took too long to react to the boulbas rolling up to the front of the wagon. One of them got in rage. The rock-person hopped out popped out of their ball form and came at Gale with child-sized mitts. Hultur chopped his hand out. A blade of geomantic force cut the boulba in half and left a scar hundreds of feet long on the road.

Geomancy was usually an unreliable magical element. It only worked on the earth, and if the caster did anything more than a push, the spell risked cave-ins and earthquakes. It was a volatile magic that was more alive than fire. That is, unless it was thrown directly at rock that had no magical resonance with the ground. Geomancy worked like a precision spell of destruction when aimed at loose boulders, stone walls, and boulbas.

The attacking boulba flew apart into rocks, pebbles, rich loamy soil, a stomach of churning lava, and a heart of quartz. They scattered in every direction like they'd never been alive at all. Rocks flew at the horses, and they panicked. Gale and Li'at tried to run off the path, shaking the wagon side to side.

Myrrel kept them from falling over, but lost her focus. Hultur helped by manifesting magical supports to steady the wagon, but all the shaking had slowed them down. Visk smacked boulba back with precision spear strikes, but they only flew back ten or twenty feet and her red electricity did very little damage to the rock-people. She had moved to Ena's side to smack out at all the returning boulba and was struggling to keep up.

Ena was too slow with one hand. She evoked a gust

of wind to help her onto the top of the wagon. She arrived in time to catch another volley of flame clods, but was close enough to feel the heat. More boulba were falling down, adding to the others that were already surrounding them. Hultur had the right idea. They couldn't keep fighting the same boulba over and over again.

Three hand positions brought an octopus of earth magic to life. With a passing thought, geomantic tendrils swept through the rolling rock-folk. Boulbas shattered into a cluster of stones and sprayed out clumps of dark, loamy soil. The sight of their quartz hearts shattering into a sparkling dust pulled at Ena's heart, spiking the ether drain through emotional disonance. Ena averted her eyes and refocused. She had to hold onto contempt for Kalta throwing their lives away, because her guilt, horror, and sorrow wouldn't help her cast geomancy.

Sal stuck out the back to yell at her. "What are you doing?!"

Narla climbed on his back to yell at him. "We don't have a choice, Sal! There are going to be a lot more deaths soon enough. Now keep your eyes open, Sal. They got a fucking crystal cannon charging up!"

"Fuck." Ena gulped.

She glanced over and saw something glowing alright. There was enough ether charging up to remind Ena of her shot against Wand-Breaker. It was a bright, spiraled pattern of red ether, the design took on the shape of a rose. It wasn't a crystal cannon. That much power was coming out of a deathstaff. Ena knew, because the red rose was Kalta's signature.

"No, it's Kalta!" Torno shouted. "But they're still too far for deathstaffs."

"Tell that to her." Visk grumbled on her way back inside the wagon.

More flame clods were incoming. Ena thrust a hand up to brush them aside, and Kalta used that moment to fire

the shot. The red rose of ether flew forward, petals falling off
the shape as it sailed across the mile between them. It was
too far, everyone could see that. But around the time Ena
was gathering her will to smack away the boulbas up front,
the red ether coalesced and popped. Flames flashed in Ena's
periphery a single moment before the sound of the explosion
deafened them.

Fire came out as a ball, but soon shaped into a hawk.
It dove at them, talons straight out and wings extended to
maximize the spread of destruction. Ena was dazed and
holding onto the feel of the octopus in her mind's eye. She
had a heart's beat to react to a forty-foot tall hawk of flames
diving in for the kill. The octopus grabbed at the flames, and
the geomantic energy passed right through it.

Screaming air hit her first, and smacked her free of the
tarp. Flames spread over Hultur's sphere, but only enough
to protect him and the front of the wagon. Wings singed the
horses and ignited their harnesses. Narla hopped to action,
willing pyromantic control to push back against the work
of a true master of magic. The tarp went up like paper. Narla
was able to push some of the flames up and back, but much
of the conflagration rebounded off Hultur's shield. The re-
angled inferno engulfed Narla, Torno, and Visk in flames. Yet
Narla's quick action saved the bed of the wagon and that let
Sal's hand find Ena's ankle.

Ena was alive. Saved by Sal and a thin aura of ice Ena
hadn't known she'd cast. Her magical aura was ripping
through Sal's hand in seconds. Large thick plates of rock were
withering down to gravel. The force of the air exploding had
dazed her. Her eyes took in the blurry sight of Visk smacking
boulbas off the back of the cart. Red lightning flashed again
and again, but the rock-people were overwhelming them. Sal
was screaming at Ena but she couldn't make out more than
the pitch of his voice. Ena canceled her ongoing spells.

"Get me up there," Ena shouted at Sal.

"Ena-"

"Now!"

In a single motion, Sal chucked Ena up over the bed and back onto the top. She couldn't pay attention to the chaos below. There was barely enough of the wagon left to hold her weight. It needed Ena's help to be reshaped with force. She tried to get Hultur to take over the task, but his attention was on the horses. He was keeping the wagon moving with reins of pure force. His mighty gerhat horses were panicked, speeding forward with a directed gallop they couldn't maintain. Another rose flickered into life, casting a sickly red glow over the dust of Kalta's army. Flame clods were falling down. More boulbas were coming in on both sides of the road. Ena didn't have a choice.

She cast haste.

The glyph was there. It had been there the entire time, renewing her with a fear that eclipsed every feeling of abandonment. Casting it was easy, holding onto the power of the glyph without running away and puking was the hard part. This was her circle. This was her power and she couldn't be afraid of it anymore. If they stopped moving, they were going to die.

She pulled up drinking water and formed it into an arch of ice to restore what was lost of the tarp. That might've taken her a minute of directed focus. Inside, a second. Breathing in panic, she exhaled her will into small pockets of kinetics. One at a time, she flicked the rolling boulbas up towards the additional boulba on their way down. With everything moving slow, she had the time to make sure every one hit their mark. Even if the boulbas survived the collision, they'd be falling down too far away for them to make a difference. She collected ethereal cold above her, quenching the fire of the flame clods as she formed the energy into a net. Flicking it like a slingshot, she threw the net at the growing hawk of flames. It surrounded the bird and smothered the spell like a match under a boot.

She let go of the spell of haste.

Her entire body was shaking. Her eyelids were stuck open wide; it burned at her retinas and dried out her eyes. Her breaths came out like hisses. Her hands were stuck in the final position of her ice spell. Some disgusting, unsettling sound was scraping through the ring in her ears. It sounded like a baby crying with a blanket over its mouth. That sound was coming out of Ena.

"Turning!" called out Hultur.

Ena grabbed the base of the tarp. They turned and slowed way down. The trebuchets had stopped. That was good, wasn't it?

"Deathstaffs Charging!" Sal screamed.

The army lit up like a sea of lanterns. They were beautiful so far away. Even the tiny little red glow quivered Ena's heart. She'd forgotten Narla's three points. Her mind had gone to shit. Ena erected a glacial wall of blue ether before them. The power of maybe a hundred deathstaffs tested the limit of Ena's power, and found her defenses unshaken.

One of the strands of red flew askew of the wall, above their heads, and further down the path. Kalta's ethereal rose bloomed in the sky and manifested into a cloud of flames. The maelstrom of fire came down on them. As it fell, the flames shaped into a lion's maw, the length of its jaw larger than the length of Captain Fascinosa's ship.

"Hultur, some help!"

"Can't!" he shouted back.

In addition to keeping the horses on harnesses of pure force, and probably guiding every impulse they had, Hultur's attention was directed forward. Kalta hadn't been the only one to fire somewhere away from the wagon. Strong bolts of yellow ether were striking the ground. The work of mages ripped apart the road, tearing at the dirt to trigger a cave in. Hultur pushed at the earth from all angles, concentrating his power to reinforce the path to the lake.

Visk climbed onto the top of the wagon. Her face was

burned, marred by the flames that had removed the long braid on her head. With spear in hand, she stood. All seven feet of her was there, ready to take on the lion of flames that threatened to swallow them. "Imbue," she told Ena.

Fear for the flames coming on, a feeling of incompetence for letting Visk and the others get hurt; Ena used these things to power Visk's spear. There was no time to doubt and not even a moment to think. She heard the command, obeyed, and power surged into the spearhead. Blue bolts of lightning danced over the length of the shaft and erupted upwards into a blade three times the length of Visk.

Laughing a challenge in her native tongue, she struck out at the falling lion of fire. Her stab cut into its head and a swirling hole was left behind. Another slash and the jaw came off and went out like a gout of flame. She stabbed and swung and the lion's head dissipated to air. Half burned and illuminated in brilliant blue light, Visk inspired Ena.

They were going to make it.

If Kalta's army was close enough to shoot with deathstaffs, then they were close enough for Ena to go on the offensive. Each of these impressive attacks from Kalta had to come with an ethereal price. She'd have to pause between the attacks to restore her power with gulda. So Ena waited for the next blast from the red rose of magic.

The fire spell came low, blasting up the ground from under Ena's glacial wall. Ena took hold of the flames and directed them out, popping ether strands of every color. With so many conflicting elemental types, the effects evened out into an explosion of white. They'd adjust by switching all to one type, but that meant they were spending this moment shouting orders while Kalta was recharging. It also meant that they'd have no time to defend.

With one hand, she gathered clouds. The other, froze the water to let it fall as a sheet of solid ice. Ena summoned a snake of roaring flame. Then a stampede of electrical elephants. Ethereal barriers arose to stop her attacks, but they came slow and weak. They barely had time to react to the falling sheet of ice and it put their ranks into chaos. Ena lost sight of them behind a copse of trees.

They were coming onto the lake.

Ena let go of the power flowing into Visk's spear. "Get healed."

Visk fell down more than she climbed.

"How are you doing, Myrrel?" Ena asked.

"Overworked and in pain, so business as usual."

"How can you all be so fucking calm about this?!" shouted Zukoch.

"Nerve training," Narla replied with no small bit of mirth.

"We're running out of gulda," Torno told her.

"Hand me the big ones."

They did. Ena stepped into haste and restored them all. It gave her a solid ten minutes to consider their situation. The army must've suffered some losses from Ena's counter attack, but they would still be coming. Obi didn't strike her as the type to give up easily and neither did Kalta. She needed the counterattack of the lake to strike fear into them. She needed to break their spirits without breaking their bodies. Hopefully the sight of Visk's spear of blue lightning was making the bulk of the army reconsider their attack. Ena had no idea how she did that, nor why it came out as two elements.

Ena climbed into the bed of the wagon and distributed the refilled gulda.

She was back into full problem-solving mode. Everything felt hazy and numb. A few of them were missing hair and the new wagon was close to falling apart. Stopping wasn't an option. They had to keep this wagon together.

"How are the horses?" Ena asked.

"They're better after the healing, but still shaken up," Hultur explained.

"This is where our final stand's gonna be?" Narla asked.

The thought of taking on that army from a stationary position shook Ena. "If it comes to that, I don't want to lure them all into a death trap."

"Didn't stop you from killing the boulba," Sal grumbled.

No time to talk that out. She just sighed and pretended she hadn't heard it.

"These homes look abandoned," said Zukoch. "Or at least partially. They might be summer homes—vacation spots for the rich."

Ena was well aware of the concept, if not the experience. "Good. Some of these building might not survive what's coming. I'm going to try to break their morale by throwing a lot of power around. If that doesn't work-"

"Incoming!" shouted Sal.

Bursts of fire and darkness tore at the trees. Kalta's army was clearing the line of sight one deathstaff shot at a time. Ena grabbed some trees out of their path and used kinetic magic to toss them in the general direction. Even if a single leaf hit the strands of ether, they'd pop, unleashing their effects early. It wouldn't stop them from felling the trees, but it might give them a little more time.

"We've arrived," called out Hultur.

The lake was ahead of them. It was blue and wide and beautiful. Sun sparkled off the water in arcs creating the illusion of a thousand smiling sprites. There were probably thousands of lifeforms living in the lake. Fish, snails, frogs, dragonflies, and that was saying nothing of the countless animals who depended on the lake for water and prey. The lake was a massive part of the life around it and Ena was about to destroy the entire ecosystem.

THE THIRTY-SEVENTH CHAPTER

Where Ngoltur Kills

N odes were emotional centers stored in a magician's memories. Some memories were easier to recall than others, and those were frequently coupled with powerful emotional reactions. Trauma typically lasted longer than memories of different types and easily resonated with similar sources of suffering. The problem with linking emotions in this manner was that they were slow to develop. Nodes cut down on a magician's search time and allowed them to access the emotion quickly. But nodes did not create emotions, rather they pulled on an existing source. Accessing a node weakened its impact. It was like biting into an apple. Sooner or later, the red skin would run out and oxidation would brown the fruit inside. Calling upon a node diluted the emotions of a memory. Some said that casting with nodes was like sacrificing one's memories for gains in power.

Ena had been saving the good ones.

She would need all the power she could grab if she was going to scare an Archmage back to Gulambar. Hultur brought the wagon close to the lake. Ena held onto the picture of that serene body of water and let out a slow exhale for the start of her aeromantic gust. Wind spells reacted best to feelings of carefree joy.

Making out with Obi in the throws of afterglow. The node kicked up the breeze. She pulled the breeze over the lake slowly, building up its power as the conflict of fulfilling this stranger's desires died in her heart. She was at peace, she was in the moment, and enjoyed the feel of the wind in her hand and the lake rippling in her mind's eye.

Fascinosa kissing Torno. Shock and bewilderment demanded a quick pushing response. She pushed at the water, scooping it with a wedge of kinetic magic. He hadn't just kissed him, he'd loved him. He'd loved Torno. He'd known his body and felt his flesh. Curiosity pulled at her, and it tickled her heart to think that she was one question away from knowing the truth of their relationship.

Jerking off Obi. Compliance, obedience, and a will to serve overpowered the resisting nature of water. Water would follow the flow of the wind and the kinetic push. All of it must flow together into a great whirlpool. She held onto that desire to please not herself, but him. It was momentary but strong, desperate enough to pull her into his satisfaction. Even as she touched herself, it was his pleasure that consumed her thoughts. Beyond the carnal, there was a pleasure she found in the act of service.

"They're following," Hultur said.

That was it, the signal for Ena to continue. She had to follow through with the plan or this army would chase them from one end of the globe to the other.

The others murmured, reacting to the actions she magically felt, but didn't see.

"Quiet," Ena snapped.

She needed to focus. Water magic was difficult to resonate with and controlling it along with air and force was harder still. The lake was flowing well, behaving as it needed to. The wind wanted to move. Kinetics were inclined towards movement far more than the stationary. *Go with it, be with it,* she told the water.

This wasn't working. The thought of pleasing Obi

was too intertwined with sex. Lust was taking hold of her thoughts. She needed an unbroken impulse to serve purely for the sake of others.

Fixing Haenir's barn. It had been during her first season. She knew so little about the world and didn't trust Torno or the others, but it had become clear to her that the Brokers were needed. With no magical work for her to do, Ena had to use her hands to hold up boards and hammer nails. She worked to the point of being covered in sweat. She saw the dedication in Narla's eyes and wanted to share that feeling. She saw the stern look of Torno's concern and wanted to please him. She wanted to be a good worker. She wanted to be on a team.

All at once, she felt the lake in its entirety. It was like holding onto a bowl of water. The lake sloshed and spun, following the whirl of Ena's desires. She lifted it with one hand on the base, and swirled it with the other. A tiny flick of the wrist and a tendril of water flung at the army.

Hawk of flames slamming into the wagon. The tendril froze. A sheet of ice thicker than buildings dropped on the army. The multitude of screams magnified their volume, sending it echoing as one unidentifiable voice. Ice slammed against the ground. The massive impact sounded with a crack.

Ena could feel her hold on the lake slipping. She flicked her wrist that held the lake, poured it out of the basin and splashed it over the armies.

Stepping into the circle. She didn't know how much of the lake she'd thrown at them, but whatever was there had frozen. She felt magical cold sap the water of its heat. Then a dissonance, a sharp fracturing of her thoughts as the joining nature of water failed to keep its form united. The singular lake was now a tendril, a pool, a torrent, a wave receding, and the million and more drops flung free. It was too much of a magical shift.

She'd lost the shape of the lake in her mind's eye. She

couldn't hold onto the wedge of force or the air. The nodes jumbled together, bleeding one moment into the other. She'd let go of the magic, but her mind was a confused mess, flooded with thoughts of conflicting emotions, rushing over her like coming out of the circle. Her muscles were stiff; lungs stagnant. She forgot how to breathe.

~ ~ ~

There was an eye in a wall. The wall was off-white and blue, a million bricks of ice laid atop each other. The eye was alive. Though it resembled no human shape, it tracked Ena's movement. The sclera was black as night including every star visible from the wilderness. Where the iris should be a hazy red cloud twinkled like a nebula in the sky. She was supposed to know the name of that nebula only it hadn't seemed important enough to remember.

Loose bricks of ice were scattered about the dirt floor. They laid been broken and cracked from the impact of the eye slamming into the wall. The bricks melted at her approach and slinked towards her like a slime on the hunt. She gasped, but they slipped harmlessly beneath her bare feet. *Melting ice looks just like slimes*, she thought. Yet the fear wouldn't let go of her mind.

Closer, Ena could see a net covering the wall of ice. It was a criss-crossed pattern of blue and white ethereal strands. Still, she could see where the force of the eye slamming into this wall had snapped some of the threads. Strands of ether were not meant to hang down loose, but they were too low for Ena to reach. Even if she could, she knew not why she felt this desire to restore the frayed stands. Strings could never be rewoven, only tied or seared together.

Between the brick was a mortar made of gold. It was old gold, thin and stained green from the oxidizing wind. But gold did not oxidize, not when it was pure. This couldn't have been gold that held this ice together. The metal had to be diluted, but what oxidized green? Green was important,

Ena was sure of this, but the reason eluded her.

She touched the wall with the very tip of her finger and it stung.

Pulling back. Her finger was pricked. Blood seeped out of a wound too small to see. She stuck it in her mouth and sucked. More crimson liquid flowed, not from the wound on her finger, but from the very wall itself. It poured out through the cracks in the ice. The green-tainted fake gold jiggled from the flow of blood pressing through the mortar. What came out in rivulets, soon flowed in a gush. Green-tinted snakes of gold wiggled free of the ice and writhed within the outpouring of crimson. Blood rushed out on the floor with enough force to bring a froth to its surface.

That simple dirt floor was covered and now, subsumed by blood, Ena felt the tilt of the world, dragging that vital flow down. Before her, the wall shook, straining from the weight of the blood it could no longer hold back.

Ena pushed forward to grab it, to support the wall with her hands, but for every step forward the rushing torrent of blood pushed her back twice as far. Her hands reached out to grab or cast but they only took on a crimson hue.

Copper, she thought. *Copper turned green.*

THE THIRTY-EIGHTH CHAPTER

In Which Ngoltur
Illuminates Secrets

It was dark with night when Ena awoke. There was a thatched roof above her and one of those candle things flickered on a nearby table. The bedroom smelled of mud and soot. Ena tried to call out. Her lips were too dry to part. She drank a full pitcher of water, but came away still feeling parched. Catching her breath, her lungs felt heavy.

A small boulba child lingered in the threshold of the now open door. She recognized the child as male by the smaller stone patches on his cheeks. He was about three feet in diameter, a look of mischief in those startled eyes.

Ena tried a smile. When it worked, she told him, "Hello."

The sudden noise startled a cat under her bed. It skittered out of the room. The boy ran after the cat, his hands slapping against the floor as he did.

Voices reverberated on a nearby window. The three interwoven warbles had to be Myrrel, Torno, and Zukoch. They were okay. Ena let out a long sigh of relief. Despite having drank all the water available, her mouth still tasted like copper. Maybe the dream meant nothing, but it felt like another message from the Gods.

The door creaked.

"*Omsa sor*," said the boulba woman. "*Ebe canta fe?*"

"Huh?" It felt like the rock woman was trying to smack the words into her skull. Ena took two steps and staggered.

The rock woman righted her and kept repeating, "*Yus hava res*," like it would mean more the fifth time.

Ena slid past and traveled into the hallway. It was dark and filled with the strong smell of sulfur. More than half of the front room was taken up by a large, indented fire pit. Two boulba men sat in the pit, roasting their feet on the open flame. One of them was young, almost the same age as Sal, and chewed on a black, flakey rock. The older waved a greeting. Ena bowed her head and went through the open front door.

The faint smell of meat and caramelizing sugar brought Ena's stomach to rumble. Half a pig was laid out alongside potatoes, corn, and foods Ena couldn't even recognize. Her body couldn't even spare the moisture to drool, but she found the strength to stumble over to the table. Utensils and plates alike had been used but the food looked fresh enough. She loaded up a plate and took huge bites.

A Leben girl of fourteen or so put a fresh pitcher before her. There was a polite smile on her lips, tempered by curiosity. When Ena drank up and thanked her, the girl pointed to her ears and shook her head. Deaf more likely than not. Ena mangled a "thanks" in Duan Si hand talk, but she didn't recognize it. No matter. This girl had brought her mead to wash down the meal and for that she was a fucking hero.

"Hi, Ena," muttered Zukoch on his way to the restroom.

"Hey." She went back to shoveling food into her mouth.

He went vertical and then jumped up and down, shouting, "Ena's awake!" as he ran back to the bonfires.

All of Ngoltur's Aides were alive and walking. Visk's

long braid was gone, replaced by close-shaved temples and a short but fuzzy hawk. There was a little bit of scarring on the left side of her face, but that was the worst of it. Torno had grown the most beardy-beard that she'd ever seen him in, and he was wearing a military cut. Sal had grown out his beard, too, filing the stones on his face into a scissor-cut pattern. Myrrel was haggard as usual, only her signature rat's nest had been replaced by a Leben style wig that touched her ears. Narla was sporting a bald look, made all the more severe by a missing eyebrow. At least Hultur and Zukoch had been untouched by the flames.

"How long was I out?" she asked.

"Almost four days," Myrrel explained with relief. "There was talk of reviving you with magic."

"I knew it was ether drain," Torno said with a false confidence.

"Are we by Toberg Monte?" Ena asked, forgetting the name of the surrounding city.

"No, this is Karzak." Sal was grinning ear to ear. "The people here are so friendly. You being sick was the only thing keeping me from relaxing. Now that you're awake, I'm drinking thick oils every night!"

"That's great, Sal, but maybe hold off on the celebrations. We all need to talk." Ena looked to her Aides.

"Deep dreams?" Hultur asked.

"I don't know. Maybe." She briefly described the dreams. "But none of that's worth worrying about. We as a group need to have regular discussions. I want us to have a group chat once a day."

"A river of blood told you to do this?" Visk asked without levity.

"It came to me back in Taulge. This is the first time we could sit down and chat."

"Maybe we should sit around a campfire," Myrrel suggested. "It would be easier to see each other's faces."

"Good idea."

"Yeah, good idea. Oh, go there without me. I gotta run off and pee. Make sure you wait for me," Zukoch insisted, scrambling over to one of the larger Leben homes.

It was then that Ena took in the size of the village. It was a modest location, maybe as big as fifty domiciles. Boulbas lived in heavy stone dwellings carved into the earth. The Leben lived in similar structures, only their roofs were shaped into triangles and their plots of land were surrounded by dirt. Leben and boulba alike stared at Ena with awe and curiosity. A few of the little ones approached, but the deaf girl of fourteen scared them off with something like a wrench.

"We had to tell them you're Ngoltur," Torno said.

"I figured. I'm just not used to the way they stare at me."

"Those jerks in your chantry wouldn't know beauty if it was melting their eyes," Torno said for maybe the hundredth time.

"Mm hmm, not like you highbrow Capital people, right?"

He stuck his nose in the air, taking on the most pompous of airs. "Undeniably."

"Torno's been doing well as leader *pro tem*," Visk informed her. "He didn't even haggle over the cost of the new horse."

"Gale?" Ena asked in fear.

"He's fine, it was Li'at that left us," Hultur informed her.

"I'm sorry." She reached over Sal to touch Hultur's arm.

"Aww, you started without me!" Zukoch pouted. He was carrying a basket in one arm and two pitchers in the other. "I knew I shouldn't have grabbed snacks."

"No, that is the work of the Gods." Ena opened the basket and found a jar full of dried beetles, smoked meat wrapped in wire, and a whole lot of rocks. She placed the basket at Sal's feet and he distributed the jars.

"How should we start?" Myrrel asked.

"We could start with your hair. I don't remember you getting it singed."

Myrrel tilted her head to show off the weave. "I shaved it as a show of solidarity for Narla."

"Which I didn't ask her to do," grumbled the expectant mother. "This is how I look when I'm ready to blow things up."

"How'd that go? The blowing people up. You all look too relaxed to be being pursued by Kalta."

They exchanged looks and Torno took it upon himself to share the news. "You froze most of them in ice. We didn't wait around to see who got out. Chances are their losses are too great to keep up the pursuit. They've been traveling for over two months, some acolytes are bound to desert."

"But you know Kalta. Do you think she'd give up that easily?"

Torno gave Ena a hard look.

"How do you know her, Torno?" Sal asked. "Her name sounds so familiar."

"He doesn't have to answer if he doesn't want to," Ena said. "I don't want this to be an interrogation, just a chat."

Torno did. "Kalta was my first lover."

"The goss is spilling out the barrel now." Myrrel leaned over to Narla. Their eyes went wide with curiosity.

"She was thirteen when they brought her to the Elite Chantry. It was during the first rounds of testing for the Great Generation. Since her merchant parents were early supporters, they were able to move their voice gem industry close to the capital.

"Kalta was an outcast. Her parents were able to continue their business, but weren't invited to the balls of the former nobility. Kalta was polite and crude and she became a target in hours. As a bastard, I was used to the abuse and came to her defense. The other kids tried to entice me to attack her too, offering me a pass into the social elite if I broke her wand, things like that. I stayed her friend, and the more they came after us, the closer we became. We were united in our hatred for them and...well, we used to play a lot of pranks.

"Then one day the Supreme Magus came to visit her parents and everything changed. He outlined his plan to create the great goss, and Kalta's parents were selected to be the sole manufacturer for vocal gems distributed throughout the country. Kalta's status was instantly elevated to the top of our class. The old nobility knew what was coming, and they forced their children to apologize and make good with Kalta. It had been easy to hate them as her enemies, but the temptation of their acceptance was too much for her to turn down. I understood when she did it. I didn't even hold it against her. I was just a bastard, after all, and Kalta was part of the new plan.

"Then the first Elite Chantry dance came. It's almost impossible to describe how electric the air was. The hype was so surreal that my stepmother took me clothes shopping. She publicly called me her son. It was all I'd ever wanted and so much more than I thought I'd deserved. But it only got better at the dance.

"Kalta's new friends, the same elite who had kicked me and spat in her food, walked up with smiles on their faces and practically pushed me out to the dance floor. Kalta was waiting, looking more beautiful than she'd ever looked before. Everyone was shouting, telling me to ask her to be my girlfriend. I knew I was beneath her, but she acted like the question was already decided. When I gave her our first kiss the entire room applauded. The great goss did a drama around that kiss and we became the Elite Chantry's 'it' couple.

"After graduation, we enrolled in the Mage's Academy. The entire academy was buzzing about Kalta and I. Women were sneaking into my room to try and seduce me. Men were picking duels with me to prove I wasn't worthy of Kalta. It did things to our relationship. It made it harder for us to find time alone. Something about all of that attention changed her.

"The more I dueled the better I became. I was scoring wins on men ranked above me. Kalta kept pushed to start fights with popular men. She said it would generate goss. I didn't want to do it, but she wouldn't let it go. It got so bad, we ended up fighting at a party and she broke up with me. She made a spectacle of destroying the brooch I made her.

"I was crushed. I felt like my entire life had ended, but that night she snuck into my room. She promised that she wouldn't push me to fight anyone. We cried, we got back together, and I thought everything was going to be okay.

"That's when the poetry started.

"She came up with this plan to have me *win her back* at a party. I'd show up and recite this grand poem and she'd give me another chance. She'd already had it drafted for me. All I had to do was perform it. I didn't want to, but it was a condition for her taking me back. I figured, what was one performance? Of course, that was only the beginning.

"Every week or two Kalta would have this new plan to keep us popular. She'd flirt with a guy that I'd beat in a challenge. If another girl came up to talk to me, I was supposed to lead her on until we gathered a crowd, and I would humiliate her. It was all about propping us up as a desirable couple. Every time we had a new breakup, it had to be bigger than the last time. Once we started throwing around spells and all of her friends had to intervene. She had me cut myself to prove my devotion after that.

"I...I know that I'm not blameless in what happened. I hadn't wanted to do it at first, but some part of me liked it. I liked the drama, I like the theatrics, and I even liked the fucking attention. But it was never enough for her. She made a dreamcast of us having sex and had it *accidentally* fell into the wrong hands.

"I was furious at Kalta. She was out shopping when I

found her, and I ended our relationship right then and there. Only it felt just like every other breakup, sans my dramatic flounce. When Kalta came to my room to talk about our reunion, I wasn't having it. I'd meant it this time. So she threatened me. If I didn't take her back, she would use her parent's influence in the great goss to destroy me. She vowed to make everyone in Caredor hate me.

"If I was a better man, I would've left and never talked to her again. Only I wasn't ready to give up the praise, the admiration, the flirtations, and all of the status I'd gained. By the end of the night I was on my knees begging her to take me back. She had me "fix" thing by challenging her new boyfriend to a duel. I burned half the man's face off. The healers couldn't remove all the scars or give him back his sight in that eye. I heard he became a mercenary.

"Kalta and I, we kept up our little act as two of the most beautiful and desirable monsters and I was miserable.

"It was draining me to always be performing for these people who were supposed to be my friends. My apologies were getting less and less convincing and my scorn during the breakups felt so real. So Kalta had us switch tactics. We could remain a couple of interest by creating rivalries with other couples. Sometimes we let the rivalries stand, but when people started to take their side we destroyed them. I was getting good at taking out my frustration on other people and I started caring less and less.

"Then we went too far. We teased Nalla Latoite, humiliating her just because she'd gotten buzz for having the best dress. I barely even remembered her the following night. I should've. Nalla was a Wizard's daughter. Her parents had enough political power to get everyone talking about her suicide attempt. I didn't hear about it until it hit the great goss.

"Kalta was in my room with me when we heard and she just laughed. She joked about making a dreamcast where we showed Nalla the proper way to kill herself. That woke me up. I left her. I didn't argue. I didn't throw a fit. I just got my stuff and my gulda and left.

"I found an eccentric Marineld sailor and paid him to take me as far away as he could. When I got back a year later, she'd dragged my name through the mud. She made up this story about me cheating on her, and I had zero standing in the Great Generation. Everything I'd worked for was gone. Yet somehow the Supreme Magus offered me a job as a Broker Captain. I thanked him with tears in my eyes. I should've known better."

Torno paused. He took the time to measure everyone's response, but he wouldn't look at Ena.

"Kalta will do anything to get what she wants," he concluded. "She's not here to get back at me. She's here because killing Ngoltur will make her a living legend. Her mages, the acolytes, they might deserve our mercy, but not her. She needs to be killed."

"Okay, but that Marineld sailor was Fascinosa, right?" Zukoch asked.

"Yes…" he sighed.

"Just making sure."

The air was heavy. No one was sure what to say.

Torno cleared his throat. "Sorry, I didn't mean to make this all about me."

"I don't mind," Zukoch said. "I'm still curious about you and Fascinosa."

"There's not much to tell. I was broken and he was sweet. We got close, had a lot of sex, and made a bunch of promises we both knew we couldn't keep. He fell in love and when I finally saw that I was using him, I ended it. There's really not much more to say than that." He shrugged. "What about you, Sal?"

"I didn't date an Archmage!"

Torno didn't even smile. "Yeah, but you're here in a country full of boulba, this has to be different for you. I've never seen you so happy, and that beard is solid."

"The boulba would say it's *cut*," he said with pride.

"What I mean is..." Torno took his time putting it to words.

Narla didn't. "You could live here."

"Sadly, being here does fall short of my expectations."

"Why's that?"

"Language. I grew up never speaking any rockspek. Only my grannie spoke the tongue. I made good money working construction, but it made it even harder to connect with my people. By the time my work rotation finished, my siblings had gone to other cities and other countries. I, alone, was there to help my father bury my mother. Becoming a Broker was a hard decision, but the sign on bonus was enough to send my father away to live with my bro. I had nothing for me in Caredor. I was happy to serve under Narla and happier still to serve under Torno. You were my friends when I had nothing. I'm not going to abandon you when you need me the most."

"You don't owe us anything, Sal," said Ena. "You can still grab some gulda and get the fuck out of here. If Karzak doesn't work you could go live with your brother and father."

"Nah, their feet stink," Sal joked, waving a hand in front of his face. "But it's more than that. My family was never close. We were too different. One of us would tell a joke and the only one laughing was the person who told it. Now that I've seen the world, I want to live with other boulba, but not until I help you, Ena. We will see this through to the end. All of us."

He was smiling and full of a confidence Ena didn't share.

Ena cleared her throat. "Are you still mad at me for killing those boulba?"

"I don't know if I was ever mad." A moment's pause made him consider that seriously. "Okay, yes, I was mad. But I think it was misplaced. This is embarrassing to admit, but the lives of boulba mean more to me than humans. I don't get to see many boulba. I forget that there are entire countries of my people. Still, some of my anger had nothing to do with that. Those were the screams of a boy too proud to admit that he was afraid."

"Afraid?" Ena asked. "What were you afraid of?"

He was reluctant to answer that question.

Many of her Aides all had the same nervous look in their eyes. It came from a combination of worry, shame, and hesitation. She'd seen that look in their eyes before, from when she first left the circle of slowed time.

Ena looked to the flames. "You're afraid of me."

"Ena, you used an entire lake as a weapon," Myrrel reminded her. "You swatted away boulbas like they were clods of dirt."

Sal let out an annoyed grunt.

"I…" Ena sighed. "I could've handled that differently. I should've kept using kinetic magic to push the boulbas away. I should've stopped after the first attack of ice from the lake. I'm sorry, Sal. I'm sorry to all of you. I get so scared when the fighting starts. I jump to extreme measures without even thinking about the consequences."

"Apologies don't help us, and I don't need them," said Narla. "You did what you had to."

"Did I? I killed a lot of people yesterday." Ena realized it had been half a week back. "On that day. You know what I mean."

Narla was adamantly on her side. "I do. They were going to kill us. Maybe you could've been more careful, but that bitch, Kalta, brought an army. She didn't give us a lot of choices. The harder we hit back, the less likely we are to meet them again. As much as those soldiers fear Kalta or even the Supreme Magus, that display of power had to make some of them think twice. They've been riding hard in a strange land and the temptation to desert is going to eat at their resolve. It was the right call to go big, Ena."

"Your not the only one to blame for what happened,"

Myrrel added. "The Archmage nearly killed us back in Caredor City. We all reacted with a lot of fear and a lot of anger. We wanted to strike back at her. We all did. In the moment, I didn't think your use of power was excessive. When you were spinning that lake I was hoping that you'd put an end to this."

"But doesn't that change how you feel about me. I know that you're scared of me now, Myrrel." Emotions gripped Ena. She scooted closer to the flames, but they couldn't melt away her shakes.

"Yes, I'm scared of your power, but I'm not scared of you as a person. The one time I was scared of you was when you lost control." Myrrel at least *sounded* sincere.

"Regardless," Narla came in. "I don't think it does us any good to look back on our actions with regret. We can only look forward. That's what we said after we got trounced by Kalta. It's still true here. In the future, you'll try not to use so much power."

Ena nodded. This was supposed to be a mission of peace. No matter what happened, killing needed to be avoided.

"Ena, can we discuss your power?" Visk asked. After a nod, she continued. "Have you reached a greater understanding of the Turall's power?"

"Honestly, no. It didn't feel any different when I moved the lake. It was like casting a regular spell right up until the moment I lost ether. If anything I'm more confused about magic than I was when I left the rug. How did you know I would be able to imbue your spear?"

Visk rose her chin. "I had faith."

"Well, don't," Ena scoffed. "My magic is becoming unpredictable. When Kalta's hawk of flames hit, I didn't consciously cast that defensive aura. It was like it cast itself."

Hultur cleared his throat. "If you remember, that was the intent of your training in the circle of time. You told me that you were only able to achieve the first of my assignments, intuitive shaping. We have seen signs of intuitive casting before."

"Yeah, and it almost got people killed," growled Narla.

"That is because her training of the second assignment is incomplete. She must feel spells more than she casts them to defend herself intuitively. We are still in possession of the rug, I think-"

"No," snapped Myrrel.

"Fuck, no," growled Torno.

"They're right, Hultur," said Ena. "I tried it once, but I can't stay in there. I'm sorry. I simply don't have your resolve."

He turned his attention back to his journal, making marks none of them could see.

"Visk, do you know why my imbuing came out as blue lightning? I've never done that before."

"Ki'an magic is not a thing of math and tables. I did not study glyphs to create my attack of red lightning. I think of my lost love and the attack takes that shape."

"It's emotional overlap," Torno explained. "When two emotions are intertwined, sometimes they can work in unison. You might be calling upon lightning, but if there's a lot of rage intertwined with your thoughts of disgust it can color it red."

"So you're saying it's possible to channel two elements at the same time?" Sal asked.

"Absolutely," Torno said. "Most casters can barely keep one spell going, but it's not unprecedented. Ena was wielding at least three elements when she was twirling that lake around like a whip. There's actually a few-"

Zukoch raised his hand. "All of this magic talk is way over my head. I can barely hold on to an empathy spell. I still don't even know how Ena was able to cast spells at the same distance as a deathstaff, let alone control a lake without even looking at it."

"Magic doesn't come from deathstaffs or wands." Ena

looked to Hultur but he wasn't interested in explaining. "Spells don't even come from incantations or emotions. Magic is part of the world and ether is our personal will stirring that magic to act. Magic systems don't control magic or ether, they're like best guesses as to how magic really works. We notice that it's easier to wield fire when we're mad, but that doesn't mean fire needs rage. I can still create fire when I'm sad or scared, but it's harder to do. In the case of using magic from a great distance, it's simply a matter of bleeding ether to extend the spells effective range.

"The world has what we call the ether-net. It's the field of magical energy that's connected to all life," she explained.

"We call it a firmament," Zukoch said with a nod. "It absorbs magical energy as things move through it. We have to work harder to make things happen the further away they are. Wands relieve that pressure by turning the spell into a concentrated strand of energy."

Sal yawned. Very little of this had anything to do with him.

Narla joined in on the yawn. "Yeah, I'm with the big guy."

"Hmm?" Hultur tilted his head.

"The other big guy. I'm tired and I ain't looking forward to a trip through Toberg Monte."

"With any luck we'll only have to fight a mega," Torno jested. "Is there anything else we needed to talk about, Ena?"

Hours and hours worth, but they'd probably have time on the upcoming journey. "That's good for now. I don't want these meetings to be too serious, but I appreciate you sharing like that. Thank you."

Torno didn't meet her gaze.

"Good night, everyone. I'll see you all in the morning. I'll take first watch and probably another three after that." Ena stood up and stretched.

The group hugged good night and Ena received a lot of extra long ones as they again expressed their relief to have her moving about. Torno tried to sneak off without a goodbye hug and Ena tracked him down.

"Hey," she called out to him when she got close. "Listen, about things with Kalta-"

"You don't have to tell me that the way she used me doesn't excuse the shitty things I've done, Ena. I know that. I've had to live with the knowledge that I'm a horrible person for a long time. I didn't want to tell any of you about my past because I was your leader and needed your respect. Maybe it'll feel different later, but right now I have too much shame to survive a dressing down. So can you spare me the shouting match just this one time? Please."

Ena was shocked into silence.

He walked off with his head held low. Again, she felt like she hadn't truly known him until that moment. Ena had worked with him for three years and she knew of him another two before that. In all of that time, everything she'd ever thought about Torno had been completely wrong. According to him, the truth was far worse, and in some ways it was. Yet, when she watched him sulk into a stranger's house, she didn't feel disgust for him. Torno's pain made her warm with sympathy.

She wanted to hug him.

THE THIRTY-NINTH CHAPTER

In Which Ngoltur First Meets
the Leader of a Nation

Karzak claimed the land on and around the great Zelyantz Mountain Range. Boulbas were natural geomancers and had crafted roads along every ridge. They used their magic constantly to push themselves along the ground like rolling rocks, but all other uses of geomancy were expressly outlawed. All things considered, it was probably for the best that Ngoltur's Aides weren't allowed to use geomancy to speed their journey. The wagon was held together by two conjoined parts after their run-in with Kalta. Fresh hewn logs and rope was the only thing keeping the two halves of the wagon together. Even on flat road, the bed shook out of sync.

Two main roads ran south along either side of the mountain range, the eastern Zel Road and the western Yan. Ngoltur's Aides had come into Karzak on the east side and stayed on the straighter Zel. Between steep peaks lay towns and cities, but neither Zel nor Yan ran through these settlements. Instead curved bridges connected the great roads to their cities. The onramps and offramps were decorated with statues depicting boulba folk heroes and strange gods that resembled monsters. Much of the art depicted the mountains themselves as grands gods of rock playing out myths.

At all times of the day, boulba traveled over Zel Road. They rolled along in connected diamond patterns. The geomancy of one boulba resonated with the next behind them aiding their travel in the same way migratory birds flew in great V shapes. Slow rollers and newcomers to the Zel came in on the mountain side. Supplies weren't carried by animal drawn wagons, except for the rare Leben riders. Instead, specialized carts called Gyeterl sat on the backs of a diamond of eight boulbas. Boulbas in ball shape carried the Gyeterl on a mechanical system of hooks and wheels that kept the rock-folk secured under the bed.

Their order and efficiency, as well as the craftsmanship and ingenuity of Karzak was fitting given the impetus of boulbas construction. Though none agreed how the boulba were created, all agreed that their purpose was the construction of roads. Made to live off rocks, they were able to build great tunnels without the need for food. Though constructed to be a slave race to humans, their freedom to eat from the very earth gave them far too much autonomy to control. Since the first generation of their liberation, they'd been employed to work in construction from one edge of the world to the other. And if the gods ever had need to make roads and buildings, they'd employ the boulbas too.

Ena had never seen so many different kinds of boulba. Earth tones were as common as those tinted gray and black. Yet some had patches of white, yellow, red, and even greens and blues. The patterning of most resembled the mountains around them, but some had clearly rolled from very far away. Ena wanted to talk to these travelers and tried to strike up conversations with the locals, but so few of them knew Dorospek.

While their journey was slow going, every village, town, and outpost welcomed the coming of Ngoltur. The diamond chain on the Zel Road was at least twice as fast as their horse drawn wagon, and so with every celebration dozens of boulba went on to the next stop to spread word of their coming. Soon they were welcomed into cities with banners, magical illuminations, and thunder songs--loud clashes of stone where boulba stomped and clapped. They never had to pay for a thing and were offered entertainment from dusk to dawn. Well, entertainment that wasn't sexual or connected to gambling. Karzak had outlawed both and had very little to offer in the way of alcohol.

By watching boulba in celebration, Ena came to understand how different Sal was. Boulba never hugged. Never. They would pat each other on the back, touch fingertips, and when they talked to close friends, only then would they greet and depart with a meeting of fists. Leben of the land told Ena that pressing hands together was like a kiss. Their hands were sensitive to vibrations, allowing them to feel the shape of nearby subterranean caverns. Pressing hands against another boulba was a very sensual experience, allowing one boulba to feel the innards of their rock and soil body. Kissing, the meeting of the mouths that took up much of their chest-head, was nothing short of sex for the boulba.

After marrying, boulba would sequester themselves for weeks as they made love through open mouthed kissing that lasted ten minutes, hours, and eventually entire days as the pair went from two balls of earth, to three. Boulba did not marry without the promise of making children and the couple spent a week gorging themselves in preparation for their wedding day.

When Ena asked people about casual sex and same gender couplings, they would not talk about either. Since these people were honoring Ngoltur and lavishing them with gifts, she suspected that they didn't want to reveal any unsavory behaviors. Ngoltur was after all a religious figure throughout the three continents. Within Ena's earshot there was no talk of crime, skirmishes, or even monsters. She wasn't allowed to see the country as it was.

Their time on the Zel Road was meant to end at the foot of Toberg Monte. Known by many as the mountain of death, Toberg Monte was an active volcano that had been spewing forth lava for millennia. In that time the boulba had feasted on the volcano's bounty and used its heat to assist them in the crafting of nations. Kingdoms and empires had risen and fallen, but the surrounding city of Ozalto had survived them all.

Karzak's capital came into view a full day before Ena and her Aides even reached the city's edge. From such a distance the buildings were little more than reflections on a pool of gold but that splendor only magnified as they drew closer. Everyone in the wagon, even Hultur and Torno were drawn to the majesty of the metropolis that lay cradled in the warmth of a volcano.

"There it is..." Zukoch said in awe. "The jewel of the world's crown."

Ena glanced over to ask Zukoch what he meant and Narla squeezed between them in the jockey seat. The spyglass was jammed against her eye. "I can see the wind turbines! They use the heat of the lava to turn their lifts and replenish the lava pools."

"I thought they kept the lava from cooling with magic," said Myrrel.

"Not all of it. Most of the city is powered by machines and architecture."

"You can see the lava casting light on their statues," beamed Sal.

"What?" gasped Ena. "That has to be candle light."

"Fires do not produce such an unwavering glow," said Visk with a stern voice. "Even if the city were ablaze, it could not light the statues in such a manner."

It unnerved Ena that Visk knew so much about the sight of a city on fire. "Good to know."

Most every building in Karzak was stone and made in the rectangular style. Bare rooftops formed the foundation for a second tiered street held together by a latticework of bridges. Resting atop those buildings laid another layer of civilization, that in turn supported an even smaller roadway. Statues of all shapes, sizes, and styles broke up flat silhouettes, with many of the larger ones serving as a fountain of fresh lava.

A gentle hand came to lay on Ena's shoulder. It was Torno. Leaning over her side to squeeze through the tarp and get a view of the city. She glanced over at his eyes and saw an honest look of wonder. He didn't even notice her. "I can't believe they call it the mountain of death."

"It is dangerous," said Zukoch. "There isn't a year that goes by where Leben don't die from a gas leak."

"Why do they live there if it's so dangerous?" Ena asked.

Zukoch shrugged. "They need to work."

"Sal!" Torno reached over Ena's back to slap Sal's arm and point. "Is that the moedkerns?!"

"Yeah, it must be! The first towers of the world," he laughed. "Oh, what a sight!"

Unique to Ozalto's skyline were the moedkerns. These extended towers were so wide and flat that they resembled free standing walls more than buildings. All of the orange glowing infrastructure was sandwiched by flat vertical slabs of black rock that rose high above the terraced roofs of the city.

"My father always said they were architectural failures," Hultur commented from the back. He was leaning out the side of the wagon adding a frightening degree of tilt to the wagon's already unstable sway. "An unsupported wall cannot withstand a shake." He chuckled. "Nothing about them looks unstable."

"They were carved from the mountain," Zukoch explained.

"But it's at the foot of the mountain." Narla took the spyglass off her eyes.

Myrrel yanked it away a second before Torno could reach for it. She stuck out her tongue and got a better view.

Zukoch continued his explanation. "There was a larger mountain here before Toberg Monte blew, supposedly it dwarfed the height of the volcano. The initial erruption was so powerful that it split the mountain. All of the southern half disappeared to feed the boulba nation. Fearing that the northern half would suffer the same fate, they planned the creation of the great castle to be made of the same black rock."

"How did you come to learn all of this?" asked Hultur. He looked more than a little miffed that Zukoch was so knowledgeable. Hultur spoke the language of Karzak and Zukoch did not.

"I told you, I studied the Grand Dream," Zukoch said with a chuckle. "You see that statue over there by the old castle? That illuminated woman is the Looming Queen. Many believe she was the third Ngoltur to ever live. It was under her magical assistance that the boulba first created Ozalto."

"I'd heard it was no longer a castle," said Sal.

"It is, but there are no monarchs inside."

"They call it their city hall," Hultur said with ironic mirth.

It was easy to spot the former castle. Though moedkerns were few, the imposing walls were packed in tight closer to the city hall—which was not only a continuation of this architectural idea, but a distortion of it. Much of the moedkern style castle was squat and cubic when compared to the standing walls of the moedkern proper. It's ancient design looked far from primitive and could likely survive a hundred more Grand Dreams.

All of these sights were a far cry from the mountain of death Ena had heard about as a teen. Here was no sweltering furnace, but a city of industry and artistry, a living embodiment of boulba ingenuity. The sight of the glowing metropolis tickled Ena's curiosity, but she would have no freedom to explore the ancient city. Ozalto was expecting her.

~ ~ ~

Great banners hung over the off ramp of Zel Road into Ozalto. They rode in with gawking strangers waving streamers and blowing horns to welcome their arrival. Making their way to the entrance, a marching band halted their progress with fanfare. Security officers rolled ahead to clear the way. A mass of people from all walks of life pushed forward to see the Turall. A marching band filled the street before them and paved the way into the heart of the capital.

Small Leben girls had painted their skin white and waved toy wands in the air. Boulba waved flags with the symbol of the Turall. Script in every tongue loudly declared, "Welcome Ngoltur! Glory Be Your Pilgrimage!" And every variation of the phrase that could be imagined. Every caster who could use a wand shot up bursts of colorful light and sounds of enthusiasm. The cheers were deafening.

Ena hung off the wagon and waved to the people and the cheers doubled in volume. The screams collected and tens of thousands of voices chanted "Ngoltur," in unison. She laughed at their awe and the sheer absurdity of it all. Throughout the entire trip, their message to the people of Karzak had been a singular one: Ena was looking for Muttur. They didn't mention that they were with Hultur, nor did they talk of their mission of peace. They simply said that Ngoltur was here to find Muttur and talk of the pilgrimage couldn't be silenced.

When she got deep into the city she began to make out signs in Dorospek, and saw amateur banners hanging from the windows of apartments. They depicted Ngoltur and Muttur kissing before a backdrop of a red heart. Many banners also depicted Ena and a Leben boy kissing over the dead corpse of Hultur. Of course, he hadn't looked like their Hultur. His hair fanned out like a lion's mane held in place by bones.

Once the procession reached the heart of the city progress slowed to a crawl. The masses cheered and pushed against a wall of boulba security. A Gulam man jumped over the wall to toss a rose and he was restrained by two guards. Four fancy horses flanked them on both sides, long streamers of blue and gold bore the defunct symbol of Doronel's royal line. It was then that she noticed that many of the white painted children were wearing tiaras and holding the wand of the queen.

It got harder to smile. She retreated into the jockey box to catch her breath. Someone handed her a letter. The envelope was marked by three sets of official seals. It's words were simple, "Wait at the steps of City Hall." She handed it to Sal, who had the reins. He tried to say something, but it was a pointless gesture with the people screaming.

Ena stopped the wind against a bubble of silence. In its own way, pure silence after so much noise hurt more.

"Ah!" Narla shouted. "Please ease into that."

"Sorry," Ena mumbled.

"Okay, this is why you need to stay in disguise," Myrrel insisted.

"We hadn't had a choice," Torno muttered. "Too many had seen her uncovered skin. It was only a few people in a small town, and every single one of them were sworn to secrecy."

"Next time make they will swear with blood," said Visk.

"We might be in trouble," Ena told them. "Have you seen some of these pictures?!"

"They enthusiastically declare my coming death," said Hultur.

"I don't understand," said Narla. "We didn't tell them anything. Why do they all think you're here to marry Muttur, reclaim your birthright, and kill Hultur?"

Wandering eyes looked for guilt and one by one they

all found Zukoch, holding his head. His blushing skin was a deep shape of indigo.

"What did you say?" asked Narla. She pulled him close by his shirt. "What did you do?!"

"I'm sorry, guys," he grumbled. "I...I didn't mean to. It's just that she was so pretty."

Groans and hands flew into the air.

"Don't feel bad, man." Torno pat his back. "I would've done the same thing."

"Well, I sure hope it was worth it," shouted a very irate Narla.

"I got my first kiss, does that count?" he asked sheepishly.

None could find the right words to voice their shock.

"What?"

Narla clapped her hands together and let out a long sigh of frustration. "You're telling us that you made up some story about Ena being on a sacred pilgrimage, and you didn't even get laid?!"

Zukoch pouted. "It felt wrong to do anything else."

"Well, I for one commend your noble spirit," said Myrrel resting an arm on his shoulders.

"Thank you."

She shook him back and forth. "But you shouldn't have lied!"

"I'm sorry," he repeated until she let him go.

Myrrel pinched the bridge of her nose. "That boy has the sense of a fucking kikaa."

He picked up Wulg the kikaa and sulked into his silky feathers.

"What are we going to do now?" Hultur asked. He was understandably nervous.

"That all depends on what's going to happen after the parade," Ena grumbled. "I think our best option is to just come clean. Explain the misunderstanding and try to sneak out of the city unnoticed."

"We're almost at city hall," Sal told them from the jockey box.

"Sal, do you know what's waiting for us inside?" Ena asked.

"No clue."

"Karzak is run by a senate," Hultur informed them. "Each mountainhome is lead by a senator voted into office every three years. The senior senator is named Senives, Oldest of the Old. Bardon Yazdel is the current Senives. He's fiscally moderate, but favors strong social reform. He wins over opposition by pushing back punitive measures while increasing the quantity being punished. While foreign matters have largely been a non-issue for the democratic country, Bardon has publicly supported Caredor which has eroded his support with Fieta."

They stared at him.

"I was right," Visk said. "You are a dangerous man."

Hultur adjusted his hat.

"Is there anything we could use to leverage him?" Torno asked.

"His daughter-"

"No. We're not here to play politics. Though, I'm curious as fuck to know why Fieta doesn't want to support Caredor." Ena shook the notion out of her head. "We sit through this pomp and then just talk to him. Do you think this Senives would favor our fake mission or our real one?"

Hultur considered that. "It is hard to say. Though Zukoch made a mistake, he seems to have stumbled on the perfect combination of lies to win over the hearts of the people. I'm curious. How did you concoct your fabrication?"

"Her fingers were in my hair and she'd pull my head back if I didn't tell her something more. I literally just said the first thing that jumped into my mind." At least Zukoch sounded apologetic.

"I think Bardon will support our anti-monarch stance. It benefits him politically to do so as well. Getting us out of

Ozalto in secret will be a problem," Hultur decided.

"Alright, I'm going out there again." Ena did her best to drop the silence slowly, but the noise still came back with a blare.

They were made to keep their wagon at rest and watch an entire parade of performers. Fire dancers, Ki'an duelists, Fieta strongmen, Doronel light weavers, and many more came. About thirty minutes into the parade a wicked idea jumped into Ena's head. She cast a slow spell on herself. Even though she flailed her hand around too fast to make out the shape, it probably just looked like a polite wave to the gathered public. The final object on the parade was a colorful float of one of their gods. The bat winged centipede was decorated with colorful panes of glass, and had clearly been used in some previous festival.

At long last boulba and Leben attendants gathered around Ena's wagon to help her down. Great boulba in shiny helmets carried their belongings inside. About thirty boulba in fancy vests and hats marched out with even more pomp than the parade itself. Each greeted Ena and tried to talk to her in a Dorospek so mangled that she couldn't make out one word in ten. They were the senators, Ena put that together. Two of them had been Leben and their chests and legs were bare in the ceremonial vest and crotch wrappings of their office. Each gave a short speech and bestowed Ngoltur and her Aides with a present to honor her arrival.

Most of it was some object of cultural significance that Ena neither understood nor had the space to keep. But the middle-aged Leben woman had gifted her with a spellbook on time. Jackpot! She also received two sets of bracelets that easily cost as much as Ena's annual salary—well, her salary back when she had a job. She did receive rings, but all nine of them were ceremonial trinkets. The last of the senators gave her a robe or a gown, she couldn't be sure. It's fabric was soft as fog; literally. The threads were constructed from clouds and held together by ethereal enchantments. It would dissipate in about three months and sat in a thin case brimming with power.

Finally, Senives Bardon Yazdel came out with flashes and bangs. His body was dark gray, striped with marbles of thick black lines. His eyes were copper and the asscher cut rocks of his beard were green-stained copper ore. He was a boulba used to the spectacle, but held no love for it. Still, he was theatrical when it counted and made a great show of having two Doronel Oracles in defunct royal robes present her with his gift.

It was a fucking warding necklace!

Each of the oval cut amethysts on the bib laced necklace could buy her a farm. Selling the largest pearl cut sapphire would pay for a life of luxury for Ena, her Aides, and probably Haenir's entire village. That was to say nothing of the enchantments humming with love, splendor, and nurturing. Holding it felt like grasping onto a hug made of precious gemstones. This wasn't just a present. This was an heirloom.

It was *her* heirloom.

She looked to the strangers in Oracle robes decorated in the same garments they probably wore when they served Ena's parents. They were old, so much older than sixty. Tears ran down their wrinkly cheeks as they looked at her with the amber eyes of the Pearlescent Line. Both were men but only one had the small nose of the Qinsys.

The man with the smaller nose didn't just share her royal blood, he was related to her. She'd seen his picture when she studied history books about the decadence of Doronel. He was her grand uncle, the exiled Prince Yeldo Noriru Vamqinsys. Upon seeing the recognition in her eyes he smiled, his cheeks shining from the flashing lights.

"I believe we have a lot to talk about, young Ena."

THE FORTIETH CHAPTER

When Ngoltur Must Accept Her Fate or Oppose the Gods

Once Ena was inside the repurposed palace, she was handled. Servants apparently still existed in democracies and they had a schedule that Ena needed to keep.

First on their itinerary was an interview with the city's press. The interpreter was a smiling Gulam man adorned with earrings bearing a modified Turall symbol, the symbol of the Pearlescent Line. Leben and Boulba journalists asked long, in depth questions, and the interpreter told Ena that they wanted to know which city had been the prettiest, or which part of the parade impressed her. No one would answer any questions she had about her Aides, their wagon, or their horses, except to say they were "taken care of."

Next, she had the honor of enjoying a private bath in one of Ozalto's famed hot springs. They moved to undress her and only stopped trying when she surrounded herself in a tunnel of wind. After a short shower, she at last entered the hot spring chamber.

Not a soul was in the tiled room fit for a king. A floor to ceiling window gave her an unbroken view of Toberg Monte. Flowing lava carried away worries. Steam melted hard thoughts. Hot water welcomed fatigue. With an exhale she sank deep. Warmth brought on serenity. Gold radiance brought on a blink and then the temptation of sleep. Rest was driven back by the sound of stiletto clacks.

With the servant's arrival, so returned Ena's stress. There was no true peace in the former palace, only tangible offers of material luxuries.

Given a drying robe, she was escorted to a masseur's private parlor. The Ki'an woman to service her was short and handsome, her angular features smooth as battleaxe's edge. This stranger was of a height with Torno and combed her finger lengthed hair down to the brow, with just enough negligence to make her look wild. She gave clipped instructions to disrobe and lay down. Strong hands rubbed fragrant oils into Ena's skin. At first sign of tension, she attacked it with precision.

Ena couldn't make sense of all the gifts and the royal treatment, and the thought kept her from enjoying any of it. She was just visiting the city on her way to find Muttur. Did they plan to keep her here until they found Muttur and brought him here to marry her? It was unsettling to know how much the people favored a marriage between two strangers. She should find a way to elope with Torno, that would really upset their plans.

Torno? Where the fuck had *that* thought come from?

Oh! The masseur was working those masterful fingers into her inner thigh. Her caress was getting progressively closer to her genitals. Handsome as the woman was, she was undeniably a servant. Ena couldn't be sure that these advances were anything more than compulsory. She brought her legs together and the masseur took the hint.

They'd given her attention, solace, treatment, and romance. Next came the dressing and with it they offered companionship.

Three humans greeted her, one from each continent. They embraced her like a wayward sister and introduced themselves in turn. Bess, the Gulam woman, was matronly and a dark shade of honey, a color Ena had only seen from those hailing from the coldest parts of Duan Si. Co, the thin Ki'an man, was adorned like a jeweler's tree. Ni, the critical Leben gentleman, showed his age, but wore his spectacles with dignity. Bess and Co spoke half to Ena as they complimented her features. Ni studied her from a distance, only making short comments to gauge the other's opinions.

In almost no time at all, Ena was presented with a dress that looked closer to a costume from a theater troupe. The form hugging dress bore the blue and gold of the Pearlescent Line and was adorned with many not so subtle triangles to imply the symbol the Turall. Yellow-tinted hair was covered with a wig of bleached silver that draped gracefully down to her waist. Two forelocks were teased out from under a tiara to frame her face. Intense debate followed over gloves and armwear, but Ena stopped paying attention when she they placed the heirloom around her neck.

Ngoltur's Necklace. One of the great artifacts of Doronel. The blue enchanted gems could supposedly snuff out a fireball cast at point blank range. Once the bib necklace was around her neck, all thoughts of annoyance eased out of her. Surrounded in an aura of magic, Ena held her head high and saw a reflection worth of a Princess.

~ ~ ~

Ena came out to applauds. She did a little twirl to pass the praise down to the fashion trio, but they hadn't followed her into the ballroom. Compliments came one after another and they kept her surrounded by senators, journalists, artists, and various well-to-dos. Though Ena spotted sign of her friends here and there, Senives Bardon Yazdel was always on one side introducing her to the public and on the other was the same soulless interpreter who deluded the meaning of every question. One drink followed another and none of it was water, but at long last the crowd was escorted into the dinning hall.

Out came the first course of some small bowl of soup

and Ena downed it like it was her last meal. The table went quiet. Some were gawking and others even had the audacity to snicker. That white skin of hers puffed up red from all the blood running through her veins. It was one thing to be made half starving because she couldn't stop for breakfast, it was another to humiliate her by expecting to follow etiquette she'd never learned. To top it all off, her friends weren't even at the table. All she could do was grit her teeth, eat slow as a glacier melting, and answer the same inane questions from that eloquently spoken tool of an interpreter.

"When are we gonna fucking talk?!" she snapped at her Grand Uncle, the exiled Prince Yeldo.

That warranted dropped utensils and open mouthed gawking. Ena couldn't care less about their sensibilities.

"After supper." Prince Yeldo went back to his greens.

Ena sank into her chair and let the sound of laughter and incomprehensible words bash against her resolve.

~ ~ ~

Prince Yeldo pulled off the hood of his robe the moment they retreated to his opulent bedroom. His lover was there with him, the infamous Vaynsta Ayra. He was just as old as the former prince and shared his same amber eyes. In a suit and tie the old man looked compassionate and attentive. He reached for a decanter and poured a drink filled with herbs.

"You want something?" Yeldo asked from the other side of the room.

"I want answers. I've been waiting half the day to get some answers, but you've been shuffling me around like a frozen flower."

Yeldo scoffed. "Those fools aren't my people. I have no more power here than you do." Vaynsta handed him the drink and sipped it with haste.

Yeldo scratched at the top of his chest. Inflamed splotches covered his ashen brown skin. They didn't look well. She reached out to sense his body with a diagnostic spell and found a weaving of magical enchantments far above her ability.

"That was rude," he chided. "Is this how Ursen teaches his Grand Generation?"

"I'm not here to be lectured about etiquette."

"Clearly. Have a seat. I'm sure you're familiar with my husband, Vaynsta Ayra," he motioned to the man.

"Hello," he offered a hand.

Ena took it. His grip was firm and bony. He smelled of chemicals Ena couldn't place. "You're the man he left the crown for?"

Vaynsta chortled. "Hardly."

"Is that what they teach you in Caredor? I hope I live long enough to see that thumb-sucker Ursen meet his end." Yeldo pulled at his upper robe, revealing a thin frame wet with sweat. "No, my dear grandniece, I did not give up the crown for love. My mother, the Queen, was very much aware of my relationship with Vaynsta and hadn't a single objection. As long as I was able to produce an heir, I would inherit the throne. I produced three, two of them men."

Ena's mind stuttered around the facts. "So...what? You were removed because of your illness? I never even knew you were sick, but you don't look well."

"I'm not. It's-" he got up and went to the privy.

"Yeldo lives with lupus," Vaynsta explained. "I've been treating him with every magical and practical application I can think of, but between his liver and his heart, he doesn't have much time left. Please forgive his mood. You seem to share that Qinsys impatience, at least."

"I'm Vamqinsys," Ena reminded him.

Yeldo screamed from the bathroom.

Vaynsta stood up. "Yeldo was removed because he was advocating for an expansion of the High Council's political powers. Excuse me." He knocked on the privy door. "Yeldo, do you need me?"

"Yes, dammit! Get in here!"

Ena tried to make sense of this. Yeldo was exiled a generation before the democratic revolution began. That had to mean that her Grandfather was a monarchist. If Yeldo had stayed in power, maybe the democratic revolution never would've happened. Ena shook her head. History didn't matter. Politics didn't matter. All that mattered was finding Muttur.

Yeldo walked out, leaning against his husband. "As you can see, all of the pomp and propaganda isn't doing me any favors, either. I didn't put that heirloom on your neck to make you listen to history."

Vaynsta helped him onto the couch and worked healing magic on his sides.

Yeldo continued. "You need to return to Doronel and take your place as Queen. Everything is in place. We will accompany you to the coast and speed back to Vyltur Castle."

Ena shook her head. "I have no claim to the throne. I am Vamqinsys."

"You may have lived your life answering to that name, but it has no basis in legal fact," Yeldo said with a drooling grin. "The King and Queen signed away their rights and the rights of their descendants from that day forth. Since you were born before they signed, you technically have the legal right to the throne."

"The President wouldn't step down to reinstate a monarchy," Ena scoffed.

"Not with a mere legal loopholes, no, but we have far more than that, little Princess." He sipped back drool and smacked away Vaynsta's dabbing handkerchief. Irate, Yeldo took the handkerchief and put it against his mouth. "We have worked over twenty years to put you back on the throne, and you come here, to the exact city where I've been living in exile. It is fate, Ena, fate."

"Allow me to explain," Vaynsta offered. His husband nodded vigorously. "Have your parents kept you abreast with our plans?"

Ena shook her head. She felt faint.

"Your parents resisted moving to Caredor City to avoid suspicion, but it was always to position them close to the Supreme Magus. They have placed assassins in his company, and several of them will act once given a signal from your parents. Solorona is too busy trying to change the laws to marry brother to sister to realize that their Cabinet is full of merchants in our pockets. New Nolda will assist-"

Yeldo hissed and waved a hand. "She needn't know everything about the other nations."

"Nothing you're saying makes any sense. Why would the people of Caredor support me? Why would Doronel abandon their democracy?"

"Gold!" Yeldo said holding up a coin. "It's all about gold! Those arrogant bulls used those little ether crystals to push out the monarchy, but it can't last. I'll admit, the idea of exchanging gulda for conjured food was clever, but it only works in times of peace. Think about it, Ena! What happens once the banners start flying and wars are being fought in earnest?

"Their military will start eating their wealth! With so much of their population busying themselves with the production of ether crystals, all it takes is a few well-placed strikes and their entire economy will collapse. Once the production of ether stops, Caredor losses its ability to feed its bloated population. They will become dependent on trade, but the value of gulda internationally will be zero. You show up with a ship filled to the brim with coin and it will buy you all the support you need. By siding with you, the people will be able to feed their families!"

"Because you're starving them!" Ena snapped back. "You plan to create a war that will force people into supporting me! That's no support at all! That is a dagger wrapped in velvet!"

Yeldo laughed. "What do you think rule is? Did you imagine that Ngoltur ruled with sweet words and beautiful smiles? Read your history! Those that came before you had to crush rebellions. Ngoltur kept taxes flowing through military action. She restricted access to food to keep the war effort going. Do you honestly think that any ruler would submit to conquerors because the sight of death brought tears to their eyes?

"Ngoltur surrenders to Hultur because the people of Gulambar are selfish, short-sighted simpletons that fight her rule even as Ki'an raiders are murdering their neighbors! Ngoltur surrenders because she cannot keep the war going *and* keep her people mollified. Without that dagger hiding in velvet, there is no kingdom! There is no rule without force, and there is no peace without rule! If you wish to bring an era of prosperity to Gulambar, that is how it is done." His hands were shaking, and the tremors spread up to his shoulders.

Vaynsta comforted him, whispering for him to calm.

"I don't want to rule," Ena said. "I'm here to break prophecy. Hultur is with me. Together, we can talk to Muttur and end this meaningless cycle of violence."

Vaynsta gasped. "What did you say?"

"That's fantastic!" Yeldo laughed. "That's great! Kill him. Kill him in his sleep and we will fully control destiny."

"I'm not going to kill Hultur! What part of us being on a mission of peace didn't you understand?!"

Vaynsta was horrified. "Hultur is pure evil."

Ena was really getting tired of hearing that.

"Child, you will be able to control the world," Yeldo said with unrestrained glee. He was bouncing up and down as he continued. "Ki'an is already in chaos after the destruction of Mu. They will not be able to rally their forces together and unite before you take all of Gulambar. Doronel alone has the forces to take Baliku after the blight of their endless summer. Prophecy gives you an excuse to invade! You can find a large male, hold up his dead corpse, and claim that you killed Hultur. This is destiny, Ena! Every cycle the

Grand Dream has costs Gulambar the most, but you can break that cycle as a conqueror!"

Ena couldn't follow all of this political talk. There was so much new information flying at her, and she was certain she didn't even have half the information she needed. She closed her eyes and tuned them out. Some itching in her heart told her that Hultur would actually get along with this man. He was pragmatic to the point of being vicious.

"No," Ena said.

"You can't-"

"Shut up!" Ena rose to her feet. "I won't kill Hultur and I won't follow your plan of gold and war! I'm not here to restore the monarchy. If gulda needs peace to thrive, then I hope it overtakes gold on every land! The monarchy was corrupt. You're proof of that. My parents are proof of that!"

"Everything they did, they did for you," Vaynsta told her calmly. Yeldo was shaking too much to talk.

"They ignored me for my own good? They locked me into rooms to be alone for days on end for my own good? They were horrible, cold, malicious monsters who were incapable of loving me! I used to think they simply didn't like children, but after seeing them with my brother, I know how twisted they truly are! If they've been working to kill the Supreme Magus in secret, then they've been doing that to get vengeance or use their daughter, but never because they love me!" Ena wiped away those treacherous tears.

"You like your friends, Ena?" Yeldo asked, calmly.

Ena held up a hand and manifested a spear of flames. "Think very carefully before threatening my friends."

"You misunderstand me," he gasped in horror. "Honestly."

She dismissed the flames.

"Maybe we should continue this conversation later," said Vaynsta.

"No," said Yeldo. The shakes were coming on much stronger now. He grimaced in pain.

"There's no need. We're done." Ena put her hand on the door knob.

"They'll be safe," Yeldo promised. "They can spend every day like this, surrounded by wealth and luxuries they've never known. You can have that, too. You don't need to rule at all. We can set you up as a figurehead. We'll make all of the difficult decisions, and you can spend every night with your husband."

She pictured a dark man with strong arms and a smile that she craved.

"We don't need to kill Hultur. If he truly is a man of peace, we trust what you say. Trust us, Ena. Everything is in place for you to rule. You will live a life of gold, parties, and happiness. The greatest worries of your friends will be what to drink, when to have supper, and who to have children with. Your children will grow as friends afforded those same luxuries."

Her friends gave up everything to help her bring about an age of peace and put an end to this cycle of death. Some of them didn't even seem to care about why they were fighting. This would mean a life of peace, not for the world, but for them. They fucking deserved to live a happy life after everything they'd been through.

Yeldo placed a compassionate hand on her arm. "Please, think it over. At least ask your friends. Don't they deserve to have some say in the matter?"

He smiled a paternal smile.

Ena nodded.

~ ~ ~

Events came and went in a blur. Ena had no idea how she ended up in a room with her friends. They were waiting around in a small personal library, maybe a magical study based on the glyph charts hanging on the walls. Hultur was at a desk surrounded by books stacked five high. He was alive and didn't seem to have a care in the world.

Narla lead the charge to greet her. "You okay?"

Ena shook her head.

"What's going on?" Torno asked. "Did they hurt you? Are we being blackmailed?"

"They can make me Queen," she told them.

"Of what?" Myrrel asked with a chuckle.

"Gulambar. They can make me Queen of Doronel and unite the continent under my rule. Decades of planning are waiting for me to take over."

Zukoch let out a long sigh. "Then you won't even have to marry Muttur. That's a relief."

They all shot him a look.

Zukoch pretended to read by holding up an upside-down book.

"I don't understand," Narla said. "Wasn't that the bad plan? The one we rejected within a few minutes of hearing about Hultur's plan?"

"Going back to Doronel would be working with prophecy." Visk pointed at Hultur. "If that happens, he will unite Ki'an and come to conquer you."

"I have no plans to conquer," said Hultur. "Regardless of your actions, I will continue on my quest to find Muttur."

"They offered to bring him to us." Ena shook her head. "All of us can wait here, or in Vytur Castle. We won't have to keep up this fighting. We'll be okay."

"We are okay," said Torno.

"I'm not," she admitted. Tears rolled down her cheeks. "I killed people, Torno. I killed so many people fighting Kalta, and for what? What was the reason for their deaths?"

"They were soldiers," Narla told her. "We're not talking about soldiers dying combat. You're talking about a continent united. That means dozens of villages set ablaze. People like Haenir will either be conscripted or starve."

"Torno started that anyway," Ena said. "For all we know, Haenir and all of the people we helped are already dead! Nothing we do can keep the world from tearing each other apart for pointless reasons. At least if we do this, I can guarantee that everyone in this room will be safe. All of us will come out of this alive. That was never a guarantee before!"

"Yes, it was," said Myrrel. "We could've just told Hultur good luck and gone back to living our lives. We could've left with Captain Fascinosa."

"Ena," said Sal, almost oblivious to Myrrel's pleading tone. "Can I see that necklace?"

Ena's first impulse was to tell Sal to fuck off. That gave her pause. This was Sal. He'd give it back. Why was she being so possessive of something she wasn't even sure she wanted? It rested on her chest. It filled her with comfort and warmth. It would protect her from harm, like the loving parents she never had. Her parents. She could have them back in her life.

"Ena?" Sal asked again, his tone gentle.

Ena took off the necklace. An emptiness settled into her chest. The bib necklace weighed down her arms as she held it out.

Sal immediately brought it from her hands to the table. "Hultur, what's in it?"

Hultur took his attention off the book. "According to legend-"

Sal interrupted him. "Feel it. Do your magic stuff and tell me what's in it?"

He blinked, took off his glasses, and studied it.

"You think it's cursed?" Myrrel asked Sal.

"I think that we can't trust anything right now."

Ena was staring at the necklace on the table. Every time Hultur raised his hand over it, Ena felt the urge to rush over it and grab it. Sal, Myrrel, and Visk were in between her and the necklace, but it would be easy to toss them aside. The necklace was hers by right and it belonged on her neck.

"I can't identify its enchantments," Hultur admitted. "There appears to be an amplifier of some kind and maybe a durability charm. This isn't any kind of spellwork that I've seen before."

"Hultur, you remember how you were telling me that glyphs represent magic?" Zukoch asked with excitement.

"That's not exactly how glyphs work," he grumbled.

"Okay, fine. Can you work the glyphs backwards? Could you feel the magic in the necklace and draw out the glyphs that you feel?"

Hultur was impressed. "Yes, I can." He wandered off to get a chalkboard.

Zukoch ran through the room, grabbing books.

"What do you think is happening?" Narla asked Sal.

"I've been thinking about the dream Ena had after she controlled that lake. She said she saw gold tainted green holding up the wall of ice. Gold is frequently used as a symbol of leadership. Bardon Yazdel is a ruler, but he has green on his face because of his copper beard."

"So you think that her dream was trying to warn her about Karzak?" Torno asked.

"I don't know..." Sal started pacing.

"He was there..." Ena closed her eyes to stop staring at the necklace. "Bardon Yazdel was there when I met Yeldo. He was elected. My grand uncle was in favor of a stronger High Council. That's why he was exiled. Maybe the green represents the will of the people or democracy itself."

"Torno, I need your help," Zukoch called out. He was flipping through books, trying to match what Hultur was drawing on the chalkboard.

Visk put her hands on Ena's shoulders and turned her away from the table. "Ena, can you trust this man? Do you believe what he says?"

"I believe he can put me back in power and that he can protect us, but I don't know about anything else. He doesn't care if people have to die. He said something about having three heirs, but he was never married." Ena swallowed.

"Three children?" Narla shook her head. "I'd heard rumors about him having an illegitimate heir, but I would've known if he had three children with the same mother. He'd have to have been with her for six years, five at the least. That doesn't fit the timeline."

"Yeah, I'm out," Myrrel admitted. "I can't follow any of this."

"Yeah," Ena agreed.

"Here," said Torno.

Zukoch saw it, nodded, and flashed through another book. He found a glyph and slid it over to Torno. They'd found two of the glyphs that Hultur had drawn on the board. Hultur was drawing a third on paper. Ena could read them. There was an impulse to invest ether into these spells. There was something familiar about the little twists and shape of them.

"Hultur, is this on it?" Zukoch pointed at another glyph.

Hultur checked the magic of the necklace. "It's faint, but yes."

Zukoch held up the first book again. "This is the one you're trying to draw now?"

"That looks accurate."

"What is it?" Myrrel asked.

"Out with it. Your silence is annoying me," Visk complained.

"They're controlling me," Ena said. "These glyphs are empathy glyphs."

"What?" Myrrel looked them over. "Oh, fuck me. How did I not see that?!"

"Because nothing like this is taught in the Chantry," Torno said. "This magic is so much more complex than anything I've seen. This is three or four levels above what I've been taught."

"This is how Ursen did it," Narla said in horror. "This is how he made the nobility side with him." She slammed the table. "That fucker had advanced empathy spells!"

"You don't know that," Myrrel said, gently.

"The fuck I don't! You weren't there during the

Liberation War, Sweetie! You didn't see people do a complete one-eighty to side with him."

"One thing at a time," Ena snapped. There was too much going on; too much that she needed to figure out. She was losing strands and forgetting important things. She felt surrounded by lies. "Is that the real necklace of Ngoltur?"

"Only one way to find out," Narla said with a shrug.

Narla blasted the necklace with a strike of pure kinetics. It wasn't stopped by a barrier of power, because it wasn't a warding necklace at all. The connecting strands shattered and with it the unifying resonance split. It let out so much raw ether that the jewels flashed from the enchantment breaking. Ena felt warmth and comfort and the need to grab onto the familiar and never let go. When it left her, she was cold and aware of the distance between her and every person she knew. They all felt so far away.

"If Yeldo has the power to make something like that, we can't trust a single thing he says," Narla growled.

Hultur was gathering up the books.

"Stop," Torno said to Hultur. He slammed the door shut to blocked Narla. "Everybody stop. We need to think."

"Fuck that! There's nothing to think about. We need to get the fuck out of here!" Narla snarled.

"Torno's right!" Ena snapped. "That much ether dispersed is going to be felt by Yeldo and probably everyone in city hall. If we rush to get to our wagon, they're going to be waiting for us."

Myrrel slumped against a bookshelf and slid to the floor. She was shaking her head.

Narla chuckled through her teeth. "Sweetie, we don't have any time for breakdowns."

"They can control people. If they can do that..." Myrrel snapped at Narla. "How do we know if anything we're doing is what we want to do?!"

"We can feel magic," Visk reminded them. "At every step we have worked against their plans and we can continue to do that. Women rise to every challenge."

Myrrel took Visk's hand and rose. Visk held her firm.

"Zukoch, what do you know about this?" Ena asked.

"Empathy magic came from Leben Erde. It was the only thing we taught Ngoltur. The *first* Ngoltur. In return, she taught us glyphs. It's why we use the same glyphs as Gulambar and the people of Ki'an don't. Books like these can be found all over the continent."

"Wait, why would Yeldo let us have access to books like this?" Narla asked. "It doesn't make any sense."

"He didn't." A realization struck Ena and she clapped to get everyone's attention. "We're going to talk to the Senives. All of us."

They followed her into the hall. Hultur came out carrying a stack of books so large, he had to waddle to keep them in his arms.

Torno rushed forward to walk beside Ena. "Hey, you know how you hate it when I won't tell anyone the plan? Well, I kind of know how you feel right now. You mind letting us know why walking into the office of the most powerful man in the country is a good idea?"

"Nope," Ena replied.

"And the reason for that?" Narla asked with an exasperated chuckle.

"Because Torno never told me how much fun it was to build up to the reveal."

THE FORTY-FIRST CHAPTER

In Which the Gods Look Away From Their Cups

Curiosity drove Senives Bardon Yazdel to call Yeldo and Vaynsta into his chambers. Ena appealed to the boulba's sense of compassion, Sal enticed him with the promise of being part of the Grand Dream, Visk promised that he would be an agent of justice, but it was curiosity that made him agree to let Ena confront Yeldo. What Ena didn't know was that this entire meeting was a violation of the terms of Senives rule. By agreeing, Bardon had committed an expellable offense, and he did it because the hundred-and-seventy-year-old boulba was curious. Such was the twisting of fate that followed Ena for working against the will of the Gods. Though she had no way of know it, fate was already scrambling to rework the path that lay before her.

Yeldo had some inkling why he'd been brought before Senives, and it was confirmed when he saw Ngoltur and her Aides. There was no shame in his eyes, nor was there fear. He accepted that he might die the moment he walked into the room. He believed that he was ready for what was coming, but he was wrong. For Yeldo had tried to play a game with the Gods as well, and for a time he had done what was thought to be impossible; he deceived the Gods. But Ena's choice had revealed that deception, and they were listening in on the proceedings of the room. Ena's words would decide how they would proceed. She did not know this. She thought she would be arguing only for the fate of herself, her friends, and two old men. She did not know she was being used to determine the future of a Grand Dream that had been twisted beyond repair.

Only Hultur felt this shifting of fate and he looked up with horror, believing that he could see the eyes of the divine staring at him. But he could not. He was only looking at a ceiling; just as Yeldo was only facing a fate he had accepted in his heart; just as Bardon was choosing to throw his career away; and just as Ena was only arguing for the survival of her and her friends. Nothing special was happening. So Hultur went back to watching the events of the room. And the Gods could once again turn their attention to Ena.

She was ready. Even though there was so much she was only guessing at, she was filled with confidence that this would all work out.

"Honorable Senives, we've brought Yeldo and Vaynsta before you because they've been manipulating people in Karzak since the moment they arrived over forty years ago. Placed on your table is a collection of expensive jewels once imbued with a priceless enchantment. We will explain to you how they've been twisting empathy magic to create the equivalent of a mental influence spell. We guarantee that you will find more enchanted objects like this necklace in the possession of senators and other key members of the city."

Senives Bardon Yazdel steepled his hands and leaned onto his knee high table.

"Senives," Yeldo stood. "This is a mockery of the judicial process. If charges are being raised against me I must be arrested. If these charges include the senate as both witnesses and victims, they must be gathered to rule on the schedule and the manner in which my trial is to be carried out."

"That could take months," Senives grumbled. He

waved his hand toward Ena. "Why not let Ngoltur speak?"

"Because it is a violation of the law," Yeldo replied.

"Perhaps," he mused. "But as a member of Karzak's government, it is in my purview to hear the formal declaration of charges before issuing a warrant for arrest. There is no law preventing the accused from being in the room when those charges are levied."

No one pointed out what laws the Senives had already broken.

"Continue," Bardon told Ena.

Yeldo did not sit.

"Prince Yeldo, I'd like you to sit down so your grandniece can announce her charges."

The exiled prince mumbled something. His hands twisted into fists and shook.

"I'm sorry, Prince Yeldo, I didn't hear you."

The once future ruler of Doronel held his head up high. "I said, I confess."

"You confess to using empathy magic to influence the decisions of Ngoltur?"

He nodded. "And to working magic on the senate, the press, and several ambassadors. Yes, I confess."

Everyone looked to each other to gauge their shock. Ena was inches away from pouting, the glory of her deductive moment stolen from her by this sudden admission of guilt. But then it came to her that she didn't know what the punishment for working empathy magic truly entailed. Empathy magic was as common as evocation spells in Leben Erde.

"This is disappointing to hear, Prince Yeldo," the Senives said. "You've been a friend to this senator for decades and our country took great risk to grant you amnesty."

"That you did," Yeldo agreed. "I ask that you allow me to apologize to my grandniece before I'm taken to prison."

Senives waved to grant it.

Yeldo walked up to Ena with confidence, but his

frail body shook so hard that it rattled his robes like sails unfurling. "Forgive me for deceiving you, Ena. I underestimated your wisdom. You must understand that I only did what I did because over twenty years of planning went into making sure that you rule over Gulambar. I didn't trust you, my sweet grandniece. Please. You must find it in your heart to forgive this old man."

Ena closed her eyes and felt for magical influence. She looked to Hultur. He should've been checking for empathy spells, but he was wasting his time gawking at a ceiling again. He did a cursory check and shook his head.

"I don't have to do anything, Yeldo," Ena told him. "I don't want any part of your schemes. You lied to me. You pushed on my sense of love and my familial bonds to coerce me into going along with your plan. How can any trust exist when our relationship starts with that?"

"Because I do not work alone. Your parents are waiting for you in Caredor City. Keeping you at a distance all these years tore at their heart." Yeldo didn't hear Ena's protest and continued. "They loved you but couldn't show it. Those moments you saw as neglect and hate were all done to protect you. They couldn't let the world see your white skin-"

"Shut up!" Ena rage threatened to boil over. Ether pulled towards that rage, readying itself for a conflagration. "Nothing forgives the way they treated me. They might've had to keep me hidden in rooms without windows and locked in closets, but I didn't have to be alone! There was an abundance of opportunities for them to show their loved. Instead, I was starved for singing and locked into rooms for running outside to play. Whatever lies they told you by letter was nothing compared to the truth that I lived. They are not my family and I want nothing to do with them."

"Fine. I'm sorry. I didn't know." His shakes were getting worse.

Vaynsta tries to get him to sit.

Yeldo smacked away his husband's hand, connecting knuckle to knuckle with a pop. He snarled at the man he loved and looked to Ena with a face melting with contrition and sorrow. He brought his hands together to plead with her as the damned so frequently plead to the Gods.

"Please, Ena. Do not let your people suffer for my mistake. Let me die. Kill me yourself, but please don't turn your back on your birthright. Go to Doronel." He talked over her objection again, getting closer as he shook to stand. "Find a Parliamentarian by the name of Rys Chaesys, he-"

Ena almost hit him as her hand struck out at the air between them. "No! I'm not going to talk to my parents or anyone that's been working on your scheme to retake the throne. I don't want to be Queen! I don't want to see democracy fall!"

"Is that why you object? You can establish a new democracy. You can elevate the lives of everyone in Caredor. You can undo every injustice you saw growing up. You can have your parents executed for treason and establish an orphanage so none will ever share in your suffering. I'm offering you the power to right every wrong. Why would you give that up? Why would you reject the power to bring about ultimate justice? Why?" Passion strained his voice.

Bardon leaned forward so hard the wood of his desk strained.

The back legs of chairs left the ground as Ena's friends did the same.

Hultur again looked up at a ceiling and saw nothing interesting.

"Because I know what the Gods have planned for me and the world. We have seen it play out countless times before, and it always ends in death and stagnation. I will not mirror the Gods and set the standard of morality! I will not magic the world as you have and compel people to do what I believe to be in their best interest! I will not scheme like my parents and deny a life lived in the name of safety!

"I reject my parents and their fake love. I reject a life of safety bought with blood. I reject the lie that one person should decide the fate of the world. I reject it all. I will not go down that path of concessions to achieve a greater good. I will not be Queen!"

The former Prince Yeldo crumpled.

One moment, Ena was screaming at a scowling, bitter old man who seemed incapable of any real empathy, and the next he was falling to the ground. It happened so suddenly that Ena didn't think to stop his fall with a cushion of air, neither did she even reach out to try and grab him. She simply watched the old man hit the floor with a crack.

Vaynsta rushed over to check on his husband. His attention went from his broken arm to his chest. Yeldo reached out for Ena, trying to grab her, to compel her to follow the plan the Gods had helped bring to fruition. She felt nothing for his plans or even the man. As Yeldo died, as life left those royal amber eyes, she thought only of Vaynsta, who had toiled for decades to keep a man with lupus alive. Her focus was on Vaynsta slowly realizing that his husband was dying without sparing him a single thought.

Yeldo's death released a great swell of ether. The intricate weave of healing magic could not maintain its power without the resonance that was Yeldo's life, and so it unraveled with a bellow of ether. There was great sorrow in that magic. Desperation was woven into every incantation, and with its parting, there was only grief. Yet, Vaynsta couldn't even find tears for the man he loved. Vaynsta closed Yeldo's eyes and rubbed at his wrist where Yeldo had smacked his hand away for the last time.

Vaynsta was slow to rise to his feet, but he did not resist his arrest. He followed the boulba out of the room with acceptance. He'd sacrificed his entire life to keep his husband happy, and in the end, Yeldo hadn't even looked at him.

Ena wiped away a tear for Vaynsta. She couldn't watch people come to collect Yeldo's body. Nor could she shake the feeling that her words had killed him. She hadn't merely rejected his plans for her future, but she had rejected him; in the same way that she had rejected her parents; in the same way that she had rejected the Gods.

"We need to get out of the city in secret," Ena told Senives Bardon. "If people know we're coming, we'll encounter men like my grand uncle in every capital, city, and town. Please, Bardon, if you have it in your power to sneak us out of here, we need it."

"There is one way out that has never been traveled by humans. If I was talking to anyone else, I wouldn't even suggest it."

"We're going to walk into the volcano!" Hultur had a wide grin on his face. It wasn't any less unsettling when he looked excited.

They stared at Hultur like he'd lost his mind.

"Ever since I first heard of Ozalto as a boy, I wanted to see the inner workings of Toberg Monte. I wish to see how the boulba harness lava like water with my own eyes. It should be a manageable task, Senives. Ena and I will get us through the tunnels safely."

Senives nodded. "Then I will have your things gathered and guide you through the tunnels. Unfortunately, there will be no way to bring your wagon. I'm sorry."

They each thought of the half-broken heap of wooden scrap that got them through Karzak.

"Terrible," said Torno.

"A true tragedy," Myrrel added.

"This is the saddest of days." Narla wiped away a fake tear.

Visk scowled at them. "It was junk on four wheels. No tears will be shed for that pile of firewood."

~ ~ ~

Their journey into the depths of Toberg Monte was one that lasted three days on horseback. In a further abuse of his power, Senives had secured each of them horses for the long ride and the journey beyond that. While not running *through* the volcano, the path was still considerably long. They were riding horses through service tunnels never made for humans, and so they got to see a great deal of the construction and lava work. Magically reinforced channels of rock and metal controlled the flow of melted earth. Vast skyward chambers lay unobstructed to vent the world's blood. Boulba scraped still wet strands of lava from the catches and wound them up like bails of hay. Workers on their breaks bathed in glowing pools beside signs prohibiting their consumption.

Ena and her Aides found rest in workstations. There were no beds down in Toberg Monte, only holes in the wall for Boulbas to crawl into. So the humans were forced to sleep on floors and knee-high dinning tables covered in left over pebbles from the workers's meals. Ena and Hultur couldn't sleep for longer than a few hours. One of them had to be awake at all times to keep the air cool and breathable.

Maintaining aeration magic in the volcano's interior was a great deal more complicated than cycling the air. The only experience Ena and Hultur had to draw on, was the process of freshening up the air in Ena's rug of time. Thankfully, Ena wasn't the first Ngoltur to step inside this domain. Glyphs thousands of years old were carved into a wall enchanted to withstand volcanic eruptions and feasting boulba. This spell of breathing had been crafted by Ngoltur's own hand and it was as complex as it was surprisingly simple in execution.

Contaminants had to be filtered out as they moved. Though happenstance or fate, the spell went through a cycle of three extended gestures. Ena picked at the air like a harpist to purify a fresh patch, she pulled the cloud in like a weaver yanking a thread, and sustained the breathable space with a smooth dip of her hand. This tiring act became a second nature and it was one Hultur had to work through as well.

By contrast the cold spell was a trivial matter. All Ena needed to do was carry about an egg of cold made into a gradient of intensity. While it was difficult to spread the egg out far enough that the horses wouldn't burn their hooves, the size became intuitive enough to bend once she and Hultur had found the way.

It took very little to get Hultur excited as they traveled along the volcano's shell. Every bubbling lake of lava drew his eyes wide with wonder. Cavities cluttered with equipment and those abandoned both brought out a torrent of questions from him. His joy was infectious and kept them all in good spirits.

Sal did eventually get permission to taste a fresh gulp of the flowing lava, and it made him so lethargic that he didn't even roll into a ball before passing out. His green granite eyes were still glossed over the next day, and he rolled off the access tunnel twice. Still, Sal had no regrets and spoke at lengths about the rejuvenating high that came with the meal. And so on the next night, when they went to rest, Senives Bardon Yazdel, elected official of Karzak, drank lava with Sal and a dozen other workers. They sang boulba work songs and Sal sang along in a tongue he didn't understand.

Their final exit came out of a small access tunnel that Gale and Hultur barely fit through. Ena fell onto the floor back-first and panted. Above them, the great bridge of the western Yan Road stood resolute against the test of time. Sheltered from the harsh sun by the solid plane of rock above, Ena could close her eyes without risk of sun exposure to her albino constitution. With her back on the ground, the gentle rumbling of Toberg Monte's endless earthquakes felt like the purr of a great panther of rock. Sleep washed over her in moments, and it lasted just as long.

Bardon shook her awake. "Ena, I wonder if I might have a moment with you in private."

She picked up her head. Everyone was ready to keep riding. "Yeah, no problem."

Ena followed him into the access tunnel's entrance. He closed the solid door of adamantium behind them, but still looked back toward the group with worry.

"I don't want to alarm you, but I think Vamere is Hultur," he whispered.

"Who?" It was amazing how Ena kept forgetting Hultur's fake name. "Oh, yeah. We know that. He's working with us, it's fine."

Bardon wasn't convinced, but he didn't press the issue. "If your mission truly is to find Muttur, there is an ancient treasury not half a day's ride away. I will show you the mountain as I open the door. Access is prohibited to all but the Turall. Place your hand upon the symbol of the Turall, and it should open. But be warned, the treasury is filled with traps to keep robbers out and hone the skills of Muttur."

Ena nodded. She knew the treasuries by their reputation and their inclusion in the Grand Dream. "What's in this one?"

"It is a key relic. Muttur will not be able to access many treasuries without it. Inside lies the famed Boulba Bracelets. They will grant Muttur the strength of a boulba. He'll need that strength to gain access to other treasuries. If the bracelets are still inside, he will come to you if you only wait."

"It's not the worst plan," she admitted. Ena opened the door and he followed her out.

"That's Rookt Monte."

She could see the mountain's rounded peak from where she stood. Traveling up the steep mountain would be difficult and might even require hiking equipment. "Thank you for the help, Senives."

Bardon shook his head. "I am Senives no longer."

"What? Why not?" asked Sal.

"I broke many of my vows bringing you here," he explained. "When I confess my crimes to the senate, they will imprison me and form a tribunal. The sentence could be carried out within a month."

"You could come with us," Ena offered. "I can't imagine you slowing us down."

"Though I'm tempted by the offer, I must refuse. As an individual breaking the law, the punishment is between me and my government. My responsibility as an elected official is greater than that. I stand as a symbol of the government itself. Every crime must be reported with honesty or it will erode the very principles that hold our country together." He spoke with pride.

"Even if your punishment could be execution, you're gonna go back?" Narla asked.

He nodded. "I am one hundred and seventy. I have lived a full life and am happy to spend it helping Ngoltur. Besides, there is still the chance that they will only take my title."

Ena almost hugged him until she remembered it would be like thanking him by cupping his balls. Instead, she held out her hand.

"No. Let us say goodbye like old boulba friends."

Ena spread her feet out and surrounded herself with a wall of kinetic magic. "Don't hold back."

He pulled his human-sized hand back, flung forward with everything he had, and slammed his fist into Ena's. She spread the kinetic magic out wide, catching his fist on an even surface. His fist stopped like he'd punched adamantium. She pushed forward the last remaining foot and touched knuckles. He stepped back and bowed. "Goodbye, Ena. I hope you bring peace to the world."

"Thank you."

~ ~ ~

Ena slept like a log on the back of Gale. Neither clopping hooves nor conversations could stir her from her slumber. Nor did the autumn sun burning down through a hazy cover of smoke make her so sweaty and uncomfortable that she itched herself conscious. Burning skin and straps cutting off blood to her toes didn't wake her up. But again, Ena was ignorant of so much of what was going on. She simply woke, and knew that something important had happened.

Sal was rolling beside her. Before her, Gale's reins were tied onto the new horse Torno rode. He was healthy and happy and looked back at the drooling Ena like he didn't have a care in the world. Behind her, Narla worked on an explosive, pressing a fresh fuse into a stick. She saw the dread in Ena's eyes and put the dynamite away.

"Hold," Narla cried out.

The caravan of horses stopped. Sal rolled back to Narla's side and stood. "What is it?"

"I think Ena had one of those big dreams."

Everyone gathered behind her. There was plenty of room in the rocky valley. There was room for them to change directions and run back to Doronel, but it was too late to go back now. They might as well have been sitting on a raft in the middle of a river for all the control they had in that moment. Their decisions had been cast, and the Gods had tallied all their actions and decided the fate of every single person there.

"It wasn't a dream." Ena shook her head. "I got a weird feeling. We can keep going."

"Ena, you are Ngoltur Reborn. We are on a quest that none of us understand," Sal said as if he had a clue how ignorant they were. "Please try to explain the feeling."

"It...um..." she swallowed. "It feels like I just woke up. It's almost like I don't remember how I got here, except without the worry."

"I felt something strange before," Hultur admitted far too late for it to matter. "Back when we were talking to Yeldo, I felt the eyes of the Gods, but stronger."

"Stronger than what?" Myrrel asked.

Hultur made a heroic attempt to identify the sensation, even going through the effort of closing his eyes.

"When I first met Ena, I felt the eyes of the Gods focusing on her. I had a similar feeling to what Ena is describing now. This sensation was amplified when Ena was yelling at Yeldo. Perhaps before, only one of the three Gods had been watching us. Now all three Gods are watching, but they are only interested in *her*."

Zukoch was holding Wulg the kikaa like those soft feathers could keep him safe from what was coming. "Guys, this is really starting to freak me out."

"We have opposed the will of the Gods," Visk said, seriously. "We should be afraid."

"Am I the only one here who doesn't actually think the Gods exist?" Torno asked in the most transparent lie he'd ever told in his entire sad life.

"It's time," Ena realized. "It's the river of time. When I woke up it was flowing, but there was a break in it. It felt like the river of time had started flowing in the exact moment that I woke."

"Well, you *did* wake up. Maybe we're just psyching ourselves up over nothing." Myrrel was earnestly trying to ease their fears, but she couldn't even alleviate her own. "We should just keep going."

One by one they all agreed with Myrrel. Each thought that they were the only one gripped by a nameless fear that they'd never known in their entire life. Each thought that they were the only one holding onto the irrational thought that they shouldn't keep moving forward, and so none of them voiced what was in their hearts. The last sad chance for them to back away from their path against the Gods ended with a few nods and half-hearted chuckles to ignore their fear.

~ ~ ~

Torno's keen eye spotted a figure running along one of Rookt Monte's winding paths. With a wave of his hand, Hultur magnified the image. There was nothing special about the look of this Leben boy. His pointed ears hung low; almost parallel to the ground, they were so horizontal. He wore the same generic clothes as farmhands all over Erchritt. His pants and hat were a faded forest green, his backpack was stuffed, his shirt was a dirt gray, and the sword at his belt was indistinguishable from any amateur blacksmith's early attempts. His pointed ears hung low; almost parallel to the ground, they were so horizontal. About the only thing slightly abnormal about his physical appearance was the sunbaked navy-blue of his skin. Only this boy of fifteen didn't have the face of a normal Leben boy.

While running uphill, carrying a backpack so overstuffed it wobbled, his brow didn't furrow from exhaustion. The only look that could be discerned from that teenager's face was one of tedium. He ran up this mountain like it was a daily chore, one that he'd done a hundred times before and would have to do a hundred times again. Beyond boredom, he looked impatient, but in the way a child was impatient for a pig to finish roasting. Those barely present eyes looked down at Ena.

Through the amplified light of Hultur's lens, she could see the red of his iris. She knew it. She knew it from the crimson splash of the jargon nebula. She'd seen it every night when she gazed up at the sky. She'd seen that color when she dreamt of an eye pushing through the wall of ice bricks. She'd seen it when she dreamt of Haenir dying.

She knew those eyes, because they were the eyes of Muttur.

THE FORTY-SECOND CHAPTER

Where The Turall Meet

Acceleration was the difference between jumping into a river and being in that river from the start. Even a minute or two after jumping in, when the flow of the river carried along the jumper at the same speed as everything else, that sensation of acceleration lingered. Ena was awake this time to feel the change in those flows. One moment she was a passive passenger and the next she felt that lingering acceleration behind every rock, crevice, and tree branch in the river of time. That feeling of falling, and drifting, and being carried away all at once, came to Ena when Muttur's eyes fell on her.

The Leben boy looked messy and poor. Muttur only regarded Ena for a moment, staring at her with a cryptic expression under the swoop of his wild hair. The moment past, he went back to his jog up the spiral path. Dust fell and cast a curtain down the side of Rookt Monte.

"That was Muttur," Ena said. "I felt it."

"Wow!" Zukoch said in awe. "I can't believe I'm here to witness this."

"Witness what?" asked Myrrel.

"The meeting of the Turall. In the thousands of years since the Turall were first born, they've only met each other a handful of time," Zukoch spoke like a child witnessing his first sunset.

"Get used to that feeling of being first." Hultur let out a great sigh of satisfaction. "We are changing history." A natural smile rested comfortably on his wide face.

"You alright?" Torno asked Ena.

Hultur was pushing on, already in motion at the head of the caravan of horses. Everyone thoughtlessly followed. They could already see the northeast side of Rookt Monte's base, where the spiral path welcomed them to their new destiny.

"Yeah," said Ena. "I just felt that time thing again." Her head ached from lack of sleep, her eyes were sore from having stared at lava and dimly lit rocks for the past three days. She rubbed her sore eyes for the tenth time in the last hour.

"I can roll on ahead," Sal offered to Hultur.

"No, we must meet him as a group, with Hultur and Ngoltur united." Hultur snapped the reins, picking up the pace of the caravan. "Ena, is your speech ready?"

"Yeah. I think so. I mean I haven't exactly written anything down."

"There is a chance he will try to kill you, Hultur," Visk said. She didn't sound broken up by the possibility.

"Why don't you move to the back?" Narla suggested.

Hultur detached and Torno kept pace at the lead.

"You sure you're okay?" Torno asked Ena again.

She felt like she was forgetting something. She'd had that feeling since she first encountered Yeldo and heard him spout out a dozen different facts that all felt important. "Just tired," Ena decided. "I'll be okay. It's only a talk."

Torno nodded. He was at the front. That wasn't right.

"Torno, move your horse behind Hultur's. I should be at the front," commanded Ena.

"No problem." Torno's helpful smile calmed her.

Ena wanted to reach out and grab his hand. She wanted him to give her a reassuring squeeze or to rub her back. But there wasn't any time for it. She needed to focus on the words she would tell Muttur. He looked like a strange boy. The sight of him was nerve wracking, like an orphaned child made wild from living alone. Maybe he was just anxious to get those Boulba Bracelets.

~ ~ ~

Ngoltur and her Aides were quiet on the ride up. It had been a longer ride than any of them anticipated. About halfway up the top, they needed to lead their horses forward on foot. There was talk about splitting up, but no one wanted to stay behind. They were all eager to see the meeting of the Turall.

Then it was like fate smiled on them. The path widened, giving them all enough room to stand four abreast. They were on the mountain's south side, where the rock was as steep on the way down as it was going up. Before them a plains hawk soared at eye level. Ena's tired eyes were drawn to the majestic creature. His top feathers were a calming shade of grass green.

Then that feeling of lingering temporal acceleration returned, and it ramped up and shifted into something new.

Time pushed on people from the tips of their toes to the edge of their chins. It never mattered if they dove underneath, or kept their heads above the river to gasp for air, because the flow of the river was the same from the bottom to the top. This was the first time Ena ever felt a difference in the levels. Not only did she feel a surface, but she felt a stillness underneath the river's surface. More than just an undertow that might be found in a real river, it felt stiller than a lake. She felt like if she could only dive under the current, she could swim backwards. But there were no such spells. There was no way to travel back in time or dive under the constant flow.

Ena slowed. They were all walking in a row, riders before their horses. Narla was behind her, then Myrrel, then Visk, Zukoch, Hultur, Torno and Sal all on foot. The second

Ena considered changing that order, rocks unsettled above them. She looked up and saw nothing strange, not even a puff of dust. Eyes back to the front a figure stood.

Muttur was there, a sword drawn in his right hand and a shield in his left. His backpack was gone and his bow rested in his quiver. Black and gray bracelets sat on his forearms. The sides of his boots were decorated with feathers of solid white. He'd taken a defensive stance. The body-sized shield was wooden and crafted into a heater design, with the bottom ending in a soft vertex. The shield was decorated with a hawk in flight soaring beside the moon. A face was drawn on that painted moon. Beady, uneven eyes, resting slant above flat teeth all painted in red. The expression was supposed to be sad, but it had been drawn so poorly that it was grimacing not out of sorrow, but anger.

Muttur looked frightened. He was hiding behind that shield, his sword held awkwardly at the level of his hip.

Ena held up her hands, her magic bracelets sliding down to her forearms. "Relax, we're not here to hurt you."

He didn't respond. He kept his shield up and twisted the sword.

Zukoch translated, repeating what Ena had just said.

Muttur glanced to Zukoch and stood up straight. The boy was maybe a hand taller than Ena.

"Zukoch, repeat what I say exactly," Ena said.

Zukoch tried to close the distance and Muttur snapped to attention. He turned about and aimed the sword tip at Zukoch.

Zukoch backed up into his horse. Wulg the Kikaa was fluttering about his tiny cage, making a racket. Zukoch tried to silence the bird.

"Maybe I should try," Hultur said. He raised his hands and walked forward.

Muttur didn't so much as shout at him, as he barked. It was the kind of sound even a child didn't make to another person, a guttural outburst of sound that had no imprint of emotion.

"No one move," Ena told them. "Zukoch translates, that's it." She smiled at him at the ragged boy. "We're not going to hurt you. Torno and Visk, drop your sword and spear onto the ground."

"Ena, I-" Visk started.

Muttur's eyes focused on Visk. He got behind his shield, taking that same low stance with his sword held back.

"Do it, Visk!"

She did. Everyone tossed anything threatening onto the ground.

Muttur stayed tense.

"We're friends," Ena told him. "We've come a very long way to see you. Maybe you've had a dream about us, but we're friendly. None of us are here to hurt you."

There was the sound of motion coming from up above. It sounded like something had jumped down from higher up. Maybe there was something sliding on the ground as well, Ena couldn't say for sure.

Muttur moved his quiver onto his belt, placing it on the side of his sword hand. He brought his shield onto his back, but kept the sword in hand. This boy was practiced with his weapons, managing them without hesitation or a single stagger of friction. Sword out, bow at the ready, he paced. His red eyes took in each of them in turn.

"We just want to talk to you. Did you have a name before you were Muttur?"

He got closer to Zukuch, looking inside his mouth while the Leben of nineteen talked. Only, between Zukoch's words, his eyes were jumpy. He continued to watch the kikaa in the cage. Wulg was settling down, but the bird seemed to unsettle him.

"The kikaa is in a cage. He's just a pet. His name is Wulg, it's a lucky name. My name is Ena, but I'm Ngoltur Reborn."

Muttur twisted about to stare at Ena. Something in eyes softened, if only a little.

"That's right, Ngoltur." She put her hand on her heart while keeping the other raised. "I'm here to see an end to the wars. We've come to Leben Erde to learn more about you. Maybe even be your friends. Do you think you could-"

Muttur was walking towards her as she talked. He'd take a long step here and then a short step there. His sword was at his side the entire time, but he was getting closer and closer to the horses and Ngoltur's Aides. He stepped past Visk, then Myrrel, who was smiling at him like an old friend. Narla looked up with shock.

Ena followed her eyes up. A monster was creeping over the edge of the path above. It was a spider-like Ekeet with a dead fish in its fangs. It dropped the fish and jumped off, drawing the attention of everyone. Hultur was casting, evoking a spear of invisible force into existence. By the time Ena realized Muttur was attacking, it was too late.

He drove his sword into Narla's belly, driving it through the battle leather like it was cloth. He pulled the sword out with a slash, cutting her open. His follow through cut her horse's neck, sending the mare into a panic. He slashed at Narla again, cutting through her ribs with such force that the blade bent. He left it stuck in her side and backflipped.

Visk retrieved her spear and imbued red lightning along the shaft. Muttur landed, grabbing an arrow and bow from the air. Visk sendt out a red bolt of with a rapid stab. Muttur was already in motion, pulling his body in tight as he followed the motion of the first backflip into a sommersault. Visk's attack missed Muttur's foot by inches. His hands worked the arrow against the bow. Ena raised a hand to evoke a wall of air between Visk and Muttur.

Myrrel was rushing forward, moving fast to heal Narla. It was her that took an arrow to the neck, even as Muttur was looking at Visk.

That all happened in the time it took the Ekeet to get slashed and fall beside Zukoch.

Torno slid his deathstaff out of the harness, and ran to the edge. Muttur was gone, sliding down the slope of the mountain at a speed fast as any horse. Torno sent out a blast of red ether. "Got him."

Ena rushed over to Narla and Myrrel. Myrrel was still focused on Narla, despite the arrow sticking out the side of her neck. As long as Ena could take care of Myrrel, they'd be okay. They'd both survive.

First thing was to push the arrow through. She did, working the incantation and glyph for a simple cut. It healed where the arrow came out. She snapped the arrowhead off. Now it was a matter of pulling the arrow out and handling the big stuff. No time to plan. Ena pulled the arrow free. An artery was cut. Blood flowed too fast for Ena to contain. She laid her hands on the wound, and slowed her heart.

"You got him?" Zukoch asked.

"He survived!" Torno shouted.

"What? How?"

Torno fired again, shooting six or seven shots in a row.

"Shut up!" Ena shouted.

She needed to focus. There was a glyph to seal up Myrrel's artery. She needed to remember the mending of arteries spell. The song, if she went through the song...

Myrrel clawed Ena's hands away. She was focusing on herself, healing the spurting wound on her neck. She looked to Ena with apologies, even as blood covered her front.

Narla.

Ena had to help Narla. She was so much worse than Myrrel. The cut to her stomach had gone through intestines, liver, pancreas, and womb. No time to process that. Save Narla. Ena needed to know the spells to heal each of those to continue the work Myrrel had started, but then the backslash against her chest might've been worse. Broken ribs. There was a small cut in the lung. Ena could heal that.

The glyph for lung repair glowed true in her mind. First the lung, then she could heal the severed veins. Myrrel would be able to handle the organs. Myrrel was a quick healer, she'd be done in two minutes, maybe less.

Incantations were on Ena's lips, reciting in a whisper the spells that would save Narla's life. They had to.

Narla gripped Ena's hand. Her fingers were firm, digging into Ena's flesh. She tried to speak. Blood came out her mouth. Narla's lungs were healed. That little bit of blood was the only fluid inside. She was going to be okay. Ena heard, "daughter," and her spells stopped working. She wasn't working on a living person anymore, but a mass of flesh in human shape.

There were spells to work on corpses. They were desperate spells used by the greatest healers in the land. They could fix a body seconds after death and then restart the heart to keep her alive. Knowing that Ena was too ignorant to help Narla only twisted the anguish in Ena's heart.

Narla was dead, and there was nothing she could do.

Beside her, Myrrel was still holding her own neck. Ena could help her. She could ease the strain. Myrrel was pale, so pale where her dark skin had pulled away in patches on her face. Tears soaked Myrrel's cheeks. "Sorry," she told Ena. "I'm sorry."

Ena shook her head. She couldn't find the words. She could barely remember the spells to heal the lesser wounds on Myrrel's neck. She had it. She was taking care of it. There was nothing Ena could do.

She half-ran, half stumbled over to the edge of the path.

Torno shook his head. "He took off behind the cliff over there. I think he had this escape planned."

"Fuck." Ena pressed a bloody hand onto her face. "Fuck." She brought her hand back and tried to wipe away the blood.

"There might-"

"Hultur, whatever you have to say I don't want to hear it," said Ena.

He bowed his head and stepped back. He didn't care. He wasn't with Visk and Myrrel, crying over a friend. He was just there. Zukoch hadn't known Narla for a month, but he was crying. He found a place beside Myrrel and rubbed her back. His knees gave out. He hugged Myrrel and cried. They were all crying, but Hultur's face was dry.

Torno found Ena. He grabbed her and sobbed onto the top of her head. She hugged him back for all the good it did either of them. Time flowed normally again. Ena hadn't noticed the shift. She only noticed it then as she held onto Torno. She felt her knees giving out. She was crying now, too.

Narla was dead.

THE FORTY-THIRD CHAPTER

In Which Ena Remembers
the Lure of Death

Ena had been sixteen when she came to work as a Broker. She'd been too young and shy for the job, but it kept her away from the capital and their great gossip. Every person in the villages was a stranger, another person to pick on her for her ugly bone-colored skin that didn't even hide her veins. Her coworkers tried to be nice, but they stared. Everyone was always staring at her.

It took months for Myrrel to talk Ena into trying to socialize at the Sorcerer's Hall. Ena did her best to stay out of the way. She stuck to corners and only ever talk to respond to someone else. She found lots of excuses to get out of conversations, but few reasons to keep them going. Weather was supposed to be a safe topic. She could talk about politics or magic, but there wasn't any reason to think of either. The problem wasn't that Ena had nothing to talk about. She didn't want to be alive.

Every day she woke up, she told herself, *do it today. Steal a horse and ride off. Find a hole to crawl into and end your sad, miserable life.* But then who would care for the horse? Worse yet, what if the horse found her dead body? She couldn't do that to Missie. She couldn't even do that to a stuck up horse like Chen. If she was going to kill herself, she needed to find a way to do it without hurting anyone.

She hadn't and now she was stuck talking to a man at the Sorcerer's Hall. Ena's tendency to hide had brought her into an unlit hallway and this lumbering butcher had taken an interest. Telltale signs of his profession came out in the way he absently thumbed a knife. His thick arms were used to moving around large slabs of meat. She could smell the rot of alcohol on his breath and see the way his glazed eyes kept looking to the unused bedrooms. A big man like him wouldn't have any trouble moving Ena. He was touching her hair and saying stuff about how she was pretty, but she knew what was happening. He wanted to use her to get off.

Maybe Ena should let him. She'd at least mean something to someone before she died. Of course it might hurt and this man was no Torno. He wasn't even the Torno that Ena had come to know as her Broker Captain. He was a gross, slobbery man that might not even remember taking her virginity. That would probably be better. Maybe she could convince him to take her far away and after he had his way with her and passed out, she could run off and end it. Maybe if they were alone and she fought, he'd do it himself. Having her death kill this man wouldn't be so bad. There was a kind of symmetry to that.

"What you doing, big man?" asked Narla.

She was sloshed. Fuck, she was probably more drunk than he was.

He looked to Narla with a smile. "Just, uh…" He sucked back some saliva. "I'm making Ena here feel welcome. She's a real pretty girl. You're not so bad yourself."

"We-heh-ell," she laughed. She leaned onto his chest, and he fell back onto the wall. "Aren't you a charmer?"

"I'm a lover, too. You can ask around. I'll keep you up all night."

Narla laughed. "I'm already gonna be up puking."

He laughed with her.

In a snap, Narla was all venom and malice. "But

you might be puking blood if you keep fucking with her." Her hand was on his throat. It was a reach for the shorter woman, but her fingers sank into his neck. "Sixteen year old girl, too shy to talk to people, and you want to make her feel welcome with a roll in the hay?"

"I's gots friends," the man slurred. He tried to use his size to intimidate her.

"You got a hundred of them? Any of them got a rat's dick worth of ether?" Narla even out the height different with a swift kick to the leg. He came down hard, slamming his knee onto the ground. Now they were eye-to-eye. "Cause I've killed thousands and I've got enough rage in me to turn your pissant village into a bed of ash. I used to stack fuckers like you ten bodies deep into the ground, 'course none of them had their pretty little faces left."

He choked.

"Summin' to say?" she asked, letting up on his throat.

"You're 'sposed to be fixin' things," he gurgled.

"I am. Impotent fuckers like you are always trouble. Shame they won't let me fix you like a horny dog."

Sal was standing in the entrance to the hall. Ena hadn't noticed him show up. With the hall lights out and the lights of the ballroom on, the rock-man looked outright sinister. Narla tossed the man face down. He was so drunk that Sal didn't have any trouble dragging him off. Ena tried to sneak off during the scuffle, finding a darker corner to hide in.

Narla followed.

"I'm fine, Narla, thanks." Ena found a door and left.

"You sure? That didn't look like you were fine."

"You saved the dumb girl from a small pissant city and a third rate Chantry," Ena grumbled. "You can pat yourself on the back and leave me alone now. I'm fine."

"Hey, I didn't do that because I pity you," she spat. Narla's foot caught a rock and she wobbled.

Ena used the trip to spin about and pass behind her. Their wagon was sitting horseless by the stables. She could get some peace and quiet there.

"Ena, you're part of the team. You might not think so, but you are. We're all trying so fucking hard to talk to you, to be your friend. But I'm not like Myrrel. If you're a bitch to me, I'll be a bitch right back!" She grabbed Ena's arm.

"Hey!"

"That's right, I got your arm. What are you gonna do about it?"

Ena stared at the ground.

"Seriously, you really gonna stand there?" she slurred.

"You won't hurt me," Ena grumbled.

Narla slapped her.

"Did that hurt?"

Ena rubbed her face. It stung. It stung like it could bleed.

Narla struck at her again.

This time Ena blocked the strike and pushed her. "What's your problem?!"

"I'm drunk. I hate my past. Every night I go to sleep, I have to remember the friends that died in my arms because it's easier than remembering the kids I killed on the battlefield or the ones that were collateral damage while our forces pushed in on civilians! What the fuck is your excuse?!" She was crying and drooling. She was a drunken mess.

Ena looked away.

"Fucking shit, girl! Talk to me!" Narla got in her face.

Ena turned around.

Narla pulled her shoulder back.

"You win, okay! Your life is worse than mine!" Ena forced herself to smile. "I'm fine now, see? Your shitty life makes mine crystal by comparison. Thank you so much for saving me." Sarcasm dripped out her mouth.

Narla tried to slap her again.

Ena blocked it, shoved her back, and called on ice. There was so much in her. It was always there, ready to freeze everything that came before her. If she froze this woman, she'd have no choice but to run away then. Maybe killing Narla was the push Ena needed to finally end her miserable life. Ena held a ball of cold. Bits of snow fell onto her clawed hand.

"There's that fight!" Narla shouted victoriously. She stumbled back and forth a bit before she caught herself. "Where the fuck was that fight back there?"

"Maybe I liked him," Ena said. "Maybe I wanted him to fuck me, did you ever think of that?"

"Head held low and shoulders pressed up against your cheeks..." Narla laughed. "Yeah, that's pretty much the universal posture for ready to fuck."

Ena dismissed the ball of cold. She couldn't kill this woman. Drunk as she was, she still fought in the Liberation War. "Leave me alone."

"No, Ena! I'm not going to leave you alone. None of us are going to leave you alone! You can't spend your life sitting in the wagon only coming out to kill a monster or freeze a stack of meat," Narla spat. "You can't go through life waiting to die! You have to live. You have to fight to get what you want!"

"What if I want to die, did you ever fucking think of that?!" Ena shouted. Fuck. She was tearing up. Ena froze the tears and flicked them off her face.

Narla chuckled. "You're so young."

"Fuck you!"

"You think I don't want to die? You think Visk doesn't spend every day of her life wish she could die and see the love of her life again?" Narla sounded serious. She almost sounded sober. "We've all been through a lot."

Ena didn't know what to say to that. She hadn't realized Visk was in pain. She looked like she never worried about anything.

"We go to parties because if we don't have fun, we can't keep going." Narla held up her flask. It had the bull of the democratic revolution on it, and a dent from where it had stopped a bit a shrapnel. "Sometimes this is the only thing keeping me going. This and the help that we bring these people. I know this isn't a life of luxury, but we do good work. I know you hate Torno, and I kind of get it, he's a Capital fuck-boy, but some of the shit that comes out of his mouth I need to hear. I'm not a good person, Ena, but I can do good work. I'm making the most of the time I have here."

"How would you do it?" Ena asked. "How would you kill yourself?"

Narla wiped away some tears. She took a long deep breath and found a rock to sit on. "Get all my stuff together and light a fuse."

"What?!" Ena laughed at the absurdity of it.

"I always hated the explosives. It would be nice to die with them, to take them out of the world as I went. Besides, I always wanted to go with a bang."

Ena laughed. She could imagine Narla's body disappearing into a fine mist, the gore and bones falling all over the ground. It was sick and it shouldn't be funny, but somehow Ena's fucked up brain couldn't stop laughing.

"What about you?" Narla asked. "You gotta have some plan, some preferred way to go."

"You only want to know so that you can stop me," Ena said with a shake of her head.

"Fuck yeah, I do," she shouted with more comedy than outrage. "We only got this one life, Ena. You are bright, mystical, and kind."

"I'm not kind," Ena snapped back. "You called me a bitch like five minutes ago."

"I said you were being a bitch." Narla shook her head. "Okay, you're kind of a bitch, but I get it. I know that you're kind, Ena. I see the way you light up when we help people. I've seen how you always go to the survivors to help them mourn when a monster has taken someone they love. You're cold now because you're afraid."

Ena made the claw and brought up her ball of cold.

"Exactly! Our magic defines us. Mine is fire because I'm fucked up and I can't stop raging at this world, but you..." Narla shook her head in awe. "Ena, you're in pain because you care. You want people to be better, you want people to feel better than they are. I know that. You have so much love to give the world, but you have to let it in."

Ena thought of Torno. She thought of him cheating on Kalta and running off to fuck everything that moved. He was with another woman tonight. She'd been as subtle as a prostitute with a coin in her hand. "Love is a lie. You're divorced, I shouldn't have to tell you that."

"I'm not talking about that love, Ena. I'm talking about the love you feel for those orphaned kids or for that horse, Missie. Or the love I feel for you. This world only stops feeling like shit when we find something to love."

Ena looked back at the Sorcerer's Hall. The lights were still on and now that the drunk had been thrown into a cell, they were laughing again. Everyone in there had something to live for, but Ena didn't. She was only holding onto life because she was too scared to die.

"How can I do that?" Ena asked. "How can I trust those strangers when so many of them are selfish and horrible?"

"We're all selfish and horrible," Narla said with a somber chuckle. "We're all pieces of shit. That means you're not better than them, but it also means you're not worse. Try living. If it doesn't work out, you know where the exit is."

Narla made it sound so simple, but maybe it was. Ena knew what it looked like when people were happy members of society. She knew where they spent their time off and what they liked to do. Even though happiness seemed elusive, she knew how people tried to find it. If she tried doing all the things that everyone else was doing, maybe she'd get closer to finding happiness. Besides, what she was doing now clearly wasn't working. "Alright. I'll try."

Narla smiled. She wanted to hug, but Ena wasn't ready for that. So Narla held out a hand to meet her halfway. Ena took it. It was a brief, but firm handshake. It lasted after the shake had come to a natural end.

~ ~ ~

It was the same grip Ena held when Narla died.

THE FORTY-FOURTH CHAPTER

In Which An End Comes

Narla's flask was in her front jacket pocket. The bull of the revolution was dented from where the symbol of her service had saved her life. The water inside was metallic and warm. Lots of things were metallic and warm when Ena handled the body. Narla's body. She's not coming back. No time to process. Get her things. Despite everything, Narla still sent her family money. They needed her support to keep their house. It kept her in Caredor because she couldn't convinced them to leave. At least Narla got one of her wishes: she didn't die in Caredor.

Aside from a few gulda and a bag of coins, Ena couldn't make sense of Narla's pockets. There were a lot of knickknacks and devices, including the sparker. She got them together and found a way to push the junk into Narla's travel bag. Her horse survived the slash. The big, ugly, off-white and gray beast was chomping on hay. It was a terrible animal to think so little of its rider!

Visk put a single hand on Ena's shoulder. She released her fist and breathed. It still wasn't time.

They needed to finalize her funeral. Once they got to the top of Rookt Monte they could say their words and mourn, but not yet. If one of them cried, they were all going to cry, and they couldn't go back to that blubbering mess.

They had so little daylight left.

Zukoch and Hultur had gone up a long time ago. The sound of people crying for over an hour had made Zukoch sick. He was sad, but he wasn't that sad. There was nothing he did or said that had any impact on the group. So he left with Hultur to examine the treasury. It felt like ten minutes since they pulled themselves out of their tears, but by the lengthening shadows they'd all cried for another two hours after Zukoch left. Ena would see the body, remember something Narla had done or said, and fall back into crying all over again. It felt like minutes had passed since she had died, but horrible purple patches were appearing on her lips. Her skin was starting to cool beyond what the sun could hide. The smell was only going to get worse.

Ena searched for a node to gain focus and found none. She had to be there; with that thing that had once been Narla. She hated it for taking Narla away. The body was somehow responsible, because it had been her. It had taken Narla away, but it wouldn't bring her back, so Ena hated it. She grabbed the legs and Torno grabbed the arms.

"Is he back?" Ena asked of Sal.

Torno shook his head.

Sal had left early on, very early on. Before anyone even knew what had happened, Sal went after Muttur. He had jumped down and rolled after the Leben boy that attacked their friends. In theory, Sal shouldn't be in any danger. Even with the Boulba Bracelets, Mutter was only as strong as Sal. The boy had lost his sword and he didn't have any arrows. None of those thoughts made Ena feel any better. They'd already lost Narla, they couldn't lose Sal too.

Visk strapped the body around the horse. He wasn't happy about it. *Good. Get startled. Hate the smell of Narla's body, just like the rest of us. Feel something for your rider, you miserable pile of meat and bones.*

Ena took a step back and bit the lapel of her coat. There wasn't time for emotion. She had to stay focused on physical things; to be present. If she didn't look at something else, Ena was going to lose it again. Seeing Myrrel didn't help. She was sitting on her horse so that when the time came to move forward, she wouldn't have to think. It was selfish. Ena would have to lead her horse forward in addition to Narla's. That was two horses without riders. Wasn't one enough? People were supposed to ride horses, not lay on them!

"We must honor Narla," said Visk. Her voice was solid as the rocks at their feet.

That helped. It helped to know that they were doing this for a reason. This was more than simply transporting a mess, it was a funeral. Narla deserved a proper funeral, but she wasn't getting that. At least this way they could say goodbye. At least this way Narla was getting things done her way. Ena lead the horses forward for Narla.

Walking was good. It kept her eyes on the path and the darkening sky. She could look out at the endless woods to the south and think that everything in there was safe. She could tell herself that there weren't any horrible lizard-people or flesh-eating children. Trees were nothing more than trees. There didn't have to be anything bad inside. Sal would be back. They hadn't lost two.

On the flattop plateau of Rookt Monte sat the symbol of the Turall. The central triangle was a hole that lead down to the treasury below. Hultur climbed out by a ladder. The giant Ki'an gabbed about something inane like the architecture. Ena wanted to end him. She left the horses with one hand ready to snap, the other twisting through the forms of haste.

Torno stepped ahead of her and place his hands on her shoulders. When she tried to look past him, Torno interposed again. "This isn't Hultur's fault. He didn't know this was going to happen."

"I am sorry, Ena," Hultur said, in a way suited for Ena losing a magic ring.

This wasn't an object, this was Narla. She deserved

some fucking respect!

"Ena, please." Torno had no fight in him. "We need to get through this."

She turned around so she wouldn't have to look at him. Of course, that meant that Ena had to look at that useless horse and that fucking body. How dare it lay there? That was supposed to be Narla. Narla didn't lay on a horse. She didn't lay flat on anything. The woman slept on a bed with her knee raised. Even when sleeping for hours, she only ever looked like she was taking a quick nap. Narla could be up and ready to cast in ten seconds. If another Ekeet hopped out of that hole, Narla was going to jump off that horse and curse and toss fire and bombs. Out climbed Zukoch and Narla didn't stir.

Something was coming. It sounded like an avalanche. They were on the top of a mountain. Rocks didn't fall up. It was Sal. He rolled all the way up to the top of the mountain, and he came fast. He whirled around the horse that held Narla and the one that held Myrrel, because Myrrel couldn't get off her ass and help them.

Sal popped out of his ball. The familiar orange and tan of his rocks look gray and cold in the night's light. Someone shined a light on him. He looked ashamed. He couldn't even look at Ena. He *should* look ashamed. He'd made all of them worry. Even if he found Muttur, none of them would be able to help. It was another selfish, poorly thought out move. He didn't even know Narla was dead. He'd rolled right past the body without even looking.

She walked up and punched his shoulder as hard as she could. Her knuckles went numb. She meant to pull her fist back and punch him again. But her hand was too heavy. She leaned into Sal's face, hugging him. She shouldn't be hugging him. It wasn't right. None of this was right. She worked her fingers into the cracks in his body and held on as tight as she could. The rocks of his face were already starting to turn cold.

It was getting so cold.

"Sal, Narla's dead," Torno said.

"No," he gasped.

He'd known it before. They'd all known it the second the blade came out in a spray of blood. But Myrrel was a miracle worker. They took her great skills for granted. It didn't matter if they took silly risks, because Myrrel would be there. Instead, it fell on Ena to heal Myrrel and she failed. She'd been too tired to heal her. She walked all of them into Muttur's traps. She ignored all of the warnings and got Narla killed.

Sal sat onto the ground. He wasn't breathing. He didn't have to. There was no spell to heal a boulba's lung, because they didn't have lungs. Lung restoration spell were only for friends that lay dying. Narla was already dying when Ena went to treat her.

They were moving it. Visk, Torno, and Myrrel were moving Narla.

"Hey," Ena snapped. "That's my job. I was moving the body. I can get *that* done right!"

Myrrel held her head down. "Ena, please..." she whimpered.

Myrrel's tears threatened to come again. They had drunk too much water after she died. That's why they were crying again, too much water.

Ena stepped out of the way.

They moved the body past her. She couldn't help Narla when it mattered. Why should she help now? She didn't deserve to help. She didn't deserve to whimper and keen. Narla was dead because of her. They'd been on the road for days, and Ena hadn't studied. Hultur studied, that's why he could do all of these wonderful, awesome things. Ena couldn't even take care of herself. Her nerves were shit and now there was no one to teach her.

~ ~ ~

She'd curled into a ball and fallen into the sorrow

again. Ena hadn't been there to help Torno, Visk, and Myrrel prepare the funeral. She was just crying with Sal, violating his body by pressing herself against his face. He was crying too. He wasn't keeping her from touching him or even trying to stop her. He was weird. They were all weird and damaged, and that's why they were all with Narla. She was weird. She was their weird, grumpy older sister.

Ena needed to pull herself out of this. It was to say goodbye. She sniffed back tears and went still as a forgotten house. Don't wipe the tears. Visk had said that. When you cry about those you love, you let those tears shine so that all can know your loss. Narla always liked that about Visk. Narla didn't hide her tears either, and she didn't hide her screams.

Narla was resting on the mouth of the treasury. No, Narla was dead. Her cold, smelly body was lying there. She looked peaceful covered in a blanket and resting on a bed of explosives. A single plank suspended the weight.

Torno spoke from Ena's side. "I'll do it. I'll speak for her."

"We all will," Ena insisted. "All of us. Hultur, why don't you go first?"

"Very well." He stepped up and adjusted his hat. "Narla was a great mind. Her intellect was squandered on meaningless fixes and the compulsive fiddling of explosive devices. It had been my hope that her technical mind could one day be focused on matters of improving the welfare of civilizations rather than small communities. Her loss robs us of that future, and so we must look back at her achievements to judge the value of her life. The world was objectively better with her in it, thus it is less with her gone."

Hultur spoke these sentimental words like a recitation of facts. It helped to solidify his words as an undeniable truth.

Zukoch was next.

"This whole funeral seems warped and twisted. Are you sure this was what she would've wanted?" He looked at the rigid faces of her mourning friends. The former Brokers didn't even crack a smile. They needed him to get on with this.

Zukoch placed Wulg down beside his feet. He unclasped his shoulder cape and laid it in his arms.

"Narla, you were the reason I came on this journey. As Commander, you were strict but compassionate. I could've thrived in an environment like that. Even though I never served under you, I learned a lot from you. You taught me about discipline. You taught me to be something more than myself." He tilted his head to let tears fall. "I will find the courage to take risks.

"One of the last things you said to me was that it was okay to be afraid of getting hit, but that a fighter must take that hit and keep moving. The next time someone comes up to punch me in the face, I won't run from it. No promises about combat, though. I still can't even cast a fireball." Zukoch laid a patch of lavender flowers onto her chest. It was a custom of Fieta to lay down a poppy, but it seemed fitting to use a weed that grew out of a mountain.

Visk stepped forward. It wasn't going to get any easier after this and Ena had to deliver hers last. It was the tradition of command.

"Smoke follows fire. I knew you as a flame and I cannot see through your ashes. You burned too bright to embrace. It is fitting that your death blinds. You illuminated the darkness in my house and helped me to clean the corners. We swept out the dust, but never tore out the moldy wood. I know you would've burned it well. Everything burned beautifully in your flames."

Visk held up her spear and slammed the bottom down hard. Tears rolled down her cheeks.

"I served under you with this spear. If you have need of it in the next world, please take it. And should I meet you in the next world, it would be my honor to take up that spear again."

She placed it into Narla's blanket, arranging her hands to rest over the spear.

There was a long, weighted pause. Some didn't want to go so soon, others wanted more time, but none wanted to be there. Ever the martyr, Sal stepped up.

"Narla, it all started with us, do you remember that? I was in that hall with you, we were waiting as strangers, and we realized it at the same time, 'This is my partner.' I remember thinking, 'This woman's a wreck, I hope she's not my Broker Captain.' Of course, you were, and we sure got into a lot of arguments. You know I supported your decision to fire Pellipet, and I still think it was shady how the Sorcerer testified in favor of her. But you just shrugged your shoulders and rolled with it. 'Life is shit,' you always used to say.

"It's hard for a Boulba to shrug his shoulders, you know? It's kind of like wiggling your brows and flailing your arms around at the same time. But, uh...I'm not really talking about that now, am I? Moving my body wasn't hard, it was my mind that was the problem. It was made of rock when I met you. I thought everything was my fault, and once something bad happened, I couldn't let go of it. You helped me with that, Narla. You helped me shrug my shoulders."

The rocks around Sal's eyes split, cracked, and broke apart into more pebbles.

"I can't shrug my shoulders this time. I'm won't be able to let go of the pain your loss brings. I can't help thinking that if I was a better soldier, I would've been on him the whole time. I hadn't even known...I wasn't ready. I wasn't ready to live without you, Narla."

He kept trying to say more, but ultimately he gave up on it. He grabbed some mud and pressed it onto his face.

They were looking at Myrrel. It had to be her next. She had her head hung low and she kept shaking it. "I can't. I'm sorry, I just...I can't."

Torno rubbed her shoulder. "Myrrel, you only get to do

this once. If you don't step forward and say something, you will regret it for the rest of your life."

Visk grabbed her hand. "Women rise to every challenge."

Sal put his hand on her back. "Cry and talk," he said, even though he was breaking up.

Ena grabbed her free hand and squeezed.

Myrrel closed her eyes. "I'm sorry I have to do it like this, Narla. I can't keep my face stiff when things get bad. We, uh, we never really got along when it came to stuff like this, did we? You were a soldier, and I was a pampered noble. You were right about me, Narla, but I couldn't learn to toughen up.

"I'm soft. I'm not ever going to stop being soft. I never served in a war. I never had to watch people die and keep fighting. I never needed to make a switch in my brain that told me, 'cry later.' I hate that you did. I hate that you had to learn how to keep going when all you wanted to do was cry. I like crying when something bad happens. I need it. You needed it too, damn it. I know you knew that about yourself, and..."

Myrrel sobbed. She gripped Ena's hand as tight as she could. She was shaking, trying to find that gumption Narla always had. She grit her teeth and muttered something.

"You're really gone. You're not here to help me through this. I know I'm letting you down again. I tried so fucking hard to learn from you, but I never did. It was hard enough to get me to swear, you remember? I'd blush every time I said 'damn,' and you'd say I looked like a berry bush."

She chuckled through her tears. "You were such a bitch, Narla. You were my bitch, and it's never going to be the same without you."

They held onto her and cried for a moment.

Torno composed himself and nodded. They all spread out. For a second, he was Broker Captain again. Serious time meant serious faces, and that meant he was in charge.

Of course he wasn't anymore, and the unsure slump of his shoulders returned. He stared at her body for a long time.

"I wasn't ready for command," he said with certainty. "Without you being the Captain in all but name, I would've been fired by the end of the month. But you made me believe it. You made me accept that I was what you all needed because I could speak asshole. Fuck, if you weren't right. I sure turned into enough of one, didn't I?"

He chuckled and held onto that smile. "I had to talk to the big people. For a time, I believed that we could work like that, with you doing all the work and me begging to the Sorcerers and Magus for more supplies. But you were a wreck. You hadn't moved on from the miscarriage, or your marriage, or the war. When I finally put my foot down, I thought I was going to have to duel you for command.

"But you were so chill about it. You said you were so proud you were gonna give up drinking." He chuckled again. "I guess you finally did that, didn't you? In a way, your death was your ultimate victory."

His mirth left him. "We should all be celebrating. But I don't feel like cheering or toasting your legacy. I don't feel much of anything right now. You died a meaningless death. What did that little shit gain from killing you? Maybe the fact that he killed you first says something about how important you really were. If the Gods really are watching us, maybe they guided his sword. Maybe they killed you because they knew it would break our resolve. Maybe you were punished for telling the Gods to fuck off."

"This isn't helping," Ena grumbled.

"No, fuck them." He looked up. "Fuck the Gods! If you're going to kill her for saying that, then fucking kill me next. Don't you dare take any of them when you have a mess like me to kill! I never did anything good without someone like her to make it happen. She's responsible for every kind thing I ever did and said. You fuckers couldn't count that in her scales of good and evil? You just had to kill her before she could be a mother, didn't you?

"Well, fuck you and your vindictive bullshit! She *was* a mother. She was a mother to all of us. And maybe she didn't always say the right thing and maybe she was going to drink herself into an early grave anyway, but couldn't you have waited to see if she could make it? Couldn't you have let her have something like a simple, happy life again before you killed her?"

Torno's head dropped. He held his head. He was crying again, struggling to find the words or the will to continue. Ena didn't step forward. He could go on, she knew he could. Myrrel stepped up and he lifted his head again. He wore those tears like medals, showing the Gods that they would not break him.

"You won't win," Torno told the Gods. "You will not break us. You want to throw her life away to try and prove Narla right in death? Fuck you! And fuck her for believing that every death is pointless. Every death has meaning, and hers means that I will not give up until we've broken your pointless cycle. You gave us the will do whatever we want, fuck you for telling us that this isn't enough. Our mistakes are our own and I will not forget Narla's. I will look back on every relapse and every drunken fight with pride. That was Narla being alive. I hope I can be that brave until my death."

He stepped back, standing beside Ena. Myrrel took his hand.

It couldn't be Ena's time to talk already. There was someone they were missing, someone they'd skipped. She looked to her opposite side and saw a blank spot where Narla should've been standing. There was no one left to talk. Ena had to say her peace so they could all move on. She stepped forward and cleared her throat.

The words didn't come. Her mind went blank.

She looked to Narla. A collection of light crystals shone a soft white light onto her. In death, she looked peaceful. Ena could poke her or drop her explosives and Narla wouldn't even react. She would lay there no matter what humiliations she was made to suffer. They had to wrap up her belly to keep her together.

"I don't think it matters why you died," Ena said at last. "I never understood why you said all deaths were meaningless before, but I think I do now. You're gone. That's it. That is the tragedy. That is the bigger message.

"You thought I would be a great leader, but you died under my command. How great of a leader can I be? As your student, I failed you. You worked so hard to break me of my tendency to freeze up. I was supposed to attack first. I didn't attack first when it mattered the most. I could've grabbed Muttur with a hand of pure cold and squeezed the life out of him." Ena gestured the action, gnashing her teeth together.

"Ena, don't," Myrrel pleaded. She looked exhausted. They were all so tired.

Ena let out a sigh. She kept her eyes on them.

"I can't help but blame myself when something like this happens. I'm Ngoltur Reborn. I am one of three chosen by the Gods. I have the power to move lakes, and I can't stop one boy without a cough of ether. This was my failure of leadership. When I took command, that meant that I took responsibility when things went bad. There's nothing worse than a preventable death, and hers was preventable."

"We're not here for you!"

Ena looked to the voice, but saw only the rock of the mountain top. There was darkness past that cold spot. Darkness and silhouettes of distant hills and treetops. Narla wasn't there to tell her to stop falling into her darkness. She wasn't there to challenge her when nobody else would. And they wouldn't. They would've let Ena rant for hours if she wanted to. She had to be strong because Narla wasn't there to make her stand tall and make those tough calls.

Crying, Ena looked back at Narla.

"I hear you, Narla. I heard you yell at me so many times for being too weak to even be alive. I'm alive now. I can feel pain and sorrow. You always said it was worth it to love. I don't know if it is. I don't know if loving you was worth the pain of watching you die."

She wasn't moving. She wasn't arguing back. She didn't yell at her. There were so many things for Narla to yell at her for, but she just lay there.

Ena approached the source of the pain. There was a flower on her chest and a spear between her hands but she was missing something. She went back to grab something from Narla's pack and placed her goggles over her eyes. She took one of the sticks of dynamite and put it in her mouth. That cold flesh of hers lingering in Ena's hands.

Ena got out the flask. She'd refilled it with whiskey in her honor. "I hope you don't mind me taking this from you. I know you fought and died to keep democracy going, but I need that reminder. This isn't about me, or us, or even you. You died because we are done with wars. People should have the right to decide what happens next in their lives and not the Gods.

"Ours is a fight for democracy, I see that now. We're not overthrowing a monarchy, we are fighting to liberate ourselves from the Gods. I'm gonna borrow this, Narla. When we win, I'll take it to back to your family, and we'll drink to you. I'll make them curse the Gods for taking you."

Ena held it up and drank from it. The whiskey inside was sour, hearty, and a little sweet. She reached down and took a big stick of dynamite off the pile, one Narla had named Revenge. "I'll find a home for this one, Narla. I promise."

~ ~ ~

Torno made sure everyone was awake when the sun was starting to rise. Ena hadn't slept. She'd been exhausted, but she couldn't get a wink while going down the mountain. They were on the edge of the woods that marked the entrance into Erchritt. This path would take them to Schlabaum and there they would meet the Grand Dreamer.

They might not have any answers, but they would at least have a map of every ancient relic in Leben Erde.

"I can't believe this is how you're saying goodbye to Narla," Zukoch said for the hundredth time.

"Believe it, kid," Torno said.

Ena took out the cigars she'd gotten from the revolution and passed them around. They stood there and puffed out the smoke of the revolution. The sun bathed the world in gold and turned the sky azure. Shadows of the eastern mountain ridge slid down the side of Rookt Monte. Soon, very soon, the light would reach the top of the plateu.

With a cigar in his mouth, Sal started counting. "Twenty..."

Everyone joined in, counting down to when they thought the shadow would reach the zenith. When they got to seven, the sun came over the mountain's peak and direct sunlight hit the ignition crystal. Fuses lit and spread out over the inner chambers of the sacred treasury, but the largest connection of wrapped fuses went down to Narla's body.

The first blasts pressed out on the mountain's rocky edge and cracked it. Some boulders flew down and jostled the paths, but it was otherwise fine. Then the poorly timed fuses hit Narla's resting place. The middle of the tower burst out with such force that it flipped chunks of rock free from the treasury. Paved stone walls and statues millennia old flew into the air. Fire spread out, kicking off the top of Rookt Monte like a thrown bottle. Ash and smoke rose up where the monument to the Grand Dream had once stood.

It had been a tower constructed to house a weapon of a great hero. Those bracelets had given Muttur the power to tear through Narla's armor. The Gods had taken Narla from this world. Now, Ena took something back. When all this was over, there would be no treasury to house the Boulba Bracelets. They were going to stop the Grand Dream or die trying.

Thank you for reading.
The Twisting the Turall saga will continue.

Book 4
Empathy

www.ingramcontent.com/pod-product-compliance
Lightning Source LLC
Chambersburg PA
CBHW051055030726
47504CB00006B/1641